I0740533

George Gilfillan, Thomas Tyrwhitt

The Canterbury Tales of Chaucer

Vol. III

George Gilfillan, Thomas Tyrwhitt

The Canterbury Tales of Chaucer
Vol. III

ISBN/EAN: 9783743388871

Manufactured in Europe, USA, Canada, Australia, Japa

Cover: Foto ©Andreas Hilbeck / pixelio.de

Manufactured and distributed by brebook publishing software (www.brebook.com)

George Gilfillan, Thomas Tyrwhitt

The Canterbury Tales of Chaucer

THE

CANTERBURY TALES

OF

CHAUCER.

TO WHICH ARE ADDED,

AN ESSAY ON HIS LANGUAGE AND VERSIFICATION,
AND AN INTRODUCTORY DISCOURSE, TOGETHER WITH
NOTES AND A GLOSSARY.

BY

THOMAS TYRWHITT, F.R.S.

With Memoir and Critical Dissert

BY THE

REV. GEORGE GILFILLAN.

IN THREE VOLS.

VOL. III.

EDINBURGH: JAMES NICHOL.
LONDON: JAMES NISBET & CO.   DUBLIN: W. ROBERTSON.
M.DCCC.LX.

THE GENIUS AND POETRY OF CHAUCER.

WE approach with a mixture of enthusiasm and of awe to the consideration of the genius and the writings of Geoffrey Chaucer, and are almost disposed to adapt and employ the well-known words of Keats addressed to Apollo—

> " Lo ! 'tis for the Father of *our* verse—
> Flush everything that has a vermeil hue,
> Let the rose smile intense," &c.

A peculiarly rich chaplet, surely, should be woven for the brow of one to whose verse, as to a fountain, we may, in a great degree, trace all the splendours, graces, and powers of English poetry: the infinite variety of Shakspeare—the linked sweetness and ethereal air of Spenser—the intricate ingenuity and involved strength of Donne, Cowley, and the rest of the metaphysical poets—the solemn grandeur of Milton—the graceful spirit of Denham and Waller—the inflamed common sense and masculine energy of Dryden—the terseness and glittering point of Pope—the rich description of Thomson—the tenderness and classical polish of Goldsmith and of Rogers—the forest-like vastness and gloom of Young—the brilliant philosophical rhetoric of Akenside—the fine frenzy of Collins—the condensed elaboration of Gray—the direct vigour and earnest spirit of Cowper—the passionate outpourings, which came, like molten lava, from the hearts of Burns and Byron—the tremulous elegance and husbanded strength of Campbell—the *Excelsior* path ever pursued by the lonely and daring genius of Shelley—the inner and inverted eye of poetry which was the differentia of Wordsworth—

the broad-winged and all-embracing sweep of Coleridge—the simple, yet fiery inspiration of Scott—the narrow, Teneriffe-like elevation of Southey—the musical and muffled song of that flower-embosomed bee, Keats—and the exquisite blending of art and nature to be found in the better poems of Tennyson, where the union of the two is so complete that you cannot distinguish between them, any more than you can determine where one colour of the rainbow melts into another;—all these, and all the rest of the efforts of our British genius, would never have existed but for the impulse given, and the example set, by Chaucer. We equal him not to one or two of his followers, such as Shakspeare and Milton—we say not that he combined the qualities of after poets in himself—we assert not that many, or any, of these succeeding writers were his slavish imitators, or his imitators at all; but, even as the oak reposes in the acorn, and as in a " cradled Hercules" we trace

> "The lines of empire in his infant face"—

so in the rhymes of Chaucer, rude as many of them are, we have the germ of the whole gigantic development of poetic growth which has since astonished the world, and to which, taking it all in all, there is nothing equal or second in the compass of literature.

Here, in reference to the poetry as well as to the life of the poet, it is no easy matter to

> " Call up him who left half told
> The story of Cambuscan bold."

Much obscurity springing from antique language and allusions rests upon many parts of Chaucer's writings. We must deduct, too, from him a good deal of the matter which he wittingly or unwittingly absorbed from the great contemporary writers of his time, and must also mark with a stern *cum nota* the offences against delicacy which unfortunately have found far too many parallels in all early literature. Early writers are, in general, great borrowers from the few sources that are open to them. They think no more of deriving thoughts and images from others than of taking stones from a mountain side, or faggots from a forest. In Scripture itself there are coincidences between different writers which can hardly be accounted for except on the supposition of appropriation, such as those between the 2d chapter of Isaiah and the 4th of Micah—not to speak of passages in which the imitations of older models is obvious, as we find in Ezekiel xxxii. 21 of Isaiah xiv. 9. Homer is probably much indebted to previous poets, although, happily perhaps for his fame, there is now no possibility of tracking him in their snow. Shakspeare is notoriously starred over with borrowed gems, although his native beauty and magnificence of form are thereby enhanced, instead of being dwindled or deformed. Milton had the magical faculty of turning pebbles into gold, and golden pieces into diamonds—he never appropriated without improving, and, when he throws a disguise over his stolen splendours, the veil is more valuable than the objects concealed. Coleridge has been compared to one of those *millionnaires* who are sometimes seized with the insane desire of stealing trifles from shops. He rather reminds us of the beautiful story told about him when a boy, detected on the Strand with his hand in a gentleman's pocket, imagining the while that he was Leander swimming in the Hellespont! So, in sheer absence of mind, he sometimes thrust his hand where it had no right to be, and was rather cavalierly treated therefore by those who were more wide awake than the "noticeable man with large gray eyes." But, for Chaucer's somewhat large transcriptions rather than transfusions from Petrarch, Dante, Boccaccio, and other writers, it may be, and has been, ingeniously pled—a plea which avails also for his numerous classical allusions—that, at the period of the revival of letters in Europe, information, and especially information connected with the history of literature, was so precious, that for a poet to exhibit the extent of his reading in his verses was deemed a perfectly legitimate mode of exciting interest, and that at that time "a thought, a sentiment, a plot, an image, a description, were all valuable to the poet wheresoever obtained, and that the duty of repeating or translating the fine passages of another author was more strongly felt than the desire of being original." Writers, and the public too, had then very different ideas from what they have now of the design of a poem. It answered then somewhat the purpose of an American store, where goods of all

kinds are collected without much regard to selection or arrangement, and in which the great point sought is, to have everything,
whether paid for or not, stowed up for all possible demands.
The readers, too, of that day were usually, to some extent,
scholars themselves, and perhaps understood recondite allusions
better than many who are reputed intelligent now.   In all
Chaucer's classicalities, however, as well as in those of Spenser
and Milton, there are a freshness and a gusto which were entirely
lost in the writers of Queen Anne's days.   And in the contrast
between them on this point, we see the difference between the
irrepressible exudation of the learning of scholars and that
forced accumulation of commonplaces in which sciolists and
schoolboys glory.   There have been three stages in the history
of the use of the classics in British poetry.   In the first instance,
Chaucer, Spenser, and others, used them with lavish profusion,
although, in general, with great felicity.   Then, in the reign of
Charles II. and Queen Anne classical figures became a nui-
sance, and the public and the critics alike began to sicken of
Delias and Phillises, Neptunes and Proserpines, although we
find Dr Moore, so late as the rise of Robert Burns, exhorting
the peasant bard to fill his poetry with these *fude* ornaments—an
advice which he very wisely did not follow.   And in fine, came
Keats, Barry Cornwall, Leigh Hunt, Shelley, and Landor, who
ventured to shoot their own genius into the dead forms of the
Pagan mythology, to give it a new glory by giving it a new interpretation, and whose object was not to imitate but to emulate
the elder models, not to garnish their sepulchres but to renew
their life.

In considering Chaucer's genius and writings, we ought never
to forget that they were written before the invention of printing,
and for the use of a manuscript-reading public.   What a curious
train of thoughts this fact opens up to the present readers or writers
of literature!   Compare the sensation which now attends the
appearance of a popular poem or novel—the hum of expectation
which precedes it—the preliminary puffs and extensive book-
selling subscription—the rush for copies on publication day—the
newspaper notices swelling out into magazine articles, and then
reverberated by the voices of the reviews—'till, through the

length and breadth of the land, there arises a storm of praise—the multiplying editions—epistles of congratulation and bank-cheques—with the cold gestation of a work in the days of our ancestors—the MS. handed round from the author to one or two of his friends—the deliberate perusal characteristic of the leisure of the times, and of the scarcity of books—the letters of acknow-ledgment travelling at a snail's pace to the patient scribe—the copies transcribed by a few earnest but tranquil admirers—the successive but slow voices by which the impulse was transmitted to a circle which was not, after all, very wide; and we may have some conception of the disadvantages under which writers and writings were then placed, notwithstanding all that princes sometimes did to reward their genius, and wandering minstrels, reciters of poetry, and peripatetic monks, to circulate their fame. The knowledge of this might probably tend to render their efforts more strenuous and more solid, and their motto more than in latter times, *Pingimus in eternitatem;* but often, too, their hearts would fail them, their fingers would drop power-less upon the lyre, or be able only to play out the *sentiment* of verses to be written in an after age—

> "Oh! who can tell how hard it is to climb
> The steep where Fame's proud temple shines afar!"

The same fact has led, according to an ingenious writer, to a peculiarity in Chaucer's writings, which he thus expounds:—"There is a LARGENESS about his poetry, as if it were written not for men of ordinary stature or moderns, but for giants or leisurely antediluvians. There is no haste about it, no literary eagerness, no deference to a standard of length or proportion, no subordina-tion of parts to the whole; all is slow, calm, arbitrary, immense, as if an Egyptian temple were a-building. Perhaps the special manifestation of this largeness which will most readily strike a reader of Chaucer, is his fondness for minute and elaborate des-criptions of scenery, ceremonials, &c. This characteristic may have been, in some degree, a constitutional peculiarity of Chaucer. We think, however, it may be referred to more general causes. In the age of manuscripts, when a reader could not turn as he pleased from one composition to another, what was written behoved to be leisurely enjoyed, and the description of a wedding procession in twenty stanzas, or of an arbour of honeysuckle in six, was less an offence against the feeling of proportion than it would be now."

There is something true as well as striking in what this writer says about the vast scale and colossal magnitude of Chaucer's works. Some of them remind us of an object we at present behold from our study window,—a great square steeple, older than "The Canterbury Tales," soaring up into the middle ages, dwelling among, but not being of the spires and mill-stalks and masts which surround it, overlooking from the height of the eleventh century a city of 100,000 souls, with what strikes the imagination as a mixture of condescending protection and calm severity of survey—the bell in which rises above all the jangling or jarring sounds beneath, like a voice from the Eternal Past, and which, in the careless grandeur and solid greatness of its structure, seems built by another species of beings, and to point, not like a finger, but like a hand, stiffened with awe, to a sublimer heaven. In this, however, it may be compared not to Chaucer's greater writings merely, but to all the Titanic products of the earlier ages of the world. Truly there were giants in those days.

Equally striking with his largeness is his simplicity. This in him reminds us of that of Nature, where one severe and simple law pervades and controls all the complex phenomena of the universe, which has one sun of one colour, not many of various, shining in the firmament—whose sky is clothed, not with rainbows, but with one beautiful and modest blue—whose earth is dyed, as its main colour, with the soft, unobtrusive green—whose ocean is just a drop of gray water, immensely magnified, and which, whether it rests or rages, obeys, both in its motion and its rest, one all-embracing principle. That fine amalgam of unity and truth, of simple proportion and complex power, we call simplicity, and which we find transferred from God's works to man's, whenever man, like God, is earnest and self-forgetting—to those piles, such as St Peter's and St Paul's, which devotion has built in honour of Heaven—to those statues which still enchant or overawe the world, such as the Venus de Medicis, the Apollo Belvedere, the Antinous, and the Hercules Farnese, the Moses

of Michael Angelo, and the Theseus of Canova—to those paint-
ings where colour is softened by taste, and splendour subdued by
the spirit of Design, such as the Cartoons of Raphael, and the
masterpieces of Leonardo da Vinci—and to those great poems
of earth, of whose very names humanity is proud, as she wears
them like many crowns around her brow—the "Iliad" and the
"Odyssey," the "Divina Comedia" and the "Macbeth," the
"Paradise Lost" and the "Samson Agonistes"—this simplicity
is nowhere better exemplified then in many portions of the poetry
of Chaucer.   From a careless hand, holding a full pen, blots are
apt to fall, but from Chaucer's half-slumbering finger drop down
many exquisite beauties.   Such is—

> "Up rose the sun, and up rose Emily ;"

the description of Emetrius—

> "And as a lion he his looking cast,
> Of five and twenty year his age I cast [guess].
> His beard was well begunnen for to spring ;
> His voice was as a trumpë thundering ;"

and a hundred more which will occur to every reader of his
poems.   How different and how inferior is Dryden's version of
these latter lines :—

> "Whose voice was heard around
> Loud as a trumpet with a silver sound."

Dryden is on the whole, and in comparison with Pope, a simple
writer, but when we read his Fables along with Chaucer's Tales,
he sinks in this point into a second-rate position.   The latter
exhibits a crag-like boldness of outline, a directness of statement,
an avoidance of all needless details, and a downright reality of
impression, which raise him almost to the level of Homer and
Dante.

> "He sets down all as plain,
> As downright Shippen or as old Montaigne."

There is no indulgence of luxurious fancy, no dalliance with pet
ideas, no delay on certain sunny spots which are favourites of his
imagination ; he goes to work in the most business-like style,
and tells his stories or writes his descriptions with a ledger-like
accuracy.   And yet no writer produces at times more powerful
and poetic effects.

Akin to this simplicity is his freshness of natural description. His landscapes wear generally a morning light. He walks through the dewy grass, with the song of the earliest birds in his ears, and with the broad sun rising in the eastern horizon. He paints nature as he finds it, and is a Pre-Raphaelite among the poets. To him no

> " visions, as poetic eyes avow,
> Hang on each branch and cling to every bough ;"

he sees nothing but the green leaves or the bare winter branches. No beautiful or terrible forms retire amidst the woods, beckoning the beholder to follow ; he is aware only of the dun deer gliding past, the raven floating over-head, or the squirrel climbing the tree and losing itself in the stream of its leaves ; and as he lies down to sleep in the afternoon glades, his dreams are of pilgrims passing by to the distant shrine of their saint, of ladies dancing in their bowers, or of knights justling in their tournaments, rather than of

> " Gay castles in the clouds that pass
> For ever flushing round a summer sky,"

of giants and wizards, of fairies and of ghosts. To this, indeed, there are exceptions among his poems, especially in " The Flower and the Leaf ; " yet in the commencement of this fine piece of imagination, we find a specimen of the quiet, photographic painting of nature, we have described as Chaucer's usual manner :—

> " When that Phœbus his chair of gold so high,
>   Had whirled up the starrie sky aloft,
>   And in the Bull was entred certainly,
>   When showers sweet of rain descended soft,
>   Causing the ground, felö timis and oft,
>   Up for to give many an wholesome air,
>   And every plainë was yclothed fair
>   With newë green.
>
>   .   .   .   .
>
>   Up I rose three hours after twelve,
>   About the springing of the gladsome day,
>   And on I put my gear and mine array,
>   And to a pleasaunt grove I 'gan to pass,
>   Long ere the bright sun uprisen was ;
>   In which were oakës great, straight as a line,
>   Under the which the grass, so fresh of hue,

> Was newly sprung, and an eight foot or nine
> Every tree well from his fellow grew,
> With branches broad laden with leavës new,
> That springen out against the sunnë shine,
> Some very red, and some a glad light green.
>
> .　　.　　.　　.　　.　　.　　.　　.
>
> On the sweet grass
> I sat me down, for as for mine intent
> The birdë's song was more convenient,
> And more pleasant to me by many fold
> Than meat or drink or any other thing ;
> Thereto the herber [grass] was so fresh and cold,
> The wholesome savours eke so comforting
> That (as I deemëd) sith the beginning
> Of the worldë was never seen ere then,
> So pleasaunt a spot of none earthly man."

The love of simple nature—of nature in its most primitive forms, of "a silent green field with the great silent sky over it"—displayed in this description is very beautiful, and discovers the child as well as the poet. And it is wonderful how one so versant with courts and camps, with the complications of politics and the annoyances of business, should retain so much youthful enthusiasm ; although his connexion with public affairs enables us, on the other hand, to comprehend the source of that common sense and that direct dealing with his subjects which are quite as remarkable as his genius.

Common sense is indeed eminently a Chaucerian gift. This has not distinguished all, or perhaps the majority of poets. Butler seems to define what it is when he says that a man who possesses wit should have

> "As much again to govern it."

Common sense, when found along with, is the Siamese twin and guardian of genius. It exists collaterally or aside the poet, and means the management he has either inherited or acquired of his own powers in their relations to his position, his purposes, and in reference to the nature and the measure of these powers themselves. In Spenser, Shelley, Byron, Southey, Wordsworth, and a host more, we do not find this faculty very largely developed. In Chapman, Lee, Smart, Leigh Hunt, and in most of the dramatists of the days of James I. and Charles II., it did not exist at all.   Milton and Coleridge soar above the sphere where it is required.   We can hardly expect common sense in them any more than in Raphael or Ariel, although we may attribute to them a species of celestial tact.   Perhaps the four poets who possess most of it are, Chaucer, Shakspeare, Cowper—semi-maniac as he was—and, with all his wild impulse and tumultuous passion, Robert Burns.   In these it is found in proportions commensurate with their genius.   In Pope, and several more of a similar class, it to some extent eclipses their poetic gift.   In Chaucer's " Canterbury Tales," particularly, we find this power strongly conspicuous.   Its calm eye looks out upon us from every page, and we are justified, were it for this alone, in applying to our poet the epithet he often gives to others, and which Thomson, in his " Castle of Indolence," gives to him—" Dan Chaucer," *i.e. Dominus*, lord of himself and of his song.

Prominent among the qualities of his poetry is the ruggedly picturesque.   Short and rapid strokes of the brush are usually more powerful than they are polished.   But in Chaucer, the ruggedness is compensated by the concentration.   He crams into a big bulging line the meaning which, in Spenser, would have filled a stanza, or a page.   In pp. 62 and 63 of our first volume, containing the description of the Temple of Mars, every line is a picture, and resembles the boss upon a buckler, or the knob on a rough goblet of gold.

> " There stood the temple of Mars Armipotent,
>   Wrought all of burned [burnished] steel, of which th' entry
>   Was long and strait, and ghastly for to see ;
>   The northern light in at the doorë shone,
>   For window on the wall ne was there none,
>   Through which men mighten any light discern,
>   The door was all of adamant etern."

What figures are carved there!   There is

> " The smiler with the knife under the cloak ;"

and—

> " The slayer of himself yet saw I there,
>   His heartë-blood hath bathed all his hair ;"

and—

> " Woodness laughing in his rage ;"

and ghastlier still—

> "The sow fretting [devouring] the child right in the cradle;
> The cook yscalded, for all his long ladle.
> Nought was forgot by th' infortune of Martë,
> The carter overridden with his cartë,
> Under the wheel full low he lay adown."

Our readers remember Spenser's powerful pictures of the Passions—of Lechery ' with whally eyes ;' Envy

>   " chawing
> Between his canker'd teeth a venomous toad ;"

and Wrath

> "Upon a lion loth for to be led,
> And in his hand a burning brand he hath,
> The which he brandisheth about his head."

But perhaps superior even to these is Chaucer's terrible Mars—

> "The god of armës was arrayed thus :
> A wolf there stood before him at his feet,
> *With eyen red, and of a man he eat.*"

This reminds us of a master-stroke of Burke, in a passage in his " Regicide Peace : "—" On that day it was thought he would have assumed the port of Mars, that he would have brought forth from their hideous kennel those impatient dogs of war *whose fierce regards affright even the minister of vengeance that feeds them.*"

When he follows the humorous style, Chaucer is equally sententious and striking. Thus he says of his Franklin :—

> " Withouten bake-meat never was his house,
> Of fish and flesh, and that so plenteous,
> *It snowed in his house of meat and drink.*"

Of the Miller—

> " His beard as any sow or fox was red,
> And thereto broad as though it were a spade.
> Upon the cop [top] right of his nose he had
> A wart, and thereon stood a tuft of hairs,
> Red as the bristles of a sowë's ears.
> His mouth widë was as a furnáce."

And of the Friar—

> " Somewhat he lisped for his wantonness,
> To make his English sweet upon his tongue,

> And in his harping, when that he had sung,
> His eyen twinkled in his head aright
> As do the starrës in a frosty night."

In this broad yet condensed style of pictorial representation Chaucer resembles Bunyan, as well as in some other qualities of his brawny genius. Bunyan, too, writes like a man of business—deals in direct strokes—puts much into few, and these simple words—has an eye for sly humour as well as for bold allegory—and with comparatively little fancy, has an immense deal of essential imagination. How different at first view the Canterbury from the Christian Pilgrims—the Friar from Evangelist—the Franklin from Great-heart—the Miller from Christian—the Sompnour from Hopeful—the Manciple from Gaius mine host—the Nun from Mercy—and the Wife of Bath from Christiana! And yet, in one very important point, they are alike; they are no cold abstractions—no stiff, formal, and half-animated figures—they are, both the pious and profane, intensely natural, and bursting at every pore with life. Nay, had it been Bunyan's cue to send a company of Pilgrims back in the wrong instead of forward in the right direction, what an odd and striking group he might have dismissed from his hand through the south gate of the City of Destruction, including Byends and Moneylove, laden with their golden bags—Mistrust and Timorous, with their reverted looks and trembling limbs—Mr Brisk pairing off with Madam Bubble—Talkative and Shame outvying each other in loud-mouthed effrontery—Mr Slowpace limping arm in arm with Mr Shortwind—besides Adam the First, and his Three Daughters—the Lust of the Eyes, the Lust of the Flesh, and the Pride of Life—wedded to Simple, Sloth, and Presumption! One, on the other hand, wishes that Chaucer had, like Bunyan, consecrated his extraordinary powers of character-painting, humour, knowledge of human nature, and strong, clear, Saxon style, to a religious purpose. But while he is only entitled to the name " Dan Chaucer," Bunyan was appropriately called by his contemporaries " Bishop Bunyan," and certainly the bench of bishops never possessed one more worthy of the name than the illustrious Baptist.

Bunyan has sometimes, although perhaps not often, reached

the sublimely ideal. In the opening of the "Pilgrim," so simply grand, in the picture of the view from Mount Clear and of the ascent to the Celestial City, in the combat with Apollyon, the Valley of the Shadow of Death, and the tremendous figure of Turnaway, he has equalled any poet that ever lived, for thrilling, curdling effect, at one time of horror, and at another of imaginative ecstasy. Chaucer, too, is chary of idealisms, but occasionally he can vault into the highest heaven of the poetic art. Witness the story of Cambuscan and the Horse of Brass, worthy of the "Arabian Nights' Entertainments." Witness many passages, some of which we shall afterwards quote, from his "House of Fame." Witness the supernatural part of "The Flower and the Leaf." And witness, in the "Pardoner's Tale," the story of the three rioters who go out to destroy Death :—

> "Heark'neth, fellóws, we three be allë ones [at one]:
> Let each of us hold up his hand to other,
> And each of us becomen other's brother,
> And we will slay this falsë traitor Death :
> He shall be slain, he that so many slay'th,
> By Goddë's dignity, ere it be night."

With the motto in their mouths,

> "Death shall be dead, if that we may him hent" [catch],

they proceed on their journey. At the close of half a mile,

> "An old man and a poorë with them met,"

who, after salutation, tells them his dismal case—

> "I cannot find
> A man, though that I walked into Ind,
> Neither in city nor in no villáge,
> That wouldë change his youthë for mine age,
> And therefore must I have mine agë still,
> As longë time as it is Goddë's will.
> Ne Death, alas! ne will not have my life.
> Thus walk I like a restëless caitiff,
> And on the ground, which is my mother's gate,
> I knockë with my staff, early and late,
> And say to her 'Levë [dear] mother, let me in.'
> . . . .
> But yet to me she will not do that grace,
> For which full pale and welked [withered] is my face."

At this old man the rioters inquire where is Death. He sends them to an oak-tree, where he says their enemy abides, and where they find gold, which leads to mutual treachery, and the death of all three. "They hear no more of the old man, *but it is Death they have encountered.*"

Hazlitt very justly remarks that this is the most powerful description of Death ever given, and contrasts it with such elaborate representations as that of Benjamin West in his "Death upon the Pale Horse," where the impalpable is made too distinct, and the gloomy shadow is changed into a substance. "Death," he adds, "is an ugly customer, who will not be invited to dinner, nor sit for his picture." Young had anticipated this remark in his "Night Thoughts," when he said—

> "That tyrant *never sate.*"

In unconscious keeping with such an ideal of Death, Milton says—

> "What *seem'd* his head
> The LIKENESS of a kingly crown had on."

And Burns—

> "I there wi' SOMETHING did foregather,
> That put me in an eerie swither."

One of the most striking and terrible stories we ever read, and which was probably founded on Chaucer's poem, was entitled the "Vision of Death," which appeared first in a Bombay newspaper. It represented Death as a man of unutterable age, appearing successively to the father of a family of devoted victims, who, before the death of one of his children, beholds the grim and grinning destroyer looking at him over the walls and through the rustling nettles of an evening churchyard; again, before that of another, feels him pulling his bed-clothes at midnight, and shewing there his "welked" face; and again, sees him sitting in the graveyard of a third child by the light of a waning moon—the awe-struck father feeling in the apparition a warning of his own end, and rushing home in horror with the cry on his lips, "I have seen Death!" Seldom has any "dismal treatise" so roused, as if "life were in 't," our "fell of hair," as this forgotten but most ghastly and powerful story.

Scarcely inferior to Chaucer's power over the terrible is his pathos. There are specimens too of this to be found in various parts of his writings, but by far the best, in point of simplicity, quiet, and completeness, is the Clerk's Tale of Griselda. The story of this we need not recount, as it is already (vol. ii.) in our readers' hands. There are in the course of it soundings of the human heart only inferior to those in the history of Joseph and his brethren, in Ruth, and in Shakspeare. What can be more touching or more truly sublime in its tenderness than Griselda's speech to her lord, when he affects to repudiate her?—

> " Here again your clothing I restore,
> And eke your wedding-ring for evermore.
>
> " The remnant of your jewels ready be
> Within your chamber, I dare it safely sayn
> Naked out of my father's house (quod she)
> I came, and naked I must turn again.
> All your pleasancë would I follow fain:
> But yet I hope it be not your intent,
> That I smocklèss out of your palace went.
>
> " Ye could not do so dishonèst a thing,
> That thilkë womb, in which your children lay,
> Shouldë before the people, in my walking,
> Be seen all barë: wherefore I you pray
> *Let me not like a worm go by the way.*
> Remember you, mine owen lord so dear,
> I was your wife, though I unworthy were."

One is reminded of the last words of the smothered Desdemona :—

> " *Emilia.*   Oh, who hath done
> This deed?
> " *Desdemona.* Nobody ; I myself ; farewell :
> Commend me to my kind lord ; oh, farewell."

And when at last Griselda returns to her father's house,

> " In her smock, with foot and head all bare,"

not Godiva herself, " clothed on with chastity," is in her Eve-like nakedness more gloriously attired.

Connected with these higher qualities of our poet, there is, as we have already incidentally noticed, a certain childlike *naïveté* distinguishing his genius. This gives to his style something of the effect which a lisp or burr does to the utterance of a strong man. You think of weakness nestling in the bosom of strength, and yet the poet becomes nearer and dearer to his readers from his share in the infirmities of their common nature, and thus what in one sense seems an imperfection, becomes in another a source of interest and power. How much marks of feebleness here and there in a writer, and occasional blunders, if not too gross, tend to lay that demon of envy which is ever ready to spring up near great excellence, and to excite that sympathy which is as much akin to pity as to admiration! Say what we please, we love Homer better because he now and then nods; Dante better for his bitterness and truculence; Livy better for his Patavinity of style; Ariosto better for his endless digressions; Shakspeare better for his puns and clenches; Dryden better for his foxhunter-like falls, while pursuing his break-neck poetic career; Wordsworth better for his childishness; Shelley better for his mist and maniacal screams; Burns better for his "ploughman graith;" Scott better for his old wives' prejudices and stories; and Chaucer better for his simplicity often approaching silliness, and his conversational tone sometimes degenerating into twaddle. We heard lately a remark that struck us forcibly, to the effect that no man has ever identified himself with, and struck a nation to the heart, unless he has been a great sufferer, an injured, persecuted man, like Wallace, Tell, and Burns. And in keeping with the spirit of this observation, we maintain that the greatest poets and authors have been influential and popular as much by their faults as by their merits as writers, and by their defects as by their virtues as men. We are all true to our species even as a *fallen* race, and dislike faultless monsters in literature as well as in life. There is, too, a secret feeling of superiority or equality which arises in the mind of the reader, in the perception of faults, which, while it lessens the ideal of his author, increases his love, and rivets his attention. Perfect, or approximately perfect writers, such as Pope and Rogers, are admired; but how poor and shallow the enthusiasm which they produce compared to that with which the initiated fight for Keats, Coleridge, and

Bailey of " Festus!" For Chaucer's blemishes there is, besides, the excuse of an early age and of imperfect culture. Rudeness is not always strength, but it sets off the appearance of strength, as nodosities do the gnarled oak, and the beard the lion. Nay, it seems somehow necessary to the full effect of all intensely original genius, since we find it not only in the early ages, but sometimes in periods of high refinement. But when found in a Chaucer or a Dunbar, in a Ben Jonson or a Shakspeare, it has certainly a more pleasing effect than in a Burns, a Landor, or a Byron.

In all great poets we are entitled to expect a purpose, whether latent or revealed, expressed or implied, good or bad, wise or foolish. Poetry without purpose is an ocean without a tide; or it may be compared to a shower of pine-cones shed on the blast with no hope of harvest, instead of the quiet seed cast into the spring soil. But men who thus scatter verses about can hardly be called poets at all. The true poet may not always be conscious of what he means, but there is a meaning in him, independent of his volition, and he is swayed toward a special end, not merely by his temperament, or by the spirit of his age, or by his genius, but to some extent, if he be a true man, by that Power which has its dwelling in

" The light of setting suns,"

and is the Soul within the pure and lofty soul. In Chaucer we find the keen observer of manners, the vigorous dissector of character, the gay, goodnatured derider of folly, and the unsparing satirist of vice; but we find, too, at least the bust and brow of a religious reformer. Indeed, this his broad sympathy with his age compelled him to be. That, as we saw in the " Life,"gave the first augury of a coming revolution in the Church. Sleeping Europe turned itself in its bed, if it did not awake. There are fine days sometimes in January, by which Nature herself would almost seem to be deceived—the birds beginning to sing and the earthworms to crawl abroad in the genial beams of the sun, although the snows of February and the winds of March are yet to come. And thus in the fourteenth century there came an early sunshine on an earth that was not ripe for bearing fruit.

The men of Wickliffe's day, including Chaucer, saw the monstrous evils connected with the Church very clearly. They discerned especially how low the clergy, through their vices, their indolence, their. ignorance, their undue *esprit de corps*, their bigotry and superstition, had sunk in public estimation. They knew that when a clergy have become just objects of contempt, especially to the lower orders, the destruction of the system of which they are the supporters is only a question of time. They saw, too, that the best method of overthrowing the Papacy was by unsheathing the Bible, and using it in the strife as the naked sword of the Spirit. But they did not feel sufficiently that they were before their day, that for yet one hundred and eighty years the pear must ripen, and that their premature efforts in defence of truth and liberty were certain to produce a reaction in favour of the old but not yet obsolete evils. Many things had to be done and suffered, discovered and changed, ere the Reformation could dawn—the blood of more martyrs must flow, the art of printing must be invented and made practically powerful in Europe, navigation and many other arts must be improved. Popery must become worse, and, above all, political movements must so operate as to create a *middle class*, as a strong soil for the reception of the new Evangel. Yet, honour to those brave spirits who arose so early to sow a seed which did not and could not then germinate, but who deserved as well as their more fortunate successors, who were permitted to return, " bringing their sheaves with them."

Chaucer's share in this movement could not be called great, but was characteristic. He did not shoot many shots against the Roman Catholic faith, but he turned his batteries in that direction. He displayed his *animus*, he made pregnant insinuations, hints where more was meant than met the ear; he did not fully unbare, but he shewed the point of that weapon of ridicule which the Church of Rome has found at various periods of her history such a formidable enemy to her claims, as wielded by the hands of Erasmus, of Sir David Lindsay, of Pascal, Voltaire, and Beranger. Chaucer's Friar and his Nun shew what he could have effected had he chosen to become the systematic caricaturist of the priests and Papacy.

In another sense, our poet paved the way for the Reformation. In hammering the English language into form, in making it pliable for every purpose of eloquence, wit, reasoning, illustration, or fancy which an author or speaker could require, he was benefiting the general advance of the nation, and forging a sword fit for the noble hands which were afterwards to draw it. The future Ridleys, Latimers, and Knoxes owed a similar debt of gratitude to the old Father of British poetry which the mettled knights of King Robert II. of Scotland's reign did to Harry Wynd for the keen-cutting blades, and steel harness, with which he armed them for the fight. Thanks to him, vernacular English had ere the Reformation become more than able to encounter Latin, the "language of Antichrist," rivalling it not in swell of sound, but exceeding it in flexibility, picturesque simplicity, and racy force. Apart from this moral effect, not to be realised till long afterwards, Chaucer was a great benefactor to the English tongue in a literary point of view. Well has it been said by a writer in the *British Quarterly Review*— "Even these love-ditties, and ballads in praise and dispraise of women, and heraldic descriptions of jousts and tournaments,— poems mostly of the fancy, and from which, by themselves, it would be unfair to infer the real nature of the man Chaucer,— what a grand result are they helping to accomplish! Not a quip, not a jest, not a simile, not a new jingle of sounds and syllables, let the intrinsic value of the sentiment of which they are the foliage and efflorescence be ever so small, but in the act of originating that quip, or jest, or simile, or jingle, Chaucer is struggling successfully with the tough element of an unformed language, and assisting to prepare it for the exigencies of the future. When we consider this, we ought to be glad that it so happened that the first great English poet was a rich descriptive genius, a man whose eye took notice of and received pleasure from the minutiæ of external appearances, the flowers and the arrangements of plots in a garden, the paraphernalia of a feast, the banners and scutcheons in a procession, the dresses and armour of knights in a tournament, the harnessing and caparison of horses. For assisting at the formation of a language and the compilation of a literary idiom, a poet with a genius for nomenclature and description, like that of Chaucer, was most suitable; and for such a genius, a life of ease and luxurious courtiership was the proper training."

On "The Canterbury Tales" we must be permitted a very few remarks. They are unquestionably the masterpiece of his genius. They owe their superiority not so much to their individual merits, as to their plan, and to the great variety and human interest secured thereby. We know not if there be a more felicitous framework in all the compass of fiction or poetry. In the "Decameron" of Boccaccio, ingenious as the plan is, the fact that the tale-tellers are there shunning the plague tends somewhat to displace the mirth and to mar the good meeting; the tie connecting so many merry stories is felt to be too dark and sombre. In "The Canterbury Tales," on the other hand, all is in fine keeping. The season is the "sweet and showery" April; the Host, a right jolly and withal gifted person, is the Greatheart of the journey; the Pilgrims are composed of the most diverse characters, picturesquely contrasted with one another—a gallant knight, his fair son, their servant, a sturdy yeoman, two nuns, a monk, a begging friar, a clerk of Oxford, a sergeant of the law, a merchant, a franklin, or gentleman farmer; a carpenter, a haberdasher, a weaver, a tapester (or maker of tapestry), a dyer, a sailor, a cook, a doctor of physic, a wife of Bath, who had buried five husbands; a holy and venerable parish priest, a reeve or land-bailiff, a ploughman, a drunken miller, a sompnour, or summoner of culprits before the ecclesiastical courts, with a blotched and pimpled countenance; a pardoner, with a wallet full of indulgences, with a weak voice, and long, yellow, womanish hair—quite a tiny Tetzel—and newly come from Rome; a manciple, or purveyor of provisions for the inns of court; and, lastly, Chaucer himself. There is a general prologue to the poem, in which these characters are described so vividly as absolutely to walk out of the canvas. Had the poem been lost all but this part, while the hiatus would have been felt very tantalising, we think the opinion entertained of the author's powers would have been as high as it is now. The tales which are told by each in rotation, as the journey proceeds, are preceded each by a short prologue, in which the progress of the pilgrims is recorded, and iu which they carry on conversations, make comments on each other's stories, or cut jests. The original plan was that each pilgrim was to tell four tales, which would have swelled the number to one hundred and twenty. The actual number is twenty-four.

In these there is great variety, and not one of them is quite unworthy of its author's genius. For the lovers of chivalric enterprise and heroic adventure, there is the Knight's Tale, the well-known story of Palamon and Arcite. For those—few, we suspect, in this age—who are disposed to pardon indecency for the sake of fun, there are the stories told by the Miller, the Reeve, the Merchant, and the Shipmaster. For the admirers of the pathetic, there is the beautiful story of Custance, the pious and persecuted daughter of the Emperor of Russia, as told by the Man of Law; and the tale, already referred to, of Griselda, or the Patient Wife, recited by the Clerk. For the lovers of quaint humour and sharp satire, there are the tales told, in emulation of each other, by the Friar and the Summoner. For those who wish specimens of Chaucer's prose style, so clear, racy, musical in cadence, and pregnant with meaning, there are the poet's own tale of Melibœus and the Parson's closing sermon on Repentance and the Seven Deadly Sins. In graceful badinage and amusing incident, the Nun's Priest's story of Chanticleer and Dame Partelot (afterwards admirably rendered in Dryden's Cock and Fox) will be found a masterpiece. The Monk's Tale is full of historical lore; the Squire's is that famous one about Cambuscan bold, so much admired by Milton. That of the Prioress, concerning the miracle of the holy Christian child murdered by the Jews, is exquisitely fine, and has been modernised by Wordsworth; and in the Pardoner's, with the search for Death which it describes, Chaucer, as we have seen, reaches a weird and haggard grandeur which has rarely been surpassed.

We promised in our Life of Chaucer, to glance in this essay at some of those poems which are not included in our edition. The first of these of any length is " The Romaunt of the Rose." This is entirely a translation from William de Lorris and John de Meun, two Frenchmen of the twelfth and thirteenth centuries.

This Romaunt is understood to have been exceedingly popular in our poet's age. Its object is to represent, under the allegory of a rose which is in a position difficult of access, and protected by magical art, "the helps and furtherances, as also the lets and impediments, that lovers have in their suits." It is quite a flowery wilderness—a magnificent but endless and pathless maze of poetry, not unlike the "Endymion" of Keats. It is now as a whole nearly illegible; but abounds in descriptive passages, one of which we may quote.

> "Hard is his heart that loveth nought
> In May, when all this mirth is wrought,
> When he may on these branches hear
> The smallë birdës singing clear
> Their blissful sweetë song piteous;
> And in this season delicious,
> When love affirmeth [informeth] allë thing,
> Methought one night, in my sleeping,
> Right in my bed full readily,
> That it was by the morrowe early,
> And up I rose, and 'gan me clothe;
> Anon I wash my handës both.
> A silver needle forth I drew,
> Out of aguiler queinte enow,*
> And 'gan this needle thread anon,
> For out of town me list to gon,
> The sound of birdës for to hear
> That on the bushes singen clear.
> Alone I went in my playing,
> The smallë fowlës' song heark'ning;
> A river I heard run fastë by,
> And fairer playen none saw I
> Than playen me by that river.
> For from a hill that stood there near,
> Came down the stream full stiff and bold,
> Clear was the water, and as cold
> As any well is, sooth to sayn,
> And somedeal less it was than Seine."

"The Legend of Good Women" relates the history of nine or ten ancient heroines. More interesting is "The Lamentation of Mary Magdalene for the Death of Christ." The following stanzas are quaint, but touching:—

---

* "Aguiler queinte enow;" A strange-enough needlecase.

> Adieu, my Lord! my love so fair of face!
> Adieu, my turtle-dove so fresh of hue!
> Adieu, my mirth! adieu, all my solace!
> Adieu, alas! my Saviour Lord Jesu,
> Adieu, the gentillest that e'er I knew!
> Adieu, my most excellent paramour! *
> Fairer than rose, sweeter than lily flower!
> Adieu, my hope of pleasure eternal!
> My life, my wealth, and my prosperity;
> Mine heart of gold! my pearl oriental!
> Mine adamant of perfect charity?
> My chief refuge, and my felicity!
> My comfort, and my recreation!
> Farewell, my perpetual salvation!
> Farewell, mine Emperor celestial,
> And most beautiful Prince of all mankind!
> Adieu, my Lord of heart most liberal!
> Farewell, my sweetest, bothë soul and mind!
> So loving a spouse shall I never find.
> Adieu, my Sovereign! very gentleman!
> Farewell, dear heart! as heartily as I can.
> My soul for anguish is now full thirsty;
> I faint, I faint right sore for heaviness,
> My Lord, my Spouse! *cur me dereliquisti?*
> Sith I for thee suffer all this distress,
> What causeth thee to seem thus merciless?
> Sith it thee pleaseth of me to make an end,
> *In manus tuas* my spirit I commend."

"Troilus and Cresseide" is a lengthy poem in five books. It tells essentially the same story with the play of Shakspeare bearing the same name, but in a very different spirit. Shakspeare's great object in his drama is to laugh; and he seems for the nonce to exchange places with its real hero Thersites, whom a modern has thus characterised :—

> " Ditch-deliver'd by a drab,
>   Early taught to filch and gab,
>   Wild as any desert donkey,
>   Wicked as an untamed monkey,
>   He laughs, he rails, he halts, he hobbles,
>   He lies, he swears, he drinks, he gobbles,
>   Who now a fool, and now a wit is,
>   And who by men is called Thersites."

---

* "Paramour:" Here, of course, understood in a pure sense.

Chaucer, on the other hand, extracts the pathos that is in the story, and uses it in his own fine way, " painting the afflicting circumstances slowly and assiduously, and descending exploringly into the caverns of tears."   As a whole, however, the poem is tedious, although fine passages are frequent.   One often quoted is that which describes Cresseide's yielding and acknowledging her love :—

> " And as the new abashed nightingale
>   That stinteth first when she beginneth sing,
>   When that she heareth any herdë's tale,
>   Or in the hedges any wight stirring,
>   And after sicker doth her voice outring ;
>   Right so Cresseide, when that her dreadë stent,
>   Open'd her heart and told him her intent."

Let us quote, too, a passage in which we find the germ of his coming " comedy "—" The Canterbury Tales :"—

> " Go, little book, go, little tragedy ;
>   There God my Maker yet ere that I die
>   So send me might to make *some comedy;*
>   But little book, make thou thee none envy,
>   But subject ben unto all poesy,
>   And kiss the steps where as thou seest pace
>   Of Virgil, Ovid, Homer, Lucan, Stace [Statius]

Excellent, too, in their way, are " The Complaint of the Black Knight," " Chaucer's Dream," " The Book of the Duchess," " The Court of Love," and " The Assembly of Fowls," wherein " all the fowls being gathered on St Valentine's Day to choose their mates, a female eagle, being beloved of three tercels (male eagles), requireth a year's respite to make her choice, upon this trial, *Qui bien aime tard oublië*—He that loveth well is slow to forget."   " The Cuckoo and the Nightingale " is the relation of a dream, in which the poet hears the two birds disputing about their comparative merits as songsters, and about love, in a very edifying and poetical manner.   The opening is striking :—

> " The god of love, ah, *benedicite!*
>   How mighty and how great a lord is he !
>   For he can maken of low heartës high,
>   And of high low and likë for to die,
>   And hardë heartes he can maken free ;
>   He can maken within a little stound

> Of sick folkö whole and fresh and sound,
> And of the whole he can ymakö seke;
> He can ybinden, and unbinden eke,
> That he will have ybounden or unbound."

From " The Flower and the Leaf" we have quoted a passage before. It is, as might have been expected from the title, full of beautiful flowers of speech and luxuriant leaves of language. Its argument is thus stated by the poet:—"A gentlewoman, out of an arbour in a grove, seeth a great company of knights and ladies in a dance upon the green grass; the which being ended, they all kneel down and do honour to the daisy, some to the flower, and some to the leaf; afterwards this gentlewoman learneth from one of these ladies the meaning thereof, which is this: they which honour the flower, a thing fading with every blast, are such as look after beauty and worldly pleasure, but they that honour the leaf, which abideth with the root, notwithstanding the frosts and storms of winter, are they which follow virtue and 'during qualities, without regard of worldly respects." We give two more specimens of the poetry :—

> " Then I saw a passing wonder sight,
> For then the nightingale, that all the day
> Had in the laurel sat and did her might
> The whole service to sing 'longing to May,
> All suddenly began to take her flight,
> And to the lady of the Leaf forthright
> She flew, and set out on her hand softly !
> Which was a thing I marvell'd at greatly.
> The goldfinch eke, that from the medlar-tree
> Was fled for heat unto the bushes cold,
> Unto the lady of the Flower 'gan flee,
> And on her hand he set him as he would,
> And pleasantly his wingës 'gan to fold,
> And for to sing they pain'd [exerted] them both as sore
> As they had done of all the day before."

She who sees all this is conversing with a lady, and addresses her thus,—

> " ' Now, fair Madám !' quod I,
> '(If I durst ask,) what is the cause and why
> That knightës have the ensign of honóur
> Rather by the Leaf than by the Flower?'
> 'Sothly [truly], daughter,' quod she, ' this is the truth,
> For knightës ever should be persévering

> To seek honóur without feintise [feigning] or sloth,
> From well to better, in all manner thing;
> In sign of which with leaves aye lasting
> They be rewarded after their degree,
> Whose lusty green may not appaired [impaired] be,
> But aye keeping their beauty fresh and green;
> For there is no stormë that may them deface,
> Ne hail nor snow, ne wind nor frostës keen;
> Wherefore they have this property and grace.
> And for [because] the Flower within a little space
> Willen be lost, so simple of natúre
> They be that they no grievance may endure,
> And every storm will blow them soon away,
> Nor they last not but for a seasón,
> That is the cause (the very truth to say)
> That they may not, by no way of reasón,
> Be put to no such occupatión.'
> 'Madám,' quod I, 'with all my whole service
> I thank you now in my most humble wise,
> For now I am ascértain'd thoroughly
> Of everything that I desired to know.'"

The most ingenious, curious, and fanciful of all Chaucer's poems is his "House of Fame." It is full of strange incidents, wild imaginations, philosophy run mad, and clever sarcastic touches. Pope, in his "Temple of Fame," has chastened and polished the conception—turning the fantastically-grand into the elegant. Chaucer dreams, and in his dream is snatched away by an eagle larger and more lustrous than any he had ever seen before—so bright that it seemed

> " As if the heaven had ywon,
> All new from God, another sun."

On his way upwards with the poet in his claws, this bird discourses some strange acoustical principles and rather doubtful philosophy to his acquiescent prey, chiefly in reference to the point to which he is conducting him—the House of Fame namely—" the central point in space, where all sounds in heaven, earth, and sea,—from the roar of the thunder to the squeak of a mouse, from the groans of an earthquake to the hum of an ephemeron's wing,—meet together; the home of sound, where, as inside a great bell, all the noises of the universe hold their booming congress."

This marvellous palace stands on a rock of ice. The poet, whom the eagle has now deserted, finds its door beset by a multitude, composed of jugglers, mimics, singers, astrologers, and troubadours. Further in, he meets a crowd of heralds and pursuivants, richly clad in chivalric devices, and shouting "Largess, largess! God save our gentle Lady Fame!" In the interior, he finds Fame herself—a singular figure, covered all over with eyes, ears, and tongues, with partridge-wings on her feet, and hair of wavy gold descending on her shoulders. She stands in the midst of a storm of everlasting music, bellowing through the golden hall. On her shoulders appear the arms and name of her two principal favourites, Hercules and Alexander—on a row of pillars stand statues of celebrated historians and poets—Josephus appearing on a pillar composed of lead mixed with iron; Homer on a very high pillar of iron; Virgil on one of iron, plated with tin; Lucan on one of iron, very strongly wrought; Ovid on one of copper; Claudian on one of sulphur; and Statius on a *pillar of iron, painted with tigers' blood.*

By and by, a great crowd rush into the room, professing to have done meritorious actions, and seeking renown from Fame. She refuses, simply "because it is her pleasure." She sends then for Æolus, the god of wind, with his two trumpets, Praise and Slander; and when a second set of suitors appear, and put in their claim, Fame admits its validity, but says she cannot grant it, but will grant the contrary of their request. Whereupon, she calls Æolus to lift his Slander-trumpet. He obeys, and such a blast follows!

> "Throughout every regioun
> Ywent this foulë trumpet's sound,
> As swift as pellet out of gun,
> When fire is in the powder run;
> And such a smoke began out-wend
> Out of the foulë trumpet's end,
> Black, blue, and greenish, swartish, red,
> As doeth where that men melt lead;
> And aye the farther that it ran,
> The greater waxen it began,
> As doth the river from a well,
> And it stank as the pit of hell."

Now comes a third company seeking renown, and Fame, in her fickleness, grants it. Æolus now takes his bright trumpet—

> " 'Full gladly, lady mine,' he said,
> And out his trump of gold he bray'd
> Anon, and set it to his mouth,
> And blew it east, and west, and south,
> And north, as loud as any thunder,
> That every wight hath it of wonder.
> So broad it ran before it stent,
> And certes all the breath that went
> Out of the trumpet's mouth y smell'd,
> As men a potful of balm held
> Among a basketful of roses."

Next comes forward a small company, saying that they wish no fame, although they had done good with all their might. The goddess grants their request; but when another set proffer the same request immediately after, she refuses, asking them if they mean to insult her in her own house, and charging Æolus to publish their names to the universe. The sixth company admit that they have done nothing, except captivate the hearts of ladies ; and, strange to tell, Lady Fame too is captivated, and makes the wind-god blow one of his very loudest blasts in their praise. The seventh, making the same acknowledgment, are treated very differently.

> " 'Fie on you,' quod she, ' every one,
> Ye nasty swine, ye idle wretches,
> Fulfill'd of rotten slowë tetches.
> What ! falsë thieves, and so ye would
> Be famëd good, and nothing would
> Deserven why, nor never thought.
> Men rather you to hangen ought ;
> For you be like the sleepy cat,
> That would have fish, but wot you what ?
> He willen nothing wet his claws.
> Evil thirst come to your jaws,
> And mine also, if I you it grant."

And Æolus follows up this testy speech with a blast upon the black trumpet, of such a peculiarly comic kind, that all, except the petitioners, fall down in fits of laughter !

Fame next refuses the request of some who admit they have done nothing but wicked actions, yet who seek renown notwithstanding; and a crowd who succeed, leaping and dancing, and seeking fame on account of their splendid sins, and gigantic acts of scoundrelism—such as burning temples, ravishing goddesses, and the like—she satisfies by ordering Æolus to make their infamy, through his black trumpet, universal and everlasting. At this moment some one taps the poet on the back—

> " And sayed, 'Friend, what is thy name?
> Art thou come hither to seek Fame?'"

Chaucer answers,—

> " ' Have Fame! nay, forsooth, friend,' quod I,
> ' I come not hither, grant mercy!
>
> .   .   .   .   .
>
> The cause why I standen here
> Is some new tidings for to hear.
> Some newe thing, I ne not what,
> Tidings either this or that,
> Of love, or of such thinges glad;
> For certainly he that me made
> To comen hither, said to me
> I should both yhear and see
> In this place many wonder things.' "

He then surveys, more particularly, under the care of his new guide, the penetralia and purlieus of the temple, and at last awakes, and behold it is a dream. The entire poem well deserves perusal, as a piece of marvellous fancy, wit, and imagination.

CONTENTS.

THE CANTERBURY TALES.

PROLOGUE TO SIR TOPAS.

WHEN said was this mirácle, every man   13621
As sober[1] was, that wonder was to see,
Till that our Host to japen[2] he began,
And then at erst[3] he looked upon me,
And saidë thus; 'What man art thou?' quod he;
'Thou lookest, as thou wouldest find an hare,
For ever upon the ground I see thee stare.

  'Approachë near, and look up merrily.
Now ware you, Sirs, and let this man have place.
He in the waist is shapen as well as I: 13630
This were a puppet in an arm t' embrace
For any woman, small and fair of face.
He seemeth elvish by his countenánce,
For unto no wight doth he dalliánce.

  'Say now somewhat, since other folk have said;
Tell us a tale of mirth and that anon.'
'Hostë,' quod I, 'ne be not evil apaid,[4]
For other talë certes can I none,

[1] Serious.

[2] Jest.

[3] For the first time.

[4] Satisfied.

But of a rhyme I learned yore[1] agone.'   13639
'Yea, that is good,' quod he, 'we shallen hear
Some dainty thing, methinketh by thy chere.'[2]

¹ Long.

² Expression.

THE RHYME OF SIR TOPÁS.

LISTENETH, lordings, in good intent,
And I will tell you *verament*
   Of mirth and of solas,[3]
All of a knight was fair and gent
In battle and in tournament,
   His name was Sir Topas.

Yborn he was in far countrý,
In Flanders, all beyond the sea,
   At Popering in the place,   13650
His father was a man full free,
And lord he was of that country,
   As it was Goddë's grace.

Sir Topas was a doughty swain,
White was his face as paindemain,[4]
   His lippës red as rose.
His rudde[5] is like scarlét in grain,
And I you tell in good certáin
   He had a seemly nose.

His hair, his beard, was like saffroún,   13660
That to his girdle reach'd adown,
   His shoes of cordëwane;[6]

³ Enjoyment.

⁴ Fine bread.

⁵ Complexion.

⁶ Spanish leather.

Of Bruges were his hosen brown;   13663
His robë was of ciclatoun,[1]
   That costë many a jane.[2]

He couldë hunt at the wild deer,
And ride on hawking for the rivére
   With gray goshawk on hand:
Thereto he was a good archére,
Of wrestling was there none his peer,   13670
   There[3] any ram should stand.

Full many a maiden bright in bow'r
They mourned for him *par amour*,
   When them were bet[4] to sleep;
But he was chaste and no lechoúr,
And sweet as is the bramble flow'r,
   That beareth the red hepe.[5]

And so it fell upon a day,
Forsooth, as I you tellen may,
   Sir Topas would out ride;   13680
He worth[6] upon his steedë gray,
And in his hand a launcëgay,[7]
   A long sword by his side.

He pricketh through a fair forést,
Therein is many a wildë beast,
   Yea, bothë buck and hare,
And as he pricked north and east,
I tell it you, him had almest
   Betid a sorry care.

There springen herbës great and smale,   13690
The liquorice and the setëwale,[8]
   And many a clove-gilofre,

---

[1] Cloth of gold.
[2] A coin of Genoa.
[3] Where.
[4] Better.
[5] Fruit of the dog-rose.
[6] Mounted.
[7] Spear.
[8] Valerian.

And nutëmeg to put in ale,   13693
Whether it be moist[1] or stale,
   Or for to lay in coffer.

The birdës singen, it is no nay,
The sperhawk and the popinjay,
   That joy it was to hear,
The throstle cock made eke his lay,
The woodë dove upon the spray   13700
   He sang full loud and clear.

Sir Topas fell in love-longing
All when he heard the throstle sing,
   And prick'd as he were wood;[2]
His fairë steed in his pricking
So swattë,[3] that men might him wring,
   His sidës were all blood.

Sir Topas eke so weary was
For pricking on the softë grass,
   So fierce was his couráge,   13710
That down he laid him in that place,
To maken his steed some solace,
   And gave him good foráge.

' Ah, Saint Mary, *benedicite,*
What aileth this lovë at me
   To bindë me so sore ?
Me dreamed all this night pardie,
An elf-queen shall my leman be,
   And sleep under my gore.

An elf-queen will I love ywis,[4]   13720
For in this world no woman is
   Worthy to be my make || in toun,—

[1] New.

[2] Mad.

[3] Sweated.

[4] Assured-ly.

All other women I forsake,   13723
And to an elf-queen I me take ·
  By dale and eke by down.'

Into his saddle he clomb anon,
And pricked over stile and stone
  An elf-queen for t' espy,
Till he so long had ridden and gone,
That he found in a privy wonne[1]   13730   [1] Haunt.
  The country of Faerie.

Wherein he soughtë north and south,
And oft he spied with his mouth
  In many a forest wild,
For in that country n'as there none,
That to him durst ride or gone,
  Neither wife nor child.

Till that there came a great giaunt,
His namë was Sir Oliphaunt,
  A perilous man of deed,   13740
He saidë, 'Child,[2] by Termagaunt,   [2] Young man.
But[3] if thou prick out of mine haunt,   [3] Except.
  Anon I slay thy steed ‖ with mace—
Here is the Queen of Faerie,
With harp, and pipe, and symphony,
  Dwelling in this place.'

The Child said, 'All so may I the,[4]   [4] Thrive.
To-morrow will I meeten thee,
  When I have mine armoúr,
And yet I hopë *par ma fay*,   13750
That thou shalt with this launcëgay
  Abyen[5] it full sour; ‖ thy maw—   [5] Pay for it.

Shall I pierce, if I may,   13753
Ere it be fully prime of the day,
    For here thou shalt be slaw.'[1]

Sir Topas drew aback full fast;
This giant at him stonës cast
    Out of a fell staff sling :
But fair escaped Child Topas,
And all it was through Goddë's grace,   13760
    And through his fair bearíng.

Yet listeneth, lordings, to my tale,
Merrier than the nightingale,
    For now I will you roun,[2]
How Sir Topas with sidës smale,
Pricking over hill and dale,
    Is come again to town.

His merry men commandeth he,
To maken them both game and glee,
    For needës must he fight,   13770
With a giánt with headës three,
For paramour and jollity
    Of one that shone full bright.

'Do[3] come,' he said, 'my minëstrales
And gestours[4] for to tellen tales
    Anon in mine arming,
Of rómances that be reales,[5]
Of popës and of cardinales,
    And eke of love-longing.'

They fet[6] him first the sweetë wine,   13780
And mead eke in a masclin,[7]
    And real spicery,

---

[1] Slain.

[2] Whisper.

[3] Cause.

[4] Narrators.

[5] Royal.

[6] Fetched.

[7] Drinking-cups.

Of ginger-bread that was full fine, 13783
And liquorice and eke cumin,
 With sugar that is trie.[1]

He diddë,[2] next his whitë lere,[3]
Of cloth of lakë[4] fine and clear
 A breech and eke a shert,
And next his shirt an haketon,[5]
And over that an habergeon,[6] 13790
 For piercing of his hert,

And over that a fine hauberk,[7]
Was all ywrought of Jewës' werk,
 Full strong it was of plate,
And over that his coat-armour,[8]
As white as is the lily flow'r,
 In which he would debate.[9]

His shield was all of gold so red,
And therein was a boarë's head,
 A charboucle[10] beside; 13800
And there he swore on ale and bread
How that the giant should be dead,
 Betide whatso betide.

His jambeux[11] were of cuirbouly,[12]
His swordë's sheath of ivory,
 His helm of laton[13] bright,
His saddle was of rewel bone,
His bridle as the sunnë shone,
 Or as the moonë light.

His spearë was of fine cypress, 13810
That bodeth war, and nothing peace,
 The head full sharp yground.

---

[1] Tried, refined.

[2] Put on.
[3] Skin.
[4] Kind of cloth.

[5] Cassock.

[6] Coat of mail.

[7] Plate-armour.

[8] Knight's surcoat.

[9] Fight.

[10] Carbuncle.

[11] Boots.
[12] Prepared leather.
[13] Brass.

His steedë was all dapple gray,   13813
It go'th an amble in the way
   Full softëly and round ‖ in lond—
Lo, Lordës mine, here is a fytt;[1]
If ye will any more of it,
   To tell it will I fond.[2]

Now hold your mouth *pour charitè*,
Both knight and lady free,   13820
   And heark'neth to my spell,
Of battle and of chivalry,
Of ladies' love and druerie,[3]
   Anon I will you tell.

Men speaken of romances of pris,[4]
Of Hornchild, and of Ipotis,
   Of Bevis, and Sir Guy,
Of Sir Libeux, and Pleindamour,
But Sir Topas, he beareth the flow'r
   Of real chivalry.   13830

His goodë steed he all bestrode,
And forth upon his way he glode,[5]
   As sparkle out of brond;[6]
Upon his crest he bare a tow'r,
And therein stick'd a lily flow'r,
   God shield his corps from shond.[7]

And for he was a knight auntrous,[8]
He n'oldë sleepen in none house,
   But liggen[9] in his hood,
His brightë helm was his wanger,[10]   13840
And by him baited his destrer[11]
   Of herbës fine and good.

---

[1] Division of a poem.
[2] Try.
[3] Gallantry.
[4] Praise.
[5] Glided, darted.
[6] Torch.
[7] Harm.
[8] Adventurous.
[9] Lie.
[10] Pillow.
[11] War-horse.

Himself drank water of the well, 13843
As did the knight Sir Percivell
  So worthy under weed,
Till on a day ——

PROLOGUE TO MELIBŒUS.

'No more of this, for Goddë's dignity,'   13847
Quod ourë Hostë, 'for thou makest me
So weary of thy very lewedness,[1]
That all so wisly[2] God my soulë bless,
Mine carës achen of thy drafty[3] speech.
Now such a rhyme the devil I beteche;[4]
This may well be rhyme doggerel,' quod he.
    'Why so?' quod I, 'why wilt thou letten[5] me
More of my talë, than another man,
Since that it is the bestë rhyme I can?'
    'By God,' quod he, 'for plainly at one word,
Thy drafty rhyming is not worth a tord:
Thou dost nought ellës but dispendest time.
Sir, at one word, thou shalt no longer rhyme.   13860
Let see whe'r thou canst tellen ought in gestc,[6]
Or tellen in prose somewhat at the lest,
In which there be some mirth or some doctrine.'
    'Gladly,' quod I, 'by Goddë's sweetë pine
I will you tell a little thing in prose,
That oughtë liken you, as I suppose,
Or else certes ye be too dangerous.[7]
It is a moral talë virtuous,

[1] Ignorance.
[2] Surely.
[3] Worthless as draff.
[4] Betake.
[5] Hinder.
[6] Narrative.
[7] Difficult.

All be it told sometime in sundry wise   13869
Of sundry folk, as I shall you devise.
  'As thus, ye wot that every' Evangelist,
That telleth us the pain of Jesus Christ,
Ne saith not all thing as his fellow doth:
But nathëless their sentence is all soth,[1]   [1] True.
And all accorden as in their senténce,[2]   [2] Meaning.
All[3] be there in their telling differénce: [3] Although.
For some of them say more, and some say less,
When they his piteous passión express;
I mean of Mark and Matthew, Luke and John;
But doubtëless their sentence is all one.   13880
Therefore, lordingës all, I you beseech,
If that ye think I vary in my speech,
As thus, though that I tellë some deal more
Of proverbës, than ye have heard before
Comprehended in this little treatise here,
To enforcen with the effect of my mattére,
And though I not the samë wordës say
As ye have heard, yet to you all I pray
Blameth me not, for, as in my senténce,
Shall ye nowhere finden no differénce   13890
From the senténce of thilkë treatise lite,[4]   [4] Little.
After the which this merry tale I write.
And therefore hearkeneth what I shall say,
And let me tellen all my tale, I pray.'

THE TALE OF MELIBŒUS.

A YOUNG man called Melibœus, mighty and rich, begat upon his wife, that called was Prudence, a daughter which that called was Sophia.

Upon a day befell, that he for his disport is went into the fields him to play. His wife and eke his daughter hath he left within his house, of which the doors were fast shut. Four of his old foes have it espied, and set ladders to the walls of his house, and by the windows been entered, and beaten his wife, and wounded his daughter with five mortal wounds, in five sundry places; this is to say, in her feet, in her hands, in her ears, in her nose, and in her mouth; and left her for dead, and went away.

When Melibœus returned was into his house, and saw all this mischief, he, like a mad man, rending his clothes, 'gan to weep and cry.

Prudence his wife, as far forth as she durst, besought him of his weeping for to stint: but not forthy[1] he 'gan to cry and weepen ever longer the more.

This noble wife Prudence remembered her upon the sentence of Ovid, in his book that cleped is the 'Remedy of Love,' whereas he saith, He is a fool that disturbeth the mother to weep, in the death of her child, till she have wept her fill, as for a certain time: and then shall a man do his diligence with

[1] Therefore.

amiable words her to recomfort and pray her of her weeping for to stint.[1] For which reason this noble wife Prudence suffered her husband for to weep and cry, as for a certain space; and when she saw her time, she said to him in this wise : 'Alas! my lord,' quod she, 'why make ye yourself for to be like a fool? Forsooth, it appertaineth not to a wise man to make such a sorrow. Your daughter, with the grace of God, shall warish[2] and escape. And all[3] were it so that she right now were dead, ye ought not as for her death yourself to destroy. Seneca saith, " The wise man shall not take too great discomfort for the death of his children, but certes he should suffer it in patience, as well as he abideth the death of his own proper person." '

This Melibœus answered anon and said: 'What man,' quod he, 'should of his weeping stint, that hath so great a cause for to weep? Jesus Christ, our Lord, himself wept for the death of Lazarus his friend.' Prudence answered, 'Certes well I wot, temperate weeping is nothing defended,[4] to him that sorrowful is, among folk in sorrow, but it is rather granted him to weep. The Apostle Paul unto the Romans writeth, " Man shall rejoice with them that make joy, and weep with such folk as weep." But though temperate weeping be granted, outrageous weeping certes is defended. Measure of weeping should be considered, after the lore[5] that teacheth us Seneca. " When that thy friend is dead," quod he, " let not thine eyes too moist be of tears, nor too much dry: although the tears come to thine eyes, let them not fall. And when thou hast forgone[1] thy friend, do diligence to get again another friend: and this is more wisdom than for to weep for thy friend which that thou hast lorn,[2] for therein is no boot."[3] And therefore if ye govern you by sapience, put away sorrow out of your heart. Remember you that Jesus Sirach saith, "A man that is joyous and glad in heart, it him conserveth flourishing in his age: but soothly a sorrowful heart maketh his bones dry." He saith eke thus, "that sorrow in heart slayeth full many a man." Solomon saith, "that right as moths in the sheep's fleece annoy[4] to the clothes, and the small worms to the tree, right so annoyeth sorrow to the heart of man." Wherefore us ought as well in the death of our children, as in the loss of our goods temporal, have patience.

'Remember you upon the patient Job, when he had lost his children and his temporal substance, and in his body endured and received full many a grievous tribulation, yet said he thus: "Our Lord hath given it to me, our Lord hath bereft it me; right as our Lord hath would, right so is it done; blessed be the name of our Lord."' To these foresaid things answered Melibœus unto his wife Prudence: 'All thy words,' quod he, 'be true, and thereto profitable, but truly mine heart is troubled with this sorrow so grievously, that I know not what to do.' 'Let call,' quod Prudence, 'thy true friends all, and thy lineage, which that be wise, and tell to them your case, and

[1] Lost.

[2] Lost.

[3] Profit.

[4] Injure.

hearken what they say in counselling, and govern you after their sentence.[1]　Solomon saith, "Work all things by counsel, and thou shalt never repent."'

Then, by counsel of his wife Prudence, this Melibœus let call a great congregation of folk, as surgeons, physicians, old folk and young, and some of his old enemies reconciled (as by their semblance) to his love and to his grace: and therewithal there come some of his neighbours, that did him reverence more for dread than for love, as it happeneth oft.　There come also full many subtle flatterers, and wise advocates learned in the law.

And when these folk together assembled were, this Melibœus in sorrowful wise shewed them his case, and by the manner of his speech, it seemed that in heart he bare a cruel ire, ready to do vengeance upon his foes, and suddenly desired that the war should begin, but nevertheless yet asked he his counsel upon this matter.　A surgeon, by licence and assent of such as were wise, uprose, and unto Melibœus said, as ye may hear.

'Sir,' quod he, 'as to us surgeons appertaineth, that we do to every wight the best that we can, where as we be withholden, and to our patient that we do no damage; wherefore it happeneth many time and oft, that when two men have each wounded other, one same surgeon healeth them both, wherefore unto our art it is not pertinent to nurse war, nor parties to support.　But certes, as to the warishing[2] of your daughter, albeit so that perilously she be wounded, we shall do so attentive business from day to night, that with the grace of God, she shall be whole and sound, as soon as is possible.' Almost right in the same wise the physicians answered, save that they said a few words more : that right as maladies be cured by their contraries, right so shall man warish war. His neighbours full of envy, his feigned friends that seemed reconciled, and his flatterers, made semblance of weeping, and impaired and agregged[1] much of this matter, in praising greatly Melibœus of might, of power, of riches, and of friends, despising the power of his adversaries: and said utterly, that he anon should wreak him on his foes, and begin war.

Uprose then an advocate that was wise, by leave and by counsel of other that were wise, and said, 'Lordings, the need for the which we be assembled in this place, is a full heavy thing, and an high matter, because of the wrong and of the wickedness that hath been done, and eke by reason of the great damages that in time coming be possible to fall for the same cause, and eke by reason of the great riches and power of the parties both, for the which reasons, it were a full great peril to err in this matter. Wherefore, Melibœus, this is our sentence;[2] we counsel you, above all things, that right anon thou do thy diligence in keeping of thy proper person, in such a wise that thou ne want no espy nor watch, thy body for to save. And after that, we counsel that in thine house thou set sufficient garrison, so that they may as well thy body as thy house defend. But certes for to move war, or suddenly for to do vengeance, we may not deem[1] in so little time that it were profitable. Wherefore we ask leisure and space to have deliberation in this case to deem; for the common proverb saith thus; "He that soon deemeth, soon shall repent." And eke men say, that that judge is wise, that soon understandeth a matter, and judgeth by leisure. For albeit so, that all tarrying be annoying, algates[2] it is not to reproof in giving of judgment, nor in vengeance taking, when it is sufficient and reasonable. And that showed our Lord Jesus Christ by example; for when that the woman that was taken in adultery, was brought in his presence to know what should be done with her person, albeit that he wist well himself what that he would answer, yet would he not answer suddenly, but he would have deliberation, and in the ground he wrote twice; and by these causes we ask deliberation: and we shall then by the grace of God counsel the thing that shall be profitable.'

Upstarted then the young folk at once, and the most part of that company have scorned this old wise man, and begun to make noise and said, 'Right so as while that iron is hot men should smite, right so men shall do[3] wreak their wrongs, while that they be fresh and new:' and with loud voice they cried, 'War! War!' Uprose then one of these old wise, and with his hand made countenance that men

[1] Decide.

[2] However.

[3] Cause.

should hold them still, and give him audience. 'Lordings,' quod he, 'there is full many a man that crieth War! war! that wot full little what war amounteth. War at his beginning hath so great an entering and so large, that every wight may enter when him liketh, and lightly[1] find war: but certes what end that shall befall, it is not light to know. For soothly when that war is once begun, there is full many a child unborn of his mother, that shall sterve[2] young, by cause of that war, or else live in sorrow, and die in wretchedness: and therefore ere that any war be begun, men must have great counsel and great deliberation.' And when this old man weened to enforce his tale by reasons, well-nigh all at once begun they to rise, for to break his tale, and bid him full oft his words for to abridge. For soothly he that preacheth to them that list not hear his words, his sermon them annoyeth. For Jesus Sirach saith, that music in weeping is a noious[3] thing. This is to say, as much availeth to speak before folk to which his speech annoyeth, as to sing before him that weepeth. And when this wise man saw that him wanted audience, all shamefast he set him down again. For Solomon saith, 'Where as thou mayest have no audience, enforce thee not to speak.' 'I see well,' quod this wise man, 'that the common proverb is sooth, that good counsel wanteth, when it is most need.'

Yet had this Meliboeus in his council many folk, that privily in his ear counselled him certain thing,

[1] Easily.

[2] Die.

[3] Trouble-some.

and counselled him the contrary in general audience. When Melibœus had heard that the greatest part of his council were accorded that he should make war, anon he consented to their counselling, and fully affirmed their sentence. Then Dame Prudence, when that she saw how that her husband shaped him for to wreak him on his foes, and to begin war, she in full humble wise, when she saw her time, said him these words: 'My lord,' quod she, 'I you beseech as heartily as I dare and can, haste you not too fast, and for all guerdons[1] as give me audience. For Piers Alphonse saith, "Whoso that doth to thee either good or harm, haste thee not to requite it, for in this wise thy friend will abide, and thine enemy shall the longer live in dread." The proverb saith, "He hasteth well that wisely can abide: and in wicked haste is no profit."'

This Melibœus answered unto his wife Prudence: 'I purpose not,' quod he, 'to work by thy counsel, for many causes and reasons: for certes every wight[2] would hold me then a fool; this is to say, if I for thy counselling would change things that be ordained and affirmed by so many wise men. Secondly, I say, that all women be wicked, and none good of them all. For of a thousand men, saith Solomon, I found one good man: but certes of all women, good woman found I never. And also certes, if I governed me by thy counsel, it should seem that I had given thee over me the mastery: and God forbid that it so were. For Jesus Sirach saith, that if the wife have the

[1] Rewards.

[2] Person.

mastery, she is contrarious to her husband. And Solomon saith, "Never in thy life to thy wife, nor to thy child, nor to thy friend, give power over thyself: for better it were that thy children ask of thee things that them needeth, than thou see thyself in the hands of thy children." And also if I will work by thy counselling, certes it must be sometime secret, till it were time that it be known: and this may not be, if I should be counselled by thee. [For it is written, "The janglerie[1] of women can nothing hide, save that which they wot not." After the Philosopher saith, "In wicked counsel women vanquish men:" and for these reasons I ought not to be counselled by thee.]'

When Dame Prudence, full debonairly[2] and with great patience, had heard all that her husband liked for to say, then asked she of him licence for to speak, and said in this wise. 'My lord,' quod she, 'as to your first reason, it may lightly be answered: for I say that it is no folly to change counsel when the thing is changed, or else when the thing seemeth otherwise than it seemed before. And moreover I say, though that ye have sworn and behight[3] to perform your emprise,[4] and nevertheless ye weive[5] to perform that same emprise by just cause, men should not say therefore ye were a liar, nor forsworn: for the book saith, that the wise man maketh no lie, when he turneth his courage[6] for the better. And albeit that your emprise be established and ordained by great multitude of folk, yet thar[7] you

[1] Prating.
[2] Courteously.
[3] Promised.
[4] Undertaking.
[5] Decline.
[6] Spirit.
[7] Behoves.

not accomplish that ordinance but[1] you liketh: for the truth of things, and the profit, be rather found in few folk that be wise and full of reason, than by great multitude of folk, there[2] every man crieth and clattereth what him liketh: soothly such multitude is not honest. As to the second reason, whereas ye say, that all women be wicked: save your grace, certes ye despise all women in this wise, and he that all despiseth, as saith the book, all displeaseth. And Seneca saith, that whoso will have sapience, shall no man dispraise, but he shall gladly teach the science that he can, without presumption or pride: and such things as he nought can, he shall not be ashamed to learn them, and to inquire of less folk than himself. And, Sir, that there hath been full many a good woman, may lightly[3] be proved: for certes, Sir, our Lord Jesus Christ would never have descended to be born of a woman, if all women had been wicked. And after that, for the great bounty[4] that is in women, our Lord Jesus Christ, when he was risen from death to life, appeared rather to a woman than to his apostles. And though that Solomon said, he found never no good woman, it followeth not therefore that all women be wicked: for though that he found no good woman, certes many another man hath found many a woman full good and true. Or else peradventure the intent of Solomon was this, that in sovereign bounty he found no woman; this is to say, that there is no wight that hath sovereign bounty, save God alone, as he himself recordeth in

[1] Unless.

[2] Where.

[3] Easily.

[4] Goodness.

his Evangels.[1] For there is no creature so good, that him ne wanteth somewhat of the perfection of God that is his maker. Your third reason is this; ye say that if that ye govern you by my counsel, it should seem that ye had given me the mastery and the lordship of your person. Sir, save your grace, it is not so; for if so were that no man should be counselled but only of them that have lordship and mastery of his person, men would not be counselled so often: for soothly[2] that man that asketh counsel of a purpose, yet hath he free choice whether he will work after that counsel or no. And as to your fourth reason, there as ye say that the janglerie[3] of women can hide things that they wot not; as whoso saith, that a woman cannot hide that she wot; Sir, these words be understood of women that be jangleresses and wicked; of which women men say that three things drive a man out of his house, that is to say, smoke, dropping of rain, and wicked wives. And of such women Solomon saith, "That a man were better dwell in desert, than with a woman that is riotous." And, Sir, by your leave, that am not I; for ye have full often assayed my great silence and my great patience, and eke how well that I can hide and hele[4] things, that men ought secretly to hide. And soothly as to your fifth reason, whereas ye say, that in wicked counsel women vanquish men; God wot that that reason stands here in no stead: for understand now, ye ask counsel for to do wickedness; and if ye will work wickedness, and your wife restraineth that wicked purpose, and overcometh you by reason and by good counsel, certes your wife ought rather to be praised than to be blamed. Thus should ye understand the philosopher that saith, "In wicked counsel women vanquish their husbands." And thereas[1] ye blame all women and their reasons, I shall shew you by many examples, that many women have been full good, and yet be, and their counsel wholesome and profitable. Eke some men have said, that the counsel of women is either too dear, or else too little of price. But albeit so that full many a woman be bad, and her counsel vile and nought worth, yet have men found full many a good woman, and discreet and wise in counselling. Lo, Jacob, through the good counsel of his mother Rebecca, won the benison[2] of his father, and the lordship over all his brethren. Judith, by her good counsel, delivered the city of Bethulia, in which she dwelt, out of the hand of Holofernes, that had it besieged, and would it all destroy. Abigail delivered Nabal her husband from David the king, that would have slain him, and appeased the ire of the king by her wit, and by her good counselling. Esther by her counsel enhanced greatly the people of God, in the reign of Assuerus the king. And the same bounty[3] in good counselling of many a good woman may men read and tell. And furthermore, when that our Lord had created Adam our forme[4] father, he said in this wise, "It is not good to be a man alone: make we to him an help semblable[5] to himself." Here may ye see that if

[1] Whereas.

[2] Blessing.

[3] Goodness.

[4] First.

[5] Like.

women were not good, and their counsel good and profitable, our Lord God of heaven would neither have wrought them, nor called them help of man, but rather confusion of man. And there said a clerk once in two verses; "What is better than gold? Jasper. What is better than jasper? Wisdom. And what is better than wisdom? Woman. And what is better than a good woman? Nothing." And, Sir, by many other reasons may ye see, that many women be good, and their counsel good and profitable. And therefore, Sir, if ye will trust to my counsel, I shall restore you your daughter whole and sound: and I will do to you so much, that ye shall have honour in this case.'

When Melibœus had heard the words of his wife Prudence, he said thus: 'I see well that the word of Solomon is sooth; for he saith, that words that be spoken discreetly by ordinance, be honeycombs, for they give sweetness to the soul, and wholesomeness to the body. And, wife, because of thy sweet words, and eke for I have proved and assayed thy great sapience and thy great truth, I will govern me by thy counsel in all things.'

'Now, Sir,' quod Dame Prudence, 'and since that ye vouchsafe to be governed by my counsel, I will inform you how that ye shall govern yourself, in choosing of your counsellors. Ye shall first in all your works meekly beseech to the high God, that he will be your counsellor, and shape you to such intent that he give you counsel and comfort, as taught

Tobias his son; "At all times thou shalt bless God, and pray him to dress[1] thy ways; and look that all thy counsels be in him for evermore." Saint James eke saith, "If any of you have need of sapience, ask it of God." And afterward, then shall ye take counsel in yourself, and examine well your own thoughts, of such things as you think that be best for your profit. And then shall ye drive from your heart three things that be contrarious to good counsel; that is to say, ire, covetousness, and hastiness.

'First, he that asketh counsel of himself, certes he must be without ire, for many causes. The first is this: he that hath great ire and wrath in himself, he weeneth alway that he may do thing that he may not do. And secondly, he that is irous and wroth, he may not well deem:[2] and he that may not well deem, may not well counsel. The third is this; he that is irous and wroth, as saith Seneca, may not speak but blameful things, and with his vicious words he stirreth other folk to anger and to ire. And eke, Sir, ye must drive covetousness out of your heart. For the Apostle saith, that covetousness is the root of all harms. And trusteth well, that a covetous man cannot deem nor think, but only to fulfil the end of his covetousness; and certes that may never be accomplished; for ever the more abundance that he hath of riches, the more he desireth. And, Sir, ye must also drive out of your heart hastiness: for certes ye may not deem for the best a sudden thought that falleth in your heart, but ye must avise you on it

[1] Order.

[2] Judge.

full oft: for as ye have heard herebefore, the common proverb is this; "He that soon deemeth, soon repenteth."

'Sir, ye be not alway in like disposition, for certes something that sometime seemeth to you that it is good for to do, another time it seemeth to you the contrary.

'And when ye have taken counsel in yourself, and have deemed by good deliberation such thing as you seemeth best, then rede[1] I you that ye keep it secret. Bewray[2] not your counsel to no person, but if so be that ye ween surely that through your bewraying your condition shall be to you more profitable. For Jesus Sirach saith, "Neither to thy foe nor to thy friend discover not thy secret, nor thy folly: for they will give you audience and looking, and supportation in your presence, and scorn you in your absence." Another clerk saith, that scarcely shalt thou find any person that may keep thy counsel secretly. The book saith, "While that thou keepest thy counsel in thine heart, thou keepest it in thy prison: and when thou bewrayest thy counsel to any wight, he holdeth thee in his snare." And therefore you is better to hide your counsel in your heart, than to pray him to whom ye have bewrayed your counsel, that he will keep it close and still. For Seneca saith, "If so be that thou mayest not thine own counsel hide, how darest thou pray any other wight thy counsel secretly to keep?" But nevertheless, if thou ween surely that thy bewraying of thy counsel

[1] Advise.
[2] Discover.

to a person will make thy condition to stand in the better plight, then shalt thou tell him thy counsel in this wise. First, thou shalt make no semblance whether thee were lever[1] peace or war, or this or that; nor shew him not thy will nor thine intent: for trust well that commonly these counsellors be flatterers, namely the counsellors of great lords, for they enforce them alway rather to speak pleasant words inclining to the lord's lust,[2] than words that be true or profitable: and therefore men say, that the rich man hath seldom good counsel, but if he have it of himself. And after that thou shalt consider thy friends and thine enemies. And as touching thy friends, thou shalt consider which of them be most faithful and most wise, and eldest and most approved in counselling: and of them shalt thou ask thy counsel, as the case requireth.

'I say, that first ye shall clepe[3] to your counsel your friends that be true. For Solomon saith, "That right as the heart of a man delighteth in savour that is sweet, right so the counsel of true friends giveth sweetness to the soul." He saith also, "There may nothing be likened to the true friend: for certes gold nor silver be not so much worth as the good will of a true friend." And eke he saith, "That a true friend is a strong defence; whoso that it findeth, certes he findeth a great treasure." Then shall ye eke consider if that your true friends be discreet and wise: for the book saith, "Ask alway thy counsel of them that be wise." And by

[1] Rather.

[2] Pleasure.

[3] Call.

this same reason shall ye clepe to your counsel your friends that be of age, such as have seen and been expert[1] in many things, and be approved in counsellings. For the book saith, "In old men is all the sapience, and in long time the prudence." And Tullius saith, that great things be not aye accomplished by strength, nor by deliverness[2] of body, but by good counsel, by authority of persons, and by science: the which three things be not feeble by age, but certes they enforce[3] and increase day by day. And then shall ye keep this for a general rule. First, ye shall clepe to your counsel a few of your friends that be especial. For Solomon saith, " Many friends have thou, but among a thousand choose thee one to be thy counsellor." For albeit so, that thou first ne tell thy counsel but to a few, thou mayest afterward tell it to more folk, if it be need. But look alway that thy counsellors have those three conditions that I have said before; that is to say, that they be true, wise, and of old experience. And work not alway in every need by one counsellor alone; for sometime behoveth it to be counselled by many. For Solomon saith, " Salvation of things is where as there be many counsellors."

' Now since that I have told you of which folk ye should be counselled, now will I teach you which counsel ye ought to eschew. First, ye shall eschew the counselling of fools: for Solomon saith, " Take no counsel of a fool; for he cannot counsel but after his own lust and his affection." The book saith,

[1] Experienced.

[2] Activity.

[3] Strengthen.

"The property of a fool is this: he troweth[1] lightly harm of every man, and lightly troweth all bounty[2] in himself." Thou shalt eke eschew the counselling of all flatterers, such as enforce them rather to praise your person by flattery than for to tell you the soothfastness of things.

'Wherefore Tullius saith, "Among all the pestilences that be in friendship, the greatest is flattery." And therefore it is more need that thou eschew and dread flatterers than any other people. The book saith, "Thou shalt rather dread and flee from the sweet words of flattering praisers than from the eager words of thy friend that saith thee sooths."[3] Solomon saith, that the words of a flatterer is a snare to catch innocents. He saith also, "He that speaketh to his friend words of sweetness and of pleasance, he setteth a net before his feet to catch him." And therefore saith Tullius, " Incline not thine ears to flatterers, nor take no counsel of words of flattery." And Cato saith, "Avise[4] thee well, and eschew words of sweetness and of pleasance." And eke thou shalt eschew the counselling of thine old enemies that be reconciled. The book saith, that no wight returneth safely into the grace of his old enemy. And Æsop saith, "Ne trust not to them to which thou hast sometime had war or enmity, nor tell them not thy counsel." And Seneca telleth the cause why. "It may not be," saith he, " there[5] as great fire hath long time endured, that there ne dwelleth some vapour of warmness." And

[1] Believeth.
[2] Goodness.
[3] Truths.
[4] Consider.
[5] Where.

therefore saith Solomon, " In thine old foe trust thou never."   For certainly, though thine enemy be reconciled, and maketh thee chere [1] of humility, and louteth [2] to thee with his head, ne trust him never : for certes he maketh that feigned humility more for his profit, than for any love of thy person; because that he deemeth to have victory over thy person by such feigned countenance, the which victory he might not have by strife of war.   And Peter Alphonse saith, " Make no fellowship with thine old enemies, for if thou do them bounty, they will pervert it to wickedness."   And eke thou must eschew the counselling of them that be thy servants, and bear thee great reverence : for peradventure they feign it more for dread than for love.   And therefore saith a philosopher in this wise : " There is no wight perfectly true to him that he too sore dreadeth."   And Tullius saith, " There n'is no might so great of any emperor that long may endure, but [3] if he have more love of the people than dread."   Thou shalt also eschew the counselling of folk that be drunken, for they ne can no counsel hide.   For Solomon saith, " There n'is no privity there as reigneth drunkenness."   Ye shall also have in suspect the counselling of such folk as counsel you one thing privily, and counsel you the contrary openly.   For Cassiodorus saith, " That it is a manner sleight to hinder his enemy when he sheweth to do a thing openly, and worketh privily the contrary."   Thou shalt also have in suspect the counselling of wicked folk, for their counsel is alway full

[1] Demeanour.
[2] Boweth.
[3] Except.

of fraud. And David saith, "Blissful is that man that hath not followed the counselling of shrews."[1] Thou shalt also eschew the counselling of young folk, for their counselling is not ripe, as Solomon saith.

'Now, Sir, since I have shewed you of which folk ye shall take your counsel, and of which folk ye shall eschew the counsel, now will I teach you how ye shall examine your counsel after the doctrine of Tullius. In examining then of your counsellors, ye shall consider many things. Alderfirst[2] thou shalt consider that in that thing that thou purposest, and upon what thing that thou wilt have counsel, that very truth be said and conserved; this is to say, tell truly thy tale: for he that saith false may not well be counselled in that case of which he lieth. And after this, thou shalt consider the things that accord to that thou purposest for to do by thy counsellors, if reason accord thereto, and eke if thy might may attain thereto, and if the more part and the better part of thy counsellors accord thereto or no. Then shalt thou consider what thing shall follow of that counselling; as hate, peace, war, grace, profit, or damage, and many other things: and in all things thou shalt choose the best, and waive all other things. Then shalt thou consider of what root is engendered the matter of thy counsel, and what fruit it may conceive and engender. Thou shalt eke consider all the causes from whence they be sprung. And when thou hast examined thy counsel, as I have said, and which part is the better and more profitable, and

[1] Evil-disposed persons.

[2] First of all.

hast approved it by many wise folk and old, then shalt thou consider if thou mayest perform it and make of it a good end. For certes reason will not that any man should begin a thing, but if he might perform it as him ought: no no wight should take upon him so heavy a charge that he might not bear it. For the proverb saith, "He that too much embraceth distraineth[1] little." And Cato saith, "Assay to do such things as thou hast power to do, lest the charge oppress thee so sore, that thee behoveth to waive thing that thou hast begun." And if so be that thou be in doubt whether thou mayest perform a thing or no, choose rather to suffer than to begin. And Peter Alphonse saith, "If thou hast might to do a thing, of which thou must repent, it is better Nay than Yea:" this is to say, that thee is better to hold thy tongue still than for to speak. Then mayest thou understand by stronger reasons, that if thou hast power to perform a work, of which thou shalt repent, then is thee better that thou suffer than begin. Well say they that defend[2] every wight to assay a thing of which he is in doubt whether he may perform it or no. And·after when ye have examined your counsel, as I have said before, and know well that ye may perform your emprise, confirm it then sadly[3] till it be at an end.

'Now is it reason and time that I shew you when, and wherefore, that ye may change your counsel, without reproof. Soothly, a man may change his purpose and his counsel, if the cause ceaseth, or

[1] Constraineth.

[2] Forbid.

[3] Steadfastly.

when a new case betideth. For the law saith, that upon things that newly betide, behoveth new counsel. And Seneca saith, " If thy counsel is come to the ears of thine enemies, change thy counsel." Thou mayest also change thy counsel, if so be that thou find that by error, or by other cause, harm or damage may betide. Also if thy counsel be dishonest, either else come of dishonest cause, change thy counsel: for the laws say, that all behests[1] that be dishonest be of no value: and eke, if so be that it be impossible, or may not goodly be performed or kept.

'And take this for a general rule, that every counsel that is affirmed so strongly, that it may not be changed for no condition that may betide, I say that that counsel is wicked.'

This Melibœus, when he had heard the doctrine of his wife Dame Prudence, answered in this wise. ' Dame,' quod he, ' as yet unto this time ye have well and covenably[2] taught me, as in general, how I shall govern me in the choosing and in the withholding of my counsellors: but now would I fain that ye would condescend in especial, and tell me how liketh you, or what seemeth you by our counsellors that we have chosen in our present need.'

' My Lord,' quod she, ' I beseech you in all humbleness, that ye will not wilfully reply against my reasons, nor distemper your heart, though I speak thing that you displease; for God wot that, as in mine intent, I speak it for your best, for your honour and for your profit eke, and soothly I hope that your

[1] Promises.

[2] Suitably.

benignity will take it in patience. And trust me well,' quod she, 'that your counsel as in this case ne should not (as to speak properly) be called a counselling, but a motion or a moving of folly, in which counsel ye have erred in many a sundry wise.

· 'First and forward, ye have erred in the assembling of your counsellors; for ye should first have cleped a few folk to your counsel, and after ye might have shewed it to more folk, if it had been need. But certes ye have suddenly cleped to your counsel a great multitude of people, full chargeant[1] and full annoyous for to hear. Also ye have erred, for whereas ye should have only cleped to your counsel your true friends, old and wise, ye have cleped strange folk, young folk, false flatterers, and enemies reconciled, and folk that do you reverence without love. And eke ye have erred, for ye have brought with you to your counsel ire, covetousness, and hastiness, the which three things be contrary to every counsel honest and profitable: the which three things ye ne have not anientissed[2] or destroyed, neither in yourself nor in your counsellors, as you ought. Ye have erred also, for ye have shewed to your counsellors your talent[3] and your affections to make war anon, and for to do vengeance, and they have espied by your words to what thing ye be inclined: and therefore have they counselled you rather to your talent, than to your profit. Ye have erred also, for it seemeth that you sufficeth to have been counselled by these counsellors only, and with little advice,

[1] Burdensome.

[2] Reduced to nothing.

[3] Desire.

whereas in so high and so great a need, it had been necessary more counsellors, and more deliberation, to perform your emprise. Ye have erred also, for ye have not examined your counsel in the foresaid manner, nor in due manner, as the case requireth. Ye have erred also, for ye have made no division betwixt your counsellors; this is to say, betwixt your true friends and your feigned counsellors: nor ye have not known the will of your true friends, old and wise, but ye have cast all their words in an hochepot,* and inclined your heart to the more part and to the greater number, and there be ye condescended;[1] and since ye wot well that men shall alway find a greater number of fools than of wise men, and therefore the counsellings that be at congregations and multitudes of folk, there as men take more regard to the number, than to the sapience of persons, ye see well, that in such counsellings fools have the mastery.' Meliboeus answered and said again, 'I grant well that I have erred; but there as thou hast told me herebefore, that he is not to blame that changeth his counsel in certain case, and for certain and just causes, I am all ready to change my counsel right as thou wilt devise. The proverb saith, "For to do sin is mannish,[2] but certes for to persevere long in sin is work of the Devil." '

To this sentence answered anon Dame Prudence, and said: 'Examine,' quod she, 'well your counsel,

[1] Yielded.

[2] Human.

* A mixture shaken together in the same pot.

and let us see the which of them have spoken most reasonably, and taught you best counsel. And forasmuch as the examination is necessary, let us begin at the surgeons and at the physicians, that first spake in this matter. I say that physicians and surgeons have said you in your counsel discreetly, as them ought: and in their speech said full wisely, that to the office of them appertaineth to do to every wight honour and profit, and no wight to annoy, and after their craft to do great diligence unto the cure of them which that they have in their governance. And, Sir, right as they have answered wisely and discreetly, right so rede[1] I that they be highly and sovereignly guerdoned[2] for their noble speech, and eke for they should do the more attentive business in the curation of thy dear daughter. For albeit so that they be your friends, therefore shall ye not suffer, that they serve you for nought, but ye ought the rather guerdon them, and shew them your largesse.[3] And as touching the proposition, which the physicians entreated in this case, this is to say, that in maladies, that a contrary is warished[4] by another contrary; I would fain know how ye understand that text, and what is your sentence?' 'Certes,' quod Meliboeus, 'I understand it in this wise; that right as they have done me a contrary, right so should I do them another; for right as they have venged them upon me and done me wrong, right so shall I venge me upon them, and do them wrong, and then have I cured a contrary by another.'

[1] Advise.

[2] Rewarded.

[3] Liberality.

[4] Healed.

'Lo, lo,' quod Dame Prudence, 'how lightly is every man inclined to his own desire and his own pleasance! Certes,' quod she, 'the words of the physicians ne should not have been understood in that wise; for certes wickedness is not contrary to wickedness, nor vengeance to vengeance, nor wrong to wrong, but they be semblable:[1] and therefore a vengeance is not warished[2] by another vengeance, nor a wrong by another wrong, but each of them increaseth and aggreggeth[3] other. But certes the words of the physicians should be understood in this wise; for good and wickedness be two contraries, and peace and war, vengeance and sufferance, discord and accord, and many other things : but certes wickedness shall be warished by goodness, discord by accord, war by peace, and so forth of other things. And hereto accordeth Saint Paul the Apostle in many places : he saith, "Ne yield not harm for harm, nor wicked speech for wicked speech, but do well to him that doth to thee harm, and bless him that saith to thee harm." And in many other places he admonisheth peace and accord. But now will I speak to you of the counsel, which that was given to you by the men of law, and the wise folk, and old folk, that said all by one accord, as ye have heard before, that over all things ye shall do your diligence to keep your person, and to warnestore[4] your house : and said also, that in this case you ought for to work full advisedly and with great deliberation. And, Sir, as to the first point, that toucheth the keeping of

[1] Alike.

[2] Healed.

[3] Aggravateth.

[4] Store, furnish.

your person, ye shall understand, that he that hath war, shall evermore devoutly and meekly pray before all things, that Jesus Christ of his mercy will have him in his protection, and be his sovereign helping at his need: for certes in this world there is no wight that may be counselled, nor kept sufficiently, without the keeping of our Lord Jesus Christ. To this sentence accordeth the Prophet David that saith, "If God ne keep the city, in idle[1] waketh he that keepeth it." Now, Sir, then shall ye commit the keeping of your person to your true friends, that be approved and known, and of them shall ye ask help your person for to keep. For Cato saith, "If thou have need of help, ask it of thy friends, for there is none so good a physician as thy true friend." And after this then shall ye keep you from all strange folk, and from liars, and have alway in suspect their company. For Piers Alphonse saith, "Ne take no company by the way of a strange man, but if so be that thou have known him of longer time;" and if so be that he fall into thy company peradventure without thine assent, inquire then, as subtilly as thou mayest, of his conversation, and of his life before, and feign thy way, saying thou wilt go thither as thou wilt not go: and if he bear a spear, hold thee on the right side, and if he bear a sword, hold thee on his left side. And after this then shall ye keep you wisely from all such manner people as I have said before, and them and their counsel eschew. And after this then shall ye keep you in such

[1] In vain.

manner, that for any presumption of your strength, that ye ne despise not, nor account not the might of your adversary so little, that ye leave the keeping of your person for your presumption; for every wise man dreadeth his enemy. And Solomon saith, "Wealful[1] is he that of all hath dread;" for certes he that through the hardiness of his heart, and through the hardiness of himself, hath too great presumption, him shall evil betide. Then shall ye evermore counterwait ambushments and all espial. For Seneca saith, that the wise man that dreadeth harms escheweth harms; nor he ne falleth into perils, that perils escheweth. And albeit so, that it seem that thou art in sure place, yet shalt thou alway do thy diligence in keeping of thy person; this is to say, ne be not negligent to keep thy person, not only from thy greatest enemy, but also from thy least enemy. Seneca saith, "A man that is well advised, he dreadeth his least enemy." Ovid saith, that the little weasel will slay the great bull and the wild hart. And the book saith, "A little thorn may prick a king full sore, and a little hound will hold the wild boar." But nevertheless, I say not thou shalt be so coward, that thou doubt whereas is no dread. The book saith, that some men [have taught their deceiver, for they have too much dreaded] to be deceived. Yet shalt thou dread to be empoisoned; and [therefore shalt thou] keep thee from the company of scorners: for the book saith, "With scorners ne make no company, but fly their words as venom."

[1] Happy.

'Now as to the second point, whereas your wise counsellors counselled you to warnestore[1] your house with great diligence, I would fain know how that ye understood these words, and what is your sentence?'

Meliboeus answered and said, 'Certes I understand it in this wise, that I shall warnestore mine house with towers, such as have castles and other manner edifices, and armour, and artilleries, by which things I may my person and mine house so keep and defend, that mine enemies shall be in dread mine house for to approach.'

To this sentence answered anon Prudence. 'Warnestoring,' quod she, 'of high towers and of great edifices, is with great cost and with great travail; and when that they be accomplished, yet be they not worth a straw, but if they be defended by true friends, that be old and wise. And understand well, that the greatest and strongest garrison that a rich man may have, as well to keep his person as his goods, is, that he be beloved with his subjects, and with his neighbours. For thus saith Tullius, that there is a manner garrison that no man may vanquish nor discomfit, and that is a lord to be beloved of his citizens, and of his people.

'Now, Sir, as to the third point, whereas your old and wise counsellors said, that you ought not suddenly nor hastily proceed in this need, but that you ought purvey and apparail[2] you in this case with great diligence and great deliberation; truly I trow that they said right wisely and right sooth. For Tullius saith, " In every need, ere thou begin it, apparail thee with great diligence." Then say I, that in vengeance-taking, in war, in battle, and in warnestoring, ere thou begin, I rede[1] that thou apparail thee thereto, and do it with great deliberation. For Tullius saith, that long apparailing before the battle, maketh short victory. And Cassiodorus saith, "The garrison is stronger, when it is long time advised."

'But now let us speak of the counsel that was accorded by your neighbours, such as do you reverence without love; your old enemies reconciled; your flatterers, that counselled you certain things privily, and openly counselled you the contrary; the young folk also, that counselled you to avenge you, and to make war anon. Certes, Sir, as I have said before, ye have greatly erred to have cleped such manner folk to your counsel, which counsellors be enough reproved by the reasons aforesaid. But, nevertheless, let us now descend to the special. Ye shall first proceed after the doctrine of Tullius. Certes the truth of this matter or of this counsel needeth not diligently to inquire, for it is well wist[2] which they be that have done to you this trespass and villainy, and how many trespassers, and in what manner they have done to you all this wrong, and all this villainy. And after this, then shall ye examine the second condition, which that the same Tullius addeth in this matter. For Tullius putteth

[1] Advise.

[2] Known.

a thing, which that he clepeth consenting : this is to say, who be they, and which be they, and how many, that consent to thy counsel in thy wilfulness, to do hasty vengeance. And let us consider also who be they, and how many be they, and which be they, that consented to your adversaries. As to the first point, it is well known which folk they be that consented to your wilfulness. For truly, all those that counselled you to make sudden war, be not your friends. Let us now consider which be they that ye hold so greatly your friends, as to your person: for albeit so that ye be mighty and rich, certes ye ne be but alone: for certes ye ne have no child but a daughter, nor ye ne have no brethren, nor cousins-germain, nor no other nigh kindred, wherefore that your enemies for dread should stint to plead with you, or to destroy your person. Ye know also, that your riches must be dispended in divers parts ; and when that every wight hath his part, they will take but little regard to avenge your death. But thine enemies be three, and they have many brethren, children, cousins, and other nigh kindred: and though so were that thou haddest slain of them two or three, yet dwell there enough to wreak their death, and to slay thy person. And though so be that your kindred be more steadfast and sure than the kin of your adversaries, yet nevertheless your 'kindred is but a far kindred; they be but little sibbe[1] to you, and the kin of your enemies be nigh sibbe to them. And certes as in that, their condition is better than

[1] Related.

yours. Then let us consider also of the counselling of them that counselled you to take sudden vengeance, whether it accord to reason: and certes, ye know well, nay; for as by right and reason, there may no man take vengeance on no wight, but the judge that hath the jurisdiction of it, when it is granted him to take that vengeance hastily, or attemprely,[1] as the law requireth. And yet moreover of that word that Tullius clepeth [2] consenting, thou shalt consider, if thy might and thy power may consent and suffice to thy wilfulness, and to thy counsellors: and certes, thou mayest well say, that nay; for certainly, as for to speak properly, we may do nothing but only such thing as we may do rightfully: and certes rightfully ye may take no vengeance as of your proper authority. Then may ye see that your power ne consenteth not, nor accordeth not to your wilfulness. Now let us examine the third point, that Tullius clepeth consequent. Thou shalt understand, that the vengeance that thou purposest for to take is the consequent, and thereof followeth another vengeance, peril, and war, and other damages without number, of which we be not ware, as at this time. And as touching the fourth point, that Tullius clepeth engendering, thou shalt consider, that this wrong which that is done to thee, is engendered of the hate of thine enemies, and of the vengeance-taking upon that would engender another vengeance, and much sorrow and wasting of riches, as I said ere.[3]

[1] Moderately.
[2] Calleth.
[3] Before.

'Now, Sir, as to the point, that Tullius clepeth causes, which that is the last point, thou shalt understand, that the wrong that thou hast received hath certain causes, which that clerks clepen *oriens*, and *efficiens*, and *causa longinqua*, and *causa propinqua*, this is to say, the far cause, and the nigh cause. The far cause, is Almighty God, that is cause of all things: the near cause, is thy three enemies; the cause accidental, was hate; the cause material, be the five wounds of thy daughter; the cause formal, is the manner of their working, that brought ladders, and climbed in at thy windows; the cause final, was for to slay thy daughter; it letted not in as much as in them was. But for to speak of tho far cause, as to what end they shall come, or what shall finally betide of them in this case, ne can I not deem,[1] but by conjecturing and supposing: for we shall suppose, that they shall come to a wicked end, because that the book of Decrees saith, "Seldom or with great pain be causes brought to a good end, when they be badly begun."

'Now, Sir, if men would ask me, why that God suffered men to do you this villainy, certes I cannot well answer, as for no soothfastness. For the Apostle saith, that the sciences and the judgments of our Lord God Almighty be full deep; there may no man comprehend nor search them sufficiently. Nevertheless, by certain presumptions and conjectures, I hold and believe, that God, which that is full of justice and of righteousness, hath suffered this betide by just cause reasonable.

[1] Decide.

'Thy name is Melibœus, this is to say, a man that drinketh honey. Thou hast drunk so much honey of sweet temporal riches, and delights, and honours of this world, that thou art drunken, and hast forgotten Jesus Christ thy Creator: thou hast not done to him such honour and reverence as thee ought, ne thou hast not well taken keep to the words of Ovid, that saith, "Under the honey of the goods of thy body is hid the venom that slayeth the soul." And Solomon saith, "If thou hast found honey, eat of it that sufficeth; for if thou eat of it out of measure, thou shalt spue, and be needy and poor." And peradventure Christ hath thee in despite, and hath turned away from thee his face, and his ears of misericord;[1] and also he hath suffered that thou hast been punished in the manner that thou hast trespassed. Thou hast done sin against our Lord Christ, for certes the three enemies of mankind, that is to say, the flesh, the fiend, and the world, thou hast suffered them enter into thine heart wilfully, by the windows of thy body, and hast not defended thyself sufficiently against their assaults, and their temptations, so that they have wounded thy soul in five places, this is to say the deadly sins that be entered into thy heart by thy five wits:[2] and in the same manner our Lord Christ hath willed and suffered that thy three enemies be entered into thy house by the windows, and have wounded thy daughter in the foresaid manner.'

[1] Mercy.

[2] Senses.

'Certes,' quod Meliboeus, 'I see well that ye enforce you much by words to overcome me, in such manner, that I shall not avenge me on mine enemies, shewing me the perils and the evils that might fall of this vengeance: but whoso would consider in all vengeances the perils and evils that might sue[1] of vengeance-taking, a man would never take vengeance, and that were harm: for by the vengeance-taking be the wicked men dissevered from the good men. And they that have will to do wickedness, restrain their wicked purpose, when they see the punishing and the chastising of the trespassers.' [To this answered Dame Prudence: 'Certes,' quod she, 'I grant you that of vengeance-taking cometh much evil and much good; but vengeance-taking appertaineth not to every one, but only to judges, and to them that have the jurisdiction over the trespassers;] and yet say I more, that right as a singular[2] person sinneth in taking vengeance of another man, right so sinneth the judge, if he do no vengeance of them that it have deserved. For Seneca saith thus: " That master," he saith, " is good, that proveth[3] shrews." And Cassiodorus saith, " A man dreadeth to do outrages, when he wot and knoweth that it displeaseth to the judges and sovereigns." And another saith, " The judge that dreadeth to do right, maketh men shrews."[4] And Saint Paul the Apostle saith in his Epistle, when he writeth unto the Romans, that the judges bear not the spear without cause, but they bear it to punish the shrews

[1] Follow.

[2] Individual.

[3] Rejects upon trial.

[4] Evil-disposed.

and misdoers, and for to defend the good men. If ye
will then take vengeance of your enemies, ye shall
return or have your recourse to the judge, that hath
the jurisdiction upon them, and he shall punish them,
as the law asketh and requireth.'

'Ah!' said Melibœus, 'this vengeance liketh me
nothing. I bethink me now, and take heed how that
Fortune hath nourished me from my childhood, and
hath helped me to pass many a strong pace; now
will I assay her, trowing, with God's help, that she
shall help me my shame for to avenge.'

'Certes,' quod Prudence, 'if ye will work by my
counsel, ye shall not assay Fortune by no way: nor
ye shall not lean or bow unto her, after the words of
Seneca; for things that be foolishly done, and those
that be done in hope of Fortune, shall never come
to good end. And as the same Seneca saith, "The
more clear and the more shining that Fortune is, the
more brittle and the sooner broke she is." Trust not
in her, for she is not steadfast nor stable: for when
thou trowest to be most certain and sure of her help,
she will fail and deceive thee. And whereas ye say,
that Fortune hath nourished you from your childhood, I say that in so much ye shall the less trust in
her, and in her wit. For Seneca saith, "What man
that is nourished by Fortune, she maketh him a great
fool." Now then since ye desire and ask vengeance,
and the vengeance that is done after the law and
before the judge liketh you not, and the vengeance
that is done in hope of Fortune is perilous and un-

certain, then have ye no other remedy, but for to have your recourse unto the Sovereign Judge, that avengeth all villainies and wrongs; and he shall avenge you, after that himself witnesseth, whereas he saith, "Leave the vengeance to me, and I shall do it." '

Meliboeus answered, 'If I no avenge me of the villainy that men have done to me, I summon or warn them that have done to me villainy, and all other, to do me another villainy. For it is written, " If thou take no vengeance of an old villainy, thou summonest thine adversaries to do thee a new villainy:" and also for my sufferance, men would do me so much villainy, that I might neither bear it nor sustain; and so should I be put and held over low. For some men say, " In much suffering shall many things fall unto thee, which thou shalt not mowe[1] suffer." '

'Certes,' quod Prudence, ' I grant you well, that overmuch sufferance is not good, but yet followeth it not thereof, that every person to whom men do villainy should take of it vengeance: for that appertaineth and belongeth all only to the judges, for they shall avenge the villainies and injuries: and therefore those two authorities, that ye have said above, be only understood in the judges: for when they suffer overmuch the wrongs and villainies to be done, without punishing, they summon not a man all only for to do new wrongs, but they command it: all so as a wise man saith, that the judge that correcteth

[1] Be able.

not the sinner, commandeth and biddeth him do sin. And the judges and sovereigns might in their land so much suffer of the shrews and misdoers, that they should by such sufferance, by process of time, wax of such power and might, that they should put out the judges and the sovereigns from their places, and at last make them lose their lordships.

'But now let us put[1] that ye have leave to avenge you: I say ye be not of might and power, as now to avenge you: for if ye will make comparison unto the might of your adversaries, ye shall find in many things, that I have shewed you ere this, that their condition is better than yours, and therefore say I, that it is good as now, that ye suffer and be patient.

'Furthermore ye know well, that after the common saw,[2] it is a woodness,[3] a man to strive with a stronger, or a more mighty man than he is himself; and for to strive with a man of even[4] strength, that is to say, with as strong a man as he is, it is peril; and for to strive with a weaker man, it is folly; and therefore should a man flee striving, as much as he might. For Solomon saith, " It is a great worship[5] to a man to keep him from noise and strife." And if it so happen, that a man of greater might and strength than thou art do thee grievance, study and busy thee rather to still the same grievance, than for to avenge thee. For Seneca saith, that he putteth him in a great peril, that striveth with a greater man than he is himself. And Cato saith, " If a man of higher estate or degree, or more mighty than thou,

[1] Suppose.

[2] Saying.
[3] Madness.

[4] Equal.

[5] Honour.

do thee annoyance or grievance, suffer him: for he that once hath grieved thee, may another time relieve thee and help thee." Yet set I case, ye have both might and licence for to avenge you, I say that there be full many things that shall restrain you of vengeance-taking, and make you for to incline to suffer, and for to have patience in the wrongs that have been done to you. First and forward, if ye will consider the defaults that be in your own person, for which defaults God hath suffered you have this tribulation, as I have said to you herebefore. For the Poet saith, that we ought patiently take the tribulations that come to us, when that we think and consider that we have deserved to have them. And Saint Gregory saith, that when a man considereth well the number of his defaults and of his sins, the pains and the tribulations that he suffereth seem the less unto him. And inasmuch as him thinketh his sins more heavy and grievous, insomuch seemeth his pain the lighter and the easier unto him. Also ye owe[1] to incline and bow your heart, to take the patience of our Lord Jesus Christ, as saith Saint Peter in his Epistles. "Jesus Christ," he saith, "hath suffered for us, and given example to every man to follow and sue him, for he did never sin, ne never came there a villain's word out of his mouth." When men cursed him, he cursed them nought; and when men beat him, he menaced them nought. Also the great patience, which saints that be in Paradise have had in tribulations that they have suffered,

<hr>

[1] Ought.

without their desert or guilt, ought much stir you to patience. Furthermore, ye should enforce you to have patience, considering that the tribulations of this world but little while endure, and soon passed be and gone, and the joy that a man seeketh to have by patience in tribulations is perdurable; after that the Apostle saith in his Epistle; "The joy of God," he saith, "is perdurable," that is to say, everlasting. Also trow and believe steadfastly, that he is not well nourished nor well taught, that cannot have patience, or will not receive patience. For Solomon saith, that the doctrine and wit of a man is known by patience. And in another place he saith, that he that is patient, governeth him by great prudence. And the same Solomon saith, "The angry and wrathful man maketh noises, and the patient man attempreth[1] and stilleth them." He saith also, "It is more worth to be patient than for to be right strong. And he that may have the lordship of his own heart, is more to praise, than he that by his force or strength taketh great cities." And therefore saith Saint James in his Epistle, that patience is a great virtue of perfection.'

'Certes,' quod Melibœus, 'I grant you, Dame Prudence, that patience is a great virtue of perfection, but every man may not have the perfection that ye seek, ne I am not of the number of the right perfect men: for mine heart may never be in peace, unto the time it be avenged. And albeit so, that it was great peril to mine enemies to do me a

[1] Moderates.

villainy in taking vengeance upon me, yet took they no heed of the peril, but fulfilled their wicked will and their courage:[1] and therefore methinketh men ought not reprove me, though I put me in a little peril for to avenge me, and though I do a great excess, that is to say, that I avenge one outrage by another.'

'Ah!' quod Dame Prudence, 'ye say your will and as you liketh; but in no case of the world a man should not do outrage nor excess, for to avenge him. For Cassiodorus saith, that as evil doth he that avengeth him by outrage, as he that doth the outrage. And therefore ye shall avenge you after the order of right, that is to say, by the law, and not by excess, nor by outrage. And also if ye will avenge you of the outrage of your adversaries, in other manner than right commandeth, ye sin. And therefore saith Seneca, that a man shall never avenge shrewedness[2] by shrewedness. And if ye say that right asketh a man to defend violence by violence, and fighting by fighting; certes ye say sooth, when the defence is done without interval, or without tarrying or delay, for to defend him, and not for to avenge. And it behoveth that a man put such temperance in his defence, that men have no cause nor matter to reprove him, that defendeth him, of outrage and excess, for else were it against reason. Pardie, ye know well, that ye make no defence as now, for to defend you, but for to avenge you: and so sheweth it, that ye have no will to do your deed attemprely:[3]

[1] Mind.

[2] Ill-nature.

[3] Moderately.

and therefore methinketh that patience is good. For
Solomon saith, that he that is not patient, shall have
great harm.'

'Certes,' quod Melibœus, 'I grant you, that when
a man is impatient and wroth of that that toucheth
him not, and that appertaineth not unto him, though
it harm him it is no wonder.   For the law saith, that
he is culpable that intermitteth or meddleth with such
thing as appertaineth not unto him.   And Solomon
saith, that he that intermitteth of the noise or strife
of another man, is like to him that taketh a strange
hound by the ears: for right as he that taketh a
strange hound by the ears is otherwhile bitten with
the hound, right in the same wise, it is reason that
he have harm that by his impatience meddleth him
of the noise of another man, whereas it appertaineth
not unto him.   But ye know well, that this deed,
that is to say, my grief and my disease,[1] toucheth me
right nigh.   And therefore though I be wroth and
impatient, it is no marvel: and (saving your grace)
I cannot see that it might greatly harm me though
I took vengeance, for I am richer and more mighty
than mine enemies be: and well know ye, that by
money and by having great possessions, be all things
of this world governed.   And Solomon saith, that
all things obey to money.'

When Prudence had heard her husband avaunt[2]
him of his riches and of his money, dispraising the
power of his adversaries, she spake and said in this
wise: 'Certes, dear Sir, I grant you that ye be rich

[1] Uneasiness.

[2] Boast.

¹ Know.

and mighty, and that riches be good to them that have well gotten them, and that well conne[1] use them. For right as the body of a man may not live without soul, no more may it live without temporal goods, and by riches may a man get him great friends. And therefore saith Pamphilus; "If a neatherd's daughter," he saith, "be rich, she may choose of a thousand men which she will take to her husband: for of a thousand men one will not forsake her nor refuse her." And this Pamphilus saith also, "If thou be right happy, that is to say, if thou be right rich, thou shalt find a great number of fellows[2] and friends; and if thy fortune change, that thou wax poor, farewell friendship and fellowship, for thou shalt be all alone without any company, but if it be the company of poor folk." And yet saith this Pamphilus moreover, that they that be bond and thrall of lineage, shall be made worthy and noble by riches. And right so as by riches there come many goods, right so by poverty come there many harms and evils: for great poverty constraineth a man to do many evils. And therefore clepeth[3] Cassiodorus poverty the mother of ruin, that is to say, the mother of overthrowing or falling down. And therefore saith Piers Alphonse, "One of the greatest adversities of this world, is when a free man by kind, or of birth, is constrained by poverty to eat the alms of his enemy." And the same saith Innocent in one of his books: he saith, that sorrowful and mishappy is the condition of a poor beggar, for if he ask not his

² Companions.

³ Calleth.

meat, he dieth for hunger, and if he ask, he dieth for shame: and algates[1] necessity constraineth him to ask. And therefore saith Solomon, that better it is to die, than for to have such poverty. And as the same Solomon saith, " Better it is to die of bitter death, than for to live in such wise." By these reasons that I have said unto you, and by many other reasons that I could say, I grant you that riches be good to them that well get them, and to them that well use those riches: and therefore will I show you how ye shall behave you in gathering of your riches, and in what manner ye shall use them.

'First, ye shall get them without great desire, by good leisure, sokingly,[2] and not over hastily; for a man that is too desiring to get riches, abandoneth him first to theft and to all other evils. And therefore saith Solomon, " He that hasteth him too busily to wax rich, he shall be none innocent." He saith also, that the riches that hastily come to a man, soon and lightly go and pass from a man, but that riches that come little and little, wax alway and multiply. And, Sir, ye shall get riches by your wit and by your travail, unto your profit, and that without wrong or harm doing to any other person. For the law saith, " There maketh no man himself rich, if he do harm to another wight;" this is to say, that nature defendeth[3] and forbiddeth by right, that no man make himself rich, unto the harm of another person. And Tullius saith, that no sorrow, nor no dread of death, nor nothing that may fall unto a man, is so much

[1] Nevertheless.

[2] Gently.

[3] Prohibits.

against nature, as a man to increase his own profit, to harm of another man. And though the great men and the mighty men get riches more lightly[1] than thou, yet shalt thou not be idle nor slow to do thy profit, for thou shalt in all wise flee idleness. For Solomon saith, that idleness teacheth a man to do many evils. And the same Solomon saith, that he that travaileth and busieth him to till his land, shall eat bread: but he that is idle, and casteth him to no business nor occupation, shall fall into poverty, and die for hunger. And he that is idle and slow, can never find covenable[2] time for to do his profit. For there is a versifier saith, that the idle man excuseth him in winter because of the great cold, and in summer by encheson[3] of the heat. For these causes saith Cato, wake, and incline you not over much to sleep, for overmuch rest nourisheth and causeth many vices. And therefore saith Saint Jerome, "Do some good deeds, that the devil which is our enemy, ne find you not unoccupied, for the devil taketh not lightly unto his working such as he findeth occupied in good works."

'Then thus in getting riches ye must flee idleness. And afterward ye shall use the riches, which ye have gotten by your wit and by your travail, in such manner, that men hold you not too scarce nor too sparing, nor fool-large, that is to say, over large a spender: for right as men blame an avaricious man, because of his scarcity and chincherie,[4] in the same wise is he to blame that spendeth over largely. And therefore

---

[1] Easily.

[2] Suitable.

[3] Occasion.

[4] Niggardliness.

saith Cato; "Use," saith he, "the riches that thou hast gotten in such manner, that men have no matter nor cause to call thee neither wretch[1] nor chinche:[2] for it is a great shame to a man to have a poor heart and a rich purse." He saith also, the goods that thou hast gotten, use them by measure, that is to say, spend measurably; for they that foolishly waste and spend the goods that they have, when they have no more proper of their own, then they shape them to take the goods of another man. I say then that ye shall flee avarice, using your riches in such manner, that men say not that your riches be buried, but that ye have them in your might and in your wielding. For a wise man reproveth the avaricious man, and saith thus in two verses; " Whereto and why burieth a man his goods by his great avarice, and knoweth well, that needs must he die, for death is the end of every man, as in this present life? and for what cause or encheson[3] joineth he him, or knitteth he him so fast unto his goods, that all his wits may not dissever him, or dispart him from his goods, and knows well, or ought to know, that when he is dead, he shall nothing bear with him out of this world?" And therefore saith Saint Augustine, that the avaricious man is likened unto hell, that the more it swalloweth, the more desire it hath to swallow and devour. And as well as ye would eschew to be called an avaricious man or chinche, as well should ye keep you and govern you in such a wise, that men call you not fool-large. Therefore saith Tullius,

[1] Miserly.
[2] Niggard.
[3] Occasion.

"The goods of thine house ne should not be hid nor kept so close, but that they might be opened by pity and debonairetee;"¹ that is to say, to give them part that have great need: nor thy goods should not be so open to be every man's goods. Afterward, in getting of your riches, and in using of them, ye shall alway have three things in your heart, that is to say, our Lord God, conscience, and good name. First, ye shall have God in your heart, and for no riches ye shall do nothing which may in any manner displease God that is your Creator and Maker. For after the word of Solomon, it is better to have a little good with love of God, than to have much good, and lose the love of his Lord God. And the Prophet saith, "That better it is to be a good man, and have little good and treasure, than to be held a shrew, and have great riches." And yet I say furthermore, that ye should alway do your business to get you riches, so that ye get them with good conscience. And the Apostle saith, that there n'is thing in this world of which we should have so great joy, as when our conscience beareth us good witness. And the wise man saith, "The substance of a man is full good, when sin is not in man's conscience." Afterward, in getting of your riches, and in using of them, ye must have great business and great diligence, that your good name be alway kept and conserved. For Solomon saith, that better it is, and more it availeth a man to have a good name, than for to have great riches: and therefore he saith in another place; "Do great diligence," saith Solomon, "in keeping of thy friends, and of thy good name, for it shall longer abide with thee than any treasure, be it never so precious." And certes, he should not be called a gentleman, that after God and good conscience, all things left, ne doth his diligence and business to keep his good name. And Cassiodorus saith, that it is a sign of a gentle heart, when a man loveth and desireth to have a good name. And therefore saith Saint Augustine, that there be two things that are right necessary and needful; and that is good conscience, and good los;[1] that is to say, good conscience to thine own person inward, and good los for thy neighbour outward. And he that trusteth him so much in his good conscience, that he despiseth and setteth at nought his good name or los, and recketh not though he keep not his good name, n'is but a cruel churl.

'Sir, now have I shewed you how ye should do in getting riches, and how ye shall use them: and I see well that for the trust that ye have in your riches, ye will move war and battle. I counsel you that ye begin no battle nor war in trust of your riches, for they suffice not wars to maintain. And therefore saith a philosopher, "That man that desireth and will algates[2] have war, shall never have sufficiency: for the richer that he is, the greater expenses must he make, if he will have worship[3] and victory." And Solomon saith, that the greater riches that a man hath, the more dispenders he hath. And, dear Sir,

[1] Praise.

[2] At all events.

[3] Honour.

albeit so that for your riches ye may have much folk, yet behoveth it not, ne it is not good to begin war, whereas ye may in other manner have peace, unto your worship and profit: for the victory of battles that be in this world, lieth not in great number or multitude of people, nor in the virtue of man, but it lieth in the will and in the hand of our Lord God Almighty. And therefore Judas Maccabæus, which was God's knight, when he should fight against his adversary, that had a greater number and a greater multitude of folk, and stronger than was the people of this Maccabæus, yet he comforted his little company, and said right in this wise; "All so lightly,"[1] said he, "may our Lord God Almighty give victory to a few folk, as to many folk; for the victory of a battle cometh not by the great number of people, but it cometh from our Lord God of heaven." And, dear Sir, forasmuch as there is no man certain, if it be worthy that God give him victory or not, after that Solomon saith, therefore every man should greatly dread wars to begin: and because that in battles fall many perils, and it happeneth other while that as soon is the great man slain as the little man; and, as it is written in the second book of Kings, the deeds of battles be adventurous, and nothing certain, for as lightly is one hurt with a spear as another; and for there is great peril in war; therefore should a man flee and eschew war in as much as a man may goodly. For Solomon saith, "He that loveth peril, shall fall in peril."

[1] Easily.

After that Dame Prudence had spoken in this manner, Melibœus answered and said, ' I see well, Dame Prudence, that by your fair words and by your reasons that ye have shewed me, that the war liketh you nothing: but I have not yet heard your counsel how I shall do in this need.'

' Certes,' quod she, ' I counsel you that ye accord with your adversaries, and that ye have peace with them. For Saint James saith in his Epistle, that by concord and peace, the small riches wax great, and by debate and discord great riches fall down. And ye know well, that one of the greatest and most sovereign things that is in this world, is unity and peace. And therefore said our Lord Jesus Christ to his Apostles in this wise: " Well happy and blessed be they that love and purchase peace, for they be called the children of God."' ' Ah!' quod Melibœus, ' now see I well, that ye love not mine honour nor my worship. Ye know well that mine adversaries have begun this debate and brige[1] by their outrage, and ye see well that they ne require nor pray me not of peace, nor they ask not to be reconciled; will ye then that I go and meek me, and obey me to them, and cry them mercy? Forsooth that were not my worship: for right as men say, that overgreat homeliness[2] engendereth dispraising, so fareth it by too great humility or meekness.'

Then began Dame Prudence to make semblance of wrath, and said, ' Certes, Sir, (save your grace,) I love your honour and your profit, as I do mine own, and ever have done; yea, ne none other saw never the contrary: and if I had said, that ye should have purchased the peace and the reconciliation, I ne had not much mistaken me, nor said amiss. For the wise man saith, "The dissension beginneth by another man, and the reconciling beginneth by thyself." And the Prophet saith, "Flee shrewedness[1] and do goodness; seek peace and follow it, in as much as in thee is." Yet say I not, that ye shall rather pursue to your adversaries for peace, than they shall to you: for I know well that ye be so hard-hearted, that ye will do nothing for me, and Solomon saith, "He that hath over hard an heart, at last he shall mishap and mistide."'

When Melibœus had heard Dame Prudence make semblance of wrath, he said in this wise: 'Dame, I pray you that ye be not displeased of things that I say, for I know well that I am angry and wroth, and that is no wonder; and they that be wroth, wot not well what they do, nor what they say. Therefore the Prophet saith, that troubled eyes have no clear sight. But say and counsel me as you liketh, for I am ready to do right as ye will desire. And if ye reprove me of my folly, I am the more held to love you and to praise you. For Solomon saith, that he that reproveth him that doth folly, he shall find greater grace than he that deceiveth him by sweet words.'

Then said Dame Prudence, 'I make no semblance of wrath nor of anger, but for your great profit. For

[1] Ill-nature.

Solomon saith, "He is more worth that reproveth or chideth a fool for his folly, shewing him semblance of wrath, than he that supporteth him and praiseth him in his misdoing, and laugheth at his folly." And this same Solomon saith afterward, that by the sorrowful visage of a man, that is to say, by the sorry and heavy countenance of a man, the fool correcteth and amendeth himself.'

Then said Melibœus, 'I shall not conne[1] answer unto so many fair reasons as ye put to me and shew: say shortly your will and your counsel, and I am all ready to perform and fulfil it.'

Then Dame Prudence discovered all her will unto him, and said: 'I counsel you,' quod she, ' above all things that ye make peace between God and you, and be reconciled unto him and to his grace, for as I have said you herebefore, God hath suffered you to have this tribulation and disease for your sins: and if ye do as I say you, God will send your adversaries unto you, and make them fall at your feet, ready to do your will and your commandments. For Solomon saith, "When the condition of man is pleasant and liking to God, he changeth the hearts of the man's adversaries, and constraineth them to beseech him of peace and of grace." And I pray you let me speak with your adversaries in privy place, for they shall not know that it be of your will or your assent; and then, when I know their will and their intent, I may counsel you the more surely.'

'Dame,' quod Melibœus, 'do your will and your

[1] Be able to.

liking, for I put me wholly in your disposition and ordinance.'

Then Dame Prudence, when she saw the good-will of her husband, deliberated unto her, and took advice in herself, thinking how she might bring this need unto good end. And when she saw her time, she sent for these adversaries to come unto her into a privy place, and shewed wisely unto them the great goods that come of peace, and the great harms and perils that be in war; and said to them, in a goodly manner, how that them ought have great repentance of the injuries and wrongs that they had done to Melibœus her lord, and unto her and to her daughter.

And when they heard the goodly words of Dame Prudence, they were so surprised and ravished, and had so great joy of her, that wonder was to tell. 'Ah lady!' quod they, 'ye have shewed unto us the blessing of sweetness, after the saying of David the Prophet; for the reconciling, which we be not worthy to have in no manner, but we ought require it with great contrition and humility, ye of your great goodness have presented unto us. Now see we well, that the science and conning[1] of Solomon is full true; for he saith, that sweet words multiply and increase friends, and make shrews to be debonaire[2] and meek.

'Certes,' quod they, 'we put our deed, and all our matter and cause, all wholly in your good-will, and be ready to obey unto the speech and commandment of my lord Melibœus. And therefore, dear and be-

[1] Knowledge.

[2] Courteous.

nign lady, we pray you and beseech you as meekly as we can and may, that it like unto your great goodness to fulfil in deed your goodly words. For we consider and acknowledge, that we have offended and grieved my lord Melibœus out of measure, so far forth that we be not of power to make him amends; and therefore we oblige and bind us and our friends, for to do all his will and his commandments; but peradventure he hath such heaviness and such wrath to usward, because of our offence, that he will enjoin us such a pain as we may not bear nor sustain; and therefore, noble lady, we beseech to your womanly pity to take such avisement in this need, that we, nor our friends, be not disinherited and destroyed, through our folly.'

'Certes,' quod Prudence, 'it is an hard thing and right perilous, that a man put him all utterly in the arbitration and judgment, and in the might and power of his enemy; for Solomon saith, "Believe me, and give credence to that that I shall say: to thy son, to thy wife, to thy friend, nor to thy brother, ne give thou never might nor mastery over thy body, while thou livest." Now, since he defendeth [1] that a man should not give to his brother, nor to his friend, the might of his body, by a stronger reason he defendeth and forbiddeth a man to give himself to his enemy. And nevertheless, I counsel you that ye mistrust not my lord: for I wot well and know verily, that he is debonaire and meek, large, courteous, and nothing desirous nor covetous of good nor riches: for there

[1] Forbiddeth.

is nothing in this world that he desireth, save only worship and honour. Furthermore, I know well, and am right sure, that he shall nothing do in this need without my counsel; and I shall so work in this case, that by the grace of our Lord God ye shall be reconciled unto us.'

Then said they with one voice, ' Worshipful lady, we put us and our goods all fully in your will and disposition, and be ready to come, what day that it like unto your nobleness to limit us or assign us, for to make our obligation and bond, as strong as it liketh unto your goodness, that we may fulfil the will of you and of my lord Melibœus.'

When Dame Prudence had heard the answer of these men, she bade them go again privily, and she returned to her lord Melibœus, and told him how she found his adversaries full repentant, acknowledging full lowly their sins and trespass, and how they were ready to suffer all pain, requiring and praying him of mercy and pity.

Then said Melibœus, 'He is well worthy to have pardon and forgiveness of his sin, that excuseth not his sin, but acknowledgeth, and repenteth him, asking indulgence. For Seneca saith, "There is the remission and forgiveness, where as the confession is; for confession is neighbour to innocence." And therefore I assent and confirm me to have peace, but it is good that we do nought without the assent and will of our friends.'

Then was Prudence right glad and joyful, and said,

'Certes, Sir, ye have well and goodly answered: for right as by the counsel, assent, and help of your friends, ye have been stirred to avenge you and make war, right so without their counsel shall ye not accord you, nor have peace with your adversaries. For the law saith, "There is nothing so good by way of kind, as a thing to be unbound by him that it was bound."'

And then Dame Prudence, without delay or tarrying, sent anon her messengers for their kin and for their old friends, which that were true and wise: and told them by order, in the presence of Melibœus, all the matter, as it is above expressed and declared; and prayed them that they would give their advice and counsel, what were best to do in this need. And when Melibœus' friends had taken their advice and deliberation of the foresaid matter, and had examined it by great business and great diligence, they gave full counsel for to have peace and rest, and that Melibœus should receive with good heart his adversaries to forgiveness and mercy.

And when Dame Prudence had heard the assent of her lord Melibœus, and the counsel of his friends accord with her will and her intention, she was wonder glad in her heart, and said: 'There is an old proverb,' quod she, 'saith, that the goodness that thou mayest do this day, do it, and abide not, nor delay it not till to-morrow: and therefore I counsel, that ye send your messengers, such as be discreet and wise, unto your adversaries, telling them on your behalf, that if they will treat of peace and of accord, that they shape them, without delay or tarrying, to come unto us.' Which thing performed was indeed. And when these trespassers and repenting folk of their follies, that is to say, the adversaries of Melibœus, had heard what these messengers said unto them, they were right glad and joyful, and answered full meekly and benignly, yielding graces and thanks to their lord Melibœus, and to all his company: and shaped them without delay to go with the messengers, and obey to the commandment of their lord Melibœus.

And right anon they took their way to the court of Melibœus, and took with them some of their true friends, to make faith for them, and for to be their borrows.[1] And when they were come to the presence of Melibœus, he said them these words: 'It stands thus,' quod Melibœus, 'and sooth it is, that ye causeless, and without skill and reason, have done great injuries and wrongs to me, and to my wife Prudence, and to my daughter also, for ye have entered into my house by violence, and have done such outrage, that all men know well that ye have deserved the death: and therefore will I know and weet of you, whether ye will put the punishing and chastising, and the vengeance of this outrage, in the will of me and of my wife, or ye will not?'

Then the wisest of them three answered for them all, and said: 'Sir,' quod he, 'we know well, that we be unworthy to come to the court of so great a lord

[1] Sureties.

and so worthy as ye be, for we have so greatly mistaken us, and have offended and aguilt[1] in such wise against your high lordship, that truly we have deserved the death; but yet for the great goodness and debonairetee,[2] that all the world witnesseth of your person, we submit us to the excellence and benignity of your gracious lordship, and be ready to obey to all your commandments, beseeching you, that of your merciable[3] pity ye will consider our great repentance and low submission, and grant us forgiveness of our outrageous trespass and offence: for well we know, that your liberal grace and mercy stretch them further into goodness, than do our outrageous guilt and trespass into wickedness; albeit that cursedly and damnably we have aguilt against your high lordship.'

Then Melibœus took them up from the ground full benignly, and received their obligations and their bonds, by their oaths upon their pledges and borrows,[4] and assigned them a certain day to return unto his court for to receive and accept sentence and judgment, that Melibœus would command to be done on them, by the causes aforesaid; which things ordained, every man returned to his house.

And when that Dame Prudence saw her time, she freined[5] and asked her lord Melibœus, what vengeance he thought to take of his adversaries.

To which Melibœus answered, and said: 'Certes,' quod he, 'I think and purpose me fully to disinherit them of all that ever they have, and for to put them in exile for ever.'

[1] Incurred guilt.

[2] Courtesy.

[3] Merciful.

[4] Sureties.

[5] Inquired.

'Certes,' quod Dame Prudence, 'this were a cruel sentence, and much against reason. For ye be rich enough, and have no need of other men's good; and ye might lightly in this wise get you a covetous name, which is a vicious thing, and ought to be eschewed of every good man: for after the saw[1] of the Apostle, covetousness is root of all harms. And therefore it were better for you to lose much good of your own, than for to take of their good in this manner. For better it is to lose good with worship,[2] than to win good with villainy and shame. And every man ought to do his diligence and his business to get him a good name. And yet shall he not only busy him in keeping his good name, but he shall also enforce him alway to do some thing by which he may renew his good name: for it is written, that the old good los,[3] or good name, of a man is soon gone and passed, when it is not 'newed. And as touching that ye say, that ye will exile your adversaries, that thinketh me much against reason, and out of measure, considered the power that they have given you upon themselves. And it is written, that he is worthy to lose his privilege, that misuseth the might and the power that is given him. And I set case, ye might enjoin them that pain by right and by law, (which I trow ye may not do,) I say, ye might not put it to execution peradventure, and then it were like to return to the war, as it was before. And therefore if ye will that men do you obeisance, ye must deem[4] more courteously, that is to say, ye must give more easy

[1] Saying.

[2] Honour.

[3] Reputation.

[4] Decide.

sentences and judgments. For it is written, "He that most courteously commandeth, to him men most obey." And therefore I pray you, that in this necessity and in this need ye cast[1] you to overcome your heart. For Seneca saith, that he that overcometh his heart, overcometh twice. And Tullius saith, "There is nothing so commendable in a great lord, as when he is debonaire[2] and meek, and appeaseth him lightly." And I pray you, that ye will now forbear to do vengeance in such a manner, that your good name may be kept and conserved, and that men may have cause and matter to praise you of pity and of mercy; and that ye have no cause to repent you of thing that ye do. For Seneca saith, "He overcometh in an evil manner, that repenteth him of his victory." Wherefore I pray you let mercy be in your heart, to the effect and intent that God Almighty have mercy upon you in his last judgment: for Saint James saith in his Epistle, "Judgment without mercy shall he do to him that hath no mercy of another wight."'

When Melibœus had heard the great skills[3] and reasons of Dame Prudence, and her wise informations and teachings, his heart 'gan incline to the will of his wife, considering her true intent, enforced him anon and assented fully to work after her counsel, and thanked God, of whom proceedeth all goodness and all virtue, that him sent a wife of so great discretion. And when the day came that his adversaries should appear in his presence, he spake to them full goodly,

[1] Endeavour.

[2] Courteous.

[3] Arguments.

and said in this wise: 'Albeit so, that of your pride and high presumption and folly, and of your negligence and unconning,[1] ye have misborne you, and trespassed unto me, yet forasmuch as I see and behold your great humility, and that ye be sorry and repentant of your guilts, it constraineth me to do you grace and mercy: wherefore I receive you into my grace, and forgive you utterly all the offences, injuries, and wrongs, that ye have done against me and mine, to this effect and to this end, that God of his endless mercy will at the time of our dying forgive us our guilts, that we have trespassed to him in this wretched world: for doubtless, if we be sorry and repentant of the sins and guilts which we have trespassed in the sight of our Lord God, he is so free and so merciable,[2] that he will forgive us our guilts, and bring us to the bliss that never hath end.' *Amen.*

[1] Ignorance.

[2] Merciful.

THE MONK'S PROLOGUE.

WHEN ended was my tale of Melibee,   13895
And of Prudénce and her benignity,
Our Hosté said, 'As I am faithful man,
And by the precious *corpus Madrian*,
I haddë lever[1] than a barrel of ale,
That goodë lefe[2] my wife had heard this tale:
For she n'is no thing of such patiénce,
As was this Melibœus' wife Prudénce.
  'By Goddë's bonës, when I beat my knaves,
She bringeth me the greatë clubbed staves,
And crieth, "Slay the doggës every one,
And break them bothë back and every bone."
  'And if that any neighëbour of mine
Will not in churchë to my wife incline,[3]
Or be so hardy to her to trespace,
When she com'th home she rampeth[4] in my face,
And crieth, "Falsë coward, wreak thy wife: 13911
By *corpus Domini*, I will have thy knife,
And thou shalt have my distaff, and go spin."
From day till night right thus she will begin.
  ' "Alas!" she saith, "that ever I was yshape
To wed a milksop, or a coward ape,
That will be overladde[5] with every wight!
Thou dar'st not standen by thy wifë's right."

[1] Rather.
[2] Dear.
[3] Bow.
[4] Flies in my face.
[5] Overborne.

'This is my life, but if that I will fight,   13919
And out at door anon I must me dight,[1]
Or ellës I am lost, but if that I
Be like a wildë lion, foolhardy.
    'I wot well she will do[2] me slay some day
Some neighëbour, and thennë go my way,
For I am perilous with knife in hand,
Albeit that I dare not her withstand:
For she is big in armës, by my faith,
That shall he find, that her misdo'th or saith.
But let us pass away from this mattere.
    'My lord the Monk,' quod he, 'be merry of chere,
For ye shall tell a talë truëly.   13931
Lo, Rochester stand'th herë fastë by.
Ride forth, mine owen lord, break not our game.
But by my truth I can not tell your name;
Whether shall I call you my lord Dan John,
Or Dan Thomas, or ellës Dan Albon?
Of what house be ye, by your father kin?
I vow to God, thou hast a full fair skin;
It is a gentle pasture there thou go'st;
Thou art not like a penant[3] or a ghost.   13940
    'Upon my faith thou art some officer,
Some worthy sexton, or some cellarer.
For by my father's soul, as to my dome,[4]
Thou art a master, when thou art at home;
No poorë cloisterer, ne no novíce,
But a govérnor bothë ware and wise,
And therewithal of brawnës and of bonës
A right well-faring person for the nonës.
I pray to God give him confusion,
That first thee brought into religion.   13950
Thou wouldst have been a treadë-fowl a right,
Hadst thou as greatë leave, as thou hast might,

---

[1] Dispose of myself.

[2] Cause.

[3] One doing penance.

[4] Judgment.

To perform all thy lust in engendrure,   13953
Thou hadst begotten many a creáture.
Alas! why wearest thou so wide a cope?
God give me sorrow, but and[1] I were pope,
Not only thou but every mighty man,
Though he were shorn full high upon his pan,[2]
Should have a wife, for all this world is lorn;
Religion hath take up all the corn   13960
Of treading, and we borel[3] men be shrimps:
Of feeble trees there comen wretched imps.
This maketh that our heirës be so slender
And feeble, that they may not well engender.
This maketh that our wivës will assay
Religious folk, for they may better pay
Of Venus' payëments than mayen we:
God wot, no lusheburghes[4] payen ye.
But be not wroth, my lord, though that I play;
Full oft in game a sooth have I heard say.'   13970
    This worthy Monk took all in patiénce,
And said, 'I will do all my diligencé,
As far as souneth[5] into honesty,
To tellen you a tale, or two or three.
And if you list to hearken hitherward,
I will you say the life of Saint Edward;
Or ellës tragedies first I will tell,
Óf which I have an hundred in my cell.
    'Tragedy is to say a certain story,
As oldë bookës maken us memóry,   13980
Of him that stood in great prosperity,
And is yfallen out of high degree
Into mis'ry, and endeth wretchedly.
And they be versified commonly
Of six feet, which men clepe[6] hexametron:
In prose eke be indited many one,

[1] If.

[2] Skull.

[3] Lay.

[4] Base coin.

[5] Is consonant to.

[6] Call.

And eke in metre, in many a sundry wise. 13987
Lo, this declaring ought enough suffice.
 'Now heark'neth, if you liketh for to hear.
But first I you beseech in this mattere,
Though I by order tellë not these things,
Be it of popës, emperors, or kings,
After their ages, as men written find,
But tell them some before and some behind,
As it now cometh to my remembránce,
Have me excused of mine ignorance.'

THE MONK'S TALE.

I WILL bewail in manner of tragedy
The harm of them, that stood in high degree,
And fellen so, that there n'as no remedy
To bring them out of their adversity. 14000
For certain when that Fortune list to flee,
There may no man of her the course withhold:
Let no man trust on blind prosperity;
Beware by these examples true and old.

LUCIFER.

 At Lucifer, though he an angel were
And not a man, at him I will begin.
For though Fortunë may no angel dere,[1]
From high degree yet fell he for his sin
Down into hell, whereas he yet is in.
O Lucifer, brightest of angels all, 14010
Now art thou Sathánas, that mayst not twin[2]
Out of mis'ry, in which that thou art fall.

[1] Hurt.

[2] Depart.

ADAM.

Lo Adam, in the field of Damascene   14013
With Goddë's owen finger wrought was he,
And not begotten of mannë's sperm unclean,
And welt[1] all Paradise saving one tree: [1] Wielded.
Had never worldly man so high degree
As Adam, till he for misgovernance
Was driven out of his prosperity
To labour, and to hell, and to mischance.   14020

SAMPSON.

Lo Sampson, which that was annunciate
By the angel, long ere his nativity:
And was to God Almighty consecrate,
And stood in nobless while he mightë see:
Was never such another as was he,
To speak of strength, and thereto hardiness:
But to his wivës told he his secreo,
Through which he slew himself for wretchedness.

Sampson, this noble and mighty champion,
Withouten weapon, save his handës tway,   14030
He slew and all to-rentë the lión,
Toward his wedding walking by the way:
His falsë wife could him so please, and pray,
Till she his counsel knew; and she untrue
Unto his foes his counsel 'gan bewray,
And him forsook, and took another new.

Three hundred foxes took Sampson for ire,
And all their tailës he together bond:
And set the foxes' tailës all on fire,

For he in every tail had knit a brond.   14040
And they burnt all the cornës in that lond,
And all their oliveres,[1] and vinës eke.
A thousand men he slew eke with his hond,
And had no weapon, but an ass's cheek.

When they were slain, so thirsted him, that he
Was well-nigh lorn,[2] for which he 'gan to pray,
That God would on his pain have some pity,
And send him drink, or ellës must he dey:
And of this ass's cheek, that was so drey,
Out of a wang-tooth[3] sprang anon a well,   14050
Of which he drank enough, shortly to say.
Thus help'd him God, as *Judicum*[4] can tell.

By very force at Gaza on a night,
Maugre the Philistines of that city,
The gatës of the town he hath up plight,[5]
And on his back ycarried them hath he
High on an hill, where as men might them see.
O noble mighty Sampson, lefe[6] and dear,
Hadst thou not told to women thy secree,
In all this world ne had there been thy peer.   14060

This Sampson never cider drank nor wine,
Nor on his head came razor none nor shear,
By precept of the messenger divine,
For all his strengthës in his hairës were:
And fully twenty winter year by year
He had of Israel the governance:
But soonë shall he weepen many a tear,
For women shall him bringen to mischance.

Unto his leman Dalida he told,

[1] Olive-trees.

[2] Lost.

[3] Cheek-tooth.

[4] Book of Judges.

[5] Pulled.

[6] Loved.

That in his hairës all his strengthë lay,　14070
And falsely to his foemen she him sold;
And sleeping in her barme[1] upon a day　　　[1] Lap.
She made to clip or shear his hair away,
And made his foemen all his craft espien;
And when that they him found in this array,
They bound him fast, and putten out his eyen.

But ere his hair was clipped or yshave,
There was no bond with which men might him bind;
But now is he in prison in a cave,
Whereas they made him at the quernë[2] grind.　14080　[2] Hand-mill.
O noble Sampson, strongest of mankind,
O whilom judge in glory and richess,
Now mayst thou weepen with thine eyen blind,
Since thou from weal art fall in wretchedness.

Th' end of this caitiff[3] was as I shall say :　　　[3] Wretched man.
His foemen made a feast upon a day,
And made him as their fool before them play :
And this was in a temple of great array.
But at the last he made a foul affray,
For he two pillars shook, and made them fall,　14090
And down fell temple and all, and there it lay,
And slew himself, and eke his foemen all.

This is to say, the princes every one,
And eke three thousand bodies were there slain
With falling of the great temple of stone.
Of Sampson now will I no morë sayn :
Beware by this example old and plain,
That no men tell their counsel to their wives
Of such thing as they would have secret fain,
If that it touch their limbës or their lives.　14100

HERCULES.

Of Hercules the sovereign conqueroúr   14101
Singen his workës' laud, and high renown;
For in his time of strength he was the flow'r.
He slew and reft the skin of the lión;
He of Centaurës laid the boast adown;
He Harpies slew, the cruel birdës fell;
He golden apples reft from the dragón;
He drew out Cerberus the hound of hell.

He slew the cruel tyrant Busirus,
And made his horse to fret[1] him flesh and bone;
He slew the fiery serpent venomous;   14111
Of Achelous' two hornës brake he one.
And he slew Cacus in a cave of stone;
He slew the giant Antæus the strong;
He slew the grisly boar, and that anon;
And bare the heaven on his neckë long.

Was never wight since that the world began,
That slew so many monsters as did he;
Throughout the widë world his namë ran,
What for his strength, and for his high bounty;
And every realmë went he for to see,   14121
He was so strong that no man might him let;
At both the world's endës, saith Trophee,
Instead of boundës he a pillar set.

A leman had this noble champion,
That hightë Dejanire, as fresh as May;
And as these clerkës maken mention,
She hath him sent a shirtë fresh and gay:
Alas! this shirt, alas and wala-wa!

[1] Devour.

Envenomed was subtlely withal,   14130
That ere that he had worn it half a day,
It made his flesh all from his bonës fall.

But nathëless some clerkës her excusen
By one, that hightë Nessus, that it maked;
Be as may be, I will not her accusen;
But on his back this shirt he wore all naked,
Till that his flesh was for the venom blaked:
And when he saw none other remedy,
In hotë coals he hath himselven raked,
For with no venom deigned him to die.   14140

Thus starf[1] this worthy mighty Hercules.
Lo, who may trust on Fortune any throw?[2]
For him that follow'th all this world of pres,[3]
Ere he be ware, is oft ylaid full low:
Full wise is he that can himselven know.
Beware, for when that Fortune list to glose,
Then waiteth she her man to overthrow,
By such a way as he would least suppose.

NABUCHODONOSOR.

The mighty throne, the precious treasor,
The glorious sceptre, and real majesty,   14150
That had the king Nabuchodonosor,
With tongue unnethës may described be.
He twiës won Jerusalem the city,
The vessels of the temple he with him lad;
At Babylonë was his sovereign see,[4]
In which his glory and his delight he had.

The fairest children of the blood real[5]

[1] Perished.
[2] Little while.
[3] Near.
[4] Seat.
[5] Royal.

Of Israel he did do geld anon,　　14158
And maked each of them to be his thrall.
Amongës other Daniel was one,
That was the wisest child of every one;
For he the dreamës of the king expounded,
Whereas in Chaldee clerk, ne was there none,
That wistë to what fin[1] his dreamës sounded.

This proudë king let make a statue of gold
Sixty cubitës long, and seven in brede,
To which imagë bothë young and old
Commanded he to lout,[2] and have in drede,
Or in a furnace, full of flamës rede,
He should be burnt, that wouldë not obey:　　14170
But never would assenten to that deed
Daniel, nor his youngë fellows twey.

This king of kingës proud was and elate;
He ween'd that God, that sits in majesty,
Ne might him not bereave of his estate:
But suddenly he lost his dignity,
And like a beast him seemed for to be,
And ate hay as an ox, and lay thereout:
In rain with wildë beastës walked he,
Till certain timë was ycome about.　　14180

And like an eagle's feathers wax'd his heres,
His nailës like a birdë's clawës were,
Till God released him at certain years,
And gave him wit, and then with many a tear
He thanked God, and ever his life in fear
Was he to do amiss, or more trespace:
And till that time he laid was on his bier,
He knew that God was full of might and grace.

[1] End.

[2] Bow.

BALTHASAR.

His sonë, which that hightë Balthasar, 14189
That held the regne[1] after his father's day,
He by his father couldë not beware,
For proud he was of heart, and of array:
And eke an idolaster was he aye.
His high estate assured him in pride;
But Fortune cast him down (and there he lay)
And suddenly his regnë 'gan divide.

A feast he made unto his lordës all
Upon a time, and made them blithë be,
And then his officerës 'gan he call;
'Go, bringeth forth the vesselës,' quod he, 14200
'Which that my father in his prosperity
Out of the temple of Jerusalem bereft,
And to our highë goddës thankë we
Of honour, that our elders with us left.'

His wife, his lordës, and his concubines
Aye drunken, while their appetitës last,
Out of these noble vessels sundry wines.
And on a wall this king his eyen cast,
And saw an hand armless, that wrote full fast,
For fear of which he quoke, and sighed sore. 14210
This hand, that Balthasar so sore aghast,
Wrote *Mane techel phares,* and no more.

In all that land magician was none,
That could expounden what this letter meant,
But Daniel expounded it anon,
And said, ' O king, God to thy father lent
Glory and honour, regne, treasúre, and rent;

[1] King-dom.

And he was proud, and nothing God ne drad;[1] 14218
And therefore God great wreche[2] upon him sent,
And him bereft the regnë that he had.

'He was out cast of mannë's company,
With asses was his habitatión;
And ate hay, as a beast, in wet and dry,
Till that he knew by grace and by reasón,
That God of heaven hath dominatión
Over every regne, and every creáture:
And then had God of him compassión,
And him restored his regne and his figúre.

'Eke thou, that art his son, art proud also,
And knowest all these thingës verily;   14320
And art rebél to God, and art his foe.
Thou drank eke of his vessels boldëly,
Thy wife eke, and thy wenches sinfully
Drank of the samë vessels sundry winës,
And heried[3] falsë goddës cursedly,
Therefore to thee yshapen full great pine is.

'This hand was sent from God, that on the wall
Wrote *Mane techel phares*, trusteth me;
Thy regne is done, thou weighest nought at all;
Divided is thy regne, and it shall be   14240
To Medës and to Perses given,' quod he.
And thilkë samë night this king was slaw;[4]
And Darius occupied his degree,
Though he thereto had neither right nor law.

Lordings, example hereby may ye take,
How that in lordship is no sikerness:[5]
For when that Fortune will a man forsake,

1 Dreaded.

2 Ven-
geance.

3 Praised.

4 Slain.

5 Certain-
ty.

She beareth away his regne and his richés,   14248
And eke his friendës, bothë more and less.
For what man that hath friendës through fortune,
Mishap will make them enemies, I guess.
This proverb is full sooth, and full commune.

ZENOBIA.

Zenobia, of Palmerie the queen,
(As writen Persians of her nobless)
So worthy was in armës, and so keen,
That no wight passed her in hardiness,
Ne in lineage, ne in other gentleness.
Of kingës' blood of Perse is she descended;
I say not that she haddë most fairness,
But of her shape she might not be amended.   14260

From her childhood I findë that she fled
Office of woman, and to wood she went;
And many a wildë hartë's blood she shed
With arrows broadë that she to them sent;
She was so swift, that she anon them hent.[1]
And when that she was older, she would kill
Lions, leopárds, and bearës all to-rent,
And in her armës wield them at her will.

She durst the wildë beastës' dennës seek,
And runnen in the mountains all the night,   14270
And sleep under the bush; and she could eke
Wrestlen by very force and very might
With any young man, were he never so wight;
There mightë nothing in her armës stond;
She kept her maidenhood from every wight,
To no man deigned her for to be bond.

[1] Caught.

But at the last her friendës have her married
To Odenate, a prince of that country;   14278
All were it so, that she them longë tarried.
And ye shall understanden, how that he
Haddë such fantasies as haddë she;
But nathëless, when they were knit in fere,[1]
They lived in joy, and in felicity,
For each of them had other lefe[2] and dear.

Save one thing, that she n'oldë never assent,
By no way, that he shouldë by her lie
But onës, for it was her plain intent
To have a child, the world to multiply:
And all so soon as that she might espy
That she was not with childë with that
     deed,   14290
Then would she suffer him do his fantasy
Eftsoon, and not but onës out of drede.

And if she were with child at thilkë cast,
No morë should he playen thilkë game
Till fully forty dayës weren past:
Then would she onës suffer him do the same.
All were this Odenatë wild or tame,
He got no more of her, for thus she said,
It was to wivës' lechery and shame,
In other case if that men with them play'd.   14300

Two sonës by this Odenate had she,
The which she kept in virtue and lettrure.[3]
But now unto our talë turnë we:
I say, so worshipful a creáture,
And wise therewith, and largë with measúre,
So penible[4] in the war, and courteous eke,

[1] Company.

[2] Pleasant.

[3] Literature.

[4] Laborious.

Ne morë labour might in war enduro,   14307
Was none, though all this world men shoulden seck.

Her rich array ne mightë not be told,
As well in vessel[1] as in her clothing:
She was all clad in pierrie[2] and in gold,
And eke she leftë not for no hunting
To have of sundry tonguës full knowing,
When that she leisure had, and for to intend[3]
To learnen bookës was all her liking,
How she in virtue might her life dispend.

And shortly of this story for to treat,
So doughty was her husband and eke she,
That they conquéred many regnës great
In the Orient, with many a fair city,   14320
Appertainant unto the majesty
Of Rome, and with strong hand held them full fast,
Ne never might their foemen do them flee,
Aye while that Odenatë's dayës last.

Her battles, whoso list them for to read,
Against Sapor the king, and other mo,
And how that all this process fell in deed,
Why she conquer'd, and what title thereto,
And after of her mischief and her woe,
How that she was besieged, and ytake,   14330
Let him unto my master Petrarch go,
That writeth enough of this, I undertake.

When Odenate was dead, she mightily
The regnës held, and with her proper hond
Against her foes she fought so cruelly,
That there n'as king nor prince in all that lond,

[1] Plate.

[2] Precious stones.

[3] Apply.

That he n'as glad, if he that gracë fond 14337
That she ne would upon his land warray;[1]
With her they maden alliánce by bond
To be in peace, and let her ride and play.

The emperor of Romë, Claudius,
Nor, him before, the Roman Galien,
Ne durstë never be so courageous,
Ne none Ermin,[2] ne none Egyptien,
Ne Surrien,[3] ne none Arabien
Within the field ne durstë with her fight,
Lest that she would them with her handës slen,[4]
Or with her meinie[5] putten them to flight.

In kingës' habit went her sonës two,
As heirës of their father's regnës all, 14350
And Heremanno and Timolao
Their namës were, as Persians them call.
But aye Fortune hath in her honey gall:
This mighty queenë may no while endure,
Fortune out of her regnë made her fall
To wretchedness and to misáventure.

Aurelian, when that the governance
Of Romë came into his handës tway,[6]
He shope [6] upon this queen to do vengeance,
And with his legións he took his way 14360
Toward Zenobie, and shortly for to say,
He made her flee, and attë last her hent,[7]
And fetter'd her, and eke her children tway,
And won the land, and home to Rome he went.

Amongës other thingës that he wan,
Her car, that was with gold wrought and pierrie,

[1] Make war.

[2] Armenian.
[3] Syrian.

[4] Slay.

[5] Servants.

[6] Purposed.

[7] Took.

This greatë Roman, this Aurelian   14367
Hath with him led, for that men should it see.
Beforen his triumphë walketh she
With giltë chainës on her neck hanging,
Crowned she was, as after her degree,
And full of pierrie charged her clothing.

Alas Fortunë! she that whilom was
Dreadful to kingës and to emperours,
Now gaureth[1] all the people on her, alas!
And she that helmed was in starkë[2] stours,
And won by forcë townës strong and tow'rs,
Shall on her head now wear a vitremite:[3]
And she that bare the sceptre full of flow'rs
Shall bear a distaff her cost for to quite.   14380

NERO.

Although that Nero were as vicious
As any fiend, that li'th full low adown,
Yet he, as telleth us Suetonius,
This widë world had in subjectióun,
Both East and West, South and Septentrioun.
Of rubies, sapphires, and of pearlës white
Were all his clothës brouded[4] up and down,
For he in gemmës greatly 'gan delight.

More delicate, more pompous of array,
More proud, was never emperor than he;   14390
That ilkë[5] cloth that he had worn one day,
After that time he n'old it never see;
Nettës of gold thread had he great plenty,
To fish in Tiber, when him list to play;

[1] Gazeth.

[2] Stiff battles.

[3] (Not known.)

[4] Embrodered.

[5] Same.

His lustës were as law, in his degree,   14395
For Fortune as his friend would him obey.

He Romë burnt for his délicacy;
The senators he slew upon a day,
To hearen how that men would weep and cry;
And slew his brother, and by his sister lay.   14400
His mother made he in piteous array,
For he her womb let slitten, to behold
Where he conceived was, so wala-wa!
That he so little of his mother told.

No tear out of his eyen for that sight
Ne came, but said, A fair woman was she.
Great wonder is, how that he could or might
Be doomësman[1] of herë dead beauty:
The wine to bringen him commanded he,
And drank anon, none other woe he made.   14410
When might is joined unto cruelty,
Alas! too deepë will the venom wade.

In youth a master had this emperour
To teachen him lettrure[2] and courtesy,
For of morality he was the flow'r,
As in his timë, but if bookës lie.
And while this master had of him mast'ry,
He maked him so conning[3] and so souple,[4]
That longë time it was ere tyranny,
Or any vicë, durst in him uncouple.   14420

This Seneca, of which that I devise,
Because Nero had of him suchë drede,
For he from vices would him aye chastise
Discreetly, as by word, and not by deed;

[1] Judge.

[2] Litera-
ture.

[3] Intelli-
gent.
[4] Pliant.

'Sir,' he would say, 'an emperor must need 14425
Be virtuous, and haten tyranny.'
For which he made him in a bath to bleed
On both his armës, till he mustë die.

This Nero had eke of a custumance
In youth against his master for to rise; 14430
Which afterward him thought a great grievance,
Therefore he made him dien in this wise.
But natheless this Seneca the wise
Chose in a bath to die in this mannere,
Rather than have another tormentise:
And thus hath Nero slain his master dear.

Now fell it so, that Fortune list no longer
The highë pride of Nero to cherice:
For though that he were strong, yet was she
stronger.
She thoughtë thus; 'By God, I am too nice 14440
To set a man, that is fulfill'd of vice,
In high degree, and emperor him call:
By God, out of his seat I will him trice;
When he least weeneth, soonest shall he fall.'

The people rose upon him on a night
For his default, and when he it espied,
Out of his doors anon he hath him dight
Alone, and there[1] he ween'd have been allied
He knocked fast, and aye the more he cried,
The faster shutten they their doorës all: 14450
Then wist he well he had himself misgied,[2]
And went his way, no longer durst he call.

The people cried and rumbled up and down,

[1] Where.

[2] Misguided.

That with his carës heard he how they said, 14454
Where is this falsë tyrant, this Neroun?
For fear almost out of his wit he braid,[1]
And to his goddës piteously he pray'd
For succour, but it mightë not betide:
For dread of this him thoughtë that he dey'd,
And ran into a garden him to hide. 14460

And in this garden found he churlës tway
That saten by a firë great and red,
And to these churlës two he 'gan to pray
To slay him, and to girden[2] off his head,
That to his body, when that he were dead,
Were no despite ydone for his defame.
Himself he slew, he coud[3] no better rede,[4]
Of which Fortunë laugh'd and had a game.

HOLOFERNES.

Was never capitain under a king,
That regnes more put in subjectióun, 14470
Nor stronger was in field of allë thing
As in his time, nor greater of renown,
Nor more pompous in high presumptióun,
Than Holoferne, which that Fortune aye kiss'd
So likerously, and led him up and down,
Till that his head was off, ere that he wist.

Not only that this world had him in awe
For losing of richés and liberty;
But he made every man reneie[5] his law.
Nabuchodonosor was God, said he; 14480
None other God ne should honoúred be.
Against his hest there dare no wight trespace,

1 Started.
2 Strike.
3 Knew.
4 Counsel.
5 Deny.

Save in Bethulia, a strong city,   14483
Where Eliachim a priest was of that place.

But take keep of the death of Holoferne:
Amid his host he drunken lay a night
Within his tentë, large as is a berne;[1]
And yet for all his pomp and all his might,
Judith, a woman, as he lay upright
Sleeping, his head off smote, and from his tent 14490
Full privily she stole from every wight,
And with his head unto her town she went.

ANTIOCHUS.

What needeth it of king Antiochus
To tell his high and royal majesty,
His great pride, and his workës venomous?
For such another was there none as he;
Readeth what that he was in Machabee.
And readeth the proud wordës that he said,
And why he fell from his prosperity,
And in an hill how wretchedly he deid.   14500

Fortune him had enhanced[2] so in pride,
That verily he ween'd he might attain
Unto the starrës upon every side,
And in a balance weighen each mountain,
And all the floodës of the sea restrain:
And Goddë's people had he most in hate,
Them would he slay in torment and in pain,
Weening that God ne might his pride abate.

And for that Nicanor and Timothee
With Jewës were vanquished mightily,   14510

[1] Barn.

[2] Lifted up.

Unto the Jewës such an hate had he,   14511
That he bade graith[1] his char[2] full hastily,
And swore and saidë full despiteously,
Unto Jerusalem he would eftsoon
To wreak his ire on it full cruelly,
But of his purpose was he let full soon.

God for his menace him so sorë smote,
With invisible wound, aye incuráble,
That in his guttës carfe[3] it so and bote,[4]
Till that his painës weren importáble;   14520
And certainly the wreche[5] was reasonáble,
For many a mannë's guttës did he pain;
But from his purpose, cursed and damnáble,
For all his smart, he n'old him not restrain:

But bade anon apparailen[6] his host.
And suddenly, ere he was of it 'ware,
God daunted all his pride, and all his
        boast;
For he so sorë fell out of his chare,[7]
That it his limbës and his skin to-tare,
So that he neither mightë go nor ride;   14530
But in a chaier men about him bare,
Allë forbruised bothë back and side.

The wreche of God him smote so cruelly,
That through his body wicked wormës crept,
And therewithal he stank so horribly,
That none of all his meinie[8] that him kept,
Whether so that he woke or ellës slept,
Ne mightë not of him the stink endure.
In this mischief he wailed and eke wept,
And knew God, Lord of every creatúre.   14540

1 Prepare.
2 Chariot.
3 Cut.
4 Bit.
5 Ven-
  geance.
6 Prepare.
7 Chariot.
8 Servants.

To all his host, and to himself also, 14541
Full wlatsom[1] was the stink of his carrain;[2]
No man ne might him bearen to nor fro.
And in this stink, and this horríble pain,
He starf[3] full wretchedly in a mountáin.
Thus hath this robber, and this homicide,
That many a man madë to weep and plain,
Such guerdon as belongeth unto pride.

[1] Loathsome.
[2] Carrion.
[3] Died.

ALEXANDER.

The story of Alexander is so commune,
That every wight, that hath discretióun, 14550
Hath heard somewhat or all of his fortúne.
This widë world, as in conclusióun,
He won by strength; or for his high renown
They weren glad for peace unto him send.
The pride of man and boast he laid adown,
Whereso he came, unto the worldë's end.

Comparison might never yet be maked
Betwixt him and another conquerour,
For all this world for dread of him hath quaked;
He was of knighthood and of freedom flow'r: 14560
Fortune him made the heir of her honóur.
Save wine and women, nothing might assuage
His high intent in armës and labóur,
So was he full of leonine couráge.

What praise were it to him, though I you told
Of Darius, and an hundred thousand mo,
Of kingës, princes, dukës, earlës bold,
Which he conquér'd, and brought them into woe?
I say, as far as man may ride or go,

The world was his, what should I more de-
  vise?   14570
For though I wrote or told you evermo
Of his knighthood, it mightë not suffice.

 Twelve years he reigned, as saith Machabee;
Philippus' son of Macedon he was,
That first was king in Greecë the country.
O worthy gentle[1] Alexander, alas
That ever should thee fallen such a case!
Enpoison'd of thine owen folk thou were;
Thy six* Fortune hath turn'd into an ace,
And yet for thee ne wept she never a tear.   14580

 Who shall me given tearës to complain
The death of gentilless, and of franchise,[2]
That all this world wielded in his demaine,[3]
And yet him thought it mightë not suffice?
So full was his couráge of high emprise.
Alas! who shall me helpen to indite
Falsë Fortune, and poison to despise?
The whichë two of all this woe I wite.[4]

JULIUS CÆSAR.

By wisdom, manhood, and by great laboúr,
From humbleness to royal majesty   14590
Uprose he, Julius the conquerour,
That won all the occident,[5] by land and sea,
By strength of hand, or ellës by treaty,
And unto Romë made them tributary;
And since of Rome the emperor was he,
Till that Fortune waxed his adversary.

* Highest cast upon a die.

1 High-born.
2 Genero-sity.
3 Manage-ment.
4 Blame.
5 West.

O mighty Cæsar, that in Thessaly   14597
Against Pompeius, father thine in law,
That of th' orient had all the chivalry,
As far as that the day beginneth daw,
That through thy knighthood hast them take and
    slaw,[1]   [1] Slain.
Save fewë folk, that with Pompeius fled,
Through which thou put all th' orient in awe,
Thankë Fortunë, that so well thee sped.

But now a little while I will bewail
This Pompeius, this noble governór
Of Romë, which that fled at this battail.
I say, one of his men, a false traitór,
His head off smote, to winnen him favór
Of Julius, and him the head he brought: 14610
Alas! Pompey, of th' orient conquerór,
That Fortune unto such a fine[2] thee brought!   [2] End.

To Rome again repaireth Julius
With his triumphë laureate full high,
But on a time Brutus and Cassius,
That ever had of his high estate envy,
Full privily had made conspiracy
Against this Julius in subtle wise:
And cast[3] the place in which he shouldë die   [3] Contriv-
                                              ed.
With bodekins,[4] as I shall you devise.[5]   14620 [4] Daggers.
                                              [5] Describe.

This Julius to the Capítol went
Upon a day, as he was wont to gon,
And in the Capitol anon him hent[6]   [6] Seized.
This falsë Brutus, and his other foen,
And sticked him with bodekins anon
With many a wound, and thus they let him lie:

But never groan'd he at no stroke but one,   14627
Or else at two, but if his story lie.

So manly was this Julius of heart,
And so well loved estately honesty,[1]
That though his deadly woundës sorë smert,
His mantle over his hippës castë he,
For no man shouldë see his privity:
And as he lay of dying in a trance,
And wistë verily that dead was he,
Of honesty yet had he remembránce.

Lucan, to thee this story' I recommend,
And to Sueton, and Valerie also,
That of this story writen word and end:
How that to these great conquerorës two   14640
Fortune was first a friend, and since a foe.
No man ne trust upon her favour long,
But have her in await[2] for evermo;
Witness on all these conquerorës strong.

CRŒSUS.

The richë Crœsus, whilom king of Lyde,
Of whichë Crœsus, Cyrus sore him drad,
Yet was he caught amiddës all his pride,
And to be burnt men to the fire him lad:
But such a rain down from the welkin shad,
That slew the fire, and made to him escape: 14650
But to beware no gracë yet he had,
Till fortune on the gallows made him gape.

When he escaped was, he cannot stint
For to begin a newë war again:

---

[1] Decency.

[2] Watch.

He weened well, for that Fortune him sent   14655
Such hap, that he escaped through the rain,
That of his foes he mighte not be slain;
And eke a sweven[1] upon a night he mette,[2]
Of which he was so proud, and eke so fain,
.That in vengeánce he all his hearte set.   14660

Upon a tree he was, as that him thought,
There Jupiter him wash'd, both back and side;
And Phœbus eke a fair towél him brought
To dry him with, and therefore wax'd his pride.
And to his daughter that stood him beside,
Which that he knew in high sciénce abound,
He bade her tell him what it signified,
And she his dream began right thus expound.

'The tree (quod she) the gallows is to mean,
And Jupiter betokeneth snow and rain,   14670
And Phœbus with his towel clear and clean,
Those be the sunne's streames, sooth to sayn:
Thou shalt anhanged be, father, certáin;
Rain shall thee wash, and sunne shall thee
    dry.'
Thus warned him full plat[3] and eke full plain
His daughter, which that called was Phanie.

Anhanged was Crœsus the proude king,
His royal throne might him not avail:
Tragedy is none other manner thing,
Ne can in singing crien nor bewail,   14680
But for that Fortune all day will assail
With unware stroke the regnes[4] that be proud:
For when men trusten her, then will she fail,
And cover her bright face with a cloud.

[1] Dream.
[2] Dreamed.
[3] Flatly.
[4] Kingdoms.

PETER OF SPAIN.

O noble, O worthy Petro, glory' of Spain, 14685
Whom Fortune held so high in majesty,
Well oughten men thy piteous death complain.
Out of thy land thy brother made thee flee,
And after at a siege by subtlety
Thou wert betray'd, and led unto his tent, 14690
Where as he with his owen hand slew thee,
Succeeding in thy regne and in thy rent.

The field of snow, with th' eagle of black therein,
Caught with the lime-rod, colour'd as the glede,[1]
He brew'd this cursedness, and all this sin;
The wicked nest was worker of this deed;
Not Charles' Oliver, that took aye heed
Of truth and honour, but of Armorike
Genelon Oliver, corrupt for meed,
Broughtë this worthy king in such a brike.[2] 14700

PETRO, KING OF CYPRUS.

O worthy Petro, king of Cypre, also,
That Alexandrie won by high mast'ry,
Full many a heathen wroughtest thou full woe,
Of which thine owen lieges had envy:
And for no thing but for thy chivalry,
They in thy bed have slain thee by the morrow;
Thus can Fortune her wheel govérn and gie,[3]
And out of joyë bringen men to sorrow.

BARNABO VISCOUNT.

Of Milan greatë Barnabo Viscount,
God of delight, and scourge of Lombardy, 14710

[1] Burning coal.

[2] Breach, ruin.

[3] Guide.

Why should I not thine infortúne account,   14711
Since in estate thou clomben were so high?
Thy brother's son, that was thy double ally,
For he thy nephew was, and son-in-law,
Within his prison made he thee to die,
But why, nor how, n'ot[1] I that thou were slaw.

  [1] Know not.

HUGOLIN OF PISA.

Of the Earl Hugolin of Pise the languor
There may no tonguë tellen for pity.
But little out of Pisa stands a tow'r,
In whichë tow'r in prison put was he,   14720
And with him be his little children three,
The eldest scarcely five year was of age:
Alas! Fortune, it was great crúelty
Such birdës for to put in such a cage.

Damned was he to die in that prison,
For Roger, which that bishop was of Pise,
Had on him made a false suggestión,
Through which the people 'gan upon him rise,
And put him in prisón, in such a wise,
As ye have heard; and meat and drink he
    had   14730
So small, that well unnethe[2] it may suffice,
And therewithal it was full poor and bad.

  [2] With difficulty.

And on a day befell, that in that hour
When that his meatë wont was to be brought,
The jailer shut the doorës of the tower;
He heared it well, but he spake right nought.
And in his heart anon there fell a thought,
That they for hunger woulden do him dien;

'Alas!' quod he, 'alas that I was wrought!' 14739
Therewith the tearës fellen from his eyen.

His youngë son, that three year was of age,
Unto him said, 'Father, why do ye weep?
When will the jailer bringen our potage?
Is there no morsel bread that ye do keep?
I am so hungry, that I may not sleep.
Now wouldë God that I might sleepen ever,
Then should not hunger in my wombë creep;
There n'is no thing, save bread, that me were lever.'[1]

Thus day by day this child began to cry,
Till in his father's barm[2] adown it lay, 14750
And saidë, 'Farewell, father, I must die;'
And kiss'd his father, and died the samë day.
And when the woful father did it sey,[3]
For woe his armës two he 'gan to bite,
And said, 'Alas! Fortune, and wala-wa!
Thy falsë wheel my woe all may I wite.'[4]

His children wenden,[5] that for hunger it was
That he his armës gnaw'd, and not for woe,
And saiden, 'Father, do not so, alas!
But rather eat the flesh upon us two. 14760
Our flesh thou gave us, take our flesh us fro,
And eat enough:' right thus they to him said,
And after that, within a day or two,
They laid them in his lap adown, and died.

Himself, despaired, eke for hunger starf.[6]
Thus ended is this mighty Earl of Pise:
From high estate Fortune away him carf.[7]
Of this tragedy it ought enough suffice;

[1] Rather.

[2] Lap.

[3] See.

[4] Blame.

[5] Thought.

[6] Died.

[7] Cut.

Whoso will hear it in a longer wise, 14769
Readeth the greatë poet of Itaille,
That hightë Dant', for he can it devise [1]
From point to point, not one word will he fail.

[1] Describe.

THE NUN'S PRIEST'S PROLOGUE.

'Ho!' quod the Knight, 'good sir, no more of this:
That ye have said, it right enough ywis,[1]   14774
And muchel more; for little heaviness
Is right enough to muchel folk, I guess.
I say for me, it is a great disease,[2]
Where as men have been in great wealth and ease,
To hearen of their sudden fall, alas!
And the contráry is joy and great solas,[3]   14780
As when a man hath been in poor estate,
And climbeth up, and waxeth fortunate,
And there abideth in prosperity:
Such thing is gladsome, as it thinketh me,
And of such thing were goodly for to tell.'
  'Yea,' quod our Hostë, 'by Saint Paulë's bell,
Ye say right sooth; this monk hath clapped loud:
He spake how Fortune cover'd with a cloud
I wot not what, and als of a tragedy
Right now ye heard: and pardie no remedy   14790
It is for to bewailen, nor complain
That that is done, and als it is a pain,
As ye have said, to hear of heaviness.
Sir Monk, no more of this, so God you bless;

[1] Surely.

[2] Trouble.

[3] Enjoyment.

Your tale annoyeth all this company;   14795
Such talking is not worth a butterfly,
For therein is there no disport nor game:
Therefore, Sir Monk, Dan Piers by your name,
I pray you heart'ly, tell us somewhat else,
For sikerly, n'ere clinking of your bells,   14800
That on your bridle hang on every side,
By heaven king, that for us allë died,
I should ere this have fallen down for sleep,
Although the slough had been never so deep:
Then had your talë all been told in vain.
For certainly, as that these clerkës sayn,
Where as a man may have no audience,
Nought helpeth it to tellen his senténce.
And well I wot the substance is in me,
If anything shall well reported be.   14810
Sir, say somewhat of hunting, I you pray.'
    'Nay,' quod this Monk, 'I have no lust to play:
Now let another tell as I have told.'
    Then spake our Host with rudë speech and bold,
And said unto the Nunnë's Priest anon,
'Come near, thou Priest, come hither, thou Sir John,
Tell us such thing as may our heartës glade.
Be blithe, although thou ride upon a jade.
What though thine horse be bothë foul and lean?
If he will serve thee, reck thee not a bean: 14820
Look that thine heart be merry evermo.'
    'Yes, Host,' quod he, 'so may I ride or go,
But I be merry', ywis I will be blamed.'
And right anon his tale he hath attamed;[1]
And thus he said unto us every one,
This sweetë priest, this goodly man, Sir John.

[1] Commenced.

THE NUN'S PRIEST'S TALE.

A POORË widow somedeal stoopen in age,   14527
Was whilom dwelling in a narrow cottáge,
Beside a grovë, standing in a dale.
This widow, which I tell you of my tale,
Since thilkë day that she was last a wife,
In patiénce led a full simple life.
For little was her chattel and her rent:
By husbandry[1] of such as God her sent,
She found herself, and eke her daughters two.
Three largë sowës had she, and no mo:
Three kine, and eke a sheep that hightë[2] Mall.
Full sooty was her bower, and eke her hall,
In which she eat many a slender meal.
Of poignant sauce ne knew she never a deal.[3]   14540
No dainty morsel passed through her throat;
Her diet was accordant to her cote.[4]
Repletión ne made her never sick;
Attemper[5] diet was all her physic,
And exercise, and heartë's suffisance.
The goutë let[6] her nothing for to dance,
No apoplexy shentë[7] not her head.
No wine ne drank she, neither white nor red:
Her board was served most with white and black,
Milk and brown bread, in which she found no lack,
Seind[8] bacon, and sometime an egg or twey;   14851
For she was as it were a mannor dey.[9]
    A yard she had, enclosed all about
With stickës, and a dry ditchë without,
In which she had a cock hight Chanticleer,
In all the land of crowing n'as[10] his peer.

1 Thrift.

2 Was called.

3 Whit.

4 Cottage.

5 Temperate.

6 Prevented.
7 Injured.

8 Singed.

9 Day-labourer.

10 Was not.

His voice was merrier than the merry' orgón,   14857
On massë days that in the churches gon.
Well sikerer[1] was his crowing in his lodge,
Than is a clock, or any abbey' orloge.[2]
By nature he knew each ascensióun
Of the equinoctial in thilkë town;
For when degreës fifteen were ascended,
Then crew he, that it might not be amended.
    His comb was redder than the fine coral,
Embattell'd, as it were a castle wall.
His bill was black, and as the jet it shone;
Like azure were his leggës and his tone;[3]
His nailës whiter than the lily flow'r,
And like the burned[4] gold was his colóur.   14870
    This gentle cock had in his governance
Seven hennës, for to do all his pleasance,
Which were his sisters and his paramours,
And wonder like to him, as of coloúrs.
Of which the fairest hued in the throat,
Was cleped fair Damoselle Partelote.
Courteous she was, discreet, and debonair,
And cómpaignáble, and bare herself so fair,
Sithen[5] the day that she was sevennight old,
That truëly she hath the heart in hold   14880
Of Chanticleer, locked in every lith:[6]
He loved her so, that well was him therewith.
But such a joy it was to hear them sing,
When that the brightë sunnë 'gan to spring,
In sweet accord, 'My lefe[7] is fare[8] in land.'
    For thilkë time, as I have understand,
Beastës and birdës coulden speak and sing.
    And so befell, that in a dawëning,
As Chanticleer among his wivës all
Sat on his perchë, that was in the hall,   14890

[1] Surer.

[2] Clock.

[3] Toes.

[4] Burnished.

[5] Since.

[6] Limb.

[7] Dear.
[8] Gone.

And next him sat his fairë Partelote,   14891
This Chanticleer 'gan groanen in his throat,
As man that in his dream is dretched[1] sore.
And when that Partelote thus heard him roar,
She was aghast, and saidë, 'Heartë dear,
What aileth you to groan in this mannere?
Ye be a very sleeper, fy for shame!'
    And he answér'd and saidë thus: 'Madame,
I pray you that ye take it not agrief:
By God, me mette[2] I was in such mischief   14900
Right now, that yet mine heart is sore affright.
Now God,' quod he, 'my sweven[3] reck aright,
And keep my body out of foul prisoún.
    'Me mette how that I roamed up and down
Within our yard, where as I saw a beast,
Was like an hound, and would have made arrest
Upon my body, and have had me dead.
His colour was betwixt yellow and red;
And tipped was his tail, and both his ears
With black, unlike the remnant of his heres.[4]   14910
His snout was small, with glowing eyen twey:
Yet for his look almost for fear I dey:
This caused me my groaning doubtëless.'
    'Away,' quod she, 'fy on you heartëless.
Alas!' quod she, 'for by that God above
Now have ye lost my heart and all my love;
I cannot love a coward, by my faith.
For certes, what so any woman saith,
We all desiren, if it mightë be,
To have an husband, hardy, wise, and free,   14920
And secret, and no niggard nor no fool,
Nor him that is aghast of every tool,
No no avantour[5] by that God above.
How dursten ye for shame say to your love,

---

[1] Oppressed.

[2] Dreamed.

[3] Dream.

[4] Hair.

[5] Boaster.

That anything might maken you afeard? 14925
Have ye no mannë's heart, and have a beard?
Alas! and can ye be aghast of swevenës?[1]   [1] Dreams.
Nothing but vanity, God wot, in sweven is.
 ' Swevens engender of repletións,
And oft of fume, and of complexións, 14930
When humours be too' abundant in a wight.
Certes this dream, which ye have mett to-night,
Cometh of the great superfluity
Of yourë redë *cholera* pardie,
Which causeth folk to dreaden in their dreams
Of arrows, and of fire with redë lemes,[2]   [2] Flames.
Of redë beastës, that they will them bite,
Of conteke,[3] and of waspës great and lite;[4] [3] Conten-
Right as the humour of meláncholy   tiou.
Causeth full many a man in sleep to cry, 14940 [4] Little.
For fear of bullës, and of bearës blake,
Or ellës that black devils will them take.
 ' Of other humours could I tell also,
That worken many a man in sleep much woe:
But I will pass, as lightly as I can.
 ' Lo Cato, which that was so wise a man,
Said he not thus? " Ne do no force[5] of dreams." [5] Take no
 ' Now, Sir,' quod she, ' when we fly from the beams heed.
For Goddë's love, as take some laxatif:
Up peril of my soul, and of my life, 14950
I counsel you the best, I will not lie,
That both of choler, and of meláncholy
Ye purge you; and for ye shall not tarry,
Though in this town be no apothecary,
I shall myself two herbës teachen you,
That shall be for your health, and for your prow;[6] [6] Profit.
And in our yard the herbës shall I find,
The which have of their property by kind

To purgen you beneath, and eke above.   14959
Sirë, forget not this for Goddë's love;
Ye be full choleric of complexión;
'Ware that the sun in his ascensión
Ne find you not replete of humours hot:
And if it do, I dare well lay a groat,
That ye shall have a fever tertiane,
Or else an ague, that may be your bane.
A day or two ye shall have digestives
Of wormës, ere ye take your laxatives,
Of laureole, centaury, and fumetere,
Or else of hellebore, that groweth there,   14970

¹ Spurge. Of catapucë,[1] or of gaitre-berries,[2]
² Dogwood berries.

Or herb ivy growing in our yard, that merry' is:
Pick them right as they grow, and eat them in.
Be merry, husband, for your father kin;
Dreadeth no dream; I can say you no more.'
    'Madame,' quod he, '*grand mercy* of your lore.
But natheless, as touching Dan Caton,
That hath of wisdom such a great renown,
Though that he bade no dreamës for to drede,
By God, men may in oldë bookës read,   14980
Of many a man, more of authority

³ Thrive. Than ever Cato was, so may I the,[3]

That all the réverse say of his senténce,
And have well founden by experience,
That dreamës be significatións
As well of joy, as tribulatións,
That folk enduren in this life present.
There needeth make of this no argument;

⁴ Trial, experience. The very prevë[4] sheweth it indeed.

    'One of the greatest authors that men read, 14990
Saith thus; that whilom two fellowës went
On pilgrimage in a full good intent;

And happen'd so, they came into a town, 14993
Where there was such a congregatióun
Of people, and eke so strait of herbergage,[1]
That they ne found as much as a cottáge,
In which they bothë might ylodged be:
Wherefore they musten of necessity,
As for that night, departen company;
And each of them go'th to his hostelry, 15000
And took his lodging as it wouldë fall.
 ' That one of them was lodged in a stall,
Far in a yard, with oxen of the plough;
That other man was lodged well enough,
As was his áventure, or his fortúne,
That us governeth all, as in commune.
 ' And so befell, that, long ere it were day,
This man mett[2] in his bed, there as he lay,
How that his fellow 'gan upon him call,
And said, " Alas! for in an ox's stall 15010
This night shall I be murder'd, there I lie.
Now help me, dearë brother, or I die;
In allë hastë come to me," he said.
 ' This man out of his sleep for fear abraid;[3]
But when that he was waked of his sleep,
He turned him, and took of this no keep;
Him thought his dream was but a vanity.
Thus twiës in his sleeping dreamed he.
 ' And at the thirdë time yet his fellaw
Came, as him thought, and said, " I now am slaw:[4]
Behold my bloody woundës, deep and wide. 15021
Arise up early, in the morrow tide,
And at the west gate of the town," quod he,
" A cartë full of dung there shalt thou see,
In which my body is hid privily.
Do thilkë cart arresten boldëly.

[1] Lodging.

[2] Dreamed.

[3] Awoke.

[4] Slain.

My gold caused my murder, sooth to sayn."   15027
And told him every point how he was slain
With a full piteous facë, pale of hue.
And trusteth well, his dream he found full true;
For on the morrow, as soon as it was day,
To his fellowë's inn he took his way:
And when that he came to this ox's stall,
After his fellow he began to call.
  'The hosteler answered him anon,
And saidë, "Sir, your fellow is agone,
As soon as day he went out of the town."
  'This man 'gan fallen in suspicioún
Rememb'ring on his dreamës that he mett,[1]
And forth he go'th, no longer would he let,[2]   15040
Unto the west gate of the town, and fond
A dung cart, as it went for to dung lond,
That was arrayed in the samë wise
As ye have heard the deadë man devise:
And with an hardy heart he 'gan to cry,
"Vengeance and justice of this felony:
My fellow murder'd is this samë night,
And in this cart he li'th, gaping upright.
I cry out on the ministers," quod he,
"That shoulden keep and rulen this city: 15050
Harow! alas! here li'th my fellow slain."
  'What should I more unto this talë sayn?
The people out start, and cast the cart to ground,
And in the middle of the dung they found
The deadë man, that murder'd was all new.
  'O blissful God! that art so good and true,
Lo, how that thou bewrayest murder alway.
Murder will out, that see we day by day.
Murder is so wlatsom[3] and abominable
To God, that is so just and reasonable,   15060

---

[1] Dreamed.
[2] Stay.
[3] Loathsome.

That he ne will not suffer it hylled[1] be:　　　15061
Though it abide a year, or two, or three,
Murder will out, this is my conclusioun.
　'And right anon, the min'sters of the town
Have hent[2] the carter, and so sore him pined,[3]
And eke the hosteler so sore engined,[4]
That they beknew[5] their wickedness anon,
And were anhanged by the neckë bone.
　'Here may ye see that dreamës be to dread.
And certes in the samë book I read,　　　15070
Right in the nextë chapter after this,
(I gabbë[6] not, so have I joy and bliss,)
Two men that would have passed o'er the sea
For certain cause into a far countrý,
If that the wind ne haddë been contrary,
That made them in a city for to tarry,
That stood full merry upon an haven side.
But on a day, against the even tide,
The wind 'gan change, and blew right as them lest.[7]
Jolly and glad they wenten to their rest,　　　15080
And casten them full early for to sail;
But to that one man fell a great marvail.
　'That one of them in sleeping as he lay,
He mett[8] a wonder dream, against the day:
Him thought a man stood by his beddë's side,
And him commanded that he should abide,
And said him thus; "If thou to-morrow wend,[9]
Thou shalt be drent;[10] my tale is at an end."
　'He woke, and told his fellow what he mett,
And prayed him his voyage for to let,[11]　　　15090
As for that day, he pray'd him for to abide.
　'His fellow, that lay by his beddë's side,
'Gan for to laugh, and scorned him full fast.
"No dream," quod he, "may so my heart aghast,

[1] Hidden.

[2] Seized.
[3] Tortured.
[4] Racked.
[5] Confess-
ed.

[6] Talk idly.

[7] Pleased.

[8] Dreamed.

[9] Go.

[10] Drown-
ed.

[11] Stay.

That I will letten for to do my things.   15095
I settë not a straw by thy dreamings,
For swevens[1] be but vanities and japes.[2]
Men dream all day of owlës and of apes,
And eke of many a masë[3] therewithal;
Men dream of thing that never was, nor shall.   15100
But since I see that thou wilt here abide,
And thus forslothen[4] wilfully thy tide,
God wot it rueth[5] me, and have good day."
And thus he took his leave, and went his way.
  'But ere that he had half his course ysail'd,
N'ot[6] I not why, nor what mischance it ail'd,
But casually the shippë's bottom rent,
And ship and man under the water went
In sight of other shippës there beside,
That with him sailed at the samë tide.   15110
  'And therefore, fairë Partelote so dear,
By such examples oldë mayst thou lere,[7]
That no man shouldë be too reckëless
Of dreamës, for I say thee doubtëless,
That many a dream full sore is for to dread.
  'Lo, in the life of Saint Kenelm I read,
That was Kenulphus' son, the noble king
Of Mercenrike, how Kenelm mett[8] a thing.
A little ere he were murder'd on a day,
His murder in his avisión[9] he say.[10]   15120
His norice[11] him expounded every del
His sweven, and bade him for to keep him well
From treason; but he n'as but seven year old,
And therefore little talë hath he told
Of any dream, so holy was his heart.
By God, I haddë lever than my shirt,
That ye had read his legend, as have I.
  'Dame Partelote, I say you truëly,

[1] Dreams.
[2] Tricks.
[3] Wild fancy.
[4] Lose by sloth.
[5] Moves my pity.
[6] Know not.
[7] Learn.
[8] Dreamed.
[9] Vision.
[10] Saw.
[11] Nurse.

Macrobius, that writ the avisión   15129
In Afric of the worthy Scipion,
Affirmeth dreamës, and saith that they be
Warning of thingës that men after see.
  'And furthermore, I pray you looketh well
In the Oldë Testament, of Daniel,
If he held dreamës any vanity.
  'Read eke of Joseph, and there shall ye see
Whe'r dreamës be sometime (I say not all)
Warning of thingës that shall after fall.
  'Look of Egypt the king, Dan Pharao,
His baker and his buteler also,   15140
Whether they ne felten none effect in dreams.
Whoso will seeken acts of sundry remes,[1]
May read of dreamës many a wonder thing.
  'Lo Crœsus, which that was of Lydie king,
Mett he not that he sat upon a tree,
Which signified he should anhanged be?
  'Lo here, Andromache, Hectorë's wife,
That day that Hector shouldë lose his life,
She dreamed on the samë night beforn,
How that the life of Hector should be lorn,   15150
If thilkë day he went into battail:
She warned him, but it might not avail;
He went forth for to fighten natheless,
And was yslain anon of Achilles.
  'But thilkë tale is all too long to tell,
And eke it is nigh day, I may not dwell.
Shortly I say, as for conclusión,
That I shall have of this avisión
Adversity: and I say furthermore,
That I ne tell[2] of laxatives no store,   15160
For they be venomous, I wot it well:
I them defy, I love them never a del.

----

[1] Realms.

[2] Set.

'But let us speak of mirth, and stint all this; 15163
Madame Partelote, so have I bliss,
Of one thing God hath sent me largë grace :
For when I see the beauty of your face,
Ye be so scarlet red about your eyen,
It maketh all my dreadë for to dien,
For, all so sicker[1] as *In principio,*
Mulier est hominis confusio. 15170
(Madam, the sentence of this Latin is,
Woman is mannë's joy and mannë's bliss.)
For when I feel a-night your softë side,
Albeit that I may not on you ride,
For that our perch is made so narrow, alas!
I am so full of joy and of solace,
That I defië bothë sweven and dream.'
    And with that word he flew down from the beam,
For it was day, and eke his hennës all;
And with a chuck he 'gan them for to call, 15180
For he had found a corn, lay in the yard.
Royal he was, he was no more afeard;
He feather'd Partelotë twenty time,
And trade her eke as oft, ere it was prime.
He looketh as it were a grim lioun;
And on his toes he roameth up and down,
Him deigned not to set his feet to ground :
He chucketh, when he hath a corn yfound,
And to him runnen then his wivës all.
    Thus royal, as a prince is in his hall, 15190
Leave I this Chanticleer in his pastúre;
And after will I tell his áventure.
    When that the month in which the world began,
That hightë March, when God first maked man,
Was cómplete, and ypassed were also,
Sithen[2] March ended, thirty days and two,

[1] Certain.

[2] Since.

Befell that Chanticleer in all his pride,   15197
His seven wivës walking him beside,
Cast up his eyen to the brightë sun,
That in the sign of Taurus had yrun
Twenty degrees and one, and somewhat more:
He knew by kind, and by none other lore,
That it was prime, and crew with blissful steven.[1]
'The sun,' he said, 'is clomben up on heaven
Twenty degrees and one, and more ywis.[2]
Madamë Partelote, my worldë's bliss,
Heark'neth these blissful birdës how they
    sing,
And see the freshë flowerës how they spring;
Full is mine heart of revel, and solace.'
    But suddenly him fell a sorrowful case;   15210
For ever the latter end of joy is woe:
God wot that worldly joy is soon ago:
And if a rethor[3] couldë fair indite,
He in a chronicle might it safely write,
As for a sovereign notability.
    Now every wise man let him hearken me:
This story is also true, I undertake,
As is the book of Launcelot du Lake,
That women hold in full great reverence.
Now will I turn again to my senténce.   15220
    A col fox, full of sly iniquity,
That in the grove had wonned[4] yearës three,
By high imaginatión forecast,
The samë night throughout the hedges brast[5]
Into the yard, there Chanticleer the fair
Was wont, and eke his wivës, to repair:
And in a bed of wortës[6] still he lay,
Till it was passed undern[7] of the day,
Waiting his time on Chanticleer to fall:

[1] Voice.

[2] Certainly.

[3] Rhetorician.

[4] Dwelt.

[5] Burst.

[6] Cabbages.

[7] Third hour.

As gladly do these homicidës all,   15230
That in await liggen[1] to murder men.
    O falsë murderer! rucking[2] in thy den!
O newë 'Scariot, newë Ganelon!
O false dissimuler, O Greek Sinon,
That broughtest Troy all utterly to sorrow!
O Chanticleer! accursed be the morrow,
That thou into thy yard flew from the beams,
Thou were full well ywarned by thy dreams,
That thilkë day was perilous to thee.
But what that God forewot[3] must needës be,   15240
After the opinion of certain clerkës.
Witness on him that any perfect clerk is,
That in school is great altercatión
In this matter, and great disputison,
And hath been of an hundred thousand men.
But I ne cannot boult[4] it to the bren,[5]
As can the holy doctor Augustin,
Or Boece, or the bishop Bradwardin,
Whether that Goddë's worthy foreweeting[6]
Straineth me needly for to do a thing,   15250
(Needly clepe I simple necessity)
Or ellës if free choice be granted me
To do that samë thing, or do it nought,
Though God forewot it ere that it was wrought;
Or if his weeting[7] straineth never a del,[8]
But by necessity conditionel.
I will not have to do of such mattére;
My tale is of a cock, as ye may hear,
That took his counsel of his wife with sorrow
To walken in the yard upon the morrow   15260
That he had mett the dream, as I you told.
Womenë's counsels be full often cold;
Womanë's counsel brought us first to woe,

[1] Lie.
[2] Crouch-
ing.
[3] Fore-
knew.
[4] Sift.
[5] Bran.
[6] Fore-
know-
ledge.
[7] Know-
ledge.
[8] Whit.

And made Adám from Paradise to go,   15264
There as he was full merry, and well at ease.
But for I n'ot,[1] to whom I might displease,
If I counsel of women wouldë blame,
Pass over, for I said it in my game.
Read authors, where they treat of such mattére,
And what they say of women ye may hear.   15270
These be the cockë's wordës, and not mine;
I can no harm of no woman divine.[2]
    Fair in the sand, to bathe her merrily,
Li'th Partelote, and all her sisters by,
Against the sun, and Chanticleer so free
Sang merrier than the mermaid in the sea,
For Physiologus saith sikerly,[3]
How that they singen well and merrily.
    And so befell that as he cast his eye
Among the wortës on a butterfly,   15280
He was 'ware of this fox that lay full low.
Nothing ne list him thennë for to crow,
But cried anon 'Cock! cock!' and up he start,
As man that was affrayed in his heart.
For naturally a beast desireth flee
From his contrary, if he may it see,
Though he ne'er erst[4] had seen it with his eye.
    This Chanticleer, when he 'gan him espy,
He would have fled, but that the fox anon
Said, 'Gentle Sir, alas! what will ye don?   15290
Be ye afraid of me that am your friend?
Now certes, I were worse than any fiend,
If I to you would harm or villainy.
I n'am not come your counsel to espy.
But truëly the cause of my coming
Was only for to hearken how ye sing:
For truëly ye have as merry a steven,[5]

[1] Know not.

[2] Conjecture.

[3] Certainly.

[4] Before.

[5] Voice.

As any angel hath that is in heaven;   15298
Therewith ye have of music more feeling,
Than had Boece, or any that can sing.
My lord your father (God his soulë bless)
And eke your mother of her gentleness
Have in mine house ybeen, to my great ease:
And certes, Sir, full fain would I you please.
But for men speak of singing, I will say,
So may I brooken[1] well mine eyen tway,
Save you, ne heard I never man so sing,
As did your father in the morrowning.
Certes it was of heart all that he sung.
And for to make his voice the morë strong,   15310
He would so pain him, that with both his eyen
He mustë wink, so loud he wouldë crien,
And standen on his tiptoes therewithal,
And stretchen forth his neckë long and small.
And eke he was of such discretión,
That there n'as no man in no región,
That him in song or wisdom mightë pass.
I have well read in Dan Burnel the ass
Among his verse, how that there was a cock,
That for a priestë's son gave him a knock   15320
Upon his leg, while he was young and nice,
He made him for to lose his benefice.
But certain there is no comparison
Betwixt the wisdom and discretión
Of yourë father, and his subtilty.
Now singeth, Sir, for Saintë Charity,
Let see, can ye your father counterfeit?'
   This Chanticleer his wingës 'gan to beat,
As man that could not his treasón espy,
So was he ravish'd with his flattery.   15330
   Alas! ye lordës, many a false flattour

---

[1] Enjoy.

Is in your court, and many a losengeour,[1]   15332
That pleaseth you well morë, by my faith,
Than he that soothfastness[2] unto you saith.
Readeth Ecclesiast of flattery,
Beware, ye lordës, of their treachery.
    This Chanticleer stood high upon his toes
Stretching his neck, and held his eyen close,
And 'gan to crowen loudë for the nones:[3]
And Dan Russel the fox start up at once,   15340
And by the gargat[4] hentë[5] Chanticleer,
And on his back toward the wood him bare.
For yet ne was there no man that him sued.[6]
    O destiny, that mayst not be eschew'd!
Alas, that Chanticleer flew from the beams!
Alas, his wife ne raughtë[7] not of dreams!
And on a Friday fell all this mischance.
    O Venus, that art goddess of pleasánce,
Since that thy servant was this Chanticleer,
And in thy service did all his powér,   15350
More for delight, than world to multiply,
Why wilt thou suffer him on thy day to die?
    O Gaufrid, dearë master sovëreign,
That, when thy worthy king Richard was slain
With shot, complainedest his death so sore,
Why ne had I now thy science and thy lore,
The Friday for to chiden, as did ye?
(For on a Friday soothly slain was he,)
Then would I shew you how that I could 'plain
For Chanticleerë's dread, and for his pain.   15360
    Certes such cry, nor lamentation
N'as ne'er of ladies made, when Ilion
Was won, and Pyrrhus with his straightë swerd
When he had hent king Priam by the beard,
And slain him, (as saith us *Eneidos*,)

---

[1] Parasite.

[2] Truth.

[3] Occasion.

[4] Throat.
[5] Seized.

[6] Followed.

[7] Recked.

As maden all the hennës in the close, 15366
When they had seen of Chanticleer the sight.
But sovereignly Dame Partelotë shright,[1]
Full louder than did Hasdrubalë's wife,
When that her husband had ylost his life,
And that the Romans hadden burnt Cartháge,
She was so full of torment and of rage,
That wilfully into the fire she start,
And burnt herselven with a steadfast heart.
    O woful hennës! right so crieden ye,
As when that Nero brentë[2] the city
Of Romë, cried the senatorës' wives
For that their husbands losten all their lives;
Withouten guilt this Nero hath them slain.
    Now will I turn unto my tale again; 15380
The sely[3] widow, and her daughters two,
Hearden these hennës cry and maken woo,
And out at the doors starten they anon,
And saw the fox toward the wood is gone,
And bare upon his back the cock away:
They crieden, 'Out! harow and wala-wa!
Aha! the fox!' and after him they ran,
And eke with stavës many another man;
Ran Coll our dog, and Talbot, and Garland,
And Malkin, with her distaff in her hand; 15390
Ran cow and calf, and eke the very hoggës
So feared were for barking of the doggës,
And shouting of the men and women eke,
They rannen so, them thought their heartës break.
They yelleden as fiendës do in hell:
The duckës crieden as men would them quell:
The geese for fearë flewen o'er the trees,
Out of the hivë came the swarm of bees,
So hideous was the noise, a *benedicite!*

[1] Shrieked.

[2] Burnt.

[3] Simple.

Certes he Jackë Straw, and his menie,[1] 15400
Ne maden never shoutës half so shrill,
When that they woulden any Fleming kill,
As thilkë day was made upon the fox.
Of brass they broughten beamës[2] and of box,
Of horn and bone, in which they blew and pooped,[3]
And therewithal they shrieked and they hooped;
It seem'd as that the heaven shouldë fall.
  Now, goodë men, I pray you heark'neth all;
Lo, how Fortunë turneth suddenly
The hope and pride eke of her enemy. 15410
This cock that lay upon the fox's back,
In all his dread, unto the fox he spake,
And saidë, 'Sir, if that I were as ye,
Yet would I say, (as wisly[4] God help me,)
"Turneth again, ye proudë churlës all;
A very pestilence upon you fall.
Now am I come unto the woodë's side,
Maugre your head, the cock shall here abide:
I will him eat in faith, and that anon."'
  The fox answer'd, 'In faith it shall be done:' 15420
And as he spake the word, all suddenly
The cock brake from his mouth deliverly,[5]
And high upon a tree he flew anon.
  And when the fox saw that the cock was gone,
'Alas!' quod he, 'O Chanticleer, alas!
I have,' quod he, 'ydone to you trespass,
Inasmuch as I maked you afeard,
When I you hent,[6] and brought out of your yard;
But, Sir, I did it in no wick' intent:
Come down, and I shall tell you what I meant.
I shall say sooth to you, God help me so.' 15431
  'Nay then,' quod he, 'I shrew[7] us bothë two.
And first I shrew myself, both blood and bones,

[1] Followers.

[2] Trumpets.
[3] Trumpeted.

[4] Surely.

[5] Actively.

[6] Took.

[7] Curse.

If thou beguile me oftener than once. 15434
Thou shalt no morë through thy flattery
Do[1] me to sing and winken with mine eye.
For he that winketh when he shouldë see,
All wilfully, God let him never the.'[2]
   'Nay,' quod the fox, 'but God give him mis-
     chance,
That is so indiscreet of governánce, 15440
That jangleth[3] when that he should hold his peace.'
   Lo, which[4] it is for to be reckëless
And negligent, and trust on flattery.
But ye that holden this tale a folly,
As of a fox, or of a cock, or hen,
Take the morality thereof, good men.
For Saint Paul saith, That all that written is,
To our doctríne it is ywritten ywis.[5]
Taketh the fruit, and let the chaff be still.
   Now goodë God, if that it be thy will, 15450
As saith my Lord, so make us all good men;
And bring us to thy highë bliss.—*Amen*.

'Sir Nunnë's Priest,' our Hostë said anon,
'Yblessed be thy breech and every stone;
This was a merry tale of Chanticleer.
But by my truth, if thou were seculere,
Thou wouldest be a treadëfowl aright:
For if thou have couráge as thou hast might,
Thee werë need of hennës, as I ween,
Yea more than seven timës seventeen. 15460
See, whichë brawnës hath this gentle priest,
So great a neck, and such a largë breast!
He looketh as a sparhawk with his eyen;
Him needeth not his colour for to dyen
With Brasil, nor with grain of Portingale.

1 Cause.
2 Thrive
3 Prateth.
4 What.
5 Certainly.

'But, Sirë, fairë fall you for your tale.' 15466
And after that, he with full merry cheer
Said to another, as ye shallen hear.

*   *   *   *   *

THE SECOND NUN'S TALE.

The minister and the norice[1] unto vices,   15469
Which that men clepe in English idleness,
That porter at the gate is of delices,[2]
T' eschewen, and by her contrary her oppress,
That is to say, by lawful business,
Well oughtë we to do all our intent,[3]
Lest that the fiend through idleness us hent.[4]

For he that with his thousand cordës sly,
Continually us waiteth to beclap,[5]
When he may man in idleness espy,
He can so lightly catch him in his trap,
Till that a man be hent right by the lappe,[6]   15480
He n'is not 'ware the fiend hath him in hand:
Well ought us work, and idleness withstand.

And though men dreaded never for to die,
Yet see men well by reason doubtëless,
That idleness is root of sluggardy,
Of which there never com'th no good increase,
And see that slothë hold'th them in a lees,[7]
Only to sleep, and for to eat and drink,
And to devouren all that others swink.[8]

1 Nurse.
2 Delights.
3 Application.
4 Take.
5 Catch.
6 Skirt.
7 Leash.
8 Labour.

And for to put us from such idleness, 15490
That cause is of so great confusión,
I have here done my faithful business
After the Legend in translatión
Right of thy glorious life and passion,
Thou with thy garland, wrought of rose and lily,
Thee mean I, maid and martyr, Saint Cecilie.

And thou, that artë flow'r of virgins all,
Of whom that Bernard list so well to write,
To thee at my beginning first I call,
Thou comfort of us wretches do me' indite 15500
Thy maiden's death, that won through her merít
The eternal life, and over the fiend victóry,
As man may after readen in her story.

Thou maid and mother, daughter of thy Son,
Thou well of mercy, sinful soulës' cure,
In whom that God of bounty chose to won;[1]
Thou humble and high over every creáture,
Thou nobledest so far forth our nature,
That no disdain the Maker had of kind,[2]
His Son in blood and flesh to clothe and wind.[3] 15510

Within the cloister blissful of thy sidës,
Took mannë's shape the eternal love and peace,
That of the trinë compass Lord and guide is,
Whom earth, and sea, and heaven out of release,
Aye herien;[4] and thou, virgín wemmëless,[5]
Bare of thy body (and dweltest maiden pure)
The Creatór of every creáture.

Assembled is in thee magnificence
With mercy, goodness, and with such pity,

[1] Dwell.

[2] Nature.

[3] Wrap.

[4] Praise.
[5] Spotless.

That thou, that art the sun of excellence,   15520
Not only helpest them that prayen thee,
But oftentime of thy benignity
Full freely, ere that men thine help beseech,
Thou go'st before, and art their livës' leech.

Now help, thou meek and blissful fairë maid,
Me flemed[1] wretch, in this desért of gall;
Think on the woman Cananee, that said
That whelpës eaten some of the crumbës all
That from their Lordë's table been yfall;
And though that I, unworthy son of Eve,   15530
Be sinful, yet accepteth my believe.

And for that faith is dead withouten werkës,
So for to worken give me wit and space,
That I be quit from thennës that most derk is;
O thou, that art so fair and full of grace,
Be thou mine advocate in that high place,
There as withouten end is sung hosanne,
Thou Christë's mother, daughter dear of Anne.

And of thy light my soul in prison light,
That troubled is by the contagión   15540
Of my bodý, and also by the weight
Of earthly lust, and false affectión:
O haven of refuge, O salvatión
Of them that be in sorrow and in distress,
Now help, for to my work I will me dress.

Yet pray I you that readen that I write,
Forgive me, that I do no diligence
This ilkë story subtlely t' indite.
For both have I the wordës and sentence

Of him, that at the sainte's reverence   15550
The story wrote, and followed her legend,
And pray you that ye will my work amend. .

First will I you the name of Saint Cecilie
Expound, as men may in her story see:
It is to say in English, Heaven's lily,
For pure chasteness of virginity,
Or for she whiteness had of honesty,
And green of conscience, and of good fame
The sweete savour, Lilie was her name.

Or Cecilie is to say, the way to blind,   15560
For she example was by good teaching;
Or else Cecilie, as I written find,
Is joined by a manner conjoining
Of heaven and *Lia*, and here in figuring
The heaven is set for thought of holiness,
And *Lia* for her lasting business.

Cecilie may eke be said in this mannere,
Wanting of blindness, for her greate light
Of sapience, and for her thewes[1] clear.
Or elles lo, this maiden's name bright   15570
Of heaven and *Leos* com'th, for which by right
Men might her well the heaven of people
    call,
Example of good and wise workes all:

For *Leos* people in English is to say;
And right as men may in the heaven see
The sun and moon, and starres every way,
Right so men ghostly,[2] in this maiden free
Sawen of faith the magnanimity,

[1] Qualities.

[2] Spiritual.

And eke the clearness whole of sapience, 15579
And sundry workës, bright of excellence.

And right so as these philosóphers write,
The heaven is swift and round, and eke burning,
Right so was fairë Cecilie the white
Full swift and busy in every good working,
And round and whole in good pérsevering,
And burning ever in charity full bright:
Now have I you declared what she hight.

This maiden bright Cecile, as her life saith,
Was come of Romans and of noble kind,
And from her cradle foster'd in the faith 15590
Of Christ, and bare his Gospel in her mind:
She never ceased, as I written find,
Of her prayér, and God to love and dread,
Beseeching him to keep her maidenhead.

And when this maiden should until a man
Ywedded be, that was full young of age,
Which that ycleped was Valerian,
And day was comen of her marriage,
She full devout and humble in her couráge,[1]
Under her robe of gold, that sat full fair, 15600
Had next her flesh yclad her in an hair.[2]

And while that th' organs maden melody,
To God alone thus in her heart sung she;
'O Lord, my soul and eke my body gie[3]
Unwemmed,[4] lest that I confounded be.'
And for his love that died upon the tree,
Every secónd or thirdë day she fast,
Aye bidding[5] in her orisons full fast.

[1] Mind.

[2] Hair-cloth.

[3] Guide.

[4] Unspotted.

[5] Praying.

The night came, and to beddë must she gon 15609
With her husbánd, as it is the mannere,
And privily she said to him anon;
'O sweet and well-beloved spousë dear,
There is a counsel, and[1] ye will it hear,
Which that right fain I would unto you say,
So that ye swear ye will it not bewray.'

Valerian 'gan fast unto her swear,
That for no case, nor thing that mightë be,
He shouldë never to none bewrayen here;[2]
And then at erst[3] thus to him saidë she;
'I have an angel which that loveth me, 15620
That with great love, where so I wake or sleep,
Is ready aye my body for to keep;

'And if that he may feelen out of drede,[4]
That ye me touch or love in villainy,
He right anon will slay you with the deed,
And in your youthë thus ye shoulden die.
And if that ye in cleanë love me gie,[5]
He will you love as me, for your cleanness,
And shew to you his joy and his brightness.'

This Valerian, corrected as God wold, 15630
Answer'd again, 'If I shall trusten thee,
Let me that angel see, and him behold;
And if that it a very angel be,
Then will I do as thou hast prayed me;
And if thou love another man, forsooth
Right with this sword then will I slay you both.'

Cecile answér'd anon right in this wise;
'If that you list, the angel shall ye see,

1 If.

2 For 'her.'

3 For the first time.

4 Doubt.

5 Guide.

So that ye trow[1] on Christ, and you baptise;   15639
Go forth to Via Appia,' quod she,
'That from this town ne stands but milës three,
And to the poorë folkës that there dwellen
Say them right thus, as that I shall you tellen.

'Tell them, that I Cecile you to them sent
To shewen you the good Urban the old,
For secret needës, and for good intent;
And when that ye Saint Urban have behold,
Tell him the wordës which I to you told;
And when that he hath purged you from sin,
Then shall ye see that angel ere ye twin.'[2]   15650

Valerian is to the placë gone,
And right as he was taught by her learning,
He found this holy old Urban anon
Among the saintës' burials[3] louting:[4]
And he anon withouten tarrying
Did his message, and when that he it told,
Urban for joy his handës 'gan uphold.

The tearës from his eyen let he fall;
'Almighty Lord, O Jesus Christ,' quod he,
'Sower of chaste counsel, herdë[5] of us all,   15660
The fruit of thilkë seed of chastity
That thou hast sown in Cecile, take to thee:
Lo, like a busy bee withouten guile
Thee serveth aye thine owen thrall Cecile.

'For thilkë spousë, that she took but new[6]
Full like a fierce lión, she sendeth here
As meek as ever was any lamb to ewe.'
And with that word anon there 'gan appear

---

[1] Believe.

[2] Depart.

[3] Burying-places.
[4] Bowing.

[5] Keeper.

[6] Newly.

An old man, clad in whitë clothës clear,   15669
That had a book with letters of gold in hand,
And 'gan before Valerian to stand.

Valerian, as dead, fell down for dread,
When he him saw; and he up hent[1] him tho,[2]
And on his book right thus he 'gan to read;
'One Lord, one faith, one God withouten mo,
One Christendom, and father of all also
Aboven all, and over all everywhere.'
These wordës all with gold ywritten were.

When this was read, then said this oldö man,
' 'Liev'st thou this thing or no? say yea or nay.' 15680
' I 'lieve all this thing,' quod Valerian,
' For soother thing than this, I dare well say,
Under the heaven no wight thinken may.'
Then vanish'd th' oldë man, he n'istë where,
And Pope Urban him christened right there.

Valerian go'th home, and finds Cecilie
Within his chamber with an angel stand:
This angel had of roses and of lily
Coronës[3] two, the which he bare in hand,
And first to Cecile, as I understand,   15690
He gave that one, and after 'gan he take
That other to Valerian her make.[4]

' With body clean, and with unwemmed[5]
    thought
Keepeth aye well these corones two,' quod he;
' From Paradise to you I have them brought,
Ne never more ne shall they rotten be,
Nor lose their sweetë savour, trusteth me,

---

[1] Took.
[2] Then.
[3] Crowns.
[4] Mate.
[5] Unspotted.

No never wight shall see them with his eye,   15698
But he be chaste, and hatë villainy.

'And thou, Valerian, for thou so soon
Assentedest to good counsel, also
Say what thee list, and thou shalt have thy boon.'
'I have a brother,' quod Valerian tho,[1]
'That in this world I lovë no man so,
I pray you that my brother may have grace
To know the truth, as I do in this place.'

The angel said, 'God liketh thy request,
And bothë with the palm of martyrdom
Ye shallen come unto his blissful rest.'
And with that word, Tiburce his brother come.   15710
And when that he the savour undernome,[2]
Which that the roses and the lilies cast,
Within his heart he 'gan to wonder fast,

And said, 'I wonder this time of the year
Whennës that sweetë savour cometh so
Of roses and lilies, that I smell here;
For though I had them in mine handës two,
The savour might in me no deeper go:
The sweetë smell, that in mine heart I find,
Hath changed me all in another kind.'   15720

Valerian said, 'Two coronës have we
Snow-white and rosë-red, that shinen clear,
Which that thine eyen have no might to see:
And as thou smellest them through my prayëre,
So shalt thou see them, levë[3] brother dear,
If it so be thou wilt withouten slouth
Believe aright, and know the very truth.'

[1] Then.

[2] Took up, received.

[3] Beloved.

Tiburcë answer'd, 'Sayest thou this to me   15728
In soothness, or in dream hearken I this?'
'In dreamës,' quod Valerian, 'have we be
Unto this timë, brother mine, ywis:[1]
But now at erst[2] in truth our dwelling is.'
'How wost[3] thou this,' quod Tiburce, 'in what wise?'
Quod Valerian, 'That shall I thee devise.

'The angel of God hath me the truth ytaught,
Which thou shalt see, if that thou wilt reney[4]
The idols, and be clean, and ellës naught.'
[And of the miracle of these corones tway
Saint Ambrose in his preface list to say;
Solemnëly this noble doctor dear   15740
Commendeth it, and saith in this mannere.

The palm of martyrdom for to receive,
Saint Cecilie, fulfilled of God's gift,
The world and eke her chamber 'gan she weive;[5]
Witness Tiburce's and Cecilë's shrift,[6]
To which God of his bounty wouldë shift[7]
Coronës two, of flowerës well smelling,
And made his angel them the corones bring.

The maid hath brought these men to bliss above;
The world hath wist what it is worth certáin   15750
Devotión of chastity to love.]
Then shewed him Cecile all open and plain,
That all idóls n'is but a thing in vain,
For they be dumb, and thereto they be deve,[8]
And charged him his idols for to leave.

'Whoso that trow'th[9] not this, a beast he is,'
Quod this Tiburce, 'if that I shall not lie.'

[1] Verily.

[2] For the first time.

[3] Knowest.

[4] Renounce.

[5] Forsake.

[6] Confession.

[7] Divide.

[8] Deaf.

[9] Believeth.

And she 'gan kiss his breast when she heard this,
And was full glad he couldë truth espy: 15759
'This day I takë thee for mine ally,'
Saidë this blissful fairë maiden dear;
And after that she said as ye may hear.

'Lo, right so as the love of Christ,' quod she,
'Made me thy brother's wife, right in that wise
Anon for mine ally here take I thee,
Sithen[1] that thou wilt thine idols despise.
Go with thy brother now and thee baptise,
And make thee clean, so that thou mayst behold
The angel's face, of which thy brother told.'

Tiburce answér'd, and saidë, 'Brother dear,   15770
First tell me whither I shall, and to what man?'
'To whom?' quod he, 'come forth with goodë cheer,
I will thee lead unto the pope Urban.'
'To Urban? brother mine Valerian,'
Quod then Tiburce; 'wilt thou me thither lead?
Methinketh that it were a wonder deed.

'Ne meanest thou not Urban,' quod he tho,
'That is so often damned to be dead,
And wonn'th[2] in halkës[3] alway to and fro,
And dare not onës putten forth his head?   15780
Men should him brennen[4] in a fire so red,
If he were found, or that men might him spy,
And we also, to bear him company.

'And while we seeken thilk[5] Divinity,
That is yhid in heaven privily,
Algate ybrent[6] in this world should we be.'
To whom Cecile answered boldily;

[1] Since.

[2] Dwelleth.
[3] Corners.

[4] Burn.

[5] That same.

[6] Burnt.

'Men mighten dreaden well and skilfully[1] 15788
This life to lose, mine owen dearë brother,
If this were living only and none other.

'But there is better life in other place,
That never shall be lost, ne dread thee nought:
Which Goddë's Son us toldë through his grace,
That Father's Son which allë thingës wrought;
And all that wrought is with a skilful thought,
The Ghost,[2] that from the Father 'gan proceed,
Hath souled[3] them withouten any drede.[4]

'By word and by mirácle he, God's Son,
When he was in this world, declared here,
That there is other life there men may wone.'[5] 15800
To whom answér'd Tiburce, 'O sister dear,
Ne saidest thou right now in this mannere,
There n'as but one God, Lord in soothfastness,
And now of three how mayst thou bear
  witness?'

'That shall I tell,' quod she, 'ere that I go.
Right as a man hath sapiences three,
Memory, ingine, and intellect also,
So in one being of divinity
Three personës mayen there right well be.'
Then 'gan she him full busily to preach 15810
Of Christë's sonde,[6] and of his painës teach,

And many pointës of his passion;
How Goddë's Son in this world was withhold[7]
To do mankindë plein[8] remissión,
That was ybound in sin and carës cold.
All this thing she unto Tiburcë told,

[1] Reasonably.

[2] Spirit.

[3] Endowed with a soul.

[4] Doubt.

[5] Dwell.

[6] Gift.

[7] Retained.

[8] Full

And after this Tiburce in good intent,   15817
With Valerian to pope Urban he went,

That thanked God, and with glad heart and light
He christen'd him, and made him in that place
Perféct in his learning and Goddë's knight.
And after this Tiburcë got such grace,
That every day he saw in time and space
The angel of God, and every manner boon
That he God asked, it was sped full soon.

It were full hard by order for to sayn
How many wonders Jesus for them wrought.
But at the last, to tellen short and plain,
The sergeants of the town of Rome them sought,
And them before Almach the prefect brought,   15830
Which them appos'd,[1] and knew all their intent,
And to th' imáge of Jupiter them sent;

And said, 'Whoso will nought do sacrifice,
Swap[2] off his head, this is my sentence here.'
Anon these martyrs, that I you devise,
One Maximus, that was an officere
Of the prefect's, and his corniculere,[3]
Them hent,[4] and when he forth the saintës lad,
Himself he wept for pity that he had.

When Maximus had heard the saintës' lore,[5]   15840
He got him of the tormentorës leave,
And led them to his house withouten more;
And with their preaching, ere that it were eve,
They gonnen[6] from the tormentors to reave,[7]
And from Maximo, and from his folk each one
The falsë faith, to trow[8] in God alone.

Cecilie came, when it was waxen night, 15847
With priestës, that them christen'd all yfere;[1]
And afterward, when day was waxen light,
Cecile them said with a full steadfast chere,[2]
'Now, Christë's owen knightës leve[3] and dear,
Cast all away the works of darkëness,
And armeth you in armës of brightness.

'Ye have forsooth ydone a great bataille;
Your course is done, your faith have ye conserved;
Go to the crown of life that may not fail;
The rightful Judgë, which that ye have served,
Shall give it you, as ye have it deserved.'
And when this thing was said, as I devise,
Men led them forth to do the sacrifice. 15860

But when they weren to the place ybrought,
To tellen shortly the conclusión,
They n'old[4] incense, nor sacrifice right nought.
But on their knees they setten them adown,
With humble heart and sad devotión,
And losten both their headës in the place;
Their soulës wenten to the King of grace.

This Maximus, that saw this thing betide,
With piteous tearës told it anon right,
That he their soulës saw to heaven glide 15870
With angels, full of clearness and of light;
And with his word converted many a wight.
For which Almachius did him to-beat
With whip of lead, till he his life 'gan lete.[5]

Cecile him took, and buried him anon
By Tiburce and Valerian softëly,

[1] Together.

[2] Mien.

[3] Beloved.

[4] Would not.

[5] Leave.

Within their burying-place, under the stone.   15877
And after this Almachius hastily
Bade his ministers fetchen openly
Cecile, so that she might in his presénce
Do sacrifice, and Jupiter incense.[1]

But they, converted at her wisë lore,[2]
Wepten full sore, and gaven full credénce
Unto her word, and crieden more and more,
' Christ, Goddë's Son, withouten difference,
Is very God, this is all our sentence,[3]
That hath so good a servant him to serve :
Thus with one voice we trowen[4] though we stervo.'[5]

Almachius, that heard of this doing,
Bade fetchen Cecile, that he might her see :   15890
And alderfirst,[6] lo, this was his asking ;
' What manner woman artë thou?' quod he.
' I am a gentlewoman born,' quod she.
' I askë thee,' quod he, ' though it thee grieve,
Of thy religion and of thy believe.'

' Why then began your question folily,'[7]
Quod she, ' that wouldest two answérs conclude
In one demand? ye asken lewedly.'[8]
Almach answér'd to that similitude,
' Of whennës com'th thine answering so rude?' 15900
' Of whennes ?' quod she, when that she was
          freined,[9]
' Of conscience, and of good faith unfeigned.'

Almachius said, ' Ne takest thou no heed
Of my powér?' and she him answer'd this ;
' Your might,' quod she, ' full little is to dread ;

For every mortal mannë's power n'is   15906
But like a bladder full of wind ywis:[1]
For with a needle's point, when it is blow,
May all the boast of it be laid full low.'

  'Full wrongfully begunnest thou,' quod he,
'And yet in wrong is all thy persev'ránce:
Wost[2] thou not how our mighty princes free
Have thus commanded and made ordinance,
That every Christian wight shall have penance
But if that he his Christendom withsay,[3]
And go all quit, if he will it reney?'[4]

  'Your princes erren, as your nobley[5] doth,'
Quod then Cecile, 'and with a wood[6] sentence
Ye make us guilty, and it is not sooth:[7]
For ye that knowen well our innocence,   15920
Forasmuch as we do aye reverence
To Christ, and for we bear a Christian name,
Ye put on us a crime and eke a blame.

  'But we that knowen thilkë namë so
For virtuous, we may it not withsay.'
Almach answered, 'Choose one of these two,
Do sacrifice, or Christendom reney,
That thou may now escapen by that way.'
At which this holy blissful fairë maid
'Gan for to laugh, and to the judgë said: 15930

  'O judge, confusë[8] in thy nicety,[9]
Wouldst thou that I reneyë innocence?
To maken me a wicked wight,' quod she,
'Lo, he dissimuleth here in audience,
He stareth and wodeth[10] in his advertence.'[11]

---

[1] Certainly.

[2] Knowest.

[3] Contradict.
[4] Deny.

[5] Nobility.
[6] Mad.
[7] True.

[8] Confounded.
[9] Folly.
[10] Grows furious.
[11] Attention.

To whom Almachius said, ' Unsely[1] wretch,   15936
Ne wost[2] thou not how far my might may stretch?

' Have not our mighty princes to me given
Yea bothe power and eke authority
To maken folk to dien or to liven ?
Why speakest thou so proudly then to me ?'
' I ne speak nought but steadfastly,' quod she,
Not proudly, for I say, as for my side,
We haten deadly thilke vice of pride.

' And if thou dread not a sooth[3] for to hear,
Then will I shew all openly by right,
That thou hast made a full great leasing[4] here.
Thou sayst, thy princes have thee given might
Both for to slay and for to quicken a wight,
Thou that ne mayst but only life bereave,   15950
Thou hast none other power ne no leave.

' But thou mayst say, thy princes have thee maked
Minister of death; for if thou speak of mo,
Thou liest; for thy power is full naked.'
' Do way thy boldness,' said Almachius tho,[5]
' And sacrifice to our gods, ere thou go.
I recke not what wrong that thou me proffer,
For I can suffer it as a philosópher.

' But thilke wronges may I not endure,
That thou speakst of our goddes here,' quod he. 15960
Cecile answer'd, ' O nice[6] creature,
Thou saidest no word since thou spake to me,
That I ne knew therewith thy nicety,[7]
And that thou wert in every manner wise[8]
A lewed[9] officer, a vain justice.

[1] Unhappy.
[2] Knowest.
[3] Truth.
[4] Falsity.
[5] Then.
[6] Foolish.
[7] Folly.
[8] Every sort of way.
[9] Ignorant.

'There lacketh nothing to thine utter[1] eyen   15966
That thou n'art blind; for thing that we see all
That is a stone, that men may well espien,
That ilkë stone a god thou wilt it call.
I rede[2] thee let thine hand upon it fall,
And taste it well, and stone thou shalt it find,
Since that thou seest not with thine eyen blind.

'It is a shamë that the people shall
So scornen thee, and laugh at thy follý:
For commonly men wot it well over all,
That mighty God is in his heavens high;
And these imáges, well mayst thou espy,
To thee nor to themselves may not profít,
For in effect they be not worth a mite.'

These and such other wordës saidë she,   15980
And he wax'd wroth, and bade men should her lead
Home to her house, 'and in her house,' quod he,
'Burn her right in a bath, with flamës red.'
And as he bade, right so was done the deed;
For in a bath they 'gun her fastë shetten,
And night and day great fire they under betten.[3]

The longë night, and eke a day also,
For all the fire, and eke the bathë's heat,
She sat all cold, and felt of it no woe,
It made her not a droppë for to sweat: 15990
But in that bath her life she mustë lete.[4]
For he, Almach, with a full wick' intent,
To slay her in the bath his sondë[5] sent.

Three strokës in the neck he smote her tho[6]
The tormentor,[7] but for no manner chance

[1] Outward.

[2] Advise.

[3] Kindle.

[4] Leave.

[5] Message.

[6] Then.
[7] Executioner.

He mightë not smite all her neck atwo: 15996
And for there was that time an ordinance
That no man shouldë do man such penance,
The fourthö stroke to smiten, soft or sore,
This tormentor ne durstë do no more;

1 Mangled.

But half dead, with her neck ycorven[1] there
He left her lie, and on his way is went.
The Christian folk, which that about her were,

2 Received. With sheetës have the blood full fair yhent:[2]
Three dayës lived she in this torment,
And never ceased them the faith to teach,
That she had foster'd them, she 'gan to preach.

3 Goods.

_4 Com-
mended._

And them she gave her mebles[3] and her thing,
And to the pope Urban betook[4] them tho,
And said, 'I asked this of heaven King,   16010
To have respite three dayës and no mo,
To recommend to you, ere that I go,

_5 Cause
make._ These soulës lo, and that I might do werche[5]
Here of mine house perpetually a cherche.'

Saint Urban with his deacons privily
6 Fetched. The body fette,[6] and buried it by night
Among his other saintës honestly:
7 Is called. Her house the church of Saintë Cecile hight;[7]
Saint Urban hallow'd it, as he well might,
In which unto this day in noble wise   16020
Men do to Christ and to his saint service.

THE CANON'S YEOMAN'S PROLOGUE.

WHEN that told was the life of Saint Cecile,   16022
Ere we had ridden fully fivë mile,
At Boughton-under-Blee us 'gan atake[1]
A man, that clothed was in clothës black,
And underneath he wore a white surplíce.
His hackney, which that was all pomelee-gris,[2]
So sweatë, that it wonder was to see,
It seem'd as he had pricked milës three.
The horse eke that his yeoman rode upon,   16030
So sweatë, that unnethes[3] might he gon.
About the peytrel[4] stood the foam full high,
He was of foam as flecked[5] as a pie.
A mailë tweifold[6] on his crupper lay,
It seemed that he carried little array,
All light for summer rode this worthy man.
And in my heartë wondren I began
What that he was, till that I understood,
How that his cloak was sewed to his hood;
For which when I had long avised[7] me,   16040
I deemed him some Canon for to be.
His hat hung at his back down by a lace,
For he had ridden more than trot or pace,
He had aye pricked like as he were wood,[8]

[1] Overtake.

[2] Dapple-grey.

[3] Scarcely.

[4] Breast.

[5] Spotted.

[6] Double.

[7] Considered.

[8] Mad.

A clote-leaf[1] he had laid under his hood   16045
For sweat, and for to keep his head from heat.
But it was joyë for to see him sweat;
His forehead dropped, as a stillatory[2]
Were full of plantain or of paritory.[3]
And when that he was come, he 'gan to cry,   16050
'God save,' quod he, 'this jolly company.
Fast have I pricked,' quod he, 'for your sake,
Becausë that I wouldë you atake,
To riden in this merry company.'
    His Yeoman was eke full of courtesy,
And saidë, 'Sirs, now in the morrow tide
Out of your hostelry I saw you ride,
And warned here my lord and sovereign,
Which that to riden with you is full fain
For his disport; he loveth dalliance.'   16060
'Friend, for thy warning God give thee good chance.'[4]
Then said our Host; 'certain it wouldë seem
Thy lord were wise, and so I may well deem;
He is full jocund also dare I lay:
Can he ought tell a merry tale or tway,
With which he gladden may this company?'
    'Who, Sir? my lord? Yea, Sir, withouten lie,
He can[5] of mirth and eke of jollity
Not but[6] enough; also, Sir, trusteth me,
And ye him knew all so well as do I,   16070
Ye woulden wonder how well and craftily
He couldë work, and that in sundry wise.
He hath take on him many a great emprise,[7]
Which were full hard for any that is here
To bring about, but[8] they of him it lear.[9]
As homely as he rid'th amongës you,
If ye him knew, it would be for your prow:[10]
Ye woulden not forego his acquaintánce

---

[1] Burdock-leaf.

[2] Still.

[3] Wall-flower.

[4] Fortune.

[5] Knows.

[6] Not less than enough.

[7] Under-taking.

[8] Unless.

[9] Learn.

[10] Profit.

For muchel good, I dare lay in balance   16079
All that I have in my possessión.
He is a man of high discretión.
I warn you well, he is a passing man.'
   'Well,' quod our Host, 'I pray thee tell me than,
Is he a clerk, or no? Tell what he is.'
   'Nay, he is greater than a clerk ywis,'[1]
Saidë this Yeoman, 'and in wordës few,
Host, of his craft somewhat I will you shew.
   'I say, my lord can such a subtlety,
(But all his craft ye may not weet[2] of me,
And somewhat help I yet to his working,)   16090
That all the ground on which we be riding
Till that we come to Canterbury town,
He could all cleanë turnen up so down,
And pave it all of silver and of gold.'
   And when this Yeoman had this tale ytold
Unto our Host, he said, '*Benedicite*,
This thing is wonder marvellous to me,
Since that thy lord is of so high prudénce,
Because of which men should him reverence,
That of his worship recketh he so lite;[3]   16100
His overest[4] slop[5] it is not worth a mite
As in effect to him, so may I go;[6]
It is all baudy[7] and to-tore also.
Why is thy lord so sluttish I thee pray,
And is of power better cloth to beye,[8]
If that his deed accorded with thy speech?
Tellë me that, and that I thee beseech.'
   'Why?' quod this Yeoman, 'whereto ask ye me?
God help me so, for he shall never the:[9]
(But I will not avowen that I say,   16110
And therefore keep it secret I you pray,)
He is too wise, in faith, as I believe.

---

[1] Certainly.

[2] Know.

[3] Little.

[4] Upper.

[5] Garment.

[6] Prosper.

[7] Soiled.

[8] Buy.

[9] Thrive.

Thing that is overdone, it will not preve[1]   16113
Aright, as clerkës say; it is a vice;
Wherefore in that I hold him lewd[2] and nice.[3]
For when a man hath overgreat a wit,
Full oft him happ'neth to misusen it:
So doth my lord, and that me grieveth sore.
God it amend; I can say now no more.'
    'Thereof no force,[4] good Yeoman,' quod our Host;
'Since of the conning[5] of thy lord thou wost,[6]   16121
Tell how he doth, I pray thee heartily,
Since that he is so crafty and so sly.
Where dwellen ye, if it to tellen be?'
    'In the suburbës of a town,' quod he,
'Lurking in hernës[7] and in lanës blind,
Whereas these robbers and these thieves by kind[8]
Holden their privy fearful residence,
As they that dare not shewen their presénce,
So faren we, if I shall say the sothë.'[9]   16130
    'Yet,' quod our Hostë, 'let me talken to thee;
Why art thou so discolour'd of thy face?'
    'Peter,' quod he, 'God give it hardë grace,
I am so used the hotë fire to blow,
That it hath changed my colóur I trow;
I n'am not wont in no mirrór to pry,
But swinkë[10] sore, and learn to multiply.[11]
We blunder ever, and poren in the fire,
And for all that we fail of our desire,
For ever we lacken our conclusión.   16140
To muchel folk we do illusión,
And borrow gold, be it a pound or two,
Or ten or twelve, or many summës mo,
And make them weenen[12] at the leastë way,
That of a pound we connen[13] maken tway,
Yet is it false; and aye we have good hope

---

[1] Stand trial.
[2] Unwise.
[3] Foolish.
[4] No matter.
[5] Skill.
[6] Knowest.
[7] Corners.
[8] Nature.
[9] Truth.
[10] Labour.
[11] Transmute metals.
[12] Think.
[13] Are able.

It for to do, and after it we grope: 16147
But that sciénce is so far us beforn,
We mowen[1] not, although we had it sworn,   [1] May.
It overtake, it slides away so fast;
It will us maken beggars at the last.'
    While this Yeoman was thus in his talking,
This Canon drew him near, and heard all thing
Which this Yeoman spake, for suspición
Of mennë's speech ever had this Canon:
For Cato saith, that he that guilty is,
Deemeth all thing be spoken of him ywis:[2]   [2] Surely.
That was the cause he 'gan so nigh him draw
To his Yeoman, to hearken all his saw,[3]   [3] Saying.
And thus he said unto his Yeoman tho;[4]   16160 [4] Then.
'Hold thou thy peace, and speak no wordës mo:
For if thou do, thou shalt it dear abie.[5]   [5] Abide.
Thou sland'rest me here in this company,
And eke discov'rest that thou shouldest hide.'
    'Yea,' quod our Host, 'tell on, whatso betide;
Of all his threat'ning reckë not a mite.'
    'In faith,' quod he, 'no more I do but lite.'
And when this Canon saw it would not be,
But his Yeoman would tell his privity,
He fled away for very sorrow and shame.   16170
    'Ah!' quod the Yeoman, 'here shall rise a game:
All that I can anon I will you tell,
Since he is gone; the foulë fiend him quell;
For never hereafter will I with him meet
For penny nor for pound, I you behete.[6]   [6] Promise.
He that me broughtë first unto that game,
Ere that he die, sorrow have he and shame.
For it is earnest[7] to me, by my faith;   [7] Serious.
That feel I well, what that any man saith;
And yet for all my smart, and all my grief,   16180

For all my sorrow, labour, and mischief,   16181
I couldë never leave it in no wise.
Now wouldë God my wit mightë suffice
To tellen all that 'longeth to that art;
But natheless, yet will I tellen part;
Since that my lord is gone, I will not spare,
Such thing as that I know I will declare.'

THE CANON'S YEOMAN'S TALE.

WITH this Canon I dwelt have seven year,
And of his science am I never the near :[1]
All that I had, I have ylost thereby,   16190
And God wot, so have many more than I.
There I was wont to be right fresh and gay
Of clothing, and of other good array,
Now may I wear an hose upon mine head;
And where my colour was both fresh and red,
Now is it wan, and of a leaden hue,
(Whoso it useth, so shall he it rue;)
And of my swink[2] yet bleared is mine eye;
Lo which[3] advantage is to multiply![4]
That sliding science hath me made so bare,   16200
That I have no good, where that ever I fare;
And yet I am indebted so thereby
Of gold, that I have borrow'd truëly,
That while I live, I shall it quiten never;
Let every man beware by me for ever.
What manner man that casteth him thereto,
If he continue, I hold his thrift[5] ydo;[6]
So help me God, thereby shall he not win,
But empt' his purse, and make his wittës thin.

[1] Nearer.
[2] Labour.
[3] What.
[4] Transmute metals.
[5] Thriving.
[6] Done.

And when he, through his madness and folly, · 16210
Hath lost his owen good through jupartie,[1]
Then he exciteth other folk thereto,
To lose their good as he himself hath do.
For unto shrewës[2] joy it is and ease
To have their fellows in painë and disease.[3]
Thus was I onës-learned of a clerk;
Of that no charge;[4] I will speak of our work.
    When we be there as we shall exercise
Our elvish[5] craft, we seemen wonder wise,
Our termës be so clergial[6] and quaint, 16220
I blow the fire till that mine heartë faint.
What should I tellen each proportión
Of thingës, whichë that we work upon,
As on five or six ounces, may well be,
Of silver, or some other quantity?
And busy me to tellen you the names,
As orpiment, burnt bonës, iron squames,[7]
That into powder grounden be full small?
And in an earthen pot how put is all,
And salt yput in, and also peppére, 16230
Before these powders that I speak of here,
And well ycover'd with a lamp of glass?
And of much other thing which that there was?
And of the pots and glasses engluting,[8] .
That of the air might passen out no thing?
And of the easy[9] fire, and smart also,
Which that was made? and of the care and woe,
That we had in our matters súbliming,
And in amalgaming, and calcining
Of quicksilver, yclep'd mercúry crude? 16240
For all our sleightës we can not conclude.
Our orpiment, and súblimed mercúry,
Our grounden litharge eke on the porphúry,[10]

[1] Jeopardy.

[2] Ill-na-
tured
persons.
[3] Uneasi-
ness.
[4] No mat-
ter.

[5] Mischiev-
ous.
[6] Learned.

[7] Scales.

[8] Luting,
cement-
ing.
[9] Slow.

[10] Por-
phyry.

Of each of these of ounces a certáin   16244
Not helpeth us, our labour is in vain.
No, neither our spirits' ascensióun,
Ne our mattérs that lie all fix adown,
May in our working nothing us avail;
For lost is all our labour and travail,
And all the cost a twenty devil way   16250
Is lost also, which we upon it lay.
     There is also full many another thing,
That is unto our craft appértaining,
Though I by order them not rehearsen can,
Becausë that I am a lewed[1] man,
Yet will I tell them as they come to mind,
Though I ne cannot set them in their kind,
As bol-armoniac, verdigris, borás;
And sundry vessels made of earth and glass,
Our urinalës, and our descensories,[2]   16260
Phials, croslettës,[3] and sublímatories,
Cucurbitës,[4] and álembikës[5] eke,
And other such gear, dear enough a leek,
What needeth it for to rehearse them all?
Waterës rubifying, and bullës' gall,
Arsenic, sal-armoniac, and brimstone?
And herbës could I tell eke many one,
As egremoine,[6] valerian, and lunary,[7]
And other such, if that me list to tarry;
Our lampës burning bothë night and day,   16270
To bring about our craft if that we may;
Our furnace eke of calcinatión,
And of waters albificatión,
Unslacked lime, chalk, and glaire[8] of an ey,[9]
Powders divérse, ashes, dung, piss, and clay,
Seared pokettës,* saltpetre, and vitriol;

     * 'Seared pokettes:' Meaning unknown.

[1] Ignorant.

[2] Vessels for making extracts.
[3] Crucibles.
[4] Retorts.
[5] Stills.

[6] Agrimony.
[7] Moonwort.

[8] White.
[9] Egg.

And divers firës made of wood and coal; 16277
Sal-tartar, alkali, and salt preparate,
And combust matters, and coagulate;
Clay made with horse and mannë's hair, and oil
Of tartar, alum, glass, barm, wort, and argoil,[1]
Rosalgar,[2] and other mattérs imbibing;
And eke of our mattérs encorporing,
And of our silver citrinatión,
Our cementing, and fermentatión,
Our ingots, tests, and many thingës mo.
    I will you tell as was me taught also
The fourë spirits, and the bodies seven,
By order, as oft I heard my lord them neven.[3]
The firstë spirit Quicksílver cleped is; 16290
The second Orpiment; the third ywis
Sal-Armoniac, and the fourth Brimstóne.
    The bodies seven eke, lo them here anon.
Sol gold is, and Luna silvér we threpe;[4]
Mars iron, Mercury quicksilver we clepe:
Saturnus lead, and Jupiter is tin,
And Venus copper, by my father kin.
    This cursed craft whoso will exercise,
He shall no good have that him may suffice,
For all the good he spendeth thereabout 16300
He losen shall, thereof have I no doubt.
Whoso that listeth utter his follý,
Let him come forth and learnen multiply:
And every man that hath ought in his coffer,
Let him appear, and wax a philosópher,
Ascauncë[5] that craft is so light to lear.[6]
Nay, nay, God wot, all be he monk or frere,
Priest or canon, or any other wight,
Though he sit at his book both day and night
In learning of this elvish[7] nicë[8] lore, 16310

[1] Potter's clay.
[2] Red arsenic.
[3] Name.
[4] Name.
[5] As if.
[6] Learn.
[7] Mischievous.
[8] Foolish.

All is in vain, and pardie muchel more   16311
To learn a lewed[1] man this subtlety;
Fie! speak not thereof, for it will not be.
And conne[2] he letterure,[3] or conne he none,
As in effect, he shall find it all one;
For bothë two, by my salvatión,
Concluden in multiplicatión[4]
Alikë well, when they have all ydo;
This is to say, they failen bothë two.
     Yet forgot I to maken rehearsale   16320
Of waters corrosive, and of limaile,[5]
And of bodies' mollificatión,
And also of their induratión,
Oilës, ablusións, metál fusíble,
To tellen all, would passen any Bible,
That owhere[6] is; wherefore as for the best
Of all these namës now will I me rest;
For as I trow, I have you told enow
To raise a fiend, all look he never so row.[7]
     Ah! nay, let be; the philosópher's stone,   16330
Elixir clep'd, we seeken fast each one,
For had we him, then were we siker[8] enow;
But unto God of heaven I make avow,
For all our craft, when we have all ydo,
And all our sleight, he will not come us to.
He hath ymade us spenden muchel good,
For sorrow of which almost we waxen wood,[9]
But that good hopë creepeth in our heart,
Supposing ever, though we sorë smart,
To be relieved of him afterward.   16340
Such súpposing and hope is sharp and hard.
I warn you well it is to seeken ever.
That future *temps* hath madë men dissever,
In trust thereof, from all that ever they had,

[1] Ignorant.
[2] Know.
[3] Literature.
[4] Art of making gold, &c.
[5] Metal filings.
[6] Anywhere.
[7] Grim, rough.
[8] Secure.
[9] Mad.

Yet of that art they cannot waxen sad,[1]   16345
For unto them it is a bitter sweet;
So seemeth it; for ne' had they but a sheet
Which that they mighten wrap them in a-night,
And a bratt[2] to walken in by daylight,
They would them sell, and spend it on this craft;
They cannot stinten,[3] till no thing be laft.   16351
And evermore, wherever that they gon,
Men may them kennen[4] by smell of brimstóne;
For all the world they stinken as a goat;
Their savour is so rammish and so hot,
That though a man a milë from them be,
The savour will infect him, trusteth me.
   Lo, thus by smelling and threadbare array,
If that men list, this folk they knowen may.
And if a man will ask them privily,   16360
Why they be clothed so unthriftily,[5]
They right anon will rounen[6] in his ear,
And sayen, if that they espied were,
Men would them slay, because of their sciénce:
Lo, thus these folk betrayen innocence.
   Pass over this; I go my tale unto.
Ere that the pot be on the fire ydo
Of metals with a certain quantity,
My lord them temp'reth, and no man but he;
(Now he is gone, I dare say boldëly;)   16370
For as men say, he can do craftily;
Algate[7] I wot well he hath such a name,
And yet full oft he runneth in a blame;
And weet[8] ye how? full oft it falleth so,
The pot to-break'th, and farewell! all is go.
These metals be of so great violence,
Our wallës may not make them résistence,
But[9] if they weren wrought of lime and stone;

---

[1] Repentant.

[2] Coarse cloak.

[3] Cease.

[4] Know.

[5] Shabbily.

[6] Whisper.

[7] However.

[8] Know.

[9] Unless.

They piercen so, that through the wall they gon;
And some of them sink down into the ground, 16380
(Thus have we lost by timës many a pound,)
And some are scatter'd all the floor about;
Some leap into the roof withouten doubt.
Though that the fiend not in our sight him shew,
I trow that he be with us, thilkë shrew,[1]
In hellë, where that he is lord and sire,
Ne is there no more woe, rancóur, nor ire.
When that our pot is broke, as I have said,
Every man chides, and holds him evil apaid.[2]
Some said it was long[3] on the fire-making; 16390
Some said nay, it was long on the blowing,
(Then was I fear'd, for that was mine office;)
'Straw!' quod the third, 'ye be lewéd and nice,[4]
It was not temper'd as it ought to be.'
'Nay,' quod the fourthë, 'stint and hearken me;
Because our firë was not made of beech,
That is the cause, and other none, so the iche.[5]
I cannot tell whereon it was along,
But well I wot great strife is us among.'
'What?' quod my lord, 'there n'is no more to don,
Of these perils I will beware eftsoon. 16401
I am right siker that the pot was crazed.
Be as be may, be ye no thing amazed.
As usage is, let sweep the floor as swithe;[6]
Pluck up your heartës and be glad and blithe.'
  The mullok[7] on an heap ysweeped was,
And on the floor ycast a canëvas,
And all this mullok in a sieve ythrow,
And sifted, and ypicked many a throw.[8]
  'Pardie,' quod one, 'somewhat of our metal 16410
Yet is there here, though that we have not all.
And though this thing mishapped hath as now,

[1] Wretch.
[2] Ill-satisfied.
[3] On account of.
[4] Foolish.
[5] So thrive I.
[6] Quickly.
[7] Rubbish.
[8] Time.

Another time it may be well enow.   16413
We musten put our good in ádventure;
A merchant pardie may not aye endure,
Trusteth me well, in his prosperity:
Sometime his good is drenched in the sea,
And sometime com'th it safe unto the lond.'
   'Peace,' quod my lord, 'the next time I will fond[1]
To bring our craft all in another plight,   16420
And but I do, Sirs, let me have the wite:[2]
There was default in somewhat, well I wot.'
   Another said, the fire was over hot.
But be it hot or cold, I dare say this,
That we concluden evermore amiss:
We fail alway of that which we would have,
And in our madness evermore we rave.
And when we be together every one,
Every man seemeth a Solomon.
But all thing, which that shineth as the gold,   16430
Ne is no gold, as I have heard it told;
Ne every apple that is fair at eye,
Ne is not good, what so men clap[3] or cry.
Right so, lo, fareth it amongës us.
He that seemeth the wisest, by Jesus,
Is most fool, when it cometh to the prefe;[4]
And he that seemeth truest, is a thief.
That shall ye know, ere that I from you wend,
By that I of my tale have made an end.
   There was a canon of religióun   16440
Amongës us, would infect all a town,
Though it as great were as was Nineveh,
Rome, Alisandre, Troy, or other three.
His sleightës and his infinite falseness
There couldë no man writen, as I guess,
Though that he mightë live a thousand year;

[1] Endeavour.

[2] Blame.

[3] Chatter.

[4] Proof.

In all this world of falseness n'is his peer.   16447
For in his termës he will him so wind,
And speak his wordës in so sly a kind,
When he communen shall with any wight,
That he will make him doaten anon right,
But¹ it a fiend be, as himselven is.
Full many a man hath he beguiled ere this,
And will, if that he may live any while:
And yet men go and riden many a mile
Him for to seek, and have his acquaintánce,
Not knowing of his falsë governance.
And if you list to give me audiénce,
I will it tellen here in your presénce.

   But, worshipful canóns religioús,   16460
Ne deemeth not that I slander your house,
Although that my tale of a canon be.
Of every order some shrew is pardie:
And God forbid that all a company
Should rue a singular² mannë's folly.
To slander you is no thing mine intent,
But to correcten that is 'miss I meant.
This talë was not only told for you,
But eke for other more: ye wot well how
That among Christë's apostelës twelve   16470
There was no traitor but Judas himselve:
Then why shóuld all the remenant have
    blame,
That guiltless were? By you I say the same.
Save only this, if ye will hearken me,
If any Judas in your convent be,
Removeth him betimës, I you rede,³
If shame or loss may causen any drede.
And be no thing displeased I you pray,
But in this case hearkeneth what I say.

¹ Except.

² Individual.

³ Advise.

In London was a priest, an annuallere,   16480
That therein dwelled hadde many a year,
Which was so pleasant and so serviceable
Unto the wife, there as he was at table,
That she would suffer him no thing to pay
For board nor clothing, went he never so gay;
And spending silver had he right enow:
Thereof no force;[1] I will proceed as now,
And tellen forth my tale of the canon,
That broughte this priest to confusión.
    This false canon came upon a day   16490
Unto the prieste's chamber, there he lay,
Beseeching him to lend him a certain
Of gold, and he would quit it him again.
'Lend me a mark,' quod he, 'but dayes three,
And at my day I will it quiten thee.
And if it so be that thou find me false,
Another day hang me up by the halse.'[2]
    This priest him took a mark, and that as swith,[3]
And this canon him thanked often sith,[4]
And took his leave, and wente forth his way: 16500
And at the thirde day brought his monéy;
And to the priest he took his gold again,
Whereof this priest was wonder glad and fain.
    'Certes,' quod he, 'nothing annoyeth me
To lend a man a noble, or two, or three,
Or what thing were in my possessión,
When he so true is of condition,
That in nowise he breaken will his day:
To such a man I can never say nay.'
    'What?' quod this canon, 'should I be untrue?
Nay, that were thing fallen all of the new.   16511
Truth is a thing that I will ever keep
Unto the day in which that I shall creep

---

[1] No matter.

[2] Neck.

[3] Quickly.

[4] Times.

Into my grave, and ellës God forbede:　16514
Believeth this as siker[1] as your creed.
God thank I, and in good time be it said,
That there n'as[2] never man yet evil apaid[3]
For gold nor silver that he to me lent,
Ne never falsehood in mine heart I meant.
　'And, Sir,' quod he, 'now of my privity,　16520
Since ye so goodly have been unto me,
And kithed to me so great gentleness,
Somewhat, to quiten with your kindëness,
I will you shew, and if you list to lear[4]
I will you teachen plainly the mannére,
How I can worken in philosophy.
Taketh good heed, ye shall well see at eye,
That I will do a mas'try ere I go.'
　'Yea?' quod the priest, 'yea, Sir, and will ye so?
Mary, thereof I pray you heartily.'　16530
　'At your commandëment, Sir, truëly,'
Quod the canón, 'and ellës God forbede.'
Lo, how this thiefë could his service bede.[5]
　Full sooth it is that such proffér'd service
Stinketh, as witnessen these oldë wise;
And that full soon I will it verify
In this canón, root of all treachery,
That evermore delight hath and gladness
(Such fiendly thoughtës in his heart impress)
How Christë's people he may to mischief bring.
God keep us from his false dissimuling.　16541
Nought wistë this priest with whom that he dealt,
Nor of his harm coming nothing he felt.
O sely[6] priest, O sely innocent,
With covetise anon thou shalt be blent;[7]
O gracëless, full blind is thy conceit,
For nothing art thou 'ware of the deceit,

[1] Sure.
[2] Was not.
[3] Satisfied.
[4] Learn.
[5] Offer.
[6] Simple.
[7] Warped.

Which that this fox yshapen hath to thee; 16548
His wily wrenches[1] thou ne mayst not flee.
Wherefore to go to the conclusión
That réferreth to thy confusión,
Unhappy man, anon I will me hie
To tellen thine unwit and thy folly,
And eke the falseness of that other wretch,
As farforth as that my conning[2] will stretch.
    This canon was my lord, ye woulden ween;[3]
Sir Host, in faith, and by the heaven queen,
It was another canon, and not he,
That can[4] an hundred part more subtlety.
He hath betrayed folkës many a time; 16560
Of his falseness it dulleth me to rhyme.
Ever when that I speak of his falsehead
For shame of him my cheekës waxen red;
Algatës[5] they beginnen for to glow,
For redness have I none, right well I know,
In my visagë, for fumës diverse
Of metals, which ye have heard me rehearse,
Consumed have and wasted my redness.
Now take heed of this canon's cursedness.
    'Sir,' quod the canon, 'let your yeoman gon 16570
For quicksílver, that we it had anon;
And let him bringen ounces two or three;
And when he cometh, as fastë shall ye see
A wonder thing, which ye saw never ere this.'
    'Sir,' quod the priest, 'it shall be done ywis.'[6]
He bade his servant fetchen him this thing,
And he all ready was at his bidding,
And went him forth, and came anon again
With this quicksilver, shortly for to sayn,
And took these ounces three to the canoun; 16580
And he them laidë well and fair adown,

[1] Strata-
  gems.

[2] Know-
  ledge.
[3] Think.

[4] Knows.

[5] At least.

[6] Certain-
  ly.

And bade the servant coalës for to bring, 16582
That he anon might go to his working.
 The coalës right anon weren yfet,[1]
And this canón took out a crossëlet[2]
Of his bosom, and shew'd it to the priest.
'This instrument,' quod he, 'which that thou seest,
Take in thine hand, and put thyself therein
Of this quicksilver an ounce, and here begin
In the name of Christ to wax a philosópher. 16590
There be full few, which that I wouldë proffer
To shewen them thus much of my sciénce:
For here shall ye see by experiénce,
That this quicksilver I will mortify,[3]
Right in your sight anon withouten lie,
And make it as good silver and as fine,
As there is any in your purse or mine,
Or ellëswhere; and make it malleable;
And ellës holdeth me false and unable
Amongës folk for ever to appear. 16600
 'I have a powder here that cost me dear,
Shall make all good, for it is cause of all
My conning,[4] which that I you shewen shall.
Voideth[5] your man, and let him be thereout;
And shut the doorë, while we be about
Our privity, that no man us espy,
While that we work in this philosophy.'
 All, as he bade, fulfilled was in deed.
This ilkë servant anon right out yede,[6]
And his master shuttë the door anon, 16610
And to their labour speedily they gon.
 This priest at this cursed canon's bidding,
Upon the fire anon he set this thing,
And blew the fire, and busied him full fast.
And this canón into the crosslet cast

[1] Fetched.

[2] Crucible.

[3] Kill.

[4] Knowledge.

[5] Send out.

[6] Went.

A powder, n'ot[1] I never whereof it was   16616
Ymade, either of chalk, either of glass,
Or somewhat ellës was not worth a fly,
To blinden with this priest; and bade him hie[2]
The coalës for to couchen[3] all above
The crosslet; 'for in tokening I thee love,'
Quod this canon, 'thine owen handës two
Shall worken all thing which that here is do.'
  '*Grand mercy*,' quod the priest, and was full glad,
And couch'd the coalës as the canon bade.
And while he busy was, this fiendly wretch,
This false canón (the foulë fiend him fetch)
Out of his bosom took a beechen coal,
In which full subtlely was made an hole,
And therein put was of silvér limaile[4]   16630
An ounce, and stopped was withouten fail
The hole with wax, to keep the limaile in.
  And understandeth, that this falsë gin[5]
Was not made there, but it was made before;
And other thingës I shall tell you more
Hereafterward, which that he with him brought;
Ere he came there, him to beguile he thought,
And so he did, ere that they went atwin:[6]
Till he had turned him, could he not blin.[7]
It dulleth me, when that I of him speak;   16640
On his falsehood fain would I me awreak,[8]
If I wist how, but he is here and there,
He is so variant, he abit[9] nowhere.
  But taketh heed, Sirs, now for Goddë's love.
He took his coal, of which I spake above,
And in his hand he bare it privily,
And whilës the priest couched busily
The coalës, as I toldë you ere this,
This canon saidë, 'Friend, ye do amiss;

[1] Know not.

[2] Hasten.

[3] Lay.

[4] Filings.

[5] Snare.

[6] Asunder.

[7] Cease.

[8] Revenge.

[9] Abideth.

[1] Laid.

This is not couched[1] as it ought to be,   16650
But soon I shall amenden it,' quod he.
' Now let me meddle therewith but a while,
For of you have I pity by Saint Gile.
Ye be right hot, I see well how ye sweat;
Have here a cloth and wipe away the wet.'
   And whilës that the priest wiped his face,
This canon took his coal, with sorry grace,
And layed it above on the midward
Of the crosslet, and blew well afterward,

[2] Began.
[3] Burn.

Till that the coalës gonnen[2] fast to bren.[3]   16660
   'Now give us drinkë,' quod this canon then,

[4] Quickly.

' As swith[4] all shall be well, I undertake.
Sittë we down, and let us merry make.'
And whennë that this canon's beechen coal
Was burnt, all the limaile out of the hole
Into the crossëlet anon fell down;
And so it mustë needës by reasoún,
Since it above so even couched was;
But thereof wist the priest nothing, alas!
He deemed all the coalës alike good,   16670
For of the sleight he nothing understood.
   And when this alchemister saw his time,
' Rise up, Sir Priest,' quod he, ' and stand by
     me;
And for I wot well ingot have ye none,
Go, walketh forth, and bringeth a chalk stone;
For I will make it of the samë shape
That is an ingot, if I may have hap.
Bring eke with you a bowl or else a pan
Full of watér, and ye shall well see than

[5] Succeed.

How that our business shall thrive and preve.[5] 16680
And yet, for ye shall have no misbelieve
No wrong conceit of me in your absence,

I ne will not be out of your presénce, 16683
But go with you, and come with you again.'
 The chamber-doorë, shortly for to sayn,
They opened and shut, and went their way,
And forth with them they carried the key,
And came again withouten any delay.
What should I tarrien all the longë day?
He took the chalk, and shaped it in the wise 16690
Of an ingot, as I shall you devise;[1]
I say, he took out of his owen sleeve
A teine[2] of silver (evil may he cheve[3])
Which that ne was but a just ounce of weight.
And taketh heed now of his cursed sleight;
He shaped his ingot, in length and in brede
Of thilkë teine, withouten any drede,[4]
So slily, that the priest it not espied;
And in his sleeve again he 'gan it hide;
And from the fire he took up his mattére, 16700
And in the ingot it put with merry cheer:
And in the water-vessel he it cast,
When that him list, and bade the priest as fast
Look what there is; 'Put in thine hand and grope;
Thou shalt there finden silver, as I hope.'
What, devil of hellë! should it ellës be?
Shaving of silver, silver is, pardie.
 He put his hand in, and took up a teine[5]
Of silver fine, and glad in every vein
Was this priest, when he saw that it was so. 16710
'Goddë's blessing, and his mother's also,
And allë hallows,[6] have ye, Sir Canón,'
Saidë this priest, 'and I their malison,[7]
But and ye vouchësafe to teachen me
This noble craft and this subtility,
I will be yours in all that ever I may.'

[1] Describe.

[2] Thin plate.
[3] End.

[4] Doubt.

[5] Plate.

[6] Praise, blessing.
[7] Curse.

    Quod the canón, 'Yet will I make assay   16717
The second time, that ye may taken heed,
And be expert of this, and in your need
Another day assay in mine absénce
This discipline, and this crafty sciénce.
Let take another ouncë,' quod he tho,[1]
'Of quicksilver, withouten wordës mo,
And do therewith as ye have done ere this
With that other, which that now silver is.'
    The priest him busieth all that ever he can
To do as this canón, this cursed man,
Commandeth him, and fastë blew the fire,
For to come to the effect of his desire.
And this canón right in the meanëwhile   16730
All ready was this priest eft[2] to beguile,
And for a countenance[3] in his hand bare
An hollow stickë, (take keep[4] and beware,)
In the end of which an ouncë and no more
Of silver limaile[5] put was, as before
Was in his coal, and stopped with wax well
For to keep in his limaile every del.[6]
And while this priest was in his business,
This canon with his stickë 'gan him dress[7]
To him anon, and his powder cast in,   16740
As he did erst,[8] (the devil out of his skin
Him turn, I pray to God, for his falsehood,
For he was ever false in thought and deed,)
And with his stick, above the crossëlet,
That was ordained with that falsë get,[9]
He stirreth the coalës, till relenten 'gan
The wax against the fire, as every man,
But he a fool be, wot well it must need.
And all that in the stickë was out yede,[10]
And in the crosslet hastily it fell.   16750

[1] Then.
[2] Again.
[3] Shew.
[4] Heed.
[5] Filings.
[6] Whit.
[7] Apply.
[8] Before.
[9] Contrivance.
[10] Went.

Now, goodë Sirs, what will ye bet[1] than well?
When that this priest was thus beguiled again,
Supposing nought but truthë, sooth to sayn,   16753
He was so glad, that I can not express
In no mannér his mirth and his gladness,
And to the canon he proffér'd eftsoon
Body and good: 'Yea,' quod the canon soon,
'Though poor I be, crafty[2] thou shalt me find:
I warn thee well, yet is there more behind.
Is there any copper here within?' said he.   16760
'Yea, Sir,' quod the priest, 'I trow there be.'
    'Ellës go buy us some, and that as swithë.[3]
Now, goodë Sir, go forth thy way and hie[4] thee.'
    He went his way, and with the copper he came,
And this canón it in his handës' name.[5]
And of that copper weighed out an ounce.
Too simple is my tonguë to pronounce,
As minister of my wit, the doubleness
Of this canon, root of all cursedness.
He seemed friendly, to them that knew him nought,
But he was fiendly, both in work and thought.   16771
It wearieth me to tell of his falseness;
And nathëless yet will I it express,
To that intent men may beware thereby,
And for none other causë truëly.
    He put this copper into the crossëlet,
And on the fire as swith[6] he hath it set,
And cast in powder, and made the priest to blow,
And in his working for to stoopen low,
As he did erst,[7] and all n'as but a jape;[8]   16780
Right as him list the priest he made his ape.
And afterward in the ingot he it cast,
And in the pannë put it at the last
Of water, and in he put his owen hand;

[1] Better.

[2] Skilful.

[3] Swiftly.
[4] Haste.

[5] Took.

[6] Quickly.

[7] At first.
[8] Trick.

And in his sleeve, as ye beforen-hand   16785
Heardë me tell, he had a silver teine;[1]
He slily took it out, this cursed heine,[2]
(Unweeting[3] this priest of his falsë craft,)
And in the pannë's bottom he it laft.
And in the water rumbleth to and fro,   16790
And wonder privily took up also
The copper teine, (not knowing thilkë priest,)
And hid it, and him hentë[4] by the breast,
And to him spake, and thus said in his game;
'Stoopeth adown; by God, ye be to blame;
Helpeth me now, as I did you whilere;[5]
Put in your hand, and looketh what is there.'
    This priest took up this silver teine anon;
And thennë said the canon, 'Let us gon
With these three teinës which that we have wrought,
To some goldsmith, and weet if they be ought: 16801
For by my faith I n'oldë[6] for my hood
But if they weren silver fine and good,
And that as swith[7] well proved shall it be.'
    Unto the goldsmith with these teinës three
They went anon, and put them in assay
To fire and hammer: might no man say nay,
But that they weren as them ought to be.
    This sotted[8] priest, who was gladdér than he?
Was never bird gladder against the day,   16810
Nor nightingale in the seasón of May
Was never none, that list bettér to sing,
Nor lady lustier in carolling,
Or for to speak of love and womanhede,
Nor knight in armës do a hardy deed
To standen in grace of his lady dear,
Than haddë this priest this craft for to lear;
And to the canon thus he spake and said;

---

[1] Thin piece.
[2] Wretch.
[3] Unsuspecting.
[4] Took.
[5] Before.
[6] Would not.
[7] Quickly.
[8] Befooled.

'For the love of God, that for us allë dey'd, 16819
And as I may deserve it unto you,
What shall this receipt cost? telleth me now.'
  'By our Lady,' quod this canon, 'it is dear.
I warn you well, that, save I and a frere,
In Engleland there can no man it make.'
  'No force,'[1] quod he; 'now, Sir, for Goddë's sake,
What shall I pay? telleth me, I you pray.'
  'Ywis,'[2] quod he, 'it is full dear I say.
Sir, at one word, if that you list it have,
Ye shall pay forty pound, so God me save;
And n'ere[3] the friendship that ye did ere this 16830
To me, ye shoulden payen more ywis.'
  This priest the sum of forty pound anon
Of nobles fet,[4] and took them every one
To this canon, for this ilkë receipt.
All his working n'as[5] but fraud and deceit.
  'Sir Priest,' he said, 'I keep[6] for to have no los[7]
Of my craft, for I would it were kept close;
And as ye love me, keepeth it secree:
For if men knewen all my subtlety,
By God, they woulden have so great envý 16840
To me, because of my philosophy,
I should be dead, there were no other way.'
  'God it forbid,' quod the priest, 'what ye say.
Yet had I lever[8] spenden all the good
Which that I have, (and ellës were I wood,[9])
Than that ye should fallen in such mischiéf.'
  'For your good will, Sir, have ye right good
      prefe,'[10]
Quod the canon, 'and farewell, *grand mercy.*'
He went his way, and never the priest him sey[11]
After that day: and when that this priest should
Maken assay, at such time as he would, 16851

[1] No matter.

[2] Certainly.

[3] Were not.

[4] Fetched.

[5] Was not.

[6] Take care.
[7] Praise.

[8] Rather.

[9] Mad.

[10] Proof, result.

[11] Saw.

Of this receipt, farewell! it n'old[1] not be.   16852
Lo, thus bejaped[2] and beguiled was he:
Thus maketh he his introductión
To bringen folk to their destructión.
    Considereth, Sirs, how that in each estate
Betwixen men and gold there is debate,
So farforth that unnethes[3] is there none.
This multiplying so blint[4] many one,
That in good faith I trowë that it be   16860
The causë greatest of such scarcity.
These philosóphers speak so mistily
In this craft, that men cannot come thereby,
For any wit that men have now-a-days.
They may well chatteren, as do these jays,
And in their termës set their lust[5] and pain,[6]
But to their purpose shall they ne'er attain.
A man may lightly learn, if he have ought,
To multiply, and bring his good to nought.
Lo, such a lucre is in this lusty[7] game;   16870
A mannë's mirth it will turn all to grame,[8]
And emptien also great and heavy purses,
And maken folk for to purchasen curses
Of them that have thereto their good ylent.
Oh, fy for shamë! they that have been brent,[9]
Alas! can they not flee the firë's heat?
Ye that it use, I rede[10] that ye it lete,[11]
Lest ye lose all; for bet[12] than never is late:
Never to thriven, were too long a date.
Though ye prowl aye, ye shall it never find: 16880
Ye be as bold as is Bayard the blind,
That blundereth forth, and peril casteth[13] none:
He is as bold to run against a stone,
As for to go besidës in the way:
So faren ye that multiply, I say.

---

[1] Would not.
[2] Befooled.
[3] Scarcely.
[4] Deceives.
[5] Delight.
[6] Trouble.
[7] Pleasant.
[8] Sorrow.
[9] Burnt.
[10] Advise.
[11] Leave.
[12] Better.
[13] Perceives no danger.

If that your eyen cannot see aright,   16886
Looketh that yourë mind lack not his sight.
For though ye look never so broad and stare,
Ye shall not win a mite on that chaffare,[1]
But wasten all that ye may rape[2] and renne.[3]
Withdraw the fire, lest it too fastë brenne;[4]
Meddleth no morë with that art, I mean;
For if ye do, your thrift is gone full clean.
And right as swith[5] I will you tellen here
What philosóphers sayn in this mattére.

    Lo, thus saith Arnold* of the newë town,
As his Rosáry maketh mentioún,
He saith right thus, withouten any lie;
'There may no man Mercúry mortify,
But it be with his brother's knowledging.'   16900
    Lo, how that he, which firstë said this thing,
Of philosóphers father was, Hermes:
He saith, how that the dragon doubtëless
Ne dieth not, but if that he be slain
With his brother.   And this is for to sayn,
By the dragon Mercury, and none other,
He understood, and Brimstone by his brother,
That out of Sol and Luna were ydraw.
    'And therefore,' said he, 'take heed to my saw.[6]
Let no man busy him this art to seech,[7]   16910
But if that he the intention and speech
Of philosóphers understanden can;
And if he do, he is a lewëd[8] man.
For this sciénce and this conning,'[9] quod he,
'Is of the secret of secrets pardie.'
    Also there was a disciple of Plato,
That on a timë said his master to,

* 'Arnold:' Arnaldus Villanovanus, a physician and chemist of the thirteenth century.

Marginal glosses:
[1] Traffic.
[2] Seize.
[3] Plunder.
[4] Burn.
[5] Quickly.
[6] Saying.
[7] Seek.
[8] Ignorant.
[9] Knowledge.

As his book Senior will bear witness,   16918
And this was his demand in soothfastness :
'Tell me the namë of thilk[1] privy stone.'
    And Plato answer'd unto him anon;
'Takë the stone that Titanos men name.'
'Which is that?' quod he. 'Magnetia is the same,'
Saidë Plato. 'Yea, Sir, and is it thus?
This is *ignotum per ignotius.*
What is magnetia, good Sir, I pray?'
    'It is a water that is made, I say,
Of the elementës fourë,' quod Plato.
    'Tell me the rootë, good Sir,' quod he tho,[2]
'Of that watér, if that it be your will.'   16930
    'Nay, nay,' quod Plato, 'certain that I n'ill.[3]
The philosophers were sworn every one,
That they ne should discover it unto none,
Nor in no book it write in no mannere ;
For unto God it is so lefe[4] and dear,
That he will not that it discover'd be,
But where it liketh to his deity
Man for to inspire, and eke for to defend[5]
Whom that him liketh ; lo, this is the end.'
    Then thus conclude I, since that God of heaven
Ne will not that the philosóphers neven,[6]   16941
How that a man shall come unto this stone,
I rede[7] as for the best to let it gon.
For whoso maketh God his adversáry,
As for to worken any thing in contráry
Of his will, certes never shall he thrive,
Though that he multiply term of his live.
And there a point ;[8] for ended is my tale.
God send every good man boot[9] of his bale.[10]

[1] That.
[2] Then.
[3] Will not.
[4] Beloved.
[5] Forbid.
[6] Name.
[7] Advise.
[8] Conclusion.
[9] Remedy.
[10] Sorrow.

THE MANCIPLE'S PROLOGUE.

———

WEET[1] ye not where standeth a little town,   16950
Which that ycleped is Bob-up-and-down,
Under the Blee,* in Canterbury way?
There 'gan our Host to japë and to play,
And saidë, 'Sirs, what? Dun[2] is in the mire.
Is there no man, for prayer nor for hire,
That will awaken our fellów behind?
A thief him might full lightly rob and bind.
See how he nappeth, see, for cockë's bones,
As he would fallen from his horse at ones.
Is that a cook of London, with mischance?   16960
Do[3] him come forth, he knoweth his penánce;
For he shall tell a talë, by my fay,[4]
Although it be not worth a bottle hay.
Awake, thou Cook,' quod he, 'God give thee sorrow;
What aileth thee to sleepen by the morrow?
Hast thou had fleas all night, or art thou drunk?
Or hast thou with some quean all night yswunk,
So that thou mayst not holden up thine head?'
    This Cook, that was full pale and nothing red,
Said to our Host, 'So God my soulë bless,   16970
As there is fall on me such heaviness,

* 'Blee:' A forest in Kent.

[1] Know.

[2] Name for an ass.

[3] Make.

[4] Faith.

N'ot [1] I not why, that me were lever [2] to sleep, 16972
Than the best gallon wine that is in Cheap.'
    'Well,' quod the Manciple, 'if it may do ease
To thee, Sir Cook, and to no wight displease,
Which that here rideth in this company,
And that our Host will of his courtesy,
I will as now excuse thee of thy tale;
For in good faith thy visage is full pale:
Thine eyen dasen, [3] soothly as me thinketh,   16980
And well I wot, thy breath full souré stinketh,
That sheweth well thou art not well disposed :
Of me certain thou shalt not be yglosed. [4]
See how he galpeth, [5] lo, this drunken wight,
As though he would us swallow anon right.
Hold close thy mouth, man, by thy father kin :
The devil of hellë set his foot therein!
Thy cursed breath infecten will us all :
Fy! stinking swine, fy! foul may thee befall.
Ah! taketh heed, Sirs, of this lusty man.   16990
Now, sweetë Sir, will ye joust at the fan ? [6]
Thereto, methinketh, ye be well yshape.
I trow that ye have drunken wine of ape,
And that is when men playen with a straw.'
    And with this speech the Cook waxed all wraw, [7]
And on the Manciple he 'gan nod fast
For lack of speech; and down his horse him cast,
Where as he lay, till that men him up took.
This was a fair chivachee [8] of a cook :
Alas that he ne had held him by his ladle!   17000
And ere that he again were in the saddle,
There was great shoving bothë to and fro
To lift him up, and muchel care and woe,
So unwieldy was this silly paled ghost :
And to the Manciple then spake our Host :

[1] Know not.
[2] Rather.
[3] Are dim.
[4] Flattered.
[5] Yawns.
[6] The quintain.
[7] Angry.
[8] Expedition.

'Because that drink hath dominatión   17006
Upon this man, by my salvatión
I trow he lewedly will tell his tale.
For were it wine, or old or moisty[1] ale,   [1] New.
That he hath drunk, he speaketh in his nose,
And sneezeth fast, and eke he hath the pose.*
He also hath to do more than enough
To keep him on his capel[2] out of the slough: [2] Horse.
And if he fall from off his capel eftsoon,
Then shall we allë have enough to don
In lifting up his heavy drunken corse.
Tell on thy tale, of him make I no force.[3]   [3] No matter.
   'But yet, Manciple, in faith thou art too nice,[4]   [4] Foolish.
Thus openly to reprove him of his vice:
Another day he will paráventure   17020
Reclaimen thee, and bring thee to the lure;
I mean, he speaken will of smallë things,
As for to pinchen at thy reckonings,
That were not honest, if it came to prefe.'[5]   [5] Proof.
   Quod the Manciple, 'That were a great mischief:
So might he lightly bring me in the snare.
Yet had I lever[6] payen for the mare   [6] Rather.
Which he rides on, than he should with me strive.
I will not wrathen him, so may I thrive;
That that I spake, I said it in my bourd.[7]   17030 [7] Jest.
And weet[8] ye what? I have here in my gourd   [8] Know.
A draught of wine, yea, of a ripë grape,
And right anon ye shall see a good jape.[9]   [9] Trick.
This cook shall drink thereof, if that I may;
Up pain of my life he will not say nay.'
   And certainly, to tellen as it was,
Of this vessél the cook drank fast, (alas!
What needeth it? he drank enough beforne,)

* 'The pose:' A defluxion obstructing the voice.

And when he haddë pouped[1] in his horn,   17039
To the Manciple he took the gourd again.
And of that drink the Cook was wonder fain,
And thanked him in such wise as he could.
    Then 'gan our Host to laughen wonder loud,
And said, 'I see well it is necessary
Where that we go good drink with us to carry;
For that will turnen rancour and disease[2]
T' accord and love, and many a wrong appease.
    'O Bacchus, Bacchus, blessed be thy name,
That so canst turnen earnest into game;
Worship and thank be to thy deity.   17050
Of that mattér ye get no more of me.
Tell on thy tale, Manciple, I thee pray.'
    'Well, Sir,' quod he, 'now heark'neth what I say.'

THE MANCIPLE'S TALE.

When Phœbus dwelled here in earth adown,
As oldë bookës maken mentióun,
He was the mostë lusty[3] bacheler
Of all this world, and eke the best archer.
He slew Python the serpent, as he lay
Sleeping against the sun upon a day;
And many another noble worthy deed   17060
He with his bow wrought, as men mayen read.
    Playen he could on every minstrelsy,
And singen, that it was a melody
To hearen of his clearë voice the soun'.
Certes the king of Thebes, Amphioun,
That with his singing walled the city,
Could never singen half so well as he.

[1] Sounded.
[2] Uneasiness.
[3] Pleasant.

Thereto he was the seemliestë man 17068
That is or was, sithen[1] the world began; · [1] Since.
What needeth it his feature to descrive?
For in this world n'is none so fair on live.
He was therewith fulfill'd of gentleness,
Of honour, and of perfect worthiness.
   This Phœbus, that was flower of bachlery,
As well in freedom,[2] as in chivalry, [2] Genero-
For his disport, in sign eke of victóry   sity.
Of Python, so as telleth us the story,
Was wont to bearen in his hand a bow.
Now had this Phœbus in his house a crow,
Which in a cage he foster'd many a day, 17080
And taught it speaken, as men teach a jay.
White was this crow, as is a snow-white swan,
And counterfeit the speech of every man
He couldë, when he shouldë tell a tale.
Therewith in all this world no nightingale·
Ne couldë by an hundred thousand del[3] [3] Part.
Singen so wonder merrily and well.
   Now had this Phœbus in his house a wife,
Which that he loved morë than his life,
And night and day did ever his diligence 17090
Her for to please, and do her reverence:
Save only, if that I the sooth shall sayn,
Jealous he was, and would have kept her fain,
For him were loth yjaped[4] for to be; [4] Tricked.
And so is every wight in such degree;
But all for nought, for it availeth nought.
A good wife, that is clean of work and thought,
Should not be kept in none await[5] certain: [5] Watch.
And truëly the labour is in vain
To keep a shrewë, for it will not be. 17100
This hold I for a very nicety,[6] [6] Folly.

To spillen labour for to keepen wives;   17102
Thus writen oldë clerkës in their lives.
   But now to purpose, as I first began.
This worthy Phœbus doth all that he can
To pleasen her, weening through such pleasance,
And for his manhood and his governance,
That no man shouldë put him from her grace:
But God it wot, there may no man embrace
As to destrain[1] a thing, which that natúre   17110
Hath naturally set in a creatúre.
   Take any bird, and put it in a cage,
And do all thine intent, and thy courage,[2]
To foster it tenderly with meat and drink
Of allë dainties that thou canst bethink,
And keep it all so cleanly as thou may;
Although the cage of gold be never so gay,
Yet had this bird, by twenty thousand fold,
Lever[3] in a forest, that is wild and cold,
Go eaten wormës, and such wretchedness.   17120
For ever this bird will do his business
T' escape out of his cage when that he may:
His liberty the bird desireth aye.
   Let take a cat, and foster her with milk
And tender flesh, and, make her couch of silk,
And let her see a mouse go by the wall,
Anon she weiveth[4] milk and flesh, and all,
And every dainty that is in that house,
Such appetite hath she to eat the mouse.
Lo, here hath kind[5] her dominatión,   17130
And appetite flemeth[6] discretión.
   A she-wolf hath also a villain's kind;
The lewedestë wolf that she may find,
Or least of reputation, will she take
In timë when her lust to have a make.[7]

[1] Con-strain.

[2] Mind.

[3] Rather.

[4] Forsak-eth.

[5] Nature.

[6] Banish-eth.

[7] Mate.

All these examples speak I by these men   17136
That be untrue, and nothing by women.
For men have ever a likerous appetite
On lower thing to pérform their delight
Than on their wivës, be they never so fair,
Ne never so truë, nor so debonaire.[1]
Flesh is so newëfangle, with mischance,
That we ne can in nothing have pleasance,
That souneth[2] unto virtue any while.
    This Phœbus, which that thought upon no guile,
Deceived was for all his jollity:
For under him another haddë she,
A man of little reputatión,
Nought worth to Phœbus in comparison:
The more harm is; it happ'neth often so;   17150
Of which there cometh muchel harm and woe.
    And so befell, when Phœbus was absént,
His wife anon hath for her leman sent.
Her leman? certes that is a knavish speech.
Forgive it me, and that I you beseech.
    The wisë Plato saith, as ye may read,
The word must need accorden with the deed;
If men shall tellen properly a thing,
The word must cousin be to the working.
I am a boistous[3] man, right thus say I;   17160
There is no differencë truëly
Betwixt a wife that is of high degree,
(If of her body dishonést she be,)
And any poorë wench, other than this,
(If it so be they worken both amiss,)
But, for the gentle is in estate above,
She shall be clep'd his lady and his love;
And, for that other is a poorë woman,
She shall be clep'd his wenchë and his leman:

[1] Court-
eous.

[2] Is accord-
ing to.

[3] Rough.

And God it wot, mine owen dearë brother,   17170
Men lay as low that one as li'th that other.
   Right so betwixt a titleless tyránt
And an outlaw, or else a thief errant,[1]
The same I say, there is no differénce,
(To Alexander told was this senténce,)
But, for the tyrant is of greater might
By force of meinie[2] for to slay downright,
And brennen[3] house and home, and make all plain,[4]
Lo, therefore is he clep'd a capitain;
And, for the outlaw hath but small meinie,   17180
And may not do so great an harm as he,
Nor bring a country to so great mischief,
Men clepen him an outlaw or a thief.
   But, for I am a man not textuel,[5]
I will not tell of textës never a del;[6]
I will go to my tale, as I began.
   When Phœbus' wife had sent for her leman,
Anon they wroughten all their lust volage.[7]
This whitë crow, that hung aye in the cage,
Beheld their work, and saidë never a word: 17190
And when that home was come Phœbus the lord,
This crowë sung, 'Cuckoo, cuckoo, cuckoo!'
   'What? bird,' quod Phœbus, 'what song sing'st
     thou now?
Ne were thou wont so merrily to sing,
That to my heart it was a réjoicing
To hear thy voice? alas! what song is this?
   'By God,' quod he, 'I singë not amiss.
Phœbus,' quod he, 'for all thy worthiness,
For all thy beauty, and all thy gentleness,
For all thy song, and all thy minstrelsy,   17200
For all thy waiting, bleared is thine eye,
With one of little reputatión,

[1] Strolling.
[2] Servants.
[3] Burn.
[4] Level.
[5] Ready at citing texts.
[6] Whit.
[7] Light.

Not worth to thee as in comparison   17203
The mountance[1] of a gnat, so may I thrive;
For on thy bed thy wife I saw him swive.'
    What will you more? the crow anon him told,
By sadë[2] tokens, and by wordës bold,
How that his wife had done her lechery
Him to great shame, and to great villainy;
And told him oft, he saw it with his eyen.   17210
    This Phœbus 'gan awayward[3] for to wrien;[4]
Him thought his woful heartë burst atwo.
His bow he bent, and set therein a flo;[5]
And in his ire he hath his wife yslain:
This is the effect, there is no more to sayn.
For sorrow of which he brake his minstrelsy,
Both harp and lutë, gitern,[6] and psalt'ry;
And eke he brake his arrows, and his bow;
And after that thus spake he to the crow.
    'Traitor,' quod he, 'with tongue of scorpión,   17220
Thou hast me brought to my confusión:
Alas that I was wrought! why n'ere[7] I dead?
    'O dearë wife, O gem of lustyhed,[8]
That were to me so sad,[9] and eke so true,
Now liest thou dead, with facë pale of hue,
Full guiltëless, that durst I swear ywis.[10]
    'O rakel[11] hand, to do so foul a mis.[12]
O troubled wit, O irë reckëless,
That unadvised smitest guiltëless.
O wantrust,[13] full of false suspición,   17230
Where was thy wit and thy discretión?
    'O, every man beware of rakelness,[14]
Ne trow[15] no thing withouten strong witnéss.
Smite not too soon, ere that ye weeten why,
And be avised[16] well and sikerly,[17]
Ere ye do any execution

---

[1] Worth.

[2] Grave.

[3] Away.
[4] Turn.

[5] Arrow.

[6] Guitar.

[7] Was not.

[8] Pleasant-
ness.
[9] Steadfast.

[10] Certain-
ly.
[11] Rash.
[12] Wrong.

[13] Distrust.

[14] Rash-
ness.
[15] Believe.

[16] Consid-
ered.
[17] Surely.

Upon your irë for suspicion.   17237
Alas! a thousand folk hath rakel ire
Foully foredone, and brought them in the mire.
¹ Slay.   Alas! for sorrow I will myselven sle.'¹
　　And to the crow, 'O falsë thief,' said he,
'I will thee quit anon thy falsë tale.
² Once.   Thou sung whilom ² like any nightingale,
Now shalt thou, falsë thief, thy song foregon,
And eke thy whitë feathers every one,
Ne never in all thy life ne shalt thou speak;
Thus shall men on a traitor be awreak.
³ Black.   Thou and thine offspring ever shall be blake,³
Ne never sweetë noisë shall ye make,
But ever cry against tempést and rain,   17250
In token that through thee my wife is slain.'
　　And to the crow he start, and that anon,
And pull'd his whitë feathers every one,
And made him black, and reft him all his song
And eke his speech, and out at door him flung
⁴ Com-   Unto the devil, which I him betake;⁴
mend to.   And for this causë be all crowës blake.
　　Lordings, by this example, I you pray,
⁵ Care.   Beware, and taketh keep⁵ what that ye say;
Ne telleth never man in all your life,   17260
How that another man hath dight his wife;
He will you haten mortally certáin.
Dan Solomon, as wisë clerkës sayn,
Teacheth a man to keep his tonguë well;
But as I said, I am not textuel.
But nathëless thus taughtë me my dame;
'My son, think on the crow, a Goddë's name.
My son, keep well thy tongue, and keep thy friend;
A wicked tongue is worsë than a fiend:
My sonë, from a fiend men may them bless.   17270

My son, God of his endöless goodness   17271
Walled a tongue with teeth, and lippës eke,
For man should him advisen what he speak.
My son, full often for too muchel speech
Hath many a man been spilt,[1] as clerkës teach;
But for a little speech advisedly
Is no man shent,[2] to speaken generally.
My son, thy tonguë shouldest thou restrain
At allë time, but when thou dost thy pain[3]
To speak of God in honour and prayere.   17280
The firstë virtue, son, if thou wilt lear,[4]
Is to restrain, and keepen well thy tongue;
Thus learnen children, when that they be young.
My son, of muchel speaking evil advised,
There[5] lessë speaking had enough sufficed,
Com'th muchel harm; thus was me told and
     taught;
In muchel speechë sinnë wanteth naught.
Wost[6] thou whereof a rakel tonguë serveth?
Right as a sword forecutteth and forecarveth
An arm atwo, my dearë son, right so   17290
A tonguë cutteth friendship all atwo.
A jangler[7] is to God abomináble.
Read Solomon, so wise and honouráble,
Read David in his Psalmës, read Senec.
My son, speak not, but with thine head thou beck,[8]
Dissimule[9] as thou were deaf, if that thou hear
A jangler speak of perilous mattére.
The Fleming saith, and learn if that thee lest,
That little jangling causeth muchel rest.
My son, if thou no wicked word hast said,   17300
Thee thar[10] not dreaden for to be bewray'd;
But he that hath missaid, I dare well sayn,
He may by no way clepe[11] his word again.

[1] Destroyed.

[2] Ruined.

[3] Trouble.

[4] Learn.

[5] Where.

[6] Knowest.

[7] Chatterer.

[8] Nod.

[9] Affect.

[10] Behoves.

[11] Call.

Thing that is said is said, and forth it go'th, 17304
Though him repent, or be him never so loth,
He is his thrall, to whom that he hath said
A tale, of which he is now evil apaid.[1]
My son, beware, and be no author new
Of tidings, whether they be false or true;
Whereso thou come, amongës high or low, 17310
Keep well thy tongue, and think upon the crow.

[1] Satisfied.

THE PARSON'S PROLOGUE.

By that the Manciple had his talë ended,   17312
The sunnë from the south line was descended
So low, that it ne was not to my sight
Degreës nine-and-twenty as of height.
Four of the clock it was then, as I guess,
For enleven [1] foot, a little more or less,   [1] Eleven.
My shadow was at thilkë time, as there,
Of such feet as my lengthë parted were
In six feet equal of proportion.   17320
Therewith the moonë's exaltatión,
In meanë [2] Libra, alway 'gan ascend,   [2] Middle.
As we were ent'ring at the thorpë's [3] end.   [3] Village.
For which our Host, as he was wont to gie,[4]   [4] Guide.
As in this case, our jolly company,
Said in this wisë ; 'Lordings, every one,
Now lacketh us no talës more than one.
Fulfill'd is my senténce and my decree ;
I trow that we have heard of each degree.
Almost fulfilled is mine ordinance ;   17330
I pray to God so give him right good chance
That telleth us this talë lustily.
   'Sir Priest,' quod he, 'art thou a vicary ? [5]   [5] Vicar.
Or art thou a Parson ? say sooth by thy fay.[6]   [6] Faith.

Be what thou be, ne break thou not our play;   17335
For every man, save thou, hath told his tale.
Unbuckle, and shew us what is in thy mail.
For truëly methinketh by thy chere [1]
Thou shouldest knit up well a great mattere.
Tell us a fable anon, for cockë's bones.'   17340
     This Parson him answéred all at ones;
'Thou gettest fable none ytold for me,
For Paul, that writeth unto Timothy,
Reproveth them that weiven [2] soothfastness,
And tellen fables, and such wretchedness.
Why should I sowen draff out of my fist,
When I may sowen wheat, if that me list?
For which I say, if that you list to hear
Morality, and virtuous mattere,
And then that ye will give me audiénce,   17350
I would full fain at Christë's reverénce
Do you pleasancë lawful, as I can.
But trusteth well, I am a southern man,
I cannot gest,[3] rom, ram, ruf, by my letter,
And, God wot, rhyme hold I but little better.
And therefore if you list, I will not glose,[4]
I will you tell a little tale in prose,
To knit up all this feast, and make an end:
And Jesu for his gracë wit me send
To shewen you the way in this viáge   17360
Of thilkë perfect glorious pilgrimage,
That hight Jerusalem celestial.
And if ye vouchësafe, anon I shall
Begin upon my tale, for which I pray
Tell your advice, I can no better say.
     'But nathëless this meditatión
I put it aye under correctión
Of clerkës, for I am not textuel;

[1] Demeanour.

[2] Forsake.

[3] Relate stories.

[4] Comment.

I take but the senténce, trusteth me well.   17369
Therefore I make a protestatión,
That I will standen to correctión.'
   Upon this word we have assented soon:
For, as us seemed, it was for to don,
To enden in some virtuous senténce,
And for to give him space and audiénce;
And bade our Host he shouldë to him say,
That allë we to tell his tale him pray.
   Our Hostë had the wordës for us all:
'Sir Priest,' quod he, 'now fairë you befall;
Say what you list, and we shall gladly hear.'   17380
And with that word he said in this mannere;
'Telleth,' quod he, 'your meditatióun,
But hasteth you, the sunnë will adown.
Be fructuous,[1] and that in little space,
And to do well God sendë you his grace.'

THE PARSON'S TALE.

Our sweet Lord God of heaven, that no man will perish, but will that we come all to the knowledge of him, and to the blissful life that is perdurable, amonesteth[2] us by the prophet Jeremiah, that saith in this wise: 'Stand upon the ways, and see and ask of the old paths;' (that is to say, of old sentences;) 'which is the good way: and walk in that way, and ye shall find refreshing for your souls.' Many be the ways spiritual that lead folk to our Lord Jesus Christ, and to the regne[3] of glory: of which ways,

[1] Fruitful.

[2] Admonisheth.

[3] Kingdom.

there is a full noble way, and well covenable,[1] which may not fail to man nor to woman, that through sin hath misgone from the right way of Jerusalem celestial; and this way is cleped penance; of which man should gladly hearken and inquire with all his heart, to weet[2] what is penance, and whence it is cleped penance, and how many manners be of actions or workings of penance, and how many species there be of penance, and which things appertain and behove[3] to penance, and which things distrouble[4] penance.

Saint Ambrose saith, that 'penance is the 'plaining of man for the guilt that he hath done, and no more to do anything for which him ought to 'plain.' And some doctor saith, 'Penance is the lamenting of man that sorroweth for his sin, and paineth himself for he hath misdone.' Penance, with certain circumstances, is very repentance of man, that holdeth himself in sorrow and other pain for his guilts: and for he shall be very penitent, he shall first bewail the sins that he hath done, and steadfastly purpose in his heart to have shrift[5] of mouth, and to do satisfaction, and never to do thing for which him ought more to bewail or complain, and to continue in good works: or else his repentance may not avail. For as Saint Isidor saith, 'He is a japer[6] and a gabber,[7] and not very[8] repentant, that eftsoons doth thing for which him oweth to repent.' Weeping, and not for to stint[9] to do sin, may not avail. But nevertheless, men should hope, that at every time that man falleth, be it never so oft, that he may arise through penance, if he have grace: but certain it is great doubt. For as saith Saint Gregory, 'Unnethes[1] ariseth he out of sin, that is charged with the charge of evil usage.' And therefore repentant folk, that stint for to sin, and forlete[2] sin ere that sin forlete them, holy church holdeth them sicker[3] of their salvation. And he that sinneth, and verily repenteth him in his last day, holy church yet hopeth his salvation, by the great mercy of our Lord Jesus Christ, for his repentance: but take ye the siker and certain way.

And now since I have declared you what thing is penance, now ye shall understand that there be three actions of penance. The first is, that a man be baptized after that he hath sinned. Saint Augustine saith, but he be penitent for his old sinful life, he may not begin the new clean life: for certes if he be baptized without penitence of his old guilt, he receiveth the mark of baptism, but not the grace, nor the remission of his sins, till he have very repentance. Another default is, that men do deadly sin after that they have received baptism. The third default is, that men fall in venial sins after their baptism, from day to day. Thereof saith Saint Augustine, that penance of good and humble folk is the penance of every day.

The species of penance be three. That one of them is solemn, another is common, and the third privy. That penance that is solemn, is in two

[1] With difficulty.

[2] Forsake.

[3] Sure.

manners; as to be put out of holy church in Lent, for slaughter of children, and such manner thing. Another is when a man hath sinned openly, of which sin the fame is openly spoken in the country: and then holy church by judgment distraineth[1] him for to do open penance. Common penance is that priests enjoin men in certain cases: as for to go peradventure naked on pilgrimage, or barefoot. Privy penance is thilk[2] that men do all day for privy sins, of which we shrive[3] us privily, and receive privy penance.

Now shalt thou understand what is behoveful[4] and necessary to every perfect penance: and this standeth on three things; contrition of heart, confession of mouth, and satisfaction. For which saith Saint John Chrysostom: 'Penance distraineth a man to accept benignly every pain that him is enjoined, with contrition of heart and shrift[5] of mouth, with satisfaction and working of all manner humility.' And this is fruitful penance against those three things, in which we wrath our Lord Jesus Christ: this is to say, by delight in thinking, by recklessness in speaking, and by wicked sinful working. And against these wicked guilts is penance, that may be likened unto a tree.

The root of this tree is contrition, that hideth him in the heart of him that is very repentant, right as the root of the tree hideth him in the earth. Of this root of contrition springeth a stalk, that beareth branches and leaves of confession, and fruit of satis-

[1] Compels.

[2] That.

[3] Confess.

[4] Profitable.

[5] Confession.

faction. Of which Christ saith in his Gospel, 'Do ye digne[1] fruit of penitence;' for by this fruit may men understand and know this tree, and not by the root that is hid in the heart of man, nor by the branches, nor the leaves of confession. And therefore our Lord Jesus Christ saith thus: 'By the fruit of them shall ye know them.' Of this root also springeth a seed of grace, which seed is mother of sikerness,[2] and this seed is eager and hot. The grace of this seed springeth of God, through remembrance on the day of doom, and on the pains of hell. Of this matter saith Solomon, that in the dread of God man forletteth[3] his sin. The heat of this seed is the love of God, and the desiring of the joy perdurable.[4] This heat draweth the heart of man to God, and doth[5] him hate his sin. For soothly there is nothing that savoureth so sweet to a child as the milk of his norice,[6] nor nothing is to him more abominable than that milk, when it is meddled[7] with other meat. Right so the sinful man that loveth his sin, him seemeth that it is to him most sweet of anything; but from that time that he loveth sadly[8] our Lord Jesus Christ, and desireth the life perdurable, there is to him nothing more abominable. For soothly the law of God is the love of God. For which David the prophet saith, 'I have loved thy law, and hated wickedness:' he that loveth God, keepeth his law and his word. This tree saw the prophet Daniel in spirit, upon the vision of Nebuchadnezzar, when he counselled him to do penance.

[1] Worthy.
[2] Security.
[3] Leaveth.
[4] Everlasting.
[5] Maketh.
[6] Nurse.
[7] Mixed.
[8] Seriously.

Penance is the tree of life, to them that it receive: and he that holdeth him in very penance, is blissful, after the sentence of Solomon.

In this penance or contrition man shall understand four things: that is to say, what is contrition; and which be the causes that move a man to contrition; and how he should be contrite; and what contrition availeth to the soul. Then is it thus, that contrition is the very sorrow that a man receiveth in his heart for his sins, with sad purpose to shrive[1] him, and to do penance, and never more to do sin. And this sorrow shall be in this manner, as saith Saint Bernard; it shall be heavy and grievous, and full sharp and poignant in heart; first, for a man hath aguilted[2] his Lord and his Creator; and more sharp and poignant, for he hath aguilted his Father celestial; and yet more sharp and poignant, for he hath wrathed and aguilted Him that bought him, that with his precious blood hath delivered us from the bonds of sin, and from the cruelty of the devil, and from the pains of hell.

The causes that ought to move a man to contrition be six. First, a man shall remember him of his sins. But look that that remembrance no be to him no delight, by no way, but great shame and sorrow for his sins. For Job saith, 'Sinful men do works worthy of confession.' And therefore saith Ezekiel, 'I will remember me all the years of my life, in the bitterness of my heart.' And God saith in the Apocalypse, 'Remember you from whence

[1] Confess.

[2] Offended.

that ye be fall,' for before the time that ye sinned, ye were children of God, and limbs of the regne[1] of God; but for your sin ye be waxen thrall and foul; members of the fiend; hate of angels; slander of holy church, and food of the false serpent; perpetual matter of the fire of hell; and yet more foul and abominable, for ye trespass so oft times, as doth the hound that turneth again to eat his own spuing; and yet fouller, for your long continuing in sin, and your sinful usage, for which ye be rotten in your sins, as a beast in his dung. Such manner thoughts make a man to have shame of his sin, and no delight; as God saith, by the prophet Ezekiel, 'Ye shall remember you of your ways, and they shall displease you.' Soothly, sins be the ways that lead folk to hell.

The second cause that ought to make a man to have disdain of sin is this, that, as saith Saint Peter, 'Whoso doth sin, is thrall to sin,' and sin putteth a man in great thraldom. And therefore saith the prophet Ezekiel, 'I went sorrowful, and had disdain of myself.' Certes, well ought a man have disdain of sin, and withdraw him from that thraldom and villainy. And lo, what saith Seneca in this matter? He saith thus: 'Though I wist that neither God nor man should never know it, yet would I have disdain for to do sin.' And the same Seneca also saith, 'I am born to greater things than to be thrall to my body, or for to make of my body a thrall.' Nor a fouller thrall may no man,

[1] Kingdom.

nor woman, make of his body, than for to give his body to sin. All were it the foulest churl, or the foulest woman that liveth, and least of value, yet is he then more foul, and more in servitude. Ever from the higher degree that man falleth, the more is he thrall, and more to God and to the world vile and abominable. O good God! well ought a man have disdain of sin, since that through sin, there[1] he was free, he is made bond. And therefore saith Saint Augustine, 'If thou hast disdain of thy servant if he offend or sin, have thou then disdain that thou thyself shouldest do sin. Take reward[2] of thine own value, that thou ne be too foul to thyself.' Alas! well ought they then have disdain to be servants and thralls to sin, and sore to be ashamed of themselves, that God of his endless goodness hath set in high estate, or given them wit, strength of body, health, beauty, or prosperity, and bought them from the death with his heart-blood, that they so unkindly[3] against his gentleness, requite him so villainously, to slaughter of their own souls. O good God! ye women that be of great beauty, remember you on the proverb of Solomon, that likeneth a fair woman, that is a fool of her body, to a ring of gold that is worn in the groine[4] of a sow: for right as a sow wroteth[5] in every ordure, so wroteth she her beauty in stinking ordure of sin.

The third cause that ought to move a man to contrition, is dread of the day of doom, and of the horrible pains of hell. For as Saint Jerome saith,

1 Where.

2 Have respect to.

3 Unnaturally.

4 Snout.

5 Diggeth.

'At every time that me remembereth of the day of doom, I quake: for when I eat or drink, or do what so I do, ever seemeth me that the trump soundeth in mine ears: Rise ye up that be dead, and come to the judgment.' O good God! much ought a man to dread such a judgment, there as we shall be all, as Saint Paul saith, before the strait[1] judgment of our Lord Jesus Christ; whereas he shall make a general congregation, whereas no man may be absent; for certes there availeth no essoine[2] nor no excusation; and not only, that our defaults shall be judged, but eke that all our works shall openly be known. And, as saith Saint Bernard, there ne shall no pleading avail, nor no sleight: we shall give reckoning of every idle word. There shall we have a judge that may not be deceived nor corrupt; and why? for certes all our thoughts be discovered as to him: nor for prayer, nor for meed, he will not be corrupt. And therefore saith Solomon, 'The wrath of God ne will not spare no wight, for prayer nor for gift.' And therefore at the day of doom there is no hope to escape. Wherefore, as saith Saint Anselm, full great anguish shall the sinful folk have at that time: there shall be the stern and wroth Judge sitting above, and under him the horrible pit of hell open, to destroy him that would not beknow[3] his sins, which sins shall openly be shewed before God and before every creature: and on the left side, more devils than any heart may think, for to hurry and draw the sinful souls to the pit of hell:

[1] Strict.

[2] Excuse.

[3] Confess.

and within the hearts of folk shall be the biting conscience, and without forth shall be the world all burning. Whither then shall the wretched soul flee to hide him? Certes he may not hide him, he must come forth and shew him. For certes, as saith Saint Jerome, the earth shall cast him out of it, and the sea, and also the air, that shall be full of thunderclaps and lightnings. Now soothly, whoso will remember him of these things, I guess that his sins shall not turn him to delight, but to great sorrow, for dread of the pain of hell. And therefore saith Job to God, 'Suffer, Lord, that I may a while bewail and beweep, ere I go without returning to the dark land, covered with the darkness of death; to the land of misease and of darkness, whereas is the shadow of death; whereas is no order nor ordinance, but grisly dread that ever shall last.' Lo, here may ye see, that Job prayed respite a while, to beweep and wail his trespass: for soothly[1] one day of respite is better than all the treasure of this world. And forasmuch as a man may acquit himself before God by penitence in this world, and not by treasure, therefore should he pray to God to give him respite a while, to beweep and bewail his trespass: for certes all the sorrow that a man might make from the beginning of the world, n'is but a little thing, at regard[2] of the sorrow of hell. The cause why that Job clepeth hell the land of darkness; understand, that he clepeth it land or earth, for it is stable and never shall fail; and dark, for he that is in hell

[1] Truly.

[2] In comparison to.

hath default[1] of light natural; for certes the dark
light, that shall come out of the fire that ever shall
burn, shall turn them all to pain that be in hell, for
it sheweth them the horrible devils that them torment. Covered with the darkness of death; that is
to say, that he that is in hell shall have default of
the sight of God; for certes the sight of God is the
life perdurable.[2] The darkness of death, be the sins
that the wretched man hath done, which that distrouble[3] him to see the face of God, right as a dark
cloud between us and the sun. It is land of misease, because that there be three manner of defaults
against three things that folk of this world have in
this present life; that is to say, honours, delights,
and riches. Against honour have they in hell
shame and confusion: for well ye wot, that men
clepe honour the reverence that man doth to man;
but in hell is no honour nor reverence; for certes no
more reverence shall be done there to a king than
to a knave.[4] For which God saith by the prophet
Jeremiah, 'The folk that me despise shall be in
despite.' Honour is also cleped great lordship.
There shall no wight serve other, but of harm and
torment. Honour is also cleped great dignity and
highness; but in hell shall they be all fortrodden of
devils. As God saith, 'The horrible devils shall
go and come upon the heads of damned folk:' and
this is, forasmuch as the higher that they were in
this present life, the more shall they be abated[5] and
defouled in hell. Against the riches of this world

[1] Want.

[2] Everlast-
ing.

[3] Disturb.

[4] Servant.

[5] Debased.

¹ Want.

² United.

shall they have misease of poverty, and this poverty shall be in four things: in default [1] of treasure; of which David saith, 'The rich folk that embraced and oned [2] all their heart to treasure of this world, shall sleep in the sleeping of death, and nothing no shall they find in their hands of all their treasure.' And moreover, the misease of hell shall be in default of meat and drink. For God saith thus by Moses, 'They shall be wasted with hunger, and the birds of hell shall devour them with bitter death, and the gall of the dragon shall be their drink, and the venom of the dragon their morsels.' And furtherover, their misease shall be in default of clothing, for they shall be naked in body, as of clothing, save the fire in which they burn, and other filths; and naked shall they be in soul, of all manner virtues, which that is the clothing of the soul. Where be then the gay robes, and soft sheets, and the fine shirts? Lo, what saith God of heaven by the prophet Isaiah, that under them shall be strewed moths, and their covertures shall be of worms of hell. And furtherover, their misease shall be in default of friends, for he is not poor that hath good friends: but there is no friend; for neither God nor no good creature shall be friend to them, and evereach of them shall hate other with deadly hate. The sons and the daughters shall rebel against father and mother, and kindred against kindred, and chide and despise each other, both day and night, as God saith by the Prophet Micah.

And the loving children, that whilome loved so fleshly, evereach of them would eat other if they might. For how should they love together in the pains of hell, when they hated each other in the prosperity of this life? For trust well, their fleshly love was deadly hate. As saith the prophet David: 'Whoso that loveth wickedness, he hateth his own soul:' and whoso hateth his own soul, certes he may love none other wight in no manner: and therefore in hell is no solace nor no friendship, but ever the more kindreds that be in hell, the more cursing, the more chiding, and the more deadly hate there is among them. And furtherover, there they shall have default of all manner delights, for certes delights be after the appetites of the five wits;[1] as sight, hearing, smelling, savouring,[2] and touching. But in hell their sight shall be full of darkness and of smoke, and their eyes full of tears; and their hearing full of waimenting[3] and grinting[4] of teeth, as saith Jesus Christ: their nostrils shall be full of stinking; and, as saith Isaiah the prophet, their savouring shall be full of bitter gall; and touching of all their body, shall be covered with fire that never shall quench, and with worms that never shall die, as God saith by the mouth of Isaiah. And forasmuch as they shall not ween[5] that they may die for pain, and by death flee from pain, that may they understand in the word of Job, that saith, 'There is the shadow of death.' Certes a shadow hath likeness of the thing of which it is

[1] Senses.
[2] Tasting.
[3] Lamenting.
[4] Gnashing.
[5] Think.

shadowed, but shadow is not the same thing of which it is shadowed: right so fareth the pain of hell; it is like death, for the horrible anguish; and why? for it paineth them ever as though they should die anon; but certes they shall not die. For as saith Saint Gregory, 'To wretched caitiffs shall be death without death, and end without end, and default[1] without failing; for their death shall alway live, and their end shall evermore begin, and their default shall never fail.' And therefore saith Saint John the Evangelist, 'They shall follow death, and they shall not find him, and they shall desire to die, and death shall flee from them.' And eke Job saith, that in hell is no order of rule. And albeit so that God hath created all thing in right order, and nothing without order, but all things be ordered and numbered, yet nevertheless they that be damned be nothing in order, nor hold no order. For the earth shall bear them no fruit; (for, as the prophet David saith, 'God shall destroy the fruit of the earth, as from them,') nor water shall give them no moisture, nor the air no refreshing, nor the fire no light. For as saith Saint Basil, 'The burning of the fire of this world shall God give in hell to them that be damned, but the light and the clearness shall be given in heaven to his children; right as the good man giveth flesh to his children, and bones to his hounds.' And for they shall have no hope to escape, saith Job at last, that there shall horror and grisly dread dwell without end. Horror is alway dread of harm that

[1] Want.

is to come, and this dread shall alway dwell in the hearts of them that be damned. And therefore have they lorn[1] all their hope for seven causes. First, for God that is their judge shall be without mercy to them; and they may not please him; nor none of his hallows;[2] nor they may give nothing for their ransom; nor they have no voice to speak to him; nor they may not flee from pain; nor they have no goodness in them that they may shew to deliver them from pain. And therefore saith Solomon, 'The wicked man dieth, and when he is dead, he shall have no hope to escape from pain.' Whoso then would well understand these pains, and bethink him well that he hath deserved these pains for his sins, certes he should have more talent[3] to sigh and to weep, than for to sing and play. For as saith Solomon, 'Whoso that had the science to know the pains that be established and ordained for sin, he would forsake sin.' 'That science,' saith Saint Austin, 'maketh a man to waiment[4] in his heart.'

The fourth point, that ought make a man have contrition, is the sorrowful remembrance of the good deeds that he hath left to do here in earth, and also the good that he hath lorn.[5] Soothly the good works that he hath left, either they be the good works that he wrought ere he fell into deadly sin, or else the good works that he wrought while he lay in sin. Soothly the good works that he did before that he fell in deadly sin, be all mortified,

[1] Lost.

[2] Holiness.

[3] Desire.

[4] Lament.

[5] Lost.

astoned,[1] and dulled by the eft[2] sinning: the other works that he wrought while he lay in sin, they be utterly dead, as to the life perdurable in heaven. Then thilk[3] good works that be mortified by eft sinning, which he did while he was in charity, may never quicken again without very[4] penitence. And thereof saith God by the mouth of Ezekiel, 'If the rightful man return again from his righteousness and do wickedness, shall he live? nay; for all the good works that he hath wrought shall never be in remembrance, for he shall die in his sin.' And upon thilk[5] chapter saith Saint Gregory thus; that we shall understand this principally, that when we do deadly sin, it is for nought then to remember or draw into memory the good works that we have wrought before: for certes in the working of deadly sin, there is no trust in no good work that we have done before; that is to say, as for to have thereby the life perdurable in heaven. But nevertheless, the good works quicken again and come again, and help and avail to have the life perdurable in heaven, when we have contrition: but soothly the good works that men do while they be in deadly sin, forasmuch as they were done in deadly sin, they may never quicken: for certes thing that never had life may never quicken: and nevertheless, albeit so that they avail not to have the life perdurable, yet avail they to abridge the pain of hell, or else to get temporal riches, or else that God will the rather illumine or light the heart of the sinful

[1] Confounded.
[2] Again.
[3] Those.
[4] True.
[5] That.

man to have repentance; and eke they avail for to use[1] a man to do good works, that the fiend have the less power of his soul. And thus the courteous Lord Jesus Christ ne will that no good work that men do be lost, for in somewhat it shall avail. But forasmuch as the good works that men do while they be in good life be all amortised[2] by sin following, and eke since all the good works that men do while they be in deadly sin be utterly dead, as for to have the life perdurable, well may that man, that no good work ne doth, sing that new French song, *J'ai tout perdu—mon temps et mon labour.* For certes sin bereaveth a man both goodness of nature, and eke the goodness of grace. For soothly the grace of the Holy Ghost fareth like fire that may not be idle; for fire faileth anon as it forletteth[3] his working, and right so grace faileth anon as it forletteth his working. Then loseth the sinful man the goodness of glory, that only is hight[4] to good men that labour and work well. Well may he be sorry then, that oweth all his life to God, as long as he hath lived, and also as long as he shall live, that no goodness ne hath to pay with his debt to God, to whom he oweth all his life: for trust well he shall give accounts, as saith Saint Bernard, of all the goods that have been given him in this present life, and how he hath them disponded, insomuch that there shall not perish an hair of his head, nor a moment of an hour shall not perish of his time, that he ne shall give thereof a reckoning.

[1] Accustom.

[2] Killed.

[3] Giveth over.

[4] Promised.

The fifth thing that ought to move a man to contrition, is remembrance of the passion that our Lord Jesus Christ suffered for our sins. For as saith Saint Bernard, 'While that I live, I shall have remembrance of the travails that our Lord Jesus Christ suffered in preaching, his weariness in travelling, his temptations when he fasted, his long wakings[1] when he prayed, his tears when he wept for pity of good people: the woe and the shame, and the filth that men said to him: of the foul spitting that men spat in his face, of the buffets that men gave him: of the foul mouths and of the foul repreves[2] that men said to him: of the nails with which he was nailed to the cross; and of all the remenant[3] of his passion, that he suffered for man's sin, and nothing for his guilt.' And here ye shall understand that in man's sin is every manner order, or ordinance, turned up so down. For it is sooth that God, and reason, and sensuality, and the body of man be ordained, that each of these four things should have lordship over that other: as thus; God should have lordship over reason, and reason over sensuality, and sensuality over the body of man. But soothly when man sinneth, all this order, or ordinance, is turned up so down; and therefore then, forasmuch as reason of man ne will not be subject nor obeisant[4] to God, that is his lord by right, therefore loseth it the lordship that it should have over sensuality, and eke over the body of man; and why? for sensuality rebelleth then against reason:

and by that way loseth reason the lordship over sensuality, and over the body. For right as reason is rebel to God, right so is sensuality rebel to reason, and the body also. And certes this disordinance, and this rebellion, our Lord Jesus Christ abought[1] upon his precious body full dear: and hearken in which wise. Forasmuch as reason is rebel to God, therefore is man worthy to have sorrow, and to be dead. This suffered our Lord Jesus Christ for man, after that he had been betrayed of his disciple, and distrained[2] and bound, so that his blood burst out at every nail of his hands, as saith Saint Augustine. And furthermore, forasmuch as reason of man will not daunt sensuality when it may, therefore is man worthy to have shame: and this suffered our Lord Jesus Christ for man, when they spat in his visage. And furtherover, forasmuch as the caitiff[3] body of man is rebel both to reason and to sensuality, therefore it is worthy the death: and this suffered our Lord Jesus Christ upon the cross, whereas there was no part of his body free, without great pain and bitter passion. And all this suffered our Lord Jesus Christ that never forfaited;[4] and thus said he, 'Too much am I pained for things that I never deserved, and too much defouled for shendship[5] that man is worthy to have.' And therefore may the sinful man well say, as saith St Bernard, 'Accursed be the bitterness of my sin, for which there must be suffered so much bitterness.' For certes, after the diverse discord-

[1] Suffered for.

[2] Constrained.

[3] Wretched.

[4] Misdid.

[5] Punishment.

ance of our wickedness was the passion of Jesus Christ ordained in diverse things; as thus. Certes sinful man's soul is betrayed of the devil, by covetousness of temporal prosperity; and scorned by deceit, when he chooseth fleshly delights; and yet it is tormented by impatience of adversity, and bespit by servage [1] and subjection of sin ; and at the last it is slain finally. For this discordance of sinful man, was Jesus Christ first betrayed ; and after that was he bound, that came for to unbind us of sin and of pain. Then was he bescorned, that only should have been honoured in all things and of all things. Then was his visage, that ought to be desired to be seen of all mankind, (in which visage angels desire to look,) villainously bespit. Then was he scourged that nothing had trespassed; and finally, then was he crucified and slain. Then were accomplished the words of Isaiah : 'He was wounded for our misdeeds, and defouled for our felonies.' Now since that Jesus Christ took on himself the pain of all our wickednesses, much ought sinful man to weep and to bewail, that for his sins God's Son of heaven should all this pain endure.

The sixth thing that should move a man to contrition is the hope of three things, that is to say, forgiveness of sin, and the gift of grace for to do well, and the glory of heaven, with which God shall guerdon [2] man for his good deeds. And forasmuch as Jesus Christ giveth us these gifts of his largeness, [3] and of his sovereign bounty, therefore is he

[1] Slavery.

[2] Reward.

[3] Liberality.

cleped, *Jesus Nazarenus Rex Judæorum.* Jesus is for to say, saviour or salvation, on whom men shall hope to have forgiveness of sins, which that is properly salvation of sins. And therefore said the angel to Joseph, 'Thou shalt clepe[1] his name Jesus, that shall save his people of their sins.' And hereof saith Saint Peter, 'There is none other name under heaven, that is given to any man, by which a man may be saved, but only Jesus.' Nazarenus is as much for to say, as flourishing, in which a man shall hope, that he that giveth him remission of sins, shall give him also grace well for to do: for in the flower is hope of fruit in time coming, and in forgiveness of sins hope of grace well to do. 'I was at the door of thine heart,' saith Jesus, 'and cleped for to enter. He that openeth to me, shall have forgiveness of his sins, and I will enter into him by my grace, and sup with him by the good works that he shall do, which works be the food of God, and he shall sup with me by the great joy that I shall give him.' Thus shall man hope, that for his works of penance God shall give him his regne,[2] as he behight[3] him in the Gospel.

Now shall man understand in which manner shall be his contrition. I say, that it shall be universal and total; this is to say, a man shall be very[4] repentant for all his sins, that he hath done in delight of his thought, for delight is perilous. For there be two manner of consentings; that one of them is cleped consenting of affection, when a

[1] Call.

[2] Kingdom.
[3] Promised.

[4] Truly.

man is moved to do sin, and then delighteth him long for to think on that sin, and his reason perceiveth it well that it is sin against the law of God, and yet his reason refraineth not his foul delight or talent, though he see well apertly,[1] that it is against the reverence of God; although his reason consent not to do that sin indeed, yet say some doctors, that such delight that dwelleth long is full perilous, albeit never so little.   And also a man should sorrow, namely for all that ever he hath desired against the law of God, with perfect consenting of his reason, for thereof is no doubt that it is deadly sin in consenting: for certes there is no deadly sin, but that it is first in man's thought, and after that in his delight, and so forth into consenting and into deed.   Wherefore I say, that many men ne repent them never of such thoughts and delights, ne never shrive[2] them of it, but only of the deed of great sins outward: wherefore I say, that such wicked delights be subtle beguilers of them that shall be damned.   Moreover man ought to sorrow for his wicked words, as well as for his wicked deeds: for certes repentance of a singular[3] sin, and not repentant of all his other sins, or else repenting him of all his other sins, and not of a singular sin, may not avail.   For certes God Almighty is all good; and therefore, either he forgiveth all, or else right nought.   And therefore saith Saint Augustine, 'I wot certainly, that God is enemy to every sinner: and how then? he that observeth[4] one sin, shall he

[1] Openly, plainly.

[2] Confess.

[3] Particular.

[4] Has regard to.

have forgiveness of the remnant of his other sins? Nay. And furtherover, contrition should be wonder sorrowful and anguishous: and therefore giveth him God plainly his mercy: and therefore when my soul was anguishous, and sorrowful within me, then had I remembrance of God, that my prayer might come to him.' Furtherover, contrition must be continual, and that man have steadfast purpose to shrive[1] him, and to amend him of his life. For soothly, while contrition lasteth, man may ever hope to have forgiveness. And of this cometh hate of sin, that destroyeth sin both in himself, and eke in other folk at his power. For which saith David, 'They that love God, hate wickedness:' for to love God, is for to love that he loveth, and hate that he hateth.

The last thing that men shall understand in contrition is this, whereof availeth contrition. I say, that contrition sometime delivereth man from sin: of which David saith; 'I say,' quod David, 'I purposed firmly to shrive me, and thou, Lord, releasedest my sin.' And right so as contrition availeth not without sad[2] purpose of shrift[3] and satisfaction, right so little worth is shrift or satisfaction without contrition. And moreover contrition destroyeth the prison of hell, and maketh weak and feeble all the strengths of the devils, and restoreth the gifts of the Holy Ghost, and of all good virtues, and it cleanseth the soul of sin, and delivereth it from the pain of hell, and from the company of the devil, and from the servage[4] of sin, and restoreth it to all

[1] Confess.

[2] Serious.
[3] Confession.

[4] Slavery.

goods spiritual, and to the company and communion of holy church. And furtherover, it maketh him that whilome[1] was son of ire, to be the son of grace: and all these things be proved by Holy Writ. And therefore he that would set his intent to these things, he were full wise: for soothly he ne should have then in all his life courage[2] to sin, but give his heart and body to the service of Jesus Christ, and thereof do him homage. For certes our Lord Jesus Christ hath spared us so benignly in our follies, that if he ne had pity on man's soul, a sorry song might we all sing.

Explicit prima pars penitentiæ; et incipit pars secunda.

The second part of penitence is confession, and that is sign of contrition. Now shall ye understand what is confession; and whether it ought needs to be done or no: and which things be covenable[3] to very[4] confession.

First shalt thou understand, that confession is very shewing of sins to the priest; this is to say very, for he must confess him of all the conditions that belong to his sin, as farforth as he can: all must be said, and nothing excused, nor hid, nor forwrapped:[5] and not avaunt him of his good works. Also, it is necessary to understand whence that sins spring, and how they increase, and which they be.

Of springing of sins saith Saint Paul in this wise: that right as by one man sin entered first into this

[1] Formerly.

[2] Mind.

[3] Suitable.

[4] True.

[5] Wrapped up, covered.

world, and through sin death, right so death entereth into all men that sin: and this man was Adam, by whom sin entered into this world, when he brake the commandment of God. And therefore he that first was so mighty, that he ne should have died, became such one that he must needs die, whether he would or no; and all his progeny in this world, that in thilk[1] manner sin, die. Look that in the estate of innocence, when Adam and Eve were naked in Paradise, and nothing ne had shame of their nakedness, how that the serpent, that was most wily of all other beasts that God had made, said to the woman, 'Why commanded God you, that ye should not eat of every tree in Paradise?' The woman answered, 'Of the fruit,' said she, 'of the trees of Paradise we feed us, but of the fruit of the tree that is in the middle of Paradise, God forbade us for to eat, ne to touch it, lest we should die.' The serpent said to the woman, 'Nay, nay, ye shall not die of death; for sooth God wot, that what day that ye eat thereof your eyes shall open, and ye shall be as gods, knowing good and harm.' 'The woman saw that the tree was good to feeding, and fair to the eyes, and delectable to the sight; she took of the fruit of the tree and did eat, and gave to her husband, and he eat; and anon the eyes of them both opened: and when they knew that they were naked, they sewed of a fig-tree leaves in manner of breeches, to hide their members.' Here may ye see, that deadly sin hath first suggestion of

[1] That same.

the fiend, as sheweth here by the adder; and afterward the delight of the flesh, as sheweth here by Eve; and after that the consenting of reason, as sheweth by Adam. For trust well, though so it were that the fiend tempted Eve, that is to say the flesh, and the flesh had delight in the beauty of the fruit defended,[1] yet certes till that reason, that is to say Adam, consented to the eating of the fruit, yet stood he in the state of innocence. Of thilk[2] Adam took we thilk sin original; from him fleshly descended be we all, and engendered of vile and corrupt matter: and when the soul is put in our bodies, right anon is contracted original sin; and that that was erst[3] but only pain of concupiscence, is afterward both pain and sin: and therefore we be all born sons of wrath, and of damnation perdurable,[4] if ne were baptism that we receive, which benimeth[5] us the culpe:[6] but forsooth the pain dwelleth with us as to temptation, which pain hight[7] concupiscence. This concupiscence, when it is wrongfully disposed or ordained in man, it maketh him covet, by covetise of flesh, fleshly sin by sight of his eyes, as to earthly things, and also covetise of highness by pride of heart.

Now as to speak of the first covetise, that is concupiscence, after the law of our members, that were lawfully made, and by rightful judgment of God, I say, forasmuch as a man is not obedient to God, that is his Lord, therefore is his heart to him disobedient through concupiscence, which is called

[1] Forbidden.

[2] That.

[3] At first.

[4] Everlasting.

[5] Taketh away.

[6] Fault.

[7] Is called

nourishing of sin, and occasion of sin. Therefore, all the while that a man hath within him the pain of concupiscence, it is impossible but he be tempted sometimes, and moved in his flesh to sin. And this thing may not fail as long as he liveth. It may well wax feeble by virtue of baptism, and by the grace of God through penitence; but fully ne shall it never quench, that he ne shall sometimes be moved in himself, but if he were refrained by sickness, or malefice[1] of sorcery, or cold drinks. For lo, what saith Saint Paul?—'The flesh coveteth against the spirit, and the spirit against the flesh: they be so contrary and so strive, that a man may not alway do as he would.' The same Saint Paul, after his great penance, in water and in land; in water by night and by day, in great peril, and in great pain; in land, in great famine and thirst, cold and clotheless, and once stoned almost to death; yet said he, 'Alas! I caitiff[2] man, who shall deliver me from the prison of my caitiff body?' And Saint Jerome, when he long time had dwelled in desert, where he had no company but of wild beasts; where he had no meat but herbs, and water to his drink, nor no bed but the naked earth, wherefore his flesh was black as an Ethiopian for heat, and nigh destroyed for cold: yet said he, that the burning of lechery boiled in all his body. Wherefore I wot well sikerly[3] that they be deceived that say they be not tempted in their bodies. Witness Saint James, that said that every wight is tempted in his own con-

[1] Enchantment.

[2] Wretched.

[3] Surely.

science; that is to say, that each of us hath matter and occasion to be tempted of the nourishing of sin that is in his body. And therefore saith Saint John the Evangelist, 'If we say that we be without sin, we deceive ourselves, and truth is not in us.'

Now shall ye understand in what manner sin waxeth and increaseth in man. The first thing is that nourishing of sin, of which I spake before, that is concupiscence: and after that cometh suggestion of the devil, this is to say, the devil's bellows, with which he bloweth in man the fire of concupiscence: and after that a man bethinketh him, whether he will do or no that thing to which he is tempted. And then if a man withstand and weive[1] the first enticing of his flesh, and of the fiend, then it is no sin: and if so be he do not, then feeleth he anon a flame of delight, and then it is good to beware and keep him well, or else he will fall anon to consenting of sin, and then will he do it, if he may have time and place. And of this matter saith Moses by the devil, in this manner, 'The fiend saith, I will chase and pursue man by wicked suggestion, and I will hent[2] him by moving and stirring of sin, and I will depart my prize, or my prey, by deliberation, and my lust[3] shall be accomplished in delight; I will draw my sword in consenting, (for certes, right as a sword departeth[4] a thing in two pieces, right so consenting departeth God from man:) and then will I slay him with my hand in deed of sin.' Thus saith the fiend; for certes then is a man all dead in

[1] Refuse.
[2] Seize.
[3] Pleasure.
[4] Divideth.

soul; and thus is sin accomplished, by temptation, by delight, and by consenting: and then is the sin actual.

Forsooth sin is in two manners, either it is venial, or deadly sin. Soothly, when a man loveth any creature more than Jesus Christ our Creator, then it is deadly sin: and venial sin it is, if a man love Jesus Christ less than him ought. Forsooth the deed of this venial sin is full perilous, for it amenuseth[1] the love that man should have to God, more and more. And therefore if a man charge himself with many such venial sins, certes but if so be that he sometimes discharge him of them by shrift,[2] they may well lightly amenuse in him all the love that he hath to Jesus Christ: and in this wise skippeth venial sin into deadly sin. For certes the more that a man chargeth his soul with venial sins, the more he is inclined to fall into deadly sin. And therefore let us not be negligent to discharge us of venial sins. For the proverb saith, that many small make a great. And hearken this example: A great wave of the sea cometh sometimes with so great a violence, that it drencheth[3] the ship: and the same harm do sometimes the small drops of water that enter through a little crevice in the thurrok,[4] and in the bottom of the ship, if men be so negligent that they discharge them not by time. And therefore, although there be difference betwixt these two causes of drenching, algates[5] the ship is dreint.[6] Right so fareth it sometime of deadly sin,

[1] Lesseneth.

[2] Confession.

[3] Drowneth.

[4] Hold.

[5] Nevertheless.

[6] Drowned.

and of anoious[1] venial sins, when they multiply in man so greatly that thilk[2] worldly things that he loveth, through which he sinneth venially, is as great in his heart as the love of God, or more: and therefore the love of everything that is not beset[3] in God, nor done principally for God's sake, although that a man love it less than God, yet is it venial sin; and deadly sin is, when the love of anything weigheth in the heart of man as much as the love of God, or more. Deadly sin, as saith Saint Augustine, is, when a man turneth his heart from God, which that is very sovereign bounty,[4] that may not change, and giveth his heart to thing that may change and flit: and certes that is every thing, save God of heaven. For sooth is, that if a man give his love, which that he oweth to God with all his heart, unto a creature, certes as much of his love as he giveth to the same creature, so much he bereaveth from God, and therefore doth he sin: for he that is debtor to God, yieldeth not to God all his debt, that is to say, all the love of his heart. ✗

Now, since man understandeth generally which is venial sin, then is it covenable[5] to tell specially of sins, which that many a man peradventure deemeth them no sins, and shriveth[6] him not of the same, and yet nevertheless they be sins soothly, as these clerks write; this is to say, at every time that man eateth and drinketh more than sufficeth to the sustenance of his body, in certain he doth sin; eke when he speaketh more than it needeth, he doth

[1] Hurtful.

[2] Those.

[3] Placed, employed.

[4] Goodness.

[5] Suitable.

[6] Confesseth.

sin; eke when he hearkeneth not benignly the complaint of the poor; eke when he is in health of body, and will not fast when other folk fast, without cause reasonable; eke when he sleepeth more than needeth, or when he cometh by that encheson[1] too late to church, or to other works of charity; eke when he useth his wife without sovereign desire of engendrure, to the honour of God, or for the intent to yield his wife his debt of his body; eke when he will not visit the sick, or the prisoner, if he may; eke if he love wife, or child, or other worldly thing, more than reason requireth; eke if he flatter or blandise[2] more than him ought for any necessity; eke if he amenuse[3] or withdraw the alms of the poor; eke if he apparaile[4] his meat more deliciously than need is, or eat it too hastily by likerousness;[5] eke if he talk vanities in the church, or at God's service, or that he be a teller of idle words of folly or villainy, for he shall yield accounts of it at the day of doom; eke when he behighteth[6] or assureth to do things that he may not perform; eke when that he by lightness of folly missayeth or scorneth his neighbour; eke when he hath any wicked suspicion of thing, where he ne wot of it no soothfastness: these things, and more without number, be sins, as saith Saint Augustine. Now shall ye understand, that albeit so that no earthly man may eschew all venial sins, yet may he refrain him, by the burning love that he hath to our Lord Jesus Christ, and by prayer and confession, and other

[1] Occasion.

[2] Fawn.

[3] Lessen.

[4] Make ready.

[5] Gluttony.

[6] Promiseth.

good works, so that it shall but little grieve. For as saith Saint Augustine, 'If a man love God in such manner that all that ever he doth is in the love of God, or for the love of God verily, for he burneth in the love of God, look how much that one drop of water, which falleth into a furnace full of fire, annoyeth or grieveth the burning of the fire, in like manner annoyeth or grieveth a venial sin unto that man which is steadfast and perfect in the love of our Saviour Jesus Christ.' Furthermore, men may also refrain and put away venial sin, by receiving worthily the precious body of Jesus Christ; by receiving eke of holy water; by alms-deed; by general confession of *Confiteor* at mass, and at prime, and at compline,[1] and by blessing of bishops and priests, and by other good works.   .

[1] Even-song.

De septem peccatis mortalibus.

Now it is behovely[2] to tell which be deadly sins, that is to say, chieftains of sins; forasmuch as all they run in one leash, but in diverse manners. Now be they cleped chieftains, forasmuch as they be chief, and of them spring all other sins. The root of these sins, then, is pride, the general root of all harms. For of this root spring certain branches: as ire, envy, accidie[3] or sloth, avarice or covetousness, (to common understanding,) gluttony, and lechery: and each of these chief sins hath his branches and his twigs, as shall be declared in their chapters following.

[2] Profit-able.

[3] Negli-gence.

De superbia.

And though so be that no man knoweth utterly the number of the twigs, and of the harms that come of pride, yet will I shew a part of them, as ye shall understand. There is inobedience, avaunting, hypocrisy, despite, arrogance, impudence, swelling of heart, insolence, elation, impatience, strife, contumacy, presumption, irreverence, pertinacity, vain-glory, and many other twigs that I cannot declare. Inobedient, is he that disobeyeth for despite to the commandments of God, and to his sovereigns, and to his ghostly[1] father. Avaunter,[2] is he that boasteth of the harm or of the bounty that he hath done. Hypocrite, is he that hideth to shew him such as he is, and sheweth him to seem such as he is not. Despiteous, is he that hath disdain of his neighbour, that is to say, of his even[3] Christian, or hath despite to do that him ought to do. Arrogant, is he that thinketh that he hath those bounties in him that he hath not, or weeneth that he should have them by his deserving, or else that deemeth that he be that he is not. Impudent, is he that for his pride hath no shame of his sins. Swelling of heart, is when man rejoiceth him of harm that he hath done. Insolent, is he that despiseth in his judgment all other folk, as in regard of his value, of his conning,[4] of his speaking, and of his bearing.[5] Elation, is when he ne may neither suffer to have master nor fellow. Impatient,

[1] Spiritual.
[2] Boaster.
[3] Equal.
[4] Knowledge.
[5] Behaviour.

is he that will not be taught, nor undernome[1] of his vice, and by strife werrieth[2] truth wittingly, and defendeth his folly. *Contumax*, is he that through his indignation is against every authority or power of them that be his sovereigns. Presumption, is when a man undertaketh an enterprise that him ought not to do, or else that he may not do, and this is called surquedrie.[3] Irreverence, is when man doth not honour there as him ought to do, and waiteth to be reverenced. Pertinacity, is when man defendeth his folly, and trusteth too much in his own wit. Vain-glory, is for to have pomp, and delight in his temporal highness, and glory him in his worldly estate. Jangling,[4] is when man speaketh too much before folk, and clappeth as a mill, and taketh no keep what he saith.

And yet there is a privy species of pride, that waiteth first to be saluted ere he will salute, all be he less worthy than that other is; and eke he waiteth to sit, or to go above him in the way, or kiss the pax, or be incensed, or go to offering before his neighbour, and such semblable[5] things, against his duty peradventure, but that he hath his heart and his intent, in such a proud desire, to be magnified and honoured before the people.

Now be there two manner of prides; that one of them is within the heart of a man, and that other is without. Of such soothly these foresaid things, and more than I have said, appertain to pride that is within the heart of man; and there be other

1 Taken up.
2 Makes war.
3 Over-weening conceit.
4 Prating.
5 Like.

species of pride that be without: but nevertheless, that one of these species of pride is sign of that other, right as the gay levesell[1] at the tavern is sign of the wine that is in the cellar. And this is in many things: as in speech and countenance, and outrageous array of clothing; for certes, if there had been no sin in clothing, Christ would not so soon have noted and spoken of the clothing of that rich man in the gospel. And, as Saint Gregory saith, that precious clothing is culpable for the dearth[2] of it, and for his softness, and for his strangeness and disguising, and for the superfluity, or for the inordinate scantness of it, alas! may not a man see as in our days the sinful costly array of clothing, and namely in too much superfluity, or else in too disordinate scantness?

As to the first sin in superfluity of clothing, which that maketh it so dear, to the harm of the people, not only the cost of the embroidering, the disguising, indenting, or barring,[3] ounding,[4] paling,[5] winding, or banding, and semblable waste of cloth in vanity; but there is also the costly furring in their gowns, so much punching of chisel to make holes, so much dagging[6] of shears, with the superfluity in length of the foresaid gowns, trailing in the dung and in the mire, on horse and eke on foot, as well of man as of woman, that all that trailing is verily (as in effect) wasted, consumed, threadbare, and rotten with dung, rather than it is given to the poor, to great damage of the foresaid poor folk, and

[1] Arbour.

[2] Dearness.

[3] Striping.
[4] Waving.
[5] Perpendicular striping.

[6] Slitting.

that in sundry wise: this is to say, the more that cloth is wasted, the more must it cost to the poor people for the scarceness; and furtherover, if so be that they would give such punched and dagged clothing to the poor people, it is not convenient to wear for their estate, nor sufficient to boot[1] their necessity, to keep them from the distemperance of the firmament. Upon that other side, to speak of the horrible disordinate scantness of clothing, as be these cutted slops or hanselines,[2] that through their shortness cover not the shameful members of man, to wicked intent; alas! some of them shew the boss and the shape of the horrible swollen members, that seem like to the malady of hernia, in the wrapping of their hosen, and eke the buttocks of them behind, that fare as it were the hinder part of a she-ape in the full of the moon. And moreover the wretched swollen members that they shew through disguising, in departing[3] of their hosen in white and red, seemeth that half their shameful privy members were flain.[4] And if so be that they depart their hosen in other colours, as is white and blue, or white and black, or black and red, and so forth; then seemeth it, as by variance of colour, that the half part of their privy members be corrupt by the fire of Saint Anthony, or by cancre, or other such mischance. Of the hinder part of their buttocks it is full horrible for to see, for certes in that part of their body there as they purge their stinking ordure, that foul part shew they to the

[1] Profit.

[2] Kind of breeches.

[3] Dividing.

[4] Flayed.

people proudly in despite of honesty,[1] which honesty that Jesus Christ and his friends observed to shew in their life. Now as to the outrageous array of women, God wot, that though the visages of some of them seem full chaste and debonaire,[2] yet notify they, in their array of attire, likerousness and pride. I say not that honesty in clothing of man or woman is uncovenable,[3] but certes the superfluity or disordinate scarcity of clothing is reprovable. Also the sin of ornament, or of apparel, is in things that appertain to riding, as in too many delicate horses, that be holden for delight, that be so fair, fat, and costly; and also in many a vicious knave,[4] that is sustained because of them; in curious harness, as in saddles, cruppers, peitrels,[5] and bridles, covered with precious cloth and rich, barred and plated of gold and silver. For which God saith by Zechariah the prophet, 'I will confound the riders of such horses.' These folk take little regard of the riding of God's Son of heaven, and of his harness, when he rode upon the ass, and had no other harness but the poor clothes of his disciples, nor we read not that ever he rode on any other beast. I speak this for the sin of superfluity, and not for honesty, when reason it requireth. And moreover, certes pride is greatly notified in holding of great meinie,[6] when they be of little profit or of right no profit, and namely when that meinie is felonous[7] and damageous to the people by hardiness of high lordship, or by way of office; for certes, such

[1] Decency.

[2] Becoming.

[3] Unsuitable.

[4] Servant.

[5] Breastplates.

[6] Servants.

[7] Violent.

lords sell then their lordship to the devil of hell, when they sustain the wickedness of their meinie. Or else, when these folk of low degree, as they that hold hostelries, sustain theft of their hostellers, and that is in many manner of deceits: that manner of folk be the flies that follow the honey, or else the hounds that follow the carrion. Such foresaid folk strangle spiritually their lordships; for which thus saith David the prophet, 'Wicked death may come unto these lordships, and God give that they may descend into hell, all down; for in their houses is iniquity and shrewedness,[1] and not God of heaven.' And certes, but if they do amendment, right as God gave his benison[2] to Laban by the service of Jacob, and to Pharaoh by the service of Joseph, right so God will give his malison[3] to such lordships as sustain the wickedness of their servants, but they come to amendment. Pride of the table appeareth eke full oft; for certes rich men be cleped to feasts, and poor folk be put away and rebuked; and also in excess of divers meats and drinks, and namely such manner bake-meats and dish-meats burning of wild fire, and painted and castled with paper, and semblable[4] waste, so that it is abuse to think. And eke in too great preciousness of vessel,[5] and curiosity of minstrelsy, by which a man is stirred more to the delights of luxury, if so be that he set his heart the less upon our Lord Jesus Christ, it is a sin; and certainly the delights might be so great in this case, that a man might lightly fall by them into deadly

[1] Cursedness.

[2] Blessing.

[3] Curse.

[4] Similar.

[5] Plate.

sin. The species that sourden[1] of pride, soothly
when they sourden of malice imagined, advised, and
forecast, or else of usage, be deadly sins, it is no
doubt. And when they sourden by frailty unadvised
suddenly, and suddenly withdraw again, all be they
grievous sins, I guess that they be not deadly.
Now might men ask, whereof that pride sourdeth
and springeth. I say that sometimes it springeth of
the goods of nature, sometimes of the goods of fortune, and sometimes of the goods of grace. Certes
the goods of nature stand only in the goods of the
body or of the soul. Certes the goods of the body
be health of body, strength, deliverness,[2] beauty,
gentry,[3] franchise;[4] the goods of nature of the soul
be good wit, sharp understanding, subtle ingine,[5]
virtue natural, good memory; goods of fortune be
riches, high degrees of lordships, and praisings of
the people; goods of grace be science, power to
suffer spiritual travail, benignity, virtuous contem-
plation, withstanding of temptation, and semblable
things: of which foresaid goods, certes it is a great
folly a man to pride him in any of them all. Now
as for to speak of goods of nature, God wot that
sometimes we have them in nature as much to our
damage as to our profit. As for to speak of health
of body, truly it passeth full lightly, and also it is
full oft encheson[6] of sickness of the soul: for God
wot, the flesh is a great enemy to the soul: and
therefore the more that the body is whole, the more
be we in peril to fall. Eke for to pride him in his

[1] Rise.

[2] Activity.

[3] High birth.

[4] Freedom.

[5] Intellect.

[6] Occasion.

strength of body, it is a great folly: for certes the flesh coveteth against the spirit: and ever the more strong that the flesh is, the sorrier may the soul be: and over all, this strength of body, and worldly hardiness, causeth full oft to many man peril and mischance. Also to have pride of gentry is right great folly: for oft time the gentry of the body benimeth[1] the gentry of the soul: and also we be all of one father and of one mother: and all we be of one nature rotten and corrupt, both rich and poor. Forsooth one manner gentry is for to praise, that apparelleth[2] man's courage[3] with virtues and moralities, and maketh him Christ's child; for trust well, that over what man that sin hath mastery, he is a very churl[4] to sin.

Now be there general signs of gentleness; as eschewing of vice and ribaldry, and servage of sin, in word, and in work and countenance, and using virtue, as courtesy, and cleanness, and to be liberal; that is to say, large by measure; for that that passeth measure is folly and sin. Another is to remember him of bounty that he of other folk hath received. Another is to be benign to his subjects; wherefore saith Seneca, 'There is nothing more covenable[5] to a man of high estate than debonairty[6] and pity: and therefore these flies that men clepe bees, when they make their king, they choose one that hath no prick wherewith he may sting.' Another is, man to have a noble heart and a diligent, to attain to high virtuous things. Now certes, a

[1] Takes away.
[2] Adorns.
[3] Spirit.
[4] Slave.
[5] Suitable.
[6] Courtesy.

man to pride him in the goods of grace, is eke an outrageous folly: for those gifts of grace that should have turned him to goodness and to medicine, turneth him to venom and confusion, as saith Saint Gregory. Certes also, whoso prideth him in the goodness of fortune, he is a great fool: for sometimes is a man a great lord by the morrow, that is a caitiff and a wretch ere it be night: and sometimes the riches of a man is cause of his death: and sometimes the delights of a man be cause of grievous malady, through which he dieth. Certes the commendation of the people is full false and brittle for to trust; this day they praise, to-morrow they blame. God wot, desire to have commendation of the people hath caused death to many a busy man.

Remedium Superbiæ.

Now since that so is that ye have understood what is pride, and which be the species of it, and how men's pride sourdeth[1] and springeth, now ye shall understand which is the remedy against it. Humility or meekness is the remedy against pride; that is a virtue through which a man hath very[2] knowledge of himself, and holdeth of himself no dainty, nor no price, as in regard of his deserts, considering ever his frailty. Now be there three manner of humilities; as humility in heart, and another in the mouth, and the third in works. The humility in heart is in four manners: that one is,

[1] Riseth.

[2] True.

when a man holdeth himself as nought worth before God of heaven: the second is, when he despiseth no other man: the third is, when he ne recketh not though men hold him nought worth: and the fourth is, when he is not sorry of his humiliation. Also the humility of mouth is in four things; in temperate speech; in humility of speech; and when he confesseth with his own mouth that he is such as he thinketh that he is in his heart: another is, when he praiseth the bounty[1] of another man and nothing thereof amenuseth.[2] Humility eke in works is in four manners. The first is, when he putteth other men before him; the second is, to choose the lowest place of all; the third is, gladly to assent to good counsel; the fourth is, to stand gladly to the award of his sovereign, or of him that is higher in degree: certain this is a great work of humility.

De Invidia.

After pride will I speak of the foul sin of envy, which that is, after the word of the philosopher, sorrow of other men's prosperity; and after the word of Saint Augustine, it is sorrow of other men's weal, and joy of other men's harm. This foul sin is platly[3] against the Holy Ghost. Albeit so that every sin is against the Holy Ghost, yet nevertheless, forasmuch as bounty appertaineth properly to the Holy Ghost, and envy cometh properly of malice, therefore it is properly against the bounty of

[1] Goodness.
[2] Lesseneth.
[3] Plainly.

the Holy Ghost. Now hath malice two species, that is to say, hardiness of heart in wickedness, or else the flesh of man is so blind, that he considereth not that he is in sin, or recketh not that he is in sin; which is the hardiness of the devil. That other species of envy is, when that a man werrieth[1] truth, when he wot that it is truth, and also when he werrieth the grace of God that God hath given to his neighbour: and all this is by envy. Certes then is envy the worst sin that is; for soothly all other sins be sometimes only against one special virtue: but certes envy is against all manner virtues and all goodness; for it is sorry of all bounty of his neighbour: and in this manner it is diverse from all other sins; for well unnethe[2] is there any sin that it ne hath some delight in himself, save only envy, that ever hath in himself anguish and sorrow. The species of envy be these. There is first sorrow of other men's goodness and of their prosperity; and prosperity ought to be kindly[3] matter of joy; then is envy a sin against kind. The second species of envy is joy of other men's harm; and that is properly like to the devil, that ever rejoiceth him of man's harm. Of these two species cometh backbiting; and this sin of backbiting or detracting hath certain species, as thus: some man praiseth his neighbour by a wicked intent, for he maketh alway a wicked knot at the last end: alway he maketh a *but* at the last end, that is dign[4] of more blame than is worth all the praising. The second species

[1] Fights against.

[2] Scarcely.

[3] Naturally.

[4] Worthy.

is, that if a man be good, or doth or saith a thing to good intent, the backbiter will turn all that goodness up so down to his shrewd[1] intent. The third is to amenuse[2] the bounty of his neighbour. The fourth species of backbiting is this, that if men speak goodness of a man, then will the backbiter say, 'Parfay, such a man is yet better than he;' in dispraising of him that men praise. The fifth species is this, for to consent gladly to hearken the harm that men speak of other folk. This sin is full great, and aye increaseth after the wicked intent of the backbiter. After backbiting cometh grutching[3] or murmurance, and sometimes it springeth of impatience against God, and sometimes against man. Against God it is when a man grutcheth against the pain of hell, or against poverty, or loss of catel,[4] or against rain or tempest, or else grutcheth that shrews[5] have prosperity, or else that good men have adversity: and all these things should men suffer patiently, for they come by the rightful judgment and ordinance of God. Sometimes cometh grutching of avarice, as Judas grutched against the Magdalene, when she anointed the head of our Lord Jesus Christ with her precious ointment. This manner murmuring is such as when man grutcheth of goodness that himself doth, or that other folk do of their own catel. Sometimes cometh murmur of pride, as when Simon the Pharisee grutched against the Magdalene, when she approached to Jesus Christ and wept at his feet for her sins: and some-

[1] Ill-natured.
[2] Lessen.
[3] Murmuring.
[4] Chattels, goods.
[5] Evil-disposed persons.

times it sourdeth[1] of envy, when men discover a man's harm that was privy, or beareth him on hand thing that is false. Murmur also is oft among servants, that grutchen when their sovereigns bid them do lawful things; and forasmuch as they dare not openly withsay the commandment of their sovereigns, yet will they say harm and grutch and murmur privily for very despite; which words they call the devil's *Pater noster*, though so be that the devil had never *Pater noster*, but that lewd[2] folk give it such a name. Sometimes it cometh of ire or privy hate, that nourisheth rancour in the heart, as afterward I shall declare. Then cometh eke bitterness of heart, through which bitterness every good deed of his neighbour seemeth to him bitter and unsavoury. Then cometh discord that unbindeth all manner of friendship. Then cometh scorning of his neighbour, all[3] do he never so well. Then cometh accusing, as when a man seeketh occasion to annoy his neighbour, which is like the craft of the devil, that waiteth both day and night to accuse us all. Then cometh malignity, through which a man annoyeth his neighbour privily if he may, and if he may not, algate[4] his wicked will shall not let,[5] as for to burn his house privily, or poison him, or slay his beasts, and semblable[6] things.

Remedium Invidiæ.

Now will I speak of the remedy against this foul

[1] Riseth.

[2] Ignorant.

[3] Although.

[4] However.

[5] Stop.

[6] Similar.

sin of envy. First is the love of God principally, and loving of his neighbour as himself: for soothly that one ne may not be without that other. And trust well, that in the name of thy neighbour thou shalt understand the name of thy brother; for certes all we have one father fleshly, and one mother; that is to say, Adam and Eve; and also one father spiritual, that is to say, God of heaven. Thy neighbour art thou bound for to love, and will him all goodness, and therefore saith God, 'Love thy neighbour as thyself;' that is to say, to salvation both of life and soul. And moreover thou shalt love him in word, and in benign amonesting[1] and chastising, and comfort him in his annoys, and pray for him with all thy heart. And in deed thou shalt love him in such wise that thou shalt do to him in charity as thou wouldest that it were done to thine own person: and therefore thou ne shalt do him no damage in wicked word, nor harm in his body, nor in his catel,[2] nor in his soul by enticing of wicked example. Thou shalt not desire his wife, nor none of his things. Understand eke that in the name of neighbour is comprehended his enemy: certes man shall love his enemy for the commandment of God, and soothly thy friend thou shalt love in God. I say thine enemy shalt thou love for God's sake, by his commandment: for if it were reason that man should hate his enemy, forsooth God n'old[3] not receive us to his love that be his enemies. Against three manner of wrongs, that his

[1] Advising.

[2] Property.

[3] Would not.

enemy doth to him, he shall do three things, as thus: against hate and rancour of heart, he shall love him in heart: against chiding and wicked words, he shall pray for his enemy: against the wicked deed of his enemy, he shall do him bounty.[1] For Christ saith, 'Love your enemies, and pray for them that speak you harm, and for them that chase and pursue you: and do bounty to them that hate you.' Lo, thus commandeth us our Lord Jesus Christ to do to our enemies: forsooth nature driveth us to love our friends, and parfay[2] our enemies have more need of love than our friends, and they that more need have, certes to them shall men do goodness. And certes in that deed have we remembrance of the love of Jesus Christ that died for his enemies: and inasmuch as that love is more grievous to perform, so much is more great the merit, and therefore the loving of our enemy hath confounded the venom of the devil. For right as the devil is confounded by humility, right so is he wounded to the death by the love of our enemy: certes then is love the medicine that casteth out the venom of envy from man's heart.

De Ira.

After envy will I declare of the sin of ire: for soothly whoso hath envy upon his neighbour, anon commonly will find him matter of wrath in word or in deed against him to whom he hath envy. And

[1] Good.

[2] In faith.

as well cometh ire of pride as of envy, for soothly he that is proud or envious is lightly[1] wroth.

This sin of ire, after the describing of Saint Augustine, is wicked will to be avenged by word or by deed. Ire, after the philosopher, is the fervent blood of man quickened in his heart, through which he would harm to him that he hateth: for certes the heart of man by enchaufing[2] and moving of his blood waxeth so troubled, that it is out of all manner judgment of reason. But ye shall understand that ire is in two manners, that one of them is good, and that other is wicked. The good ire is by jealousy of goodness, through the which man is wroth with wickedness, and against wickedness. And therefore saith the wise man, that ire is better than play. This ire is with debonairtee,[3] and it is wroth without bitterness: not wroth against the man, but wroth with the misdeed of the man: as saith the prophet David, *Irascimini, et nolite peccare.* Now understand that wicked ire is in two manners, that is to say, sudden ire or hasty ire without advisement and consenting of reason; the meaning and the sense of this is, that the reason of a man ne consenteth not to that sudden ire, and then it is venial. Another ire is that is full wicked, that cometh of felony of heart, advised and cast before, with wicked will to do vengeance, and thereto his reason consenteth: and soothly this is deadly sin. This ire is so displeasant to God, that it troubleth his house, and chaseth the Holy Ghost

[1] Easily.

[2] Heat.

[3] Gentleness.

out of man's soul, and wasteth and destroyeth that likeness of God, that is to say the virtue that is in man's soul, and putteth in him the likeness of the devil, and benimeth[1] the man from God, that is his rightful Lord. This ire is a full great pleasance to the devil, for it is the devil's furnace, that he enchaufeth[2] with the fire of hell. For certes right so as fire is more mighty to destroy earthly things than any other element, right so ire is mighty to destroy all spiritual things. Look how that fire of small gledes,[3] that be almost dead under ashes, will quicken again when they be touched with brimstone; right so ire will evermore quicken again when it is touched with pride that is covered in man's heart. For certes fire ne may not come out of nothing, but if it were first in the same thing naturally: as fire is drawn out of flints with steel. And right so as pride is many times matter of ire, right so is rancour norice[4] and keeper of ire. There is a manner tree, as saith Saint Isidore, that when men make a fire of the said tree, and cover the coals of it with ashes, soothly the fire thereof will last all a year or more: and right so fareth it of rancour, when it is once conceived in the heart of some men, certes it will last peradventure from one Easter day until another Easter day, or more. But certes the same man is full far from the mercy of God all that while.

In this foresaid devil's furnace there forge three shrews:[5] pride, that aye bloweth and increaseth the

[1] Takes away.

[2] Heateth.

[3] Burning coals.

[4] Nurse.

[5] Evil ones.

fire by chiding and wicked words: then standeth envy, and holdeth the hot iron upon the heart of man, with a pair of long tongs of long rancour: and then standeth the sin of contumely or strife and cheste,[1] and battereth and forgeth by villain's reprovings. Certes this cursed sin annoyeth both to the man himself, and eke his neighbour. For soothly almost all the harm or damage that any man doth to his neighbour cometh of wrath: for certes, outrageous wrath doth all that ever the foul fiend willeth or commandeth him; for he ne spareth neither for our Lord Jesus Christ, nor his sweet mother; and in his outrageous anger and ire, alas! alas! full many one at that time feeleth in his heart full wickedly, both of Christ and also of all his hallows.[2] Is not this a cursed vice? Yes certes. Alas! it benimmeth[3] from man his wit and his reason, and all his debonaire[4] life spiritual, that should keep his soul. Certes it benimmeth also God's due lordship (and that is man's soul) and the love of his neighbours; it striveth also all day against truth; it reaveth[5] him the quiet of his heart, and subverteth his soul.

Of ire come these stinking engendrures: first, hate, that is old wrath; discord, through which a man forsaketh his old friend that he hath loved full long; and then cometh war, and every manner of wrong that a man doth to his neighbour in body or in catel.[6] Of this cursed sin of ire cometh eke manslaughter. And understand well that homicide

[1] Debate.

[2] Holiness.

[3] Taketh away.

[4] Gentle.

[5] Robbeth.

[6] Goods.

(that is, manslaughter) is in diverse wise. Some manner of homicide is spiritual, and some is bodily. Spiritual manslaughter is in six things. First, by hate, as saith Saint John, 'He that hateth his brother is an homicide.' Homicide is also by back-biting; of which backbiters saith Solomon, that they have two swords, with which they slay their neighbours; for soothly as wicked it is to benime[1] of him his good name as his life. Homicide is also in giving of wicked counsel by fraud, as for to give counsel to areise[2] wrongful customs and talages;[3] of which saith Solomon, ' A lion roaring, and a bear hungry, be like to cruel lords, in withholding or abridging of the hire or of the wages of servants, or else in usury, or in withdrawing of the alms of poor folk.' For which the wise man saith, ' Feed him that almost dieth for hunger; for soothly but if thou feed him thou slayest him.' And all these be deadly sins. Bodily manslaughter is when thou slayest him with thy tongue in other manner, as when thou commandest to slay a man, or else givest counsel to slay a man. Manslaughter in deed is in four manners. That one is by law, right as a justice damneth him that is culpable to the death: but let the justice beware that he do it rightfully, and that he do it not for delight to spill blood, but for keeping of righteousness. Another homicide is done for necessity, as when a man slayeth another in his defence, and that he ne may none otherwise escape from his own death: but certain,

[1] Take away.

[2] Raise.
[3] Taxes.

and[1] he may escape without slaughter of his adversary, he doth sin, and he shall bear penance as for deadly sin. Also if a man by cas[2] or adventure shoot an arrow or cast a stone, with which he slayeth a man, he is an homicide. And if a woman by negligence overlieth her child in her sleep, it is homicide and deadly sin. Also when a man disturbeth conception of a child, and maketh a woman barren by drinks of venomous herbs, through which she may not conceive, or slayeth her child by drinks, or else putteth certain material thing in her secret place to slay her child, or else doth unkind[3] sin, by which man, or woman, sheddeth his nature in place there as a child may not be conceived: or else if a woman hath conceived, and hurteth herself, and by that mishap the child is slain, yet is it homicide. What say we eke of women that murder their children for dread of worldly shame? Certes, it is an horrible homicide. Eke if a man approach to a woman by desire of lechery, through which the child is perished ; or else smiteth a woman wittingly, through which she loseth her child ; all these be homicides, and horrible deadly sins. Yet come there of ire many more sins, as well in word as in thought and in deed; as he that arretteth[4] upon God, or blameth God of the thing of which he is himself guilty; or despiseth God and all his hallows,[5] as do these cursed hazarders[6] in divers countries. This cursed sin do they, when they feel in their heart full wickedly of God and of his hallows: also

[1] If.

[2] Chance.

[3] Unnatural.

[4] Imputeth.

[5] Holiness.

[6] Gamblers.

when they treat unreverently the sacrament of the altar, that sin is so great, that unneth[1] it may be released, but that the mercy of God passeth all his works, it is so great, and he so benign. Then cometh also of ire attry[2] anger, when a man is sharply amonested[3] in his shrift[4] to leave his sin, then will he be angry, and answer hokerly[5] and angrily, to defend or excuse his sin by unsteadfastness of his flesh; or else he did it for to hold company with his fellows; or else he saith the fiend enticed him; or else he did it for his youth; or else his complexion is so courageous that he may not forbear; or else it is his destiny, he saith, unto a certain age; or else he saith it cometh him of gentleness of his ancestors, and semblable[6] things. All these manner of folk so wrap them in their sins, that they ne will not deliver themselves; for soothly no wight that excuseth himself wilfully of his sin, may not be delivered of his sin, till that he meekly beknoweth[7] his sin. After this then cometh swearing, that is express against the commandment of God: and that befalleth often of anger and of ire. God saith, 'Thou shalt not take the name of thy Lord God in idle.' Also our Lord Jesus Christ saith by the word of Saint Matthew, 'Ne shall ye not swear in all manner, neither by heaven, for it is God's throne: nor by earth, for it is the bench of his feet: nor by Jerusalem, for it is the city of a great King: nor by thine head, for thou ne mayst not make an hair white nor black:' but he saith, 'Be your word

[1] Scarcely.

[2] Pernicious.
[3] Admonished.
[4] Confession.
[5] Frowardly.

[6] Like.

[7] Confesseth.

yea, yea, nay, nay; and what that is more, it is of evil.' Thus saith Christ. For Christ's sake swear not so sinfully, in dismembering of Christ, by soul, heart, bones, and body: for certes it seemeth that ye think that the cursed Jews dismembered him not enough, but ye dismember him more. And if so be that the law compel you to swear, then rule you after the law of God in your swearing, as saith Jeremiah, 'Thou shalt keep three conditions; thou shalt swear in truth, in doom,[1] and in righteousness.' This is to say, thou shalt swear sooth; for every leasing[2] is against Christ; for Christ is very truth: and think well this, that every great swearer, not compelled lawfully to swear, the plague shall not depart from his house while he useth unlawful swearing. Thou shalt swear also in doom, when thou art constrained by the doomsman to witness a truth. Also thou shalt not swear for envy, neither for favour, nor for meed, but only for righteousness, and for declaring of truth to the honour and worship of God, and to the aiding and helping of thine even[3] Christian. And therefore every man that taketh God's name in idle, or falsely sweareth with his mouth, or else taketh on him the name of Christ, to be called a Christian man, and liveth against Christ's living and his teaching: all they take God's name in idle. Look also what saith Saint Peter, *Actuum* iv., *Non est aliud nomen sub cœlo*, &c. There is no other name (saith Saint Peter) under heaven given to men, in which they may be saved;

[1] Judgment.

[2] Lie.

[3] Fellow.

that is to say, but the name of Jesus Christ. Take keep eke how precious is the name of Jesus Christ, as saith Saint Paul, *ad Philippenses* ii., *In nomine Jesu*, &c.; that in the name of Jesus every knee of heavenly creature, or earthly, or of hell, should bow; for it is so high and so worshipful, that the cursed fiend in hell should tremble for to hear it named. Then seemeth it that men that swear so horribly by his blessed name, that they despise it more boldly than did the cursed Jews, or else the devil, that trembleth when he heareth his name.

Now certes, since that swearing (but if it be lawfully done) is so highly defended,[1] much worse is for to swear falsely, and eke needless.

What say we eke of them that delight them in swearing, and hold it a genterie[2] or manly deed to swear great oaths? And what of them that of very usage ne cease not to swear great oaths, all be the cause not worth a straw? Certes this is horrible sin. Swearing suddenly without avisement[3] is also a great sin. But let us go now to that horrible swearing of adjuration and conjuration, as do these false enchanters and necromancers in basins full of water, or in a bright sword, in a circle, or in a fire, or in a shoulder-bone of a sheep: I cannot say, but that they do cursedly and damnably against Christ, and all the faith of holy church.

What say we of them that believe on divinals,[4] as by flight or by noise of birds or of beasts, or by

[1] Forbidden.

[2] Gentility.

[3] Consideration.

[4] Divination.

sort[1] of geomancy,* by dreams, by chirking of doors, or creaking of houses, by gnawing of rats, and such manner wretchedness? Certes, all these things be defended[2] by God and holy church, for which they be accursed, till they come to amendment, that on such filth set their belief. Charms for wounds, or for maladies of men or of beasts, if they take any effect, it may be peradventure that God suffereth it, for folk should give the more faith and reverence to his name.

Now will I speak of leasings,[3] which generally is false significance of word, in intent to deceive his even[4] Christian. Some leasing is, of which there cometh no advantage to no wight; and some leasing turneth to the profit and ease of a man, and to the damage of another man. Another leasing is, for to save his life or his catel.[5] Another leasing cometh of delight for to lie, in which delight they will forge a long tale, and paint it with all circumstances, where all the ground of the tale is false. Some leasing cometh, for he will sustain his word: and some leasing cometh of recklessness without avisement,[6] and semblable[7] things.

Let us now touch the vice of flattery, which ne cometh not gladly, but for dread, or for covetousness. Flattery is generally wrongful praising. Flatterers be the devil's nourices,[8] that nourish his children with milk of losengerie.[9] Forsooth Solomon saith, that flattery is worse than detraction: for sometimes

* 'Geomancy:' Divination by figures made on the earth.

---

[1] Chance.

[2] Forbidden.

[3] Falsehoods.

[4] Fellow.

[5] Goods.

[6] Consideration.

[7] Similar.

[8] Nurses.

[9] Flattery.

detraction maketh an haughty man be the more humble, for he dreadeth detraction, but certes flattery maketh a man to enhaunce[1] his heart and his countenance. Flatterers be the devil's enchanters, for they make a man to ween himself be like that he is not like. They be like to Judas, that betrayed God; and these flatterers betray man to sell him to his enemy, that is the devil. Flatterers be the devil's chaplains, that ever sing *Placebo*. I reckon flattery in the vices of ire: for oft time if a man be wroth with another, then will he flatter some wight to sustain him in his quarrel.

Speak we now of such cursing as cometh of irous[2] heart. Malison generally may be said every manner power of harm: such cursing bereaveth man the regne[3] of God, as saith Saint Paul. And oft time such cursing wrongfully returneth again to him that curseth, as a bird returneth again to his own nest. And over all thing men ought eschew to curse their children, and to give to the devil their engendrure, as far forth as in them is: certes it is a great peril and a great sin.

Let us then speak of chiding and reproving, which be full great wounds in man's heart, for they unsow the seams of friendship in man's heart: for certes unnethe[4] may a man be plainly accorded with him that he hath openly reviled, reproved, and slandered: this is a full grisly[5] sin, as Christ saith in the Gospel. And take ye keep now, that he that reproveth his neighbour, either he reproveth him by some harm

[1] Lift up.

[2] Passionate.

[3] Kingdom.

[4] Scarcely.

[5] Dreadful.

¹ Leper.

² Command.

³ Leprosy.

⁴ Whoremonger.

of pain that he hath upon his body, as 'Mesel,'[1] 'Crooked harlot,' or by some sin that he doth. Now if he reprove him by harm of pain, then turneth the reproof to Jesus Christ: for pain is sent by the righteous sond[2] of God, and by his sufferance, be it meselrie,[3] or maim, or malady: and if he reprove him uncharitably of sin, as, 'Thou holour,'[4] 'Thou drunken harlot,' and so forth, then appertaineth that to the rejoicing of the devil, which ever hath joy that men do sin. And certes, chiding may not come but out of a villain's heart, for after the abundance of the heart speaketh the mouth full oft. And ye shall understand, that look by any way, when any man chastiseth another, that he beware from chiding or reproving: for truly, but he beware, he may full lightly quicken the fire of anger and of wrath, which he should quench: and peradventure slayeth him, that he might chastise with benignity. For, as saith Solomon, the amiable tongue is the tree of life; that is to say, of life spiritual. And soothly, a dissolute tongue slayeth the spirit of him that reproveth, and also of him which is reproved. Lo, what saith Saint Augustine, 'There is nothing so like the devil's child as he which oft chideth.' A servant of God behoveth not to chide. And though that chiding be a villain's thing betwixt all manner folk, yet it is certes most uncovenable[5] between a man and his wife, for there is never rest. And therefore saith Solomon, 'An house that is uncovered in rain and dropping, and a

⁵ Unbecoming.

chiding wife be like.' A man which is in a dropping house in many places, though he eschew the dropping in one place, it droppeth on him in another place; so fareth it by a chiding wife; if she chide him not in one place, she will chide him in another: and therefore, 'Better is a morsel of bread with joy, than an house filled full of delices[1] with chiding,' saith Solomon. And Saint Paul saith, 'O ye women, be ye subjects to your husbands, as you behoveth in God; and ye men love your wives.'

Afterward speak we of scorning, which is a wicked sin, and namely, when he scorneth a man for his good works: for certes such scorners fare like the foul tod,[2] that may not endure to smell the sweet savour of the vine, when it flourisheth. These scorners be parting fellows with the devil, for they have joy when the devil winneth, and sorrow if he loseth. They be adversaries to Jesus Christ, for they hate that he loveth; that is to say, salvation of soul.

Speak we now of wicked counsel, for he that wicked counsel giveth is a traitor, for he deceiveth him that trusteth in him. But nevertheless, yet is wicked counsel first against himself: for, as saith the wise man, every false living hath this property in himself, that he that will annoy another man, he annoyeth first himself. And men shall understand, that man shall not take his counsel of false folk, nor of angry folk, or grievous folk, nor of folk that love specially their own profit, nor of too much worldly folk, namely, in counselling of man's soul.

[1] Delights.

[2] Fox.

Now cometh the sin of them that make discord among folk, which is a sin that Christ hateth utterly; and no wonder is, for he died for to make concord. And more shame do they to Christ than did they that him crucified: for God loveth better that friendship be among folk, than he did his own body, which that he gave for unity. Therefore be they likened to the devil, that ever is about to make discord.

Now cometh the sin of double tongue; such as speak fair before folk, and wickedly behind; or else they make semblant as though they spake of good intention, or else in game and play, and yet they speak of wicked intent.

Now cometh betraying of counsel, through which a man is defamed: certes unnethe[1] may he restore the damage. Now cometh menace, that is an open folly: for he that oft menaceth, he threateneth more than he may perform full oft time. Now come idle words, that be without profit of him that speaketh the words, and eke of him that hearkeneth the words: or else idle words be those that be needless, or without intent of natural profit. And albeit that idle words be sometimes venial sin, yet should men doubt them, for we shall give reckoning of them before God. Now cometh jangling,[2] that may not come without sin: and, as saith Solomon, it is a sign of apert[3] folly. And therefore a philosopher said, when a man asked him how that he should please the people, he answered, 'Do many good works, and

[1] Scarcely.

[2] Prating.

[3] Open.

speak few janglings.' After this cometh the sin of japers,[1] that be the devil's apes, for they make folk to laugh at their japerie, as folk do at the gaudes[2] of an ape: such japes defendeth[3] Saint Paul. Look how that virtuous words and holy comfort them that travail in the service of Christ, right so comfort the villain's words, and the knacks[4] of japers, them that travail in the service of the devil. These be the sins of the tongue, that come of ire, and other sins many more.

Remedium Iræ.

The remedy against ire is a virtue that cleped is mansuetude, that is debonairtee:[5] and eke another virtue, that men clepe patience or sufferance.

Debonairtee withdraweth and refraineth the stirrings and movings of man's courage[6] in his heart, in such manner that they ne skip not out by anger nor ire. Sufferance suffereth sweetly all the annoyance and the wrong that is done to man outward. Saint Jerome saith this of debonairtee, that it doth no harm to no wight, nor saith: nor for no harm that men do nor say, he ne chafeth not against reason. This virtue sometimes cometh of nature; for, as saith the philosopher, a man is a quick thing, by nature debonaire, and tractable to goodness: but when debonairtee is informed of grace, then it is the more worth.

Patience is another remedy against ire, and is a virtue that suffereth sweetly every man's goodness,

[1] Buffoons.
[2] Tricks.
[3] Forbids.
[4] Tricks.
[5] Gentleness.
[6] Spirit.

and is not wroth for no harm that is done to him. The philosopher saith, that patience is the virtue that suffereth debonairly[1] all the outrage of adversity, and every wicked word. This virtue maketh a man like to God, and maketh him God's own child, as saith Christ. This virtue discomfiteth thine enemies. And therefore saith the wise man, 'If thou wilt vanquish thine enemy, see thou be patient.' And thou shalt understand, that a man suffereth four manner of grievances in outward things, against the which four he must have four manner of patiences.

The first grievance is of wicked words. That grievance suffered Jesus Christ, without grutching,[2] full patiently, when the Jews despised him and reproved him full oft. Suffer thou therefore patiently, for the wise man saith, 'If thou strive with a fool, though the fool be wroth, or though he laugh, algate[3] thou shalt have no rest.' That other grievance outward is to have damage of thy catel.[4] Thereagainst suffered Christ full patiently, when he was despoiled of all that he had in this life, and that was not but his clothes. The third grievance is a man to have harm in his body. That suffered Christ full patiently in all his passion. The fourth grievance is in outrageous labour in works: wherefore I say, that folk that make their servants to travail too grievously, or out of time, as in holy days, soothly they do great sin. Hereagainst suffered Christ full patiently, and taught us patience, when he bare upon his blessed shoulders the cross, upon which he should suffer despiteous death.   Here may men learn to be patient; for certes not only Christian men be patient for love of Jesus Christ, and for guerdon[1] of the blissful life that is perdurable,[2] but certes the old pagans, that never were christened, commended and used the virtue of patience.

A philosopher upon a time, that would have beaten his disciple for his great trespass, for which he was greatly moved, and brought a yard[3] to beat the child, and when this child saw the yard, he said to his master, 'What think ye to do?' 'I will beat thee,' said the master, 'for thy correction.' 'Forsooth,' said the child, 'ye ought first correct yourself, that have lost all your patience for the offence of a child.' 'Forsooth,' said the master all weeping, 'thou sayest sooth: have thou the yard, my dear son, and correct me for mine impatience.' Of patience cometh obedience, through which a man is obedient to Christ, and to all them to which he ought to be obedient in Christ.   And understand well, that obedience is perfect, when that a man doth gladly and hastily, with good heart entirely, all that he should do.   Obedience generally, is to perform hastily the doctrine of God, and of his sovereigns, to which him ought to be obedient in all righteousness.

De Accidia.

After the sin of wrath, now will I speak of the

[1] Recompence.
[2] Everlasting.
[3] Rod.

sin of accidie[1] or sloth: for envy blindeth the heart of a man, and ire troubleth a man, and accidie maketh him heavy, thoughtful, and wraw.[2] Envy and ire make bitterness in heart, which bitterness is mother of accidie; and benimeth[3] him the love of all goodness; then is accidie the anguish of a troubled heart. And Saint Augustine saith, ' It is annoy of goodness and annoy of harm.' Certes this is a damnable sin, for it doth wrong to Jesus Christ, inasmuch as it benimeth the service that men should do to Christ with all diligence, as saith Solomon: but accidie doth no such diligence. He doth all thing with annoy, and with wrawness, slackness, and excusation, with idleness and unlust.[4] For which the book saith, ' Accursed be he that doth the service of God negligently.' Then is accidie enemy to every estate of man. For certes the estate of man is in three manners: either it is the estate of innocence, as was the estate of Adam, before that he fell into sin, in which estate he was held to work, as in herying[5] and adoring of God. Another estate is the estate of sinful men: in which estate men be held to labour in praying to God, for amendment of their sins, and that he would grant them to rise out of their sins. Another estate is the estate of grace, in which estate he is held to works of penitence: and certes, to all these things is accidie enemy and contrary, for he loveth no business at all. Now certes this foul sin of accidie is eke a full great enemy to the livelihood of the body; for it ne hath no purveyance against

[1] Indolence.

[2] Peevish.

[3] Taketh from.

[4] Unwillingness.

[5] Praising.

temporal necessity; for it forsleutheth,[1] forsluggeth, and destroyeth all goods temporal by recklessness.

The fourth thing is that accidie is like them that be in the pain of hell, because of their sloth and of their heaviness: for they that be damned be so bound that they may neither do well nor think well. Of accidie cometh first, that a man is annoyed and cumbered to do any goodness, and that maketh that God hath abomination of such accidie, as saith Saint John.

Now cometh sloth, that will not suffer no hardness nor no penance: for soothly, sloth is so tender and so delicate, as saith Solomon, that he will suffer no hardness nor penance, and therefore he shendeth[2] all that he doth. Against this rotten sin of accidie and sloth should men exercise themselves, and use themselves to do good works, and manly and virtuously catch courage well to do, thinking that our Lord Jesus Christ requireth every good deed, be it never so little. Usage of labour is a great thing; for it maketh, as saith Saint Bernard, the labourer to have strong arms and hard sinews; and sloth maketh them feeble and tender. Then cometh dread for to begin to work any good works: for certes, he that inclineth to sin him thinketh it is too great an emprise for to undertake the works of goodness, and casteth in his heart that the circumstances of goodness be so grievous and so chargeant[3] for to suffer, that he dare not undertake to do works of goodness, as saith Saint Gregory.

[1] Loses by sloth.

[2] Ruins.

[3] Burdensome.

Now cometh wanhope, that is despair of the mercy of God, that cometh sometimes of too much outrageous sorrow, and sometimes of too much dread, imagining that he hath done so much sin, that it would not avail him though he would repent him and forsake sin: through which despair or dread, he abandoneth all his heart to every manner sin, as saith Saint Augustine. Which damnable sin, if it continue unto his end, it is cleped[1] the sin of the Holy Ghost. This horrible sin is so perilous, that he that is despaired, there n'is no felony, nor no sin, that he doubteth[2] for to do, as shewed well by Judas. Certes, above all sins then, is this sin most displeasant and most adversary to Christ. Soothly he that despaireth him is like to the coward champion recreant, that flieth without need. Alas! alas! needless is he recreant, and needless despaired. Certes the mercy of God is ever ready to the penitent person, and is above all his works. Alas! cannot a man bethink him on the Gospel of Saint Luke, chap. xv., whereas Christ saith, that as well shall there be joy in heaven upon a sinful man that doth penitence, as upon ninety and nine rightful men that need no penitence? Look further, in the same Gospel, the joy and the feast of the good man that had lost his son, when his son was returned with repentance to his father. Can they not remember them also (as saith Saint Luke, chap. xxiii.) how that the thief that was hung beside Jesus Christ said, 'Lord, remember on me when

[1] Called.

[2] Hesitates.

thou comest in thy regne?'[1] 'Forsooth,' said Christ, 'I say to thee, To-day shalt thou be with me in Paradise.' Certes, there is none so horrible sin of man, that ne may in his life be destroyed by penitence, through virtue of the passion and of the death of Christ. Alas! what needeth man then to be despaired, since that his mercy is so ready and large? Ask and have. Then cometh somnolence, that is sluggy slumbering, which maketh a man heavy and dull in body and in soul, and this sin cometh of sloth: and certes the time that by way of reason man should not sleep is by the morrow,[2] but if there were cause reasonable. For soothly in the morrow tide is most covenable[3] to a man to say his prayers, and for to think on God, and to honour God, and to give alms to the poor that come first in the name of Jesus Christ. Lo, what saith Solomon? 'Whoso will by the morrow awake to seek me, he shall find me.' Then cometh negligence or recklessness that recketh of nothing. And though that ignorance be mother of all harms, certes negligence is the norice.[4] Negligence ne doth no force,[5] when he shall do a thing, whether he do it well or badly.

The remedy of these two sins is, as saith the wise man, that he that dreadeth God, spare not to do that him ought to do; and he that loveth God, he will do diligence to please God by his works, and abandon himself, with all his might, well for to do. Then cometh idleness, that is the gate of all harms. An idle man is like to a place that hath no walls;

[1] Kingdom.

[2] Morning.

[3] Suitable.

[4] Nurse.
[5] Cares not.

thereas devils may enter on every side, or shoot at him at discovert[1] by temptation on every side. This idleness is the thurrok[2] of all wicked and villain's thoughts, and of all jangles, trifles, and all ordure. Certes heaven is given to them that will labour, and not to idle folk. Also David saith, 'They ne be not in the labour of men, ne they shall not be whipped with men,' that is to say, in purgatory. Certes then seemeth it they shall be tormented with the devil in hell, but if they do penance.

Then cometh the sin that men clepe *tarditas*, as when a man is latered[3] or tarried ere he will turn to God: and certes that is a great folly. He is like him that falleth in the ditch, and will not arise. And this vice cometh of false hope, that thinketh that he shall live long, but that hope faileth full oft.

Then cometh lachesse,[4] that is, he that when he beginneth any good work, anon he will forlete[5] it and stint,[6] as do they that have any wight to govern, and ne take of him no more keep, anon as they find any contrary or any annoy. These be the new shepherds, that let their sheep wittingly go run to the wolf that is in the briars, and do no force[7] of their own governance. Of this cometh poverty and destruction, both of spiritual and temporal things. Then cometh a manner coldness, that freezeth all the heart of man. Then cometh undevotion, through which a man is so blunt, as saith Saint Bernard, and hath such languor in his soul, that he may neither read-nor sing in holy church, nor hear nor think of

[1] Uncovered.
[2] Hold.
[3] Delayed.
[4] Slackness.
[5] Leave.
[6] Stop.
[7] Care not.

no devotion, nor travail with his hands in no good work, that it n'is to him unsavoury and all apalled. Then waxeth he sluggish and slumbry, and soon will he be wroth, and soon is inclined to hate and to envy. Then cometh the sin of worldly sorrow such as is cleped *tristitia*, that slayeth a man, as saith Saint Paul. For certes such sorrow worketh to the death of the soul and of the body also, for thereof cometh that a man is annoyed of his own life. Wherefore such sorrow shorteneth the life of many a man, ere that his time is come by way of kind.[1]

[1] Nature.

Remedium Accidiæ.

Against this horrible sin of accidie,[2] and the branches of the same, there is a virtue that is called *fortitudo* or strength, that is, an affection through which a man despiseth noyous[3] things. This virtue is so mighty and so vigorous, that it dare withstand mightily, and wrestle against the assaults of the devil, and wisely keep himself from perils that be wicked; for it enhaunseth[4] and enforceth[5] the soul, right as accidie abateth and maketh it feeble: for this *fortitudo* may endure with long sufferance the travails that be covenable.[6]

This virtue hath many species. The first is cleped magnanimity, that is to say, great courage. For certes there behoveth great courage against accidie, lest that it swallow the soul by the sin of sorrow, or destroy it with wanhope.[7] Certes, this virtue maketh

[2] Negligence.

[3] Hurtful.

[4] Lifteth up.
[5] Strengtheneth.

[6] Suitable.

[7] Despair.

folk to undertake hard and grievous things by their own will, wisely and reasonably. And forasmuch as the devil fighteth against man more by queintise[1] and sleight than by strength, therefore shall a man withstand him by wit, by reason, and by discretion. Then be there the virtues of faith, and hope in God and in his saints, to achieve and accomplish the good works, in the which he purposeth firmly to continue. Then cometh surety or sickerness, and that is when a man ne doubteth no travail in time coming of the good works that he hath begun. Then cometh magnificence, that is to say, when a man doth and performeth great works of goodness that he hath begun, and that is the end why that men should do good works. For in the accomplishing of good works lieth the great guerdon. Then is there constance, that is stableness of courage, and this should be in heart by steadfast faith, and in mouth, and in bearing, in chere,[2] and in deed. Eke there be more special remedies against accidie, in divers works, and in consideration of the pains of hell and of the joys of heaven, and in trust of the grace of the Holy Ghost, that will give him might to perform his good intent.

De Avaritia.

After accidie will I speak of avarice, and of covetousness. Of which sin Saint Paul saith, 'The root of all harms is covetousness.' For soothly, when the heart of man is confounded in itself and

[1] Cunning.

[2] Demeanour.

troubled, and that the soul hath lost the comfort of God, then seeketh he an idle solace of worldly things.

Avarice, after the description of Saint Augustine, is a likerousness[1] in heart to have earthly things. Some other folk say that avarice is for to purchase[2] many earthly things, and nothing to give to them that have need. And understand well, that avarice standeth not only in land or catel,[3] but sometimes in science and in glory, and in every manner outrageous thing is avarice. And the difference between avarice and covetousness is this: covetousness is for to covet such things as thou hast not; and avarice is to withhold and keep such things as thou hast, without rightful need. Soothly this avarice is a sin that is full damnable, for all holy writ curseth it, and speaketh against it, for it doth wrong to Jesus Christ; for it bereaveth him the love that men to him owe, and turneth it backward against all reason, and maketh that the avaricious man hath more hope in his catel than in Jesus Christ, and doth more observance in keeping of his treasure than he doth in the service of Jesus Christ. And therefore saith Saint Paul, that an avaricious man is the thraldom of idolatry.

What difference is there betwixt an idolater and an avaricious man, but that an idolater peradventure ne hath not but one maumet[4] or two, and the avaricious man hath many? for certes every florin in his coffer is his maumet. And

[1] Greediness.
[2] Acquire.
[3] Goods.
[4] Idol.

certes the sin of maumetrie is the first that God defended in the ten commandments, as beareth witness Exodus, cap. xx., 'Thou shalt have no false gods before me, nor thou shalt make to thee no graven thing.' Thus is an avaricious man, that loveth his treasure before God, an idolater. And through this cursed sin of avarice and covetousness cometh these hard lordships, through which men be distrained by tallages,[1] customs, and carriages, more than their duty or reason is: and eke take they of their bondmen amercements,[2] which might more reasonably be called extortions than amercements. Of which amercements, or ransoming of bondmen, some lords' stewards say that it is rightful, forasmuch as a churl hath no temporal thing that it ne is his lord's, as they say. But certes these lordships do wrong that bereave their bondmen things that they never gave them. *Augustinus de Civitate Dei*, lib. ix. Sooth is that the condition of thraldom, and the first cause of thraldom, was for sin, (Genesis v.)

Thus may ye see, that the guilt deserved thraldom, but not nature. Wherefore those lords ne should not too much glorify them in their lordships, since that they by natural condition be not lords of their thralls, but that thraldom came first by the desert of sin. And furtherover, thereas[3] the law saith that temporal goods of bondfolk be the goods of their lord, yea, that is for to understand the goods of the emperor to defend them in their right,

[1] Taxes.
[2] Fines.
[3] Whereas.

but not to rob them nor to reave them. Therefore saith Seneca, 'The prudent should live benignly with the thrall. Those that thou clepest thy thralls, be God's people: for humble folk be Christ's friends; they be contubernial[1] with the Lord thy king.'

Think also, that of such seed as churls spring, of such seed spring lords; as well may the churl be saved as the lord. The same death that taketh the churl, such death taketh the lord. Wherefore I rede,[2] do right so with thy churl as thou wouldest that thy lord did with thee, if thou were in his plight. Every sinful man is a churl to sin; I rede thee, thou lord, that thou rule thee in such wise that thy churls rather love thee than dread thee. I wot well that there is degree above degree, as reason is, and skill is, that men do their devoir there as it is due: but certes extortion, and despite of your underlings, is damnable.

And furthermore understand well, that these conquerors or tyrants make full oft thralls of them that be born of as royal blood as be they that them conquer. This name of thraldom was never erst[3] couth,[4] till that Noah said that his son Ham should be thrall to his brethren for his sin. What say we then of them that pille[5] and do extortions to holy church? Certes the sword that men give first to a knight when he is new dubbed, signifieth that he should defend holy church, and not rob it nor pille it: and whoso doth is traitor to Christ. As saith

[1] Familiar.

[2] Advise.

[3] Before.

[4] Known.

[5] Pillage.

Saint Augustine, 'Those be the devil's wolves, that strangle the sheep of Jesus Christ, and do worse than wolves: for soothly, when the wolf hath full his womb, he stinteth to strangle sheep; but soothly, the pillers[1] and destroyers of holy church's goods ne do not so, for they ne stint never to pill.' Now as I have said, since so is that sin was first cause of thraldom, then is it thus, that at the time that all this world was in sin, then was all this world in thraldom and in subjection: but certes, since the time of grace came, God ordained that some folk should be more high in estate and in degree, and some folk more low, and that each should be served in his estate and his degree. And therefore in some countries there as they be thralls, when they have turned them to the faith, they make their thralls free out of thraldom: and therefore certes the lord oweth to his man, that the man oweth to the lord. The Pope clepeth himself servant of the servants of God. But forasmuch as the estate of holy church ne might not have been, nor the common profit might not have been kept, nor peace nor rest in earth, but if God had ordained that some men have higher degree and some men lower; therefore was sovereignty ordained to keep, and maintain, and defend her underlings or her subjects in reason, as farforth as it lieth in her power, and not to destroy them nor confound. Wherefore I say, that those lords that be like wolves, that devour the possessions or the catel[2] of poor folk wrongfully, without mercy

[1] Robbers.

[2] Goods.

or measure, they shall receive by the same measure that they have measured to poor folk the mercy of Jesus Christ, but they it amend. Now cometh deceit betwixt merchant and merchant. And thou shalt understand, that merchandise is in two manners, that one is bodily, and that other is ghostly:[1] that one is honest and lawful, and that other is dishonest and unlawful. The bodily merchandise, that is lawful and honest, is this: that thereas God hath ordained that a regne[2] or a country is sufficient to himself, then it is honest and lawful that of the abundance of this country men help another country that is needy: and therefore there must be merchants to bring from one country to another their merchandise. That other merchandise, that men haunt with fraud, and treachery, and deceit, with leasings,[3] and false oaths, is right cursed and damnable. Spiritual merchandise is properly simony, that is, attentive desire to buy thing spiritual, that is, thing which appertaineth to the sanctuary of God and to the cure of the soul. This desire, if so be that a man do his diligence to perform it, albeit that his desire ne take none effect, yet it is to him a deadly sin: and if he be ordered[4] he is irregular. Certes simony is cleped of Simon Magus, that would have bought for temporal catel[5] the gift that God had given by the Holy Ghost to Saint Peter and to the apostles: and therefore understand ye, that both he that selleth and he that buyeth things spiritual be called simoniacs, be it by catel, be it by procuring,

[1] Spiritual.

[2] Kingdom.

[3] Lies.

[4] In holy orders.

[5] Goods.

or by fleshly prayer of his friends, fleshly friends or spiritual friends, fleshly in two manners, as by kindred or other friends: soothly, if they pray for him that is not worthy and able, it is simony, if he take the benefice; and if he be worthy and able, there is none. That other manner is, when man, or woman, prayeth for folk to advance them only for wicked fleshly affection which they have unto the persons, and that is foul simony, But certes in service, for which men give things spiritual unto their servants, it must be understood that the service must be honest, or else not, and also that it be without bargaining, and that the person be able. For, as saith Saint Damascen, all the sins of the world, at regard[1] of this sin, be as thing of nought, for it is the greatest sin that may be after the sin of Lucifer and of Antichrist: for by this sin God forloseth the church and the soul, which he bought with his precious blood, by them that give churches to them that be not dign,[2] for they·put in thieves, that steal the souls of Jesus Christ, and destroy his patrimony. By such undign priests and curates, have lewd[3] men less reverence of the sacraments of holy church: and such givers of churches put the children of Christ out, and put into churches the devil's own sons: they sell the souls that lambs should keep to the wolf, which strangleth them: and therefore shall they never have part of the pasture of lambs, that is, in the bliss of heaven. Now cometh hazardry with his appertenants, as

[1] In comparison.

[2] Worthy.

[3] Ignorant.

tables[1] and raffles,[2] of which cometh deceit, false oaths, chidings, and all raving, blaspheming, and reneying[3] of God, hate of his neighbours, waste of goods, misspending of time, and sometimes manslaughter. Certes hazarders[4] ne may not be without great sin. Of avarice come eke leasings,[5] theft, false witness, and false oaths: and ye shall understand that these be great sins, and express against the commandments of God, as I have said. False witness is eke in word and in deed: in word, as for to bereave thy neighbour's good name by thy false witness, or bereave him his catel[6] or his heritage by thy false witnessing, when thou for ire, or for meed, or for envy, bearest false witness, or accusest him, or excusest thyself falsely. 'Ware ye questmongers[7] and notaries: certes for false witnessing was Susanna in full great sorrow and pain, and many another more. The sin of theft is also express against God's hest,[8] and that in two manners, temporal and spiritual: the temporal theft is, as for to take thy neighbour's catel against his will, be it by force or by sleight; be it in meting[9] or measure; by stealing; by false indictments upon him; and in borrowing of thy neighbour's catel, in intent never to pay it again, and semblable[10] things. Spiritual theft is sacrilege, that is to say, hurting of holy things, or of things sacred to Christ, in two manners: by reason of the holy place, as churches or churches' hawes,[11] (for every villain's sin, that men do in such places, may be called sacrilege, or every violence in sembla-

[1] A game.
[2] Plays with dice.
[3] Denying.
[4] Gamblers.
[5] Lies.
[6] Goods.
[7] Packers of juries.
[8] Command.
[9] Measuring.
[10] Like.
[11] Yards.

ble places;) also they that withdraw falsely the rents and rights that belong to holy church; and plainly and generally, sacrilege is to reave holy thing from holy place, or unholy thing out of holy place, or holy thing out of unholy place.

Remedium Avaritiæ.

Now shall ye understand, that relieving of avarice is misericord[1] and pity largely taken. And men might ask, why that misericord and pity are relieving of avarice; certes the avaricious man sheweth no pity nor misericord to the needful man. For he delighteth him in the keeping of his treasure, and not in the rescuing nor relieving of his even[2] Christian. And therefore speak I first of misericord. Then is misericord, as saith the philosopher, a virtue, by which the courage[3] of man is stirred by the misease of him that is miseased. Upon which misericord followeth pity, in performing and fulfilling of charitable works of mercy, helping and comforting him that is miseased. And certes this moveth a man to misericord of Jesus Christ, that he gave himself for our offence, and suffered death for misericord, and forgave us our original sins, and thereby released us from the pain of hell, and amenused[4] the pains of purgatory by penitence, and giveth us grace well to do, and at last the bliss of heaven. The species of misericord be for to lend, and eke for to give, and for to forgive and release, and for to

[1] Compassion.

[2] Fellow.

[3] Spirit.

[4] Lessened.

have pity in heart, and compassion of the mischief
of his even Christian, and also to chastise there as
need is. Another manner of remedy against avarice
is reasonable largesse:[1] but soothly, here behoveth
the consideration of the grace of Jesus Christ, and
of the temporal goods, and also of the goods perdurable that Jesus Christ gave to us, and to have
remembrance of the death which he shall receive,
he wot not when: and eke that he shall forego all
that he hath, save only that which he hath dispensed
in good works.

But forasmuch as some folk be unmeasurable, men
ought for to avoid and eschew fool-largesse, the which
men clepen[2] waste. Certes he that is fool-large,
he giveth not his catel,[3] but he loseth his catel.
Soothly, what thing that he giveth for vain-glory, as
to minstrels, and to folk that bear his renown in the
world, he hath done sin thereof, and no alms: certes
he loseth foul his good, that ne seeketh with the
gift of his good nothing but sin. He is like to an
horse that seeketh rather to drink drovy[4] or troubled
water, than for to drink water of the clear well.
And forasmuch as they give there as they should not
give, to them appertaineth that malison[5] that Christ
shall give at the day of doom to them that shall be
damned.

De Gula.

After avarice cometh gluttony, which is express
against the commandment of God. Gluttony is un-

[1] Bounty.

[2] Call.
[3] Goods.

[4] Dirty.

[5] Curse.

measurable appetite to eat or to drink: or else to do in ought to the unmeasurable appetite and disordained[1] covetousness to eat or drink. This sin corrupted all this world, as is well showed in the sin of Adam and of Eve. Look also what saith Saint Paul of gluttony: 'Many,' saith he, 'go, of which I have oft said to you, and now I say it weeping, that they be the enemies of the cross of Christ, of which the end is death, and of which their womb is their God and their glory;' in confusion of them that so serve earthly things. He that is usant[2] to this sin of gluttony, he no may no sin withstand, he must be in servage[3] of all vices, for it is the devil's horde,* there he hideth him and resteth. This sin hath many species. The first is drunkenness, that is the horrible sepulture of man's reason: and therefore when a man is drunk, he hath lost his reason: and this is deadly sin. But soothly, when that a man is not wont to strong drinks, and peradventure ne knoweth not the strength of the drink, or hath feebleness in his head, or hath travailed, through which he drinketh the more, all be he suddenly caught with drink, it is no deadly sin, but venial. The second species of gluttony is, that the spirit of a man waxeth all trouble for drunkenness, and bereaveth a man the discretion of his wit. The third species of gluttony is, when a man devoureth his meat, and hath not rightful manner of eating. The fourth is, when, through the great abundance of

* 'Horde:' A private place for keeping treasure.

[1] Disorderly.

[2] Accustomed.
[3] Slavery.

his meat, the humours in his body be distempered. The fifth is, forgetfulness by too much drinking, for which sometimes a man forgetteth by the morrow what he did over eve.

In other manner be distinct the species of gluttony, after Saint Gregory. The first is, for to eat before time. The second is, when a man getteth him too delicate meat or drink. The third is, when men take too much over measure. The fourth is, curiosity[1] with great intent to make and apparel[2] his meat. The fifth is, for to eat greedily. These be the five fingers of the devil's hand, by which he draweth folk to the sin.

Remedium Gulæ.

Against gluttony the remedy is abstinence, as saith Galen: but that I hold not meritorious, if he do it only for the health of his body. Saint Augustine will that abstinence be done for virtue, and with patience. Abstinence, saith he, is little worth, but if a man have good will thereto, and but it be enforced by patience and charity, and that men do it for God's sake, and in hope to have the bliss in heaven.

The fellows of abstinence be temperance, that holdeth the mean in all things; also shame, that escheweth all dishonesty;[3] sufficiency, that seeketh no rich meats nor drinks, nor doth no force[4] of no outrageous apparelling of meat; measure also, that restraineth by reason the unmeasurable appetite of

[1] Nicety.
[2] Prepare.
[3] Indecency.
[4] Cares not for.

eating; soberness also, that restraineth the outrage of drink; sparing also, that restraineth the delicate ease, to sit long at meat, wherefore some folk stand of their own will when they eat, because they will eat at less leisure.

De Luxuriâ.

After gluttony cometh lechery, for these two sins be so nigh cousins, that oft time they will not depart.[1] God wot this sin is full displeasant to God, for he said himself, Do no lechery. And therefore he putteth great pain against this sin. For in the old law, if a woman thrall were taken in this sin, she should be beaten with staves to the death; and if she were a gentlewoman, she should be slain with stones; and if she were a bishop's daughter, she should be burnt by God's commandment. Moreover, for the sin of lechery God dreint[2] all the world, and after that he burnt five cities with thunder and lightning, and sank them down into hell.

Now let us speak then of the said stinking sin of lechery, that men clepen avoutrie,[3] that is of wedded folk, that is to say, if that one of them be wedded, or else both. Saint John saith, that avouterers shall be in hell in a stack burning of fire and of brimstone, in fire for their lechery, in brimstone for the stench of their ordure. Certes the breaking of this sacrament is a horrible thing: it

[1] Separate.

[2] Drowned.

[3] Adultery.

was made of God himself in paradise, and confirmed by Jesus Christ, as witnesseth Saint Matthew in the Gospel, 'A man shall let[1] father and mother, and take him to his wife, and they shall be two in one flesh.' This sacrament betokeneth the knitting together of Christ and holy church. And not only that God forbade avoutrie in deed, but also he commanded that thou shouldest not covet thy neighbour's wife. In this hest, saith Saint Augustine, is forbidden all manner coveting to do lechery. Lo, what saith Saint Matthew in the Gospel, that whoso seeth a woman, to covet of his lust, he hath done lechery with her in his heart. Here may ye see, that not only the deed of this sin is forbidden, but eke the desire to do that sin. This cursed sin annoyeth grievously them that it haunt: and first to the soul, for he obligeth it to sin and to pain of death, which is perdurable; and to the body annoyeth it grievously also, for it drieth him and wasteth, and shent[2] him, and of his blood he maketh sacrifice to the fiend of hell: it wasteth eke his catel[3] and his substance. And certes, if it be a foul thing a man to waste his catel on women, yet is it a fouler thing, when that for such ordure women dispend upon men their catel and their substance. This sin, as saith the prophet, bereaveth man and woman their good fame and all their honour, and it is full pleasant to the devil: for thereby winneth he the most part of this wretched world. And right as a merchant delighteth him most in that chaffare[4]

[1] Leave.

[2] Ruins.

[3] Goods.

[4] Traffic.

which he hath most advantage and profit of, right so delighteth the fiend in this ordure.

This is that other hand of the devil, with five fingers, to catch the people to his villainy. The first finger is the fool looking of the fool woman and of the fool man, that slayeth right as the basilisk slayeth folk by venom of his sight: for the coveting of the eyes followeth the coveting of the heart. The second finger is the villain's touching in wicked manner. And therefore saith Solomon, that whoso toucheth and handleth a woman, he fareth as the man that handleth the scorpion, which stingeth and suddenly slayeth through his envenoming; or as whoso that toucheth warm pitch it shendeth his fingers. The third is foul words, which fareth like fire, which right anon burneth the heart. The fourth finger is kissing: and truly he were a great fool that would kiss the mouth of a burning oven or of a furnace; and more fools be they that kiss in villainy, for that mouth is the mouth of hell; and namely these old dotards holours,[1] which will kiss, and flicker, and busy themselves, though they may nought do. Certes they be like to hounds: for an hound when he cometh by the roser,[2] or by other bushes, though so be that he may not piss, yet will he heave up his leg and make a countenance to piss. And for that many man weeneth that he may not sin for no likerousness that he doth with his wife, truly that opinion is false: God wot a man may slay himself with his own knife, and make himself

[1] Whore-mongers.

[2] Rose-bush.

drunk of his own tun. Certes be it wife, be it child, or any worldly thing, that he loveth before God, it is his maumet,[1] and he is an idolater. A man should love his wife by discretion, patiently and attemprely,[2] and then is she as though it were his sister. The fifth finger of the devil's hand, is the stinking deed of lechery. Truly the five fingers of gluttony the fiend putteth in the womb of a man: and with his five fingers of lechery he gripeth him by the reins, for to throw him into the furnace of hell, there as they shall have the fire and the worms that ever shall last, and weeping and wailing, and sharp hunger and thirst, and grisliness of devils, which shall all-to-tread them without respite and without end. Of lechery, as I said, sourden[3] and spring divers species: as fornication, that is between man and woman which be not married, and is deadly sin, and against nature. All that is enemy and destruction to nature, is against nature. Parfay, the reason of a man eke telleth him well that it is deadly sin; forasmuch as God forbade lechery. And Saint Paul giveth them the regne[4] that n'is due to no wight but to them that do deadly sin. Another sin of lechery is, to bereave a maid of her maidenhood, for he that so doth, certes he casteth a maiden out of the highest degree that is in this present life, and bereaveth her that precious fruit that the book clepeth the hundredth fruit. I ne can say it no otherwise in English, but in Latin it hight[5] *Centesimus fructus.* Certes he that

[1] Idol.

[2] Moderately.

[3] Rise.

[4] Kingdom.

[5] Is named.

so doth is the cause of many damages and villainies, more than any man can reckon: right as he sometimes is cause of all damages that beasts do in the field, that breaketh the hedge of the closure through which he destroyeth that may not be restored: for certes no more may maidenhood be restored, than an arm that is smitten from the body may return again and wax:[1] she may have mercy, this wot I well, if that she have will to do penitence, but never shall it be but that she is corrupt. And albeit so that I have spoken somewhat of avoutrie, it is good to shew the perils that belong to avoutrie, for to eschew that foul sin. Avoutrie, in Latin, is for to say, approaching of another man's bed, through which those, that some time were one flesh, abandon their bodies to other persons. Of this sin, as saith the wise man, follow many harms: first, breaking of faith; and certes faith is the key of Christendom,[2] and when that key is broken and lorn,[3] soothly Christendom is lorn, and stands vain and without fruit. This sin also is theft, for theft generally is to reave a wight his things against his will. Certes, this is the foulest theft that may be, when that a woman stealeth her body from her husband, and giveth it to her holour to defoul it: and stealeth her soul from Christ, and giveth it to the devil: this is a fouler theft than for to break a church and steal away the chalice, for these avouterers break the temple of God spiritually, and steal the vessel of grace; that is, the body and the soul: for which

[1] Grow.

[2] Christianity.
[3] Lost.

Christ shall destroy them, as saith Saint Paul. Soothly of this theft doubted greatly Joseph, when that his lord's wife prayed him of villainy, when he said, 'Lo, my lady, how my lord hath taken to me under my ward all that he hath in this world, nor nothing is out of my power, but only ye that be his wife: and how should I then do this wickedness, and sin so horribly against God, and against my lord? God it forbid.' Alas! all too little is such truth now found. The third harm is the filth, through which they break the commandment of God, and defoul the altar of matrimonies, that is, Christ. For certes, insomuch as the sacrament of marriage is so noble and so dign,[1] so much is it the greater sin for to break it: for God made marriage in Paradise in the estate of innocency, to multiply mankind to the service of God, and therefore is the breaking thereof the more grievous, of which breaking come false heirs oft time, that wrongfully occupy folk's heritages: and therefore will Christ put them out of the regne[2] of heaven, that is heritage to good folk. Of this breaking cometh eke oft time that folk unware wed or sin with their own kindred: and namely these harlots, that haunt bordels of these foul women, that may be likened unto a common gong,[3] whereas men purge their ordure. What say we also of putours,[4] that live by the horrible sin of puterie, and constrain women to yield them a certain rent of their bodily puterie, yea, sometimes his own wife or his child, as do these bawds? certes, these

[1] Worthy.

[2] King-dom.

[3] Privy.

[4] Whore-mongers.

be cursed sins. Understand also, that avoutrie is set in the ten commandments between theft and manslaughter, for it is the greatest theft that may be, for it is theft of body and of soul, and it is like to homicide, for it carveth a-two and breaketh a-two them that first were made one flesh. And therefore by the old law of God they should be slain, but nevertheless, by the law of Jesus Christ, that is the law of pity, when he said to the woman that was found in avoutrie, and should have been slain with stones, after the will of the Jews, as was their law; 'Go,' said Jesus Christ, 'and have no more will to do sin;' soothly, the vengeance of avoutrie is awarded to the pain of hell, but if so be that it be discumbered by penitence. Yet be there more species of this cursed sin, as when that one of them is religious, or else both, or of folk that be entered into order, as sub-deacon, deacon, or priest, or hospitallers: and ever the higher that he is in order, the greater is the sin. The things that greatly agrege[1] their sin, is the breaking of their vow of chastity, when they received the order: and moreover sooth is, that holy order is chief of all the treasury of God, and is a special sign and mark of chastity, to shew that they be joined to chastity, which is the most precious life that is: and these ordered folk be specially titled to God, and of the special meinie[2] of God: for which, when they do deadly sin, they be the special traitors of God and of his people, for they live by the people to pray for

[1] Aggravate.

[2] Servants.

the people, and whiles they be such traitors their prayers avail not to the people. Priests be as angels, as by the mystery of their dignity: but forsooth Saint Paul saith, that Satan transformeth him in an angel of light. Soothly, the priest that haunteth deadly sin, he may be likened to an angel of darkness transformed into an angel of light: he seemeth an angel of light, but forsooth he is an angel of darkness. Such priests be the sons of Eli, as is shewed in the book of Kings, that they were the sons of Belial, that is, the devil. Belial is to say, without judge, and so fare they; them thinketh that they be free, and have no judge, no more than hath a free bull, that taketh which cow that him liketh in the town. So fare they by women; for right as one free bull is enough for all a town, right so is a wicked priest corruption enough for all a parish, or for all a country : these priests, as saith the book, ne cannot minister the mystery of priesthood to the people, nor they know not God, nor they hold them not apaid,[1] as saith the book, of sodden flesh that was to them offered, but they take by force the flesh that is raw. Certes, right so these shrews ne hold them not apaid of roasted flesh and sodden, with which the people feed them in great reverence, but they will have raw flesh, as folk's wives and their daughters: and certes, these women that consent to their harlotry, do great wrong to Christ and to holy church, and to all hallows,[2] and to all souls, for they bereave all these

[1] Satisfied.

[2] Holiness.

them that should worship Christ and holy church, and pray for Christian souls: and therefore have such priests, and their lemans also that consent to their lechery, the malison[1] of the court Christian, till they come to amendment. The third species of avoutrie is sometimes betwixt a man and his wife, and that is when they take no regard in their assembling but only to their fleshly delight, as saith Saint Jerome, and ne reckon of nothing but that they be assembled because they be married, all is good enough, as thinketh to them. But in such folk hath the devil power, as said the angel Raphael to Tobit, for in their assembling, they put Jesus Christ out of their heart, and give themselves to all ordure. The fourth species is of them that assemble with their kindred, or with them that be of one affinity, or else with them with which their fathers or their kindred have dealt in the sin of lechery: this sin maketh them like to hounds, that take no keep of kindred. And certes, parentele[2] is in two manners: either ghostly[3] or fleshly: ghostly is for to deal with their godsibs:[4] for right so as he that engendereth a child is his fleshly father, right so is his godfather his father spiritual: for which a woman may in no less sin assemble with her godsib than with her own fleshly brother. The fifth species is that abominable sin, of which abominable sin no man unneth[5] ought to speak nor write, nevertheless it is openly rehearsed in holy writ. This cursedness do men and women in diverse intent and in diverse manner: but though

[1] Curse.

[2] Kindred.

[3] Spiritual.

[4] God-fathers.

[5] Scarcely.

that holy writ speak of horrible sin, certes holy writ may not be defouled, no more than the sun that shineth on the mixen.[1] Another sin appertaineth to lechery, that cometh in sleeping, and this sin cometh often to them that be maidens, and eke to them that be corrupt; and this sin men call pollution, that cometh of four manners: sometimes it cometh of languishing of the body, for the humours be too rank and abundant in the body of man; sometimes of infirmity, for feebleness of the virtue retentive, as physic maketh mention; sometimes of surfeit of meat and drink; and sometimes of villain's thoughts that be enclosed in man's mind when he goeth to sleep, which may not be without sin; for which men must keep them wisely, or else may they sin full grievously.

Remedium Luxuriæ.

Now cometh the remedy against lechery, and that is generally chastity and continence, that restraineth all disordinate movings that come of fleshly talents:[2] and ever the greater merit shall he have that most restraineth the wicked enchaufing[3] or ardour of this sin; and this is in two manners: that is to say, chastity in marriage, and chastity in widowhood. Now shalt thou understand, that matrimony is lawful assembling of man and woman, that receive by virtue of this sacrament the bond through which they may not be departed[4] in all their life, that is to say, while that they live both. This, as saith the

[1] Dunghill.

[2] Desires.

[3] Heat.

[4] Divided.

book, is a full great sacrament; God made it (as I have said) in paradise, and would himself be born in marriage: and for to hallow marriage he was at a wedding, whereas he turned water into wine, which was the first miracle that he wrought in earth before his disciples. The true effect of marriage cleanseth fornication, and replenisheth holy church of good lineage, for that is the end of marriage, and changeth deadly sin into venial sin between them that be wedded, and maketh the hearts all one of them that be wedded, as well as the bodies. This is very marriage that was established by God ere that sin began, when natural law was in his right point in paradise; and it was ordained, that one man should have but one woman, and one woman but one man, as saith Saint Augustine, by many reasons.

First, for marriage is figured betwixt Christ and holy church; and another is, for a man is head of the woman; (algate[1] by ordinance it should be so;) for if a woman had more men than one, then should she have more heads than one, and that were an horrible thing before God; and also a woman might not please many folk at once: and also there should never be peace nor rest among them, for evereach of them would ask his own right. And furthermore, no man should know his own engendrure, nor who should have his heritage, and the woman should be the less beloved for the time that she were conjunct to many men.

Now cometh how that a man should bear him

[1] However.

with his wife, and namely in two things, that is to say, in sufferance and in reverence, and this shewed Christ when he first made woman. For he ne made her of the head of Adam, for she should not claim too great lordship; for there[1] as the woman hath the mastery, she maketh too much disarray; there need no examples of this, the experience that we have day by day ought enough suffice. Also certes, God ne made not woman of the foot of Adam, for she should not be holden too low, for she cannot patiently suffer: but God made woman of the rib of Adam, for woman should be fellow unto man. Man should bear him to his wife in faith, in truth, and in love; as saith Saint Paul, that a man should love his wife as Christ loved holy church, that loved it so well that he died for it: so should a man for his wife, if it were need.

Now how that a woman should be subject to her husband, that telleth Saint Peter; first in obedience. And eke, as saith the decree, a woman that is a wife, as long as she is a wife, she hath no authority to swear nor bear witness, without leave of her husband, that is her lord; algate he should be so by reason. She should also serve him in all honesty, and be attempre[2] of her array. I weet[3] well that they should set their intent to please their husbands, but not by queintise[4] of their array. Saint Jerome saith, 'Wives that be apparelled in silk and precious purple, ne may not clothe them in Jesus Christ.' Saint Gregory saith also, that no

[1] Where.

[2] Moderate.
[3] Know.
[4] Excessive trimness.

wight seeketh precious array, but only for vain-glory to be honoured the more of the people. It is a great folly, a woman to have a fair array outward, and herself to be foul inward. A wife should also be measurable in looking, in bearing, and in laughing, and discreet in all her words and her deeds, and above all worldly things, she should love her husband with all her heart, and to him be true of her body: so should every husband eke be true to his wife: for since that all the body is the husband's, so should her heart be also, or else there is betwixt them two, as in that, no perfect marriage. Then shall men understand, that for three things a man and his wife fleshly may assemble. The first is, for the intent of engendrure of children, to the service of God, for certes that is the cause final of matrimony. Another cause is, to yield each of them to other the debts of their bodies: for neither of them hath power of his own body. The third is, for to eschew lechery and villainy. The fourth is, for sooth deadly sin. As to the first, it is merito-rious: the second also; for, as saith the decree, she hath merit of chastity that yieldeth to her husband the debt of her body, yea though it be against her liking, and the lust of her heart. The third manner is venial sin; truly, scarcely may any of these be without venial sin, for the corruption and for the delight thereof. The fourth manner is for to under-stand, if they assemble only for amorous love, and for none of the foresaid causes, but for to accomplish their burning delight, they reck not how oft, soothly it is deadly sin; and yet, with sorrow, some folk will pain them more to do than to their appetite sufficeth.

The second manner of chastity is for to be a clean widow, and eschew the embracing of a man, and desire the embracing of Jesus Christ. These be those that have been wives, and have foregone their husbands, and eke women that have done lechery, and been relieved by penance. And certes, if that a wife could keep her all chaste by license of her husband, so that she gave no cause nor no occasion that he aguilted, it were to her a great merit. This manner of women, that observe chastity, must be clean in heart as well as in body and in thought, and measurable in clothing and in countenance, abstinent in eating and drinking, in speaking, and in deed, and then is she the vessel or the boiste[1] of the blessed Magdalene, that fulfilleth holy church of good odour. The third manner of chastity is virginity, and it behoveth that she be holy in heart, and clean of body; then is she the spouse of Jesus Christ, and she is the life of angels: she is the praising of this world, and she is as these martyrs in equality: she hath in her that tongue may not tell, nor heart think. Virginity bare our Lord Jesus Christ, and virgin was himself.

Another remedy against lechery is specially to withdraw such things as give occasion to that villainy, as ease, eating, and drinking; for certes,

[1] Box.

when the pot boileth strongly, the best remedy is to withdraw the fire. Sleeping long in great quiet is also a great nurse to lechery.

Another remedy against lechery is, that a man or a woman eschew the company of them by which he doubteth to be tempted: for albeit so that the deed be withstood, yet is there great temptation. Soothly a white wall, although it ne burn not fully with sticking of a candle, yet is the wall black of the leyte.[1]   Full oft time I read, that no man trust in his own perfection, but he be stronger than Samson, or holier than David, or wiser than Solomon.

Now, after that I have declared you as I can of the seven deadly sins, and some of their branches, and the remedies, soothly, if I could, I would tell you the ten commandments, but so high doctrine I let[2] to divines.   Nevertheless, I hope to God they be touched in this treatise evereach of them all.

Now, forasmuch as the second part of penitence standeth in confession of mouth, as I began in the first chapter, I say Saint Augustine saith, 'Sin is every word and every deed, and all that men covet against the law of Jesus Christ;' and this is for to sin, in heart, in mouth, and in deed, by the five wits,[3] which be sight, hearing, smelling, tasting or savouring, and feeling.   Now is it good to understand the circumstances that agrege[4] much every sin.   Thou shalt consider what thou art that dost the sin, whether thou be male or female, young or old, gentle or thrall, free or servant, whole or sick,

[1] Flame.

[2] Leave.

[3] Senses.

[4] Aggravate.

wedded or single, ordered[1] or unordered, wise or fool, clerk or secular; if she be of thy kindred, bodily or ghostly, or not; if any of thy kindred have sinned with her or no, and many more things.

Another circumstance is this, whether it be done in fornication, or in advoutrie, or no, in manner of homicide or no, a horrible great sin or small, and how long thou hast continued in sin. The third circumstance is the place there thou hast done sin, whether in other men's houses, or in thine own, in field, in church, or in churchhawe,[2] in church dedicate, or not. For if the church be hallowed, and man or woman spill his kind within that place, by way of sin or by wicked temptation, the church were interdicted till it were reconciled by the bishop; and if it were a priest that did such villainy, the term of all his life he should no more sing mass; and if he did, he should do deadly sin, at every time that he so sung mass. The fourth circumstance is, by which mediators, as by messengers, or for enticement, or for consentment, to bear company with fellowship; for many a wretch, for to bear fellowship, will go to the devil of hell. Wherefore, they that egg[3] or consent to the sin, be partners of the sin, and of the damnation of the sinner. The fifth circumstance is, how many times that he hath sinned, if it be in his mind, and how oft he hath fallen. For he that oft falleth in sin, he despiseth the mercy of God, and increaseth his sin, and is unkind to Christ, and he waxeth the more feeble to with-

[1] In orders.

[2] Churchyard.

[3] Incite.

stand sin, and sinneth the more lightly, and the later ariseth, and is more slow to shrive him, and namely to him that hath been his confessor. For which that folk, when they fall again to their old follies, either they forlete[1] their old confessor all utterly, or else they depart[2] their shrift in divers places; but soothly such departed shrift deserveth no mercy of God for their sins. The sixth circumstance is, why that a man sinneth, as by what temptation; and if himself procure that temptation, or by exciting of other folk; or if he sin with a woman by force or by her own assent; or if the woman maugre her head have been enforced or no, this shall she tell, and whether it were for covetousness or poverty, and if it were by her procuring or no, and such other things. The seventh circumstance is, in what manner he hath done his sin, or how that she hath suffered that folk have done to her. And the same shall the man tell plainly, with all the circumstances, and whether he hath sinned with common bordel[3] women or no, or done his sin in holy times or no, in fasting times or no, or before his shrift, or after his later shrift, and hath peradventure broken thereby his penance enjoined, by whose help or whose counsel, by sorcery or craft, all must be told. All these things, after that they be great or small, engrege[4] the conscience of man or woman. And eke the priest that is thy judge, may the better be advised of his judgment in giving of penance, and that shall be after thy con-

---

[1] Abandon.
[2] Divide.
[3] Brothel.
[4] Aggravate.

trition. For understand well, that after the time that a man hath defouled his baptism by sin, if he will come to salvation, there is none other way but by penance, and shrift, and satisfaction; and namely by those two, if there be a confessor to whom he may shrive him, and that he first be very contrite and repentant, and the third if he have life to perform it.

Then shall a man look and consider, that if he will make a true and a profitable confession, there must be four conditions. First, it must be in sorrowful bitterness of heart, as saith the king Hezekiah to God, 'I will remember all the years of my life in the bitterness of my heart.' This condition of bitterness hath five signs: The first is, that confession must be shamefast,[1] not for to cover nor hide his sin, but for he hath aguilted[2] his God and defouled his soul. And hereof saith Saint Augustine, 'The heart travaileth for shame of his sin, and for he hath great shamefastness he is dign[3] to have great mercy of God.' Such was the confession of the publican, that would not heave up his eyes to heaven for he had offended God of heaven: for which shamefastness he had anon the mercy of God. And therefore saith Saint Augustine, that such shamefast folk be next forgiveness and mercy. Another sign is, humility in confession: of which saith Saint Peter, 'Humble you under the might of God:' the hand of God is mighty in confession, for thereby God forgiveth thee thy sins, for he alone

[1] Modest.

[2] Sinned against.

[3] Worthy.

hath the power. And this humility shall be in heart, and in sign outward: for right as he hath humility to God in his heart, right so should he humble his body outward to the priest, that sitteth in God's place. For which in no manner, since that Christ is sovereign, and the priest mean and mediator betwixt Christ and the sinner, and the sinner is last by way of reason, then should not the sinner sit as high as his confessor, but kneel before him or at his feet, but if malady distrouble[1] it: for he shall not take keep who sitteth there, but in whose place he sitteth. A man that hath trespassed to a lord, and cometh for to ask mercy and make his accord, and setteth him down anon by the lord, men would hold him outrageous, and not worthy so soon for to have remission nor mercy. The third sign is, that the shrift should be full of tears, if men may weep, and if they may not weep with their bodily eyes, then let them weep in their heart. Such was the confession of Saint Peter; for after that he had forsaken Jesus Christ, he went out and wept full bitterly. The fourth sign is, that he ne let[2] not for shame to shrive him and shew his confession. Such was the confession of Magdalene, that ne spared, for no shame of them that were at the feast, to go to our Lord Jesus Christ and beknow[3] to him her sins. The fifth sign is, that a man or a woman be obedient to receive the penance that them is enjoined. For certes Jesus Christ for the guilt of man was obedient to the death.

---

[1] Disturb.

[2] Leave.

[3] Confess.

The second condition of very[1] confession is, that it be hastily done: for certes, if a man had a deadly wound, ever the longer that he tarried to warish[2] himself, the more would it corrupt and haste him to his death, and also the wound would be the worse for to heal. And right so fareth sin, that long time is in a man unshewed. Certes a man ought hastily to shew his sins for many causes; as for dread of death, that cometh oft suddenly, and is in no certain what time it shall be, nor in what place; and eke the drenching[3] of one sin draweth in another; and also the longer that he tarrieth, the further is he from Christ. And if he abide to his last day, scarcely may he shrive him or remember him of his sins, or repent him, for the grievous malady of his death. And forasmuch as he ne hath in his life hearkened Jesus Christ, when he hath spoken unto him, he shall cry unto our Lord at his last day, and scarcely will he hearken him. And understand that this condition must have four things. First, that the shrift be purveyed[4] afore, and avised,[5] for wicked haste doth not profit; and that a man con[6] shrive him of his sins, be it of pride, or envy, and so forth, with the species and circumstances; and that he have comprehended in his mind the number and the greatness of his sins, and how long he hath lain in sin; and eke that he be contrite for his sins, and be in steadfast purpose (by the grace of God) never eft[7] to fall into sin; and also that he dread and counterwait[8] himself, that he flee the occasions of

[1] True.
[2] Cure.
[3] Drowning.
[4] Foreseen.
[5] Considered.
[6] Knows how.
[7] Again.
[8] Watch against.

sin to which he is inclined. Also, thou shalt shrive thee of all thy sins to one man, and not parcelmele[1] to one man, and parcelmele to another; that is to understand, in intent to depart[2] thy confession for shame or dread; for it is but strangling of thy soul. For certes Jesus Christ is entirely all good, in him is not imperfection, and therefore either he forgiveth all perfectly, or else never a deal. I say not that if thou be assigned to thy penitencer* for certain sin, that thou art bound to shew him all the remnant of thy sins, of which thou hast been shriven of thy curate, but if it like thee of thy humility; this is no departing of shrift. Ne I say not, there as I speak of division of confession, that if thou have licence to shrive thee to a discreet and an honest priest, and where thee liketh, and by the licence of thy curate, that thou ne mayest well shrive thee to him of all thy sins: but let no blot be behind, let no sin be untold as far as thou hast remembrance. And when thou shalt be shriven of thy curate, tell him eke all the sins that thou hast done since thou were last shriven. This is no wicked intent of division of shrift.

Also, the very shrift asketh certain conditions. First, that thou shrive thee by thy free will, not constrained, ne for shame of folk, nor for malady, or such other things: for it is reason, that he that trespasseth by his free will, that by his free will he confess his trespass; and that no other man tell

---

* 'Penitencer:' A priest who enjoins penance in extraordinary cases.

[1] By parts.

[2] Divide.

his sin but himself: ne he shall not nay nor deny his sin, nor wrath him against the priest for amonesting[1] him to lete[2] his sin. The second condition is, that thy shrift be lawful, that is to say, that thou that shrivest thee, and eke the priest that heareth thy confession, be verily in the faith of holy church, and that a man ne be not despaired of the mercy of Jesus Christ, as Cain and Judas were. And eke a man must accuse himself of his own trespass and not another: but he shall blame and wite[3] himself of his own malice and of his sin, and none other: but nevertheless, if that another man be encheson[4] or enticer of his sin, or the estate of the person be such by which his sin is agregged,[5] or else that he may not plainly shrive him but he tell the person with which he hath sinned, then may he tell, so that his intent ne be not to backbite the person, but only to declare his confession.

Thou ne shalt not also make no leasings[6] in thy confession for humility, peradventure, to say that thou hast committed and done such sins, of which that thou ne were never guilty. For Saint Augustine saith, 'If that thou, because of thy humility, makest a leasing on thyself, though thou were not in sin before, yet art thou then in sin through thy leasing.' Thou must also shew thy sin by thy proper mouth, but thou be dumb, and not by no letter: for thou that hast done the sin, thou shalt have the shame of the confession. Thou shalt not eke paint thy confession, with fair and subtle words,

[1] Admonishing.
[2] Leave.
[3] Impute to.
[4] Occasion.
[5] Aggravated.
[6] Falsehoods.

to cover the more thy sin; for then beguilest thou thyself, and not the priest: thou must tell it plainly, be it never so foul nor so horrible. Thou shalt eke shrive thee to a priest that is discreet to counsel thee: and eke thou shalt not shrive thee for vain-glory, nor for hypocrisy, nor for no cause, but only for the doubt[1] of Jesus Christ, and the health of thy soul. Thou shalt not eke run to the priest all suddenly, to tell him lightly thy sin, as who telleth a jape[2] or a tale, but advisedly and with good devotion; and generally shrive thee oft: if thou oft fall, oft arise by confession. And though thou shrive thee oftener than once of sin which thou hast been shriven of, it is more merit; and, as saith Saint Augustine, thou shalt have the more lightly release and grace of God, both of sin and of pain. And certes once a year at the least way it is lawful to be houseled,[3] for soothly once a year all things in the earth renovelen.[4]

[1] Fear.

[2] Jest.

[3] Receive the sacrament.

[4] Are renewed.

Explicit secunda pars penitentiæ: et sequitur tertia pars.

Now have I told you of very confession, that is the second part of penitence: The third part is satisfaction, and that standeth most generally in alms-deeds and in bodily pain. Now be there three manner of alms: contrition of heart, where a man offereth himself to God; another is, to have pity of the default of his neighbour; and the third is, in giving of good counsel, ghostly and bodily, where as men have need, and namely in sustenance of man's food. And take keep that a man hath need of these things generally: he hath need of food, of clothing, and of herberow,[1] he hath need of charitable counselling and visiting in prison and in malady, and sepulture of his dead body. And if thou mayest not visit the needful in prison in thy person, visit them with thy message and thy gifts. These be generally the alms and works of charity, of them that have temporal riches, or discretion in counselling. Of these works shalt thou hear at the day of doom.

This alms shouldest thou do of thy proper things, and hastily, and privily if thou mayest; but nevertheless, if thou mayest not do it privily, thou shalt not forbear to do alms, though men see it, so that it be not done for thank of the world, but only to have thank of Jesus Christ. For, as witnesseth Saint Matthew, cap. v., 'A city may not be hid that is set on a mountain, nor men light not a lantern to put it under a bushel, but set it upon a candlestick, to light the men in the house: right so shall your light lighten before men, that they may see your good works, and glorify your Father that is in heaven.'

Now as for to speak of bodily pain, it standeth in prayers, in waking,[2] in fasting, and in virtuous teaching. Of orisons ye shall understand, that orisons or prayers is to say, a piteous will of heart, that setteth it in God, and expresseth it by word

[1] Lodging.

[2] Watching.

outward, to remove harms, and to have things spiritual and perdurable, and sometimes temporal things. Of which orisons, certes in the orison of the *Pater noster* hath Jesus Christ enclosed most things. Certes it is privileged of three things in his dignity, for which it is more dign[1] than any other prayer: for that Jesus Christ himself made it; and it is short, for it should be coude[2] the more lightly, and to hold it the more easy in heart, and help himself the oftener with this orison, and for a man should be the less weary to say it, and for a man may not excuse him to learn it, it is so short and so easy; and for it comprehendeth in himself all good prayers. The exposition of this holy prayer, that is so excellent and so dign, I betake[3] to the masters of theology; save thus much will I say, that when thou prayest that God should forgive thee thy guilts, as thou forgivest them that have aguilted thee, be well ware that thou be not out of charity. This holy orison amenuseth[4] eke venial sin, and therefore it appertaineth specially to penitence.

This prayer must be truly said, and in perfect faith, and that men pray to God ordinately, discreetly, and devoutly: and alway a man shall put his will to be subject to the will of God. This orison must eke be said with great humbleness and full pure, and honestly, and not to the annoyance of any man or woman. It must eke be continued with works of charity. It availeth eke against the

[1] Worthy.

[2] Known.

[3] Commit.

[4] Lesseneth.

vices of the soul; for, as saith Saint Jerome, by fasting be saved the vices of the flesh, and by prayer the vices of the soul.

After this thou shalt understand, that bodily pain stands in waking, For Jesus Christ saith, 'Wake ye and pray ye, that ye ne enter into wicked temptation.' Ye shall understand also, that fasting stands in three things: in forbearing of bodily meat and drink, in forbearing of worldly jollity, and in forbearing of deadly sin: this is to say, that a man shall keep him from deadly sin with all his might.

And thou shalt understand also, that God ordained fasting, and to fasting appertaineth four things. Largeness[1] to poor folk; gladness of heart spiritual; not to be angry nor annoyed, nor grutch[2] for he fasteth; and also reasonable hour for to eat by measure, that is to say, a man shall not eat in untime,[3] nor sit the longer at the table, for he fasteth.

Then shalt thou understand, that bodily pain standeth in discipline, or teaching, by word, or by writing, or by example. Also in wearing of hair[4] or of stamin,[5] or of habergeons[6] on their naked flesh, for Christ's sake; but 'ware thee well that such manner penances ne make not thine heart bitter or angry, nor annoyed of thyself; for better is to cast away thine hair than to cast away the sweetness of our Lord Jesus Christ. And therefore saith Saint Paul, 'Clothe you, as they that be chosen of God in heart, of misericord,[7] debonairtee,[8]

[1] Bounty.
[2] Murmur.
[3] Unseasonable time.
[4] Haircloth.
[5] Woollen.
[6] Mail.
[7] Pity.
[8] Gentleness.

sufferance, and such manner of clothing,' of which Jesus Christ is more pleased than with the hairs or habergeons.

Then is discipline eke in knocking of thy breast, in scourging with yards,[1] in kneeling, in tribulation, in suffering patiently wrongs that be done to thee, and eke in patient suffering of maladies, or losing of worldly catel,[2] or wife, or child, or other friends.

Then shalt thou understand which things disturb penance, and this is in four manners; that is dread, shame, hope, and wanhope, that is desperation. And for to speak first of dread, for which he weeneth that he may suffer no penance, there against is remedy for to think that bodily penance is but short and little at regard of the pain of hell, that is so cruel and so long that it lasteth without end.

Now against the shame that a man hath to shrive[3] him, and namely these hypocrites, that would be holden so perfect that they have no need to shrive them, against that shame should a man think, that by way of reason he that hath not been ashamed to do foul things, certes him ought not to be ashamed to do fair things, and that is confessions. A man should also think, that God seeth and knoweth all his thoughts, and all his works, and to him may nothing be hid nor covered. Men should eke remember them of the shame that is to come at the day of doom, to them that be not penitent in this present life; for all the creatures in heaven, and in

[1] Rods.

[2] Goods.

[3] Confess.

earth, and in hell, shall see apertly[1] all that they hide in this world.

Now for to speak of the hope of them that be so negligent and slow to shrive them: that standeth in two manners. That one is, that he hopeth for to live long, and for to purchase much riches for his delight, and then he will shrive him: and, as he sayeth, he may, as him seemeth, then timely enough come to shrift: another is, the surquedrie[2] that he hath in Christ's mercy. Against the first vice, he shall think that our life is in no sikerness,[3] and eke that all the riches in this world be in adventure, and pass as a shadow on a wall; and, as saith Saint Gregory, that it appertaineth to the great righteousness of God, that never shall the pain stint[4] of them that never would withdraw them from sin their thanks,[5] but ever continue in sin: for that perpetual will to do sin shall they have perpetual pain.

Wanhope[6] is in two manners. The first wanhope is, in the mercy of God: that other is, that they think that they ne might not long persevere in goodness. The first wanhope cometh of that he deemeth that he hath sinned so greatly and so oft, and so long lain in sin, that he shall not be saved. Certes against that cursed wanhope should he think, that the passion of Jesus Christ is more strong for to unbind than sin is strong for to bind. Against the second wanhope he shall think, that as often as he falleth, he may arise again by penitence: and though he never so long hath lain in sin, the

[1] Openly.

[2] Presumption.

[3] Security.

[4] Cease.

[5] With their will

[6] Despair.

mercy of Christ is alway ready to receive him to mercy. Against that wanhope that he deemeth he should not long persevere in goodness, he shall think, that the feebleness of the devil may nothing do but if men will suffer him: and eke he shall have strength of the help of Jesus Christ, and of all his church, and of the protection of angels, if him list.

Then shall men understand what is the fruit of penance; and after the words of Jesus Christ, it is an endless bliss of heaven, there joy hath no contrariosity of woe nor grievance; there all harms be passed of this present life; there as is sickerness[1] from the pains of hell; there as is the blissful company, that rejoice them evermore evereach of other's joy; there as the body of man, that whilom[2] was foul and dark, is more clear than the sun; there as the body that whilom was sick and frail, feeble and mortal, is immortal, and so strong and so whole, that there ne may nothing appeire[3] it; there as is neither hunger, nor thirst, nor cold, but every soul replenished with the sight of the perfect knowing of God. This blissful regne[4] may men purchase by poverty spiritual, and the glory by lowliness, the plenty of joy by hunger and thirst, and the rest by travail, and the life by death and mortification of sin: to which life He us bring that bought us with his precious blood. Amen.

Now pray I to them all that hearken this little treatise or read it, that if there be anything in it

[1] Safety.

[2] Once.

[3] Impair.

[4] Kingdom.

that liketh them, that thereof they thank our Lord Jesus Christ, of whom proceedeth all wit and all goodness; and if there be anything that displeaseth them, I pray them also that they arrette[1] it to the default of my unkonning,[2] and not to my will, that would fain have said better if I had had konning; for our book saith, all that is written is written for our doctrine, and that is my intent. Wherefore I beseech you meekly for the mercy of God that ye pray for me, that Christ have mercy of me and forgive me my guilts, [and namely of my translations and inditings of worldly vanities, the which I revoke in my Retractions, as the book of Troilus, the book also of Fame, the book of the Five-and-twenty Ladies, the book of the Duchess, the book of Saint Valentine's day of the Parliament of Birds, the Tales of Canterbury, those that sounen[3] unto sin, the book of the Lion, and many another book, if they were in my remembrance, and many a song and many a lecherous lay, Christ of his great mercy forgive me the sin. But of the translation of Boece of Consolation, and other books of legends of saints, and of homilies, and morality, and devotion, that thank I our Lord Jesus Christ, and his blissful mother, and all the saints in heaven, beseeching them that they from henceforth unto my life's end send me grace to bewail my guilts, and to study to the salvation of my soul,] and grant me grace of very penance, confession, and satisfaction to do in this present life, through the benign grace of Him

[1] Impute.

[2] Unskilfulness.

[3] Harmonise with.

that is King of kings and Priest of all priests, that bought us with the precious blood of his heart, so that I may be one of them at the last day of doom that shall be saved; *qui cum Deo Patre et Spiritu Sancto vivis et regnas Deus per omnia secula. Amen.*

NOTES

ON

THE CANTERBURY TALES.

Ver. 13623. 'To japen he began:' So MS. E.   Some MSS. read 'tho began.'

Ver. 13650. 'At Popering:' 'Poppering,' or 'Poppeling,' was the name of a parish in the marches of Calais.   Our famous antiquary Leland was once rector of it. (Tanner, 'Bib. Brit.,' in v. 'Leland.')

Ver. 13655. 'Paindemain:' That this must have been a sort of remarkably white bread is clear enough.   Skinner derives it from 'Panis matutinus,' 'Pain de matin;' and indeed Du Cange mentions a species of loaves or rolls called 'Matinelli.' However I am more inclined to believe that it received its denomination from the province of Maine, where it was, perhaps, made in the greatest perfection.   I find it twice in a northern tale called 'The Freiris of Berwick,' MS. Maitland:—

'And als that creil is full of breid of mane.'

And again, 'The mane breid.'

Ver. 13664. 'Ciclatoun'—Edit. 1775, 'Chekelatoun:' The Glossaries suppose this word to be compounded of 'cheke' and 'latoun,' a species of base metal like gold: but it seems rather to be merely a corruption of the Fr. 'Ciclaton;' which originally signified 'a circular robe of state,' from the Gr. Lat. 'Cyclas;' and afterwards 'the cloth of gold,' of which such robes were generally made.   Du Cange, in v. 'Cyclas,' has produced

instances enough of both senses.   In fact several MSS. read
'ciclaton;' and I have no excuse for not having followed them,
but that I was misled by the authority of Spenser, as quoted by
Mr Warton, ('Obs. on Sp.,' v. i. p. 194.)   Upon further consideration, I think it is plain that Spenser was mistaken in the
very foundation of his notion, 'that the quilted Irish jacket
embroidered with gilded leather' had any resemblance to 'the
robe of shecklaton.'   He supposes that Chaucer is here describing Sir Topas, as he went to fight against the giant in his robe
of Shecklaton; whereas, on the contrary, it is evident that Sir
Topas is here described in his usual habit in time of peace.   His
warlike apparel, when he goes to fight against the giant, is
described below, (ver. 13786 and foll.,) and is totally different.

Ver. 13665. 'A jane:' A coin of Janua (Genoa), called in
our statutes 'galley halfpence.'   (See the quotations from Stow
in Mr Warton's 'Obs. on Sp.,' v. i. p. 180.)

Ver. 13667. 'Hawking for the rivere:' See the note on ver. 6466.

Ver. 13671. 'There any ram :' See the note on ver. 550.

Ver. 13682. 'A launcegay :' The Editt. have split this im-
properly into two words, as if 'gay' were an epithet.   It occurs
as one word in Rot. Parl. 29 H. VI. n. 8: 'And the said Evan
then and there with a launcegay, smote the said William
Tresham threughe the body a foote and more, whereof he died.'
Nicot describes a 'zagaye' to be a Moorish lance, longer and
slenderer than a pike ; from the Span. Arab. ' azagáya.'

Ver. 13692. 'Clove-gilofre:' 'Clou de girofle,' Fr., 'Cary-
ophyllus,' Lat.   A clove-tree, or the fruit of it.   Sir J. Mandeville, (c. xxvi.,) describing a country beyond Cathay, says—
'And in that contree, and in other contrees thereabouten, growen
many trees, that beren clowe gylofres and notemuges, and grete
notes of Ynde, and of canelle and of many other spices.'

But the most apposite illustration of this passage is a similar
description in Chaucer's 'R. R.,' ver. 1360–1372—in the Original, ver. 1347–1350.   See also a note of 'an ingenious corre-
spondent' in Mr Warton's 'Obs. on Sp.,' v. i. p. 139, Ed. 1762,
where this passage is very properly adduced to shew 'that the
Rime of Sire Thopas was intended as a burlesque on the old
ballad romances.'

Ver. 13722. '‖ In town:' These two last words, which are plainly superfluous, are distinguished by a mark of this kind in MS. C. 1; and the same mark is repeated in ver. 13743, 13752, and 13815, where the two final syllables are also superfluous to the metre. Whether in all these cases the words thus separated are to be considered as idle additions, for the purpose of introducing the rhyme which answers to them, or whether some lines, which originally connected them with the context, have been lost, it is not easy to determine. Upon the latter supposition, which, I confess, appears to me the most probable, we may imagine, that, in the present instance, the three last lines of this stanza and the three first of the following, except the words ' in town,' have dropped out. In the three other instances, only two lines and the two first feet of the third may be supposed to be wanting.

In support of this hypothesis it may be observed, that in the very next stanza, the last line, ver. 13731, and the following line, in MS. C. 1, stand thus :—

> 'The contree of Faerie so wilde
> For in that contree n'as ther non
> [That to him durst ride or gon]
> Neither wif ne childe.'

Whether the two lines and part of another which I have inserted before ' wilde' from other MSS. be genuine, I will not be positive; but it is very clear, I think, that something is wanting. The line between hooks, which is inserted in MS. C. 1, in a later hand, is in MSS. HA., D.

Ver. 13733. ' He spied:' Ed. Urr. reads 'spired;' I know not upon what authority. But the emendation is probable enough; as the expression of ' spying with the mouth' seems to be too extravagantly absurd even for this composition. To ' spire,' or ' spere,' Gl. Doug., signifies ' to inquire,' from the Sax. ' spyrian.' (See ' P. L.,' p. 327; Gower, ' Conf. Am.,' fol. 182.)

Ver. 13739. ' Sir Oliphaunt:' Sir ' Elephant;' a proper name for a giant. Mandeville, p. 283 :—' And there ben also many wylde bestes, and nameliche of Olyfauntes.' The very learned and ingenious author of ' Letters on Chivalry,' &c., supposes

' that the "Boke" of " The Giant Olyphant and Chylde Thopas"
was not a fiction of Chaucer's own, but a story of antique fame,
and very celebrated in the days of chivalry.'   I can only say,
that I have not been so fortunate as to meet with any traces of
such a story of an earlier date than ' The Canterbury Tales.'

Ver. 13741. ' By Termagaunt:' This Saracen deity, in an old
romance (MS. Bod., 1624) is constantly called ' Tervagan : '—

> ' De devant sei fait porter sun dragon,
> E l'estendart tervagan e mahum,
> E un ymagene apolin le felun.'

And again :—

> ' Pleignent lur deus tervagan et mahum,
> E apollin, dunt il mie rien unt.'

This romance, which in the MS. has no title, may possibly be
an older copy of one which is frequently quoted by Du Cange
under the title of ' Le Roman de Roncevaux.'   The author's
name was Turold, as appears from the last line :—

> ' Ci falt le geste que Turold' declinet.'

He is not mentioned by any of the writers of French literary
history that I have seen.

Ver. 13758. ' A fell staff sling :' This is the reading of the
best MSS. ; but what kind of sling is meant I know not.

Ver. 13775. 'Gestours for to tellen tales :' The proper business
of a ' gestour' was ' to recite tales,' or ' gestes ;' which was only
one of the branches of the minstrel's profession.

' Minstrels ' and ' gestours ' are mentioned together in the
following lines, from William of Nassyngton's translation of a
religious treatise by John of Waldby (MS. Reg. 17 C., viii.
p. 2) :—

> ' I warne you furst at the begynninge,
> That 1 will make no vain carpinge
> Of dedes of armys ne of amours,
> As dus mynstrelles and jestours,
> That makys carpinge in many a place
> Of Octoviane and Isembrase,
> And of many other jestes,
> And namely when they come to festes ;
> Ne of the life of Bevys of Hampton,
> That was a knight of gret renoun,

> Ne of Sir Gye of Warwyke,
> All if it might sum men lyke.'

I cite these lines to shew the species of tales related by the ancient gestours, and how much they differed from what we now call ' jests.'

Ver. 13777. 'Of romances that be reales :' So in the 'Rom. of Ywain and Gawain' (MS. Cott., Galb. E. ix.) :—

> ' He fund a knight under a tre ;
> Upon a cloth of gold he lay ;
> Byfor him sat a ful fayr may :
> A lady sat with tham in fere ;
> The maiden red, that thai might here,
> A *real romance* in that place.'

The original of this title, which is an uncommon one, I take to have been this. When the French romances found their way into Italy, (not long before the year 1300, Crescimb., t. i. p. 336,) some Italian undertook to collect together all those relating to Charlemagne and his family, and to form them into a regular body of history. The six first books of this work come down to the death of Pepin. They begin thus : ' Qui se comenza la hystoria el Real de Franza comenzando a Constantino imperatore secondo molte lezende che io ho attrovate e racolte insieme.' (Edit. Mutinæ, 1491, fol.)   It was reprinted in 1537 under this title, ' I reali di Franza, nel quale si contiene la generazione di tutti i Re, Duchi, Principi e Baroni di Franza, e delli Paladini, colle battaglie da loro fatte,' &c. (Quadrio, t. vi. p. 530.) Salviati had seen a MS. of this work, written about 1350 (Crescimb., t. i. p. 330), and I do not believe that any mention of a ' Real,' or ' Royal Romance ' is to be found, in French or English, prior to that date.

Ver. 13786. ' He didde next his white lere :' ' He did,' or ' put, on ' next his white ' skin.' To ' don,' ' do on,' and ' doff,' ' do off,' have been in use, as vulgar words, long since Chaucer's time. ' Lere ' seems to be used for ' skin ' in Isumbras (MS. Cott., Cal. 11, fol. 129) :—

> ' His lady is white as wales bone,
> Here lere brygte to se upon,
> So faire as blosme on tre.'

Though it more commonly signifies only what we call 'complexion.'

In the Romance of 'Li Beau Desconus,' his arming is thus
described (fol. 42) :—

> 'They caste on him a scherte of selk,
> A gypell as white as melk
> In that semely sale,
> And syzt an hawberk brygt,
> That richely was adygt
> With mayles thykke and smale.'

Ver. 13793. 'Of Jewes' werk :' I do not recollect to have seen
the Jews celebrated anywhere as remarkable artificers. I am
therefore inclined to adopt an explanation of this word, which I
find in a note of the learned editor of 'Anc. Scott. Poems,' p. 230:
'This Jow,' not this Jew, but this juggler or magician. The
words ' to jowk,' ' to deceive,' and 'jowkery-pawkry,' 'juggling
tricks,' are still in use. In Lord Hyndford's MS., p. 136, there
is a fragment of a sort of fairy tale, where 'Scho is the Quene
of Jowis' means, 'She is the queen of magicians.'

According to this explanation, 'Jewes' werk' may signify the
work of magicians or fairies.

Ver. 13800. 'A charboucle :' 'A carbuncle' (' Escarboucle,'
Fr.) was a common bearing. (Guillim's 'Heraldry,' p. 109.)

Ver. 13804. 'Cuirbouly :' 'Cuir bouilli,' of which Sir Topas's boots were made, was also applied to many other purposes.
(See Froissart, v. i. c. 110, 120, and v. vi. c. 19.) In this last
passage, he says the Saracens covered their targes with 'cuir
bouilli de Capadoce, où nul ſer ne peut prendre n'attacher; si le
cuir n'est trop échaufé.'

Ver. 13807. 'Rewel bone ·' What kind of material this was
I profess myself quite ignorant. In the 'Turnament of Totten-
ham,' ver. 75, ('Anc. Poet.,' v. ii. p. 18,) Tibbe is introduced
with ' a garland on her head full of ruell bones.' The derivation
in Gloss. Urr. of this word from the Fr. 'riolé,' diversely
coloured, has not the least probability. The other, which de-
duces it from the Fr. ' rouelle ;' ' rotula ;' the ' whirl-bone,' or
' knee-pan,' is more plausible; though, as the Glossarist observes,
that sense will hardly suit here.

Ver. 13823. 'Of ladies' love and druerie:' I have taken the liberty here of departing from the MSS., which read—

'And of ladies' love druerie.'

Upon second thoughts I am more inclined to throw out 'love' as a gloss for 'druerie,' and to read thus:—

'And of ladies' druerie.'

'Druerie' is strangely explained in Gloss. Urr. 'Sobriety,' 'modesty.' It means 'courtship,' 'gallantry.'

Ver. 13828. 'Of Sir Libeux:' His romance is in MS. Cott., Cal. ii. In the 12th stanza we have his true name, and the reason of it. King Arthur speaks :—

> 'Now clepeth him alle thus,
> *Ly beau desconus,*
>   For the love of me,
> Than may ye wete arowe,
> *The fayre unknowe*
>   Certes so hatte he.'

Ibid. 'Pleindamour:' This is the reading of the MSS., and I know not why we should change it for 'Blandamour,' as both names sound equally well.

Ver. 13833. 'As sparkle:' The same simile is in 'Isumbras,' fol. 130, b. :—

> 'He spronge forth, as sparke on [f. of] glede.'

'Glode' in the preceding verse is probably for 'glowde,' 'glowed;' from the Sax. 'glowan,' 'candere.'

Ver. 13844. 'Sir Percivell:' The 'Romance of Perceval le Galois,' or 'de Galis,' was composed in octosyllable French verse by Chrestien de Troyes, one of the oldest and best French romancers, before the year 1191, (Fauchet, l. ii. c. x.) It consisted of above sixty thousand verses ('Bibl. des Rom.,' t. 11. p. 250), so that it would be some trouble to find the fact which is probably here alluded to. The romance under the same title, in French prose, printed at Paris, 1530, fol., can be only an abridgment, I suppose, of the original poem.

Ver. 13845. 'So worthy under weed:' This phrase occurs repeatedly in the 'Romance of Emaré:'—

> Fol. 70, b. 'Than sayde that worthy unther wede.'

> Fol. 74, b. 'The childe was worthy unther wede,
> And sate upon a nobyl stede.'

See also fol. 71, b. 73, a.

Ver. 13852. 'The devil I beteche:' I 'betake,' 'recommend,' or 'give,' to the devil. See ver. 3748—

> 'My soul betake I unto Sathanas;'

and ver. 8037, 17256, where the preposition is omitted, as here. 'To take,' in our old language, is also used for 'To take to;' 'To give.' See ver. 13334—

> 'He took me certain gold, I wot it well;'

and compare ver. 13224, 13286.

The change of 'betake' into 'beteche' was not so great a license formerly as it would be now, as 'ch' and 'k' seem once to have been pronounced in nearly the same manner. See ver. 3307, 3308, 3311, 3312, where 'werk' is made to rhyme to 'cherche' and 'clerk.' It may be observed, too, that the Saxons had but one verb, 'tæcau,' to signify 'capere' and 'docere;' and though our ancestors, even before Chaucer's time, had split that single verb into two, 'to take' and 'to teche,' and had distinguished each from the other by a different mode of inflection, yet the compound verb 'betake,' which, according to that mode of inflection, ought to have formed its past time 'betoke,' formed it often 'betaught,' as if no such distinction had been established. (See 'R. R.,' ver. 4428; 'Gamelyn,' 666.) The regular past time 'betoke' occurs in ver. 16009.

Ver. 13879. 'I mean of Mark and Matthew:' The conjunction 'and' has been added for the sake of the metre, without authority, and perhaps without necessity; as 'Mark' was probably written by Chaucer 'Marke,' and pronounced as a dissyllable.

The Tale of Melibœus: Mr Thomas has observed that this tale seems to have been written in blank verse. (MS. notes upon Chaucer, Ed. Urr., in Brit. Mus.) It is certain that in the former part of it we find a number of blank verses intermixed, in a much greater proportion than in any of our author's other prose writings. But this poetical style is not, I think, remarkable beyond the first four or five pages.

P. 12, l. 23. ‘ The sentence of Ovid : ’ ‘ Rem. Am.’ 125 :—

‘ Quis matrem, nisi mentis inops, in funere nati
    Flere vetet ?’ &c.

It would be a laborious and thankless task to point out the exact places of all the quotations which are made use of in this treatise. I shall therefore confine my observations of that kind to a few passages, which are taken from authors not commonly to be met with.

P. 19, l. 12. ‘ Piers Alphonse : ’ He calls himself ‘ Petrus Alphunsi ’ in his ‘ Dialogus contra Judæos.’ (MS. Harl., 3861.) He there informs us, that he was himself originally a Jew, but converted and baptized in the year 1106, in July ‘ die natalis App. Petri et Pauli ;’ upon which account he took the name of Peter. ‘ Fuit autem pater meus spiritualis Alfunsus, gloriosus Hispanie imperator—(the first king of Arragon of that name and the seventh of Castile)—quare, nomen ejus prefato nomini meo apponens, Petrus Alfunsi mihi nomen imposui.’ After his conversion, he wrote the ‘ Dialogue’ above mentioned, and also another work, which is here quoted by Chaucer, and of which, therefore, I think myself obliged to give some account.

It is extant in MS. in many libraries, but the only copy which I have had an opportunity of examining is in the Museum, Bib. Reg., 10 B. xii. It is there entitled ‘ Petri Adelfonsi de Clericali Disciplinâ,’ and begins thus :—‘ Dixit Petrus Adelfonsus, servus xp̄ı ı͠hu, compositor hujus libri—Libellum compegi partim ex proverbiis et castigationibus Arabicis et fabulis et versibus, et partim ex animalium et volucrum similitudinibus.’ After a short proem, he enters thus upon his main subject :— ‘ Eboc igitur philosophus, qui linguâ Arabicâ cognominatur Edric, dixit filio suo ; Timor Domini sit tua negotiatio,’ &c. The work then proceeds in the form of a dialogue between the philosopher and his son, in which the precepts of the former are for the most part illustrated by apposite fables and examples. ‘ Edris,’ according to D’Herbelot in v., was the name of Enoch among the Arabians, who attribute to him many fabulous compositions. Whether Alfonsus had any of them in his view I know not, nor is it material. The manner and style of his work both shew many marks of an Eastern original, and one of his stories, ‘ Of a trick put upon a thief,' is entirely taken from the 'Calilah u Damnah,'* a celebrated collection of Oriental apologues.

In this part of the world, however, Alfonsus may be considered as an original writer. His work was very early translated into French verse. In an old copy (MS. Reg., 16, E. VIII.), the translation is entitled 'Proverbes Peres Anforse;' and there is a short introduction by the translator, in which he says, 'Voil Peres Anfors translater.' In a later copy (MS. Bod., 1687) the introduction is omitted, but the poem is entitled 'Le romaunz Peres Aunfour coment il aprist et chastia sun fils belement.' In another copy (MS. Harl., 4388), there is neither

* Though the exact age of the 'Calilah u Damnah' be by no means clear, we know that it was translated out of Arabic into Greek by Symeon Seth several years before Alfonsus wrote. The story mentioned here is not in that copy of Symeon's translation which Starkius has printed under the title of 'Specimen Sapientiæ Indorum' (Berolin., 1697, 8vo), but it is in MS. Bod., 510 ; and in the Latin version of Symeon's book, which Poussin published by way of Appendix to the history of Pachymeres, 'inter Script. Hist. Byzant.' The various titles under which this Eastern romance has passed through Europe, may be seen in the preface of Starkius, and in Fabric. ('Bib. Gr.,' vi. 460, and x. 324,) though neither of them has taken notice of an Italian translation, or imitation, by Firenzuola, entitled, 'Discorsi degli animali.' (See his Prose, Fir. 1548.) The other Italian version which they mention, by Doni, was translated into English, under the title of 'The Moral Philosophy of Doni, out of Italian, by Sir Thomas North, Knight,' 4to, 1601 (Ames, p. 435), and is alluded to, I suppose, by Jonson in his 'Epicœne,' p. 494, by the name of 'Done's Philosophy,' though he has made the speaker, Sir Am. La-Fool, whether designedly or not I am uncertain, confound it with 'Reynard the fox.' Since they wrote, there has been an edition at Paris, in 1724, with this title, 'Contes et Fables Indiennes, de Bidpai et de Lokman, traduites D'Ali Tchelebi-Ben-Saleh, Auteur Turc. Œuvre posthume, par M. Galland.' The words 'et de Lokman' in this title I suspect to have been added by the bookseller, for I cannot find anything of Lokman in the work itself. Perhaps M. Galland might have intended to annex the fables of Lokman, but was prevented by death. For the rest, there is no material difference between this edition and a former French version, which was made from the Persic, and printed in 1698, except in the style. They both differ very considerably from the Greek.

I will just take notice, that one of the fables in Greek (p. 444) has been inserted, but with great variations, by Matthew Paris in his History, ad ann. 1195, as a parable, which Richard I., after his return from the East, was used frequently to relate 'ingratos redarguendo.'

introduction nor title; so that, by the mere omissions of transcribers, the French translation has put on the appearance of an original work, and is quoted as such by M. le Comte de Caylus in his ' Memoire sur les Fabliaux' ('Acad. des Ins.,' t. xx. p. 361), under the general title of ' Le chastoiement du pere au fils.' The fable of ' the Sheep,' of which M. de Caylus has there given an abstract, is in the Latin Alfonsus (Fab. ix.) I will add, that the same fable, in the 'Cento Novelle Antiche,' N. xxx., is fathered upon ' uno novellatore di Messer Azzolino ;' and Cervantes, changing the sheep for goats, has put it into the mouth of Sancho, (' Don Quix.,' p. 1, c. xx.) Cervantes indeed has also altered the application of it, but, I think, not for the better.

I am inclined to believe that Hebers, the author or translator of the French romance called ' Dolopatos,' in the beginning of the thirteenth century, had read this work of Alfonsus, perhaps before it was translated into French. The story of the stone thrown into the well (' Decameron,' vii. 4), which Fauchet supposes Boccaccio to have taken from Hebers, is in Alfonsus (Fab. xi.) It is not in the Greek ' Syntipas,'* which I imagine to

---

* The only copy which I have ever seen of ' Syntipas' is in MS. Harl., 5560. I should guess that it agreed in substance with that which Du Cange made use of in his ' Glossarium Med. et Inf. Græcitatis' (see his ' Index Auctorum,' p. 33), though it seems to be of a later age, and in a more depraved dialect. They differ in this, that the Harleian copy is said to have been translated from the Persic (απο Περσιακης βιβλου εις Ρωμαϊκην γλωτταν), and Du Cange's from the Syriac (απο Συριακης βιβλου, ὡς ειχεν αυταις λεξεσιν, εις την Ελλαδα γλωτταν). However, I would not vouch that it really was translated either from the Persic or Syriac. Among the Oriental MSS. in the Bodleian Library, the catalogue mentions one in Turkish (Rawlinson, 31), ' De uxore Chafikini Turcarum regis et filio,' which I suspect to contain this same story, translated perhaps from the Greek, or from the Italian ' Erasto.'

' Syntipas' is said to have been printed at Venice, ' lingua Græca vulgari' (Fabric. ' Bibl. Gr.' x. 515). How far that edition may agree with the Harleian MS. I cannot say, having never seen it. To judge by the MS. only, it seems probable, that if ' Syntipas' was the groundwork of the ' Dolopatos,' Hebers must have departed as much from his original as the succeeding compilers of ' Les Sept Sages' and of ' Erasto' have from Hebers. Neither the story mentioned in the text, nor the two others which Fauchet refers to as borrowed by Boccaccio from Hebers, viz.,

have been the groundwork of the 'Dolopatos,' and therefore I
presume that it was inserted by Hebers, or the monk whose Latin
he translated, and possibly from Alfonsus.   At least it is not more
probable that Boccaccio should take it from Hebers than from
Alfonsus, with whose work he appears to have been well ac-
quainted. One of his novels ('Decam.,' vii. 6) is plainly copied
from thence (Fab. viii.); and his celebrated novel of the two
friends, 'Tito and Gisippo,' (Decam.' x. 8,) is borrowed, with
hardly any variation, except in the names of persons and places,
from the second of Alfonsus, or, which is the same thing, from
the 'Gesta Romanorum,' * into which collection, after a time,
almost all the best fables of Alfonsus were incorporated.

'Decam.,' iii. 2, and viii. 8, are to be found in the MS. 'Syntipas.' On the
other hand, the story in the 'Decam.,' vii. 6, which is said in the text to
be probably copied from Alfonsus, is also in 'Syntipas,' though, from the
silence of Fauchet, we may presume that it was not in the 'Dolopatos.'
　　The plan of 'Syntipas' is exactly the same with that of 'Les Sept
Sages,' the Italian 'Erasto,' the French 'Eraste,' and our own little story-
book, 'The Seven Wise Masters,' except that, instead of Dioclesian of
Rome, the king is called Cyrus of Persia, and, instead of one tale, each of
the philosophers tells two. This last circumstance is an argument, I
think, for the originality of 'Syntipas;' and another may be drawn from
the insipidity of the greatest part of the tales. The only one of them
which, as I remember, is retained in the modern 'Erastus,' is that of the
knight who in a fit of groundless passion killed a faithful dog. ('Eraste,'
ch. viii.) It is plainly borrowed from a story in the 'Calilah u Damnah,'
p. 339 of the Greek translation, though there, instead of a dog, the animal
is called Νυμφη, by some mistake, as I suspect, of the translator.
　　There is a translation of this romance in English octosyllable verse, not
later than Chaucer's time, as I imagine, in MS. Cotton., Galba. E. ix. It is
entitled, 'The Proces of the Seven Sages,' and agrees exactly with 'Les Sept
Sages de Rome,' in French prose, in MS. Harl, 3860.
　　* The title in the printed copies is 'Ex gestis Romanorum historie
notabiles collecte ; de viciis virtutibusque tractantes ; cum applicationibus
moralisatis et mysticis.' The author of this strange work is quite unknown,
nor is it easy to fix with precision the time of its composition. Upon the
whole, I have no doubt that it is of a later date than Alfonsus, viz., the
beginning of the twelfth century, and I should guess that it was composed about the end of that century, or the beginning of the thirteenth.
　　Three couplets of English verses in ch. 68, and some English names in ch.
128, which are to be found in several old MSS. (the former chapter being
there numbered liii., and the latter xxviii.), though they have been left out

This last circumstance, though certainly very honourable to Alfonsus, has been very prejudicial to his fame. For instance, a

of the editions, afford a reasonable ground for conjecturing that one of our own countrymen was the author.

As it continued to be a popular book at the time of the invention of printing, it was very early put to the press, and several editions of it were published in different places before the year 1500. The earliest editions that I have seen agree together exactly, and contain 152 chapters. The edition at Rouen, in 1521, contains 181 chapters, the History of Apollonius Tyrius being the first of the additional chapters. (See 'Discourse,' &c., p. cxviii., note.) An edition of 'Gesta Romanorum,' printed in 1488, (probably at Argentina, Strasbourg,) agrees exactly with the edition of 1521. In MSS. Harl., 2270 and 5259, which are both seemingly complete, the number of chapters does not exceed 102; and yet, notwithstanding there are so many more stories in the printed books, there are still several in the MSS. which, I apprehend, have never been printed. See a note upon the plot of Shakspeare's 'Merchant of Venice,' with the signature of 'T. T.,' vol. iii. p. 224, and an addition to it in Appendix ii. See also a note of Mr Farmer's in the same Appendix, where he mentions his having found 'The Story of the Caskets' 'in an old translation of the "Gesta Romanorum," first printed by Winkin de Worde.' As he says nothing of 'The Story of the Bond,' we may presume, from the known accuracy of Mr Farmer's researches, that it is not contained in that translation.

It has been said above, that several of the fables in the 'Gesta Romanorum' are taken from Alfonsus. The author has also borrowed from the 'Calilah u Damnah,' by the help, I suppose, of some Latin translation from the Greek of Symeon Seth. The originals of the greatest part of his stories are not so easy to be traced. I speak of those which are found in the MSS., for of those in the Editt. many are plainly taken from well-known authors, some of which are quoted by name, as Aulus Gellius, Macrobius, Augustinus, Gervasius Tilberiensis, and others.

I will add here a few instances, which occur to me at present, of stories which writers of the fourteenth century have, or rather may have, borrowed from the 'Gesta Romanorum;' for in some of these instances it is possible that they may have had recourse to the very books from which the compiler of that work drew his materials. I shall cite the chapters as they are numbered in the edition of 1521, and in MS. Harl., 2270. Where reference is made to only one of these, it should be understood that I have not observed that story in the other.

Ch. viii., MS. 96, is copied by Gower, 'Conf. Am.,' b. v. fol. 122 b.— Ch. lvii., MS. 16: This story is in the 'Cento Novelle Antiche,' N. vi.—Ch. lxi. is in Gower, 'Conf. Am.' b. iii. fol. 54.—Ch. lxxxix. This is the story of 'The Three Rings,' which has been said, but I think without any reason, to have been of use to Swift in his 'Tale of a Tub.' It is in the 'C. N. A.,' Nov.

translation, as I suppose, of his last-mentioned story of 'The Two Friends,' is entitled, in a MS. of Lydgate, belonging to the late Dr Askew, 'A Tale of Two Marchants of Egypt and of Baldad, ex Gestis Romanorum,' (Mr Farmer's Notes on the 'Merch. of Ven.,' last ed. of Shakesp., App. ii.,) as if the tale had first appeared in that work. However, somebody, not long after the invention of printing, as I guess, did a little more justice to Alfonsus, by putting together his principal tales, and inserting them, with his name, in a collection of the fables of Æsop and other eminent fabulists in Latin. This collection was soon turned into French; and from that version Caxton made the translation into English which has been mentioned in the 'Discourse,' &c., p. cxxiv., note. Caxton's book has been reprinted more than once. I have seen an edition of it in 1647, and I doubt whether there has been one since.

P. 20, l. 9. ' For it is written,' &c. : What is included between

lxxi., and in the 'Decameron,' i. 3.—Ch. cix. There is a great similitude between this story and one which is told in the ' C. N. A.,' Nov. lxv., and in the ' Decameron,' x. 1. See also Gower, ' Conf. Am.,' b. v. fol. 96, 97.—Ch. cxviii. is from Alfonsus. It is repeated in the 'C. N. A.,' Nov. lxxxiv.—Ch. cxix., MS. 102, has been versified by Gower, ' Conf. Am.' b. v. fol. 110, b. It has been mentioned in a former note as taken originally from the 'Sapientia Indorum,' p. 444.—Ch. cxxiv., MS. 20, makes the last Novel of the 'C. N. A.'—Ch. clvii. makes the 50th Novel of the 'C. N. A.,' but it may have been taken from Alfonsus.—Ch. clxxi., MS. 55, is the story of ' The Two Friends,' mentioned in the text.—Ch. xlviii. MS. contains the story of ' The Caskets,' and Ch. xcix. MS. that of ' The Bond,' the two principal incidents in Shakspeare's ' Merchant of Venice.' It is said in the additional note, App. ii. last ed. of Shaksp., that Ser. Giovanni had ' worked up these two stories into one, as they are in the play.' But that is a mistake, which I beg leave to retract here. The novel of 'Ser. Giovanni' ('Pecorone,' Giorn. iv., Nov. 1) is founded only upon the story of 'The Bond.' It is probable, therefore, that Shakspeare took the story of 'The Caskets' from the English ' Gesta Romanorum,' and engrafted it upon the other.—Ch. xcviii. MS. is copied with very little alteration in the 'C. N. A.,' Nov. lxviii.

Many more stories in Gower, which seem to be founded upon ancient history, will appear upon examination to be taken from this book. It would lead me too far to particularise those which Lydgate, Occleve, and other later writers have borrowed from it. I will only mention, for the credit of the collection, that Ch. lxxx. contains the complete fable of Parnell's ' Hermit.'

hooks is wanting in all the MSS. which I have examined. It is plainly necessary to the sense, as it shews us what the fourth and fifth reasons of Meliboeus were, to which Prudence replies in pp. 22, 23. I have therefore inserted as literal a translation as I imagine Chaucer might have made of the following passage in the French 'Melibée' (MS. Reg., 19 C. vii.) :—'Car il est escript, la genglerie des femmes ne peut riens celler fors ce qu'elle ne scet. Apres le philosophre dit, en mauvais conseil les femmes vainquent les hommes, et par ces raisons je ne dois point user de ton conseil.'

P. 29, l. 20. 'Avise thee well:' He refers, I presume, to Cato, l. iii. dist. 6 :—

'Sermones blandos blæsosque cavere memento.'

P. 32, l. 8. 'Assay to do such things:' This precept of Cato is in l. iii. dist. 16 :—

'Quod potes id tentato ; operis ne pondere pressus
Succumbat labor, et frustra tentata relinquas.'

P. 38, l. 13. 'If thou have need :' Cato, l. iv. dist. 14 :—

'Auxilium a notis petito, si forte laboras ;
Nec quisquam melior medicus quam fidus amicus.'

P. 39, l. 25. 'Some men,' &c.: This passage, which is defective in all the MSS., I have patched up as well as I could by adding the words between hooks from the French ' Melibée,' where it stands thus :—' Aucunes gens ont enseigne leur decevour, car ils ont trop doubte que on ne les deceust. Apres tu te dois garder de venim, et si te dois garder de compaignie de moqueurs, car il est escript, Avec les moqueurs n'aies compaignie, et fuy leurs paroles comme le venim.'

P. 46, l. 12. 'Of the trespassers :' The following passage, which the reader will see to be very material to the sense, I have translated from the French, and inserted between hooks, as before :—'Et a ce respont dame Prudence : Certes, dist elle, Je t'ottroye que de vengeance vient molt de maulx et de biens, mais vengeance n'appartient pas a un chascun, fors seulement aux juges et a ceulx qui ont la juridicion sur les malfaiteurs.'

P. 49, l. 29. 'If a man of higher estate:' This prudent advice is from Cato, l. iv. dist. 40 :—

> 'Cede locum læsus, fortunæ cede potenti [f. potentis]
> Lædere qui potuit, prodesse aliquando valebit.'

P. 54, l. 6. 'If a neatherd's daughter:' The Editt. have strangely corrupted this into 'a nerthes daughter.' The reading, which I have restored from the MSS., is confirmed by the original passage in 'Pamphilus' (MS. Bod., 3703) :—

> 'Dummodo sit dives cujusdam nata bubulci,
> Eligit e mille quem libet illa virum.'

P. 56, l. 16. 'Wake,' &c. I can find nothing nearer to this in Cato, than the maxim (l. iii. dist. 7), 'Segnitiem fugito.' For the quotations from the same author in the following page, l. 1 and 5, see l. iv. dist. 17, and l. iii. dist. 23.

Ver. 13898. '*Corpus Madrian:*' The relics of St Maternus, Gloss. Urr. But I can find no such saint in the common legendaries.

Ver. 13948. 'A right well-faring:' I have no better authority for the insertion of 'right' than Ed. Urr.

Ver. 13968. 'Lusheburghes:' Base coins, probably, first imported, as Skinner thinks, from Luxemburg. They are mentioned in the Stat. 25 E. III. c. 2., 'la monoie appelle Lucynbourg;' and in 'P. P.,' fol. 82, b—

> 'As in lushburgh is a luther alay, yet loketh like sterling.'

Ver. 14013. 'In the field of Damascene:' So Lydgate, from Boccaccio, speaks of Adam and Eve ('Trag.,' b. i. c. 1.)—

> 'Of slime of the erth in Damascene the felde,
> God made them above ech creature.'

Boccaccio is much longer in relating their story, which is the first of his tragedies.

Ver. 14021. 'Samson:' His tragedy is also in Boccaccio (b. i. c. 19); but our author seems rather to have followed the original, Judges xiv., xv., xvi.

Ver. 14080. 'The quern:' 'The mill.' 'Kuerna,' 'mola,' Island.

Ver. 14101. 'Hercules:' In this account of the labours of Hercules, Chaucer has evidently copied Boethius, l. iv. met. 7.

Many of the expressions he had used before in his prose translation of that author.

Ver. 14116. 'The heaven on his neckë long:' This is the reading of the best MSS., and is agreeable to Boethius, loc. cit., thus translated by Chaucer:—'And the last of his labors was, that he susteined the heven upon his necke unbowed.' The margin of MS. C. 1 explains 'long' to mean 'diu.' The Editt. read—

'And bare his hed upon his spere long.'

Ver. 14123. 'Saith Trophee:' As all the best MSS. agree in this reading, I have retained it, though I cannot tell what author is alluded to. The margin of C. 1 has this note—'Ille vates Chaldæorum Tropheus.'

The Editt. read ' for trophee.'

Ver. 14149. 'Nabuchodonosor:' For this history, and the following of Balthasar, see Daniel i.–v. The latter only is related by Boccaccio, (b. ii. c. xxiii.)

Ver. 14253. 'Zenobia:' Her story is told by Boccaccio, 'De cas. Vir.,' l. iii. c. 7, but more at large in his book 'De claris Mulieribus;' from which our author has plainly taken almost every circumstance of his narration: though in ver. 14331 he seems to refer to Petrarch as his original. Perhaps Boccaccio's book had fallen into Chaucer's hands under the name of Petrarch.

Ver. 14295. 'Till fully forty days:' There is a confusion in this passage, which might have been avoided if our author had recurred to Trebellius Pollio, 'Trig. Tyrann.,' c. xxix. de Zenobia :—'Quum semel concubuisset, expectatis menstruis, continebat se si prægnans esset; sin minus, iterum potestatem quærendis liberis dabat.'

Ver. 14378. 'A vitremite:' This word is differently written in the MSS. 'vitrymite,' 'witermite,' 'wintermite,' 'vitryte.' The Editt. read 'autremite,' which is equally unintelligible.

Ver. 14385. 'South and Septentrioun:' The MSS. read 'north;' but there can be no doubt of the propriety of the correction, which was first made, I believe, in Ed. Urr. In the 'Rom. de la R.,' from whence great part of this tragedy of Nero is translated, the passage stands thus (ver. 6501) :—

> ' Ce desloyal, que je te dy,
> Et d'Orient et de Midy,
> D'Occident, de Septentrion,
> Tint-il la jurisdicion.'

Ver. 14408. 'Doomsman:' 'Judge.' The word in Boethius, who has also related this story, is 'censor' (l. ii. met. vi.) :—

> ' Ora non tinxit lacrymis, sed esse
> Censor extincti potuit decoris;'

which our author has thus rendered in his prose version :—'Ne no tere wette his face, but he was so harde-herted, that he might be domesman, or judge, of her dedde beautee.'

· Ver. 14484. 'Where Eliachim:' I cannot find any priest of this name in the Book of Judith. The High Priest of Jerusalem is called Joacim in c. iv., which name would suit the verse better than Eliachim.

Ver. 14493. 'Antiochus:' This tragedy is a poetical para-phrase of 2 Maccabees ix.

Ver. 14639. 'Word and end:' Dr Hicks, in his 'Gr. A.-S.,' p. 70, has proposed to read 'ord and end,' both here and in 'Tro.,' b. v. ver. 1668. He has shewn very clearly that 'ord and end' was a common Saxon expression for 'the whole' of a thing; the 'beginning and end' of it. But all the MSS. that I have examined read 'word,' and therefore I have left it in the text, as possibly the old Saxon phrase, in Chaucer's time, might have been corrupted.

Ver. 14645. 'Crœsus:' In the opening of this story, our author has plainly copied the following passage of his own version of 'Boethius,' b. ii. pro. 2 :—'Wiste thou not how Crœsus, king of Lydiens, of whiche king Cyrus was ful sore agaste a litel before,' &c. But the greatest part is taken from the 'Rom. de la R.,' ver. 6847–6912.

14679. 'Tragedy is:' This reflection seems to have been suggested by one which follows soon after the mention of Crœsus in the passage just cited from Boethius :—'What other thing bewaylen the cryinges of tragedyes but onely the dedes of fortune, that with an aukewarde stroke overtourneth the realmes of grete nobleye?'

Ver. 14685. 'Peter of Spain:' This tragedy, and the three

following, in several MSS. are inserted before, after ver. 14380.
So that the Monk's Tale ends with ver. 14684 :—

    ' And cover her bright face with a cloud.'

In favour of this arrangement, it may be observed, that when
the Monk is interrupted, the Host alludes to this line as fresh
in his memory (ver. 14788) :—

    ' He spake how Fortune cover'd with a cloud
      I wot not what, and als of a tragedy
      Right now ye heard.'

Where ' tragedy ' may be supposed to allude to ver. 14679.
On the other hand, though the Monk professedly disregards
chronological order, these very modern stories in the midst of
the ancient make an awkward appearance; and as the Host
declares himself to have been half asleep, he may very well be
supposed to speak from a confused recollection of what had been
said eighty-eight verses before. And what he says of ' tragedy '
may be referred to ver. 14768.
I have followed the order observed in the best MSS.—C. 1,
Ask. 1, 2, HA.
Ver. 14697. ' Not Charles' Oliver :' Not the Oliver of Charles
(Charlemagne), but an Oliver of Armorica, a second Genelon,
or Ganelon. (See ver. 13124, 15233.) So this passage is to
be understood, which in Ed. Urr. has been changed to ' Not
Charles, ne Oliver.' But who this ' Oliver of Bretagne ' was,
whom our author charges as ' worker ' of the death of King
Petro, is not so clear. According to Mariana, (l. xvii. c. 13,)
such a charge might most properly be brought against Bertrand du Guesclin, a Breton, afterwards Constable of France;
as it was in consequence of a private treaty with him that Petro
came to his tent, where he was killed by his brother Henry,
and partly, as some said, ' con ayuda de Beltran.' But how he
should come to be called ' Oliver ' I cannot guess; unless, perhaps, Chaucer confounded him with Olivier de Clisson, another
famous Breton of those times, who was also Constable of France
after Bertrand. Froissart mentions an Olivier de Manny, nephew to Bertrand du Guesclin, as receiving large rewards from

King IIenry (vol. i. ch. 245), but he does not represent him as particularly concerned in the death of Petro.

The person meant, whoever he was, must have been sufficiently pointed out at the time by his coat of arms, which is described in ver. 14693, 14694. The 'eagle of black' in 'a field of snow' is plain enough, but the rest of the blazonry I cannot pretend to decipher.

Ver. 14701. 'Petro, king of Cypre:' Concerning the taking of Alexandria by this prince, and his other exploits, see the note on ver. 51, and the authors there cited. He was assassinated in 1369. ('Acad. des Ins.,' t. xx. p. 439.)

Ver. 14709. 'Barnabo Viscount:' Bernabo Visconti, duke of Milan, was deposed by his nephew and thrown into prison, where he died in 1385.

I did not attend to this circumstance, when I stated the insurrection of Straw in 1381, as the latest historical fact mentioned in these tales, ('Discourse,' &c., p. cv., note.) The death of Bernabo was certainly later. Fortunately, however, this difference of four years has no other consequence than that it makes the supposed date of the Pilgrimage, in 1383, which was before very doubtful, still more improbable. The Knight might as probably be upon a pilgrimage in 1387 as in 1383, according to the precedent of Sir Mathew de Gourney. (See note on ver. 43.)

Ver. 14717. 'Hugolin of Pise:' Chaucer himself has referred us to Dante for the original of this tragedy. (See 'Inferno,' c. xxxiii.)

Ver. 14765, 14766. These two verses in the Editt. have been transposed, to the confusion of the sense as well as of the metre.

Ver. 14811. 'Say somewhat of hunting:' For the propriety of this request, see the note on ver. 166 of the Monk's Character.

Ver. 14816. 'Thou Sir John:' I know not how it has happened, that in the principal modern languages, John, or its equivalent, is a name of contempt, or at least of slight. So the Italians use 'Gianni,' from whence 'Zani;' the Spaniards 'Juan,' as 'Bobo Juan,' a foolish John; the French 'Jean,' with various additions; and in English, when we call a man 'a John,' we do not mean it as a title of honour. Chaucer, in ver. 3708, uses 'Jack fool' as the Spaniards do 'Bobo Juan;' and I suppose 'Jack ass' has the same etymology.

The title of Sir was usually given by courtesy to priests, both secular and regular.

Ver. 14852. 'A manner dey:' 'A kind of dey;' but what 'a dey' was it is not easy to determine precisely. It is mentioned, as the last species of labourers in husbandry, in the Stat. 25 Edw. III., St. i. c. 1:—'Qe chescun charetter, caruer, chaceour des carues, bercher, porcher, deye, et tous autres servantz.' And again, in the Stat. 37 Edw. III., c. 14:—'Item qe charetters, charuers, chaceours des carues, bovers, vachers, berchers, porchers, deyes, et tous autres gardeins des bestes, bateurs des bleez, et toutes maneres des genz d'estate de garson entendantz a husbandrie.' It probably meant originally 'a day-labourer' in general, though it may since have been used to denote particularly the superintendent of a 'dayerie.' (See Du Cange, in v. 'Daeria,' 'Dayeria,' 'Dagascalci.'

Ver. 14857. 'The merry orgon:' This is put licentiously for orgons, or organs. It is plain, from 'gon,' in the next line, that Chaucer meant to use this word as a plural, from the Lat. Gr. 'Organa.' He uses it so in ver. 15602:—

'And while that th' organs maden melody.'

Ver. 14876. 'Was cleped fair Damoselle Partelote:' I suspect that 'fair' has been added by some one who was unnecessarily alarmed for the metre.

After this verse, the Editt. (except Ca. 1) have the two following:—

'He feather'd her a hundred times a day,
And she him pleaseth all that ever she may.'

But as I found them in only two MSS., HA. and D., I was glad to leave them out as an injudicious interpolation. See below, ver. 15183.

Whoever wishes to see a great deal of uncertain etymology concerning the name Partelote, may consult Gl. V. in v. 'Partelot.'

Ver. 14881. 'Loken in every lith :' 'Locked in every limb.' The Editt. read 'loking.' 'Loken' is used by Occleve, in the first of his poems mentioned above in note on ver. 5002 :—

> 'Lefte was the Erles chamber dore unstoken,
> To which he came, and fonde it was not *loken*.

Ver. 14885. 'My lefe is fare in land :' 'Fare,' or 'faren ;' gone. So the best MSS. Ed. Ca. 2 reads 'fer.' It is not easy to determine which of these is the true reading, unless we should recover the old song from which this passage seems to be quoted.

Ver. 14914. 'Away, quod she :' I have here inadvertently followed the printed copies. But instead of 'away,' the best MSS. read 'avoy,' which is more likely to have been used by Chaucer. The word occurs frequently in the French 'Fabliaux,' &c. (See t. ii. p. 243, 245.) The vocabulary, at the end of that volume, renders 'Avoi,' 'Helas !' but it seems to signify no more than our 'Away!' The Italians use 'Via!' in the same manner. 'Roman de Troye,' MS. :—

> ' Lors dit Thoas, *Avoi, avoi*,
> Sire Achilles, vous dites mal.'

Ver. 14946. ' Lo Cato :' L. ii. dist. 32, 'Somnia ne cures.' I observe, by the way, that this distich is quoted by John of Salisbury ('Polycrat.,' l. ii. c. 16) as a precept 'viri sapientis.' In another place (l. vii. c. 9) he introduces his quotation of the first verse of dist. 20, l. iii. in this manner :—' Ait vel Cato, vel alius, nam autor incertus est.'

Ver. 14971. ' Catapuce :' ' Catapuzza,' Ital. ; ' Catapuce,' Fr. A kind of spurge.

Ver. 14990. ' One of the greatest authors :' Cicero (' De Divin.,' l. i. c. 27) relates this and the following story, but in a contrary order, and with so many other differences, that one might be led to suspect that he was here quoted at second hand, if it were not usual with Chaucer, in these stories of familiar life, to throw in a number of natural circumstances, not to be found in his original authors.

Ver. 15116. ' Saint Kenelm :' See his life in all the Editt. of the English ' Golden Legende.'

Ver. 15147. 'Lo her, Andromache:' We must not look for this dream of Andromache in Homer. The first author who relates it is the fictitious Dares (c. xxiv.); and Chaucer very probably took it from him, or from Guido de Columnis; or perhaps from Benoit de Saint More, whose 'Roman de Troye' I believe to have been that history of Dares which Guido professes to follow, and has indeed almost entirely translated. A full discussion of this point, by a comparison of Guido's work with the 'Roman de Troye,' would require more time and pains than I am inclined to bestow upon it. I will just mention a circumstance which, if it can be verified, will bring the question to a much shorter decision. The 'Versio Daretis Phrygii Gallico metro,' in the Ambrosian Library, of which Montfaucon speaks, ('Diar. Ital.' p. 19,) is undoubtedly the 'Roman de Troye' by Benoit de Sainte More. The verses which are there quoted differ no otherwise from the beginning of Benoit's poem in MS. Harl., 4482, than as an old copy usually does from a more modern one. If, therefore, we can depend upon Montfaucon's judgment, that the MS. which he saw was written in the twelfth century, it will follow that Benoit wrote near a hundred years before Guido, whose work, in all the MSS. that I have seen or heard of, is uniformly said to have been finished in the year 1287. There can be no doubt that the later of these two writers copied from the former.

Ver. 15169. 'So sicker as *In principio:*' See the note on ver. 256.

The next line is taken from the fabulous conference between the Emperor Adrian and Secundus the Philosopher, of which some account has been given in note on ver. 6777. 'Quid est mulier? Hominis confusio, insaturabilis bestia,' &c.

Ver. 15196. 'Sithen March ended:' I have ventured to depart from the MSS. and Editt. in this passage. They all read 'began' instead of 'ended.' At the same time MS. C. 1 has this note in the margin: 'i. 2° die Maii,' which plainly supposes that the thirty-two days are to be reckoned from the end of March. As the vernal equinox, according to our author's hypothesis, ('Discourse,' &c., p. civ.,) happened on the 12th of March, the place of the sun (as described in ver. 15200, 15201) in

22° of Taurus, agrees very nearly with his true place on the 2d of May, the fifty-third day inclusive from the equinox. MS. C. reads thus :—

> ‘ Syn March began tway monthes and dayes two ;’

which brings us to the same day, but, I think, by a less probable correction of the faulty copies.

Ver. 15205. ‘ Twenty degrees :’ The reading of the greatest part of the MSS. is ‘ forty degrees.’ But that is evidently wrong; for Chaucer is speaking of the altitude of the sun at or about prime—*i. e.* six o’clock A.M. (See ver. 15203.) When the sun is in 22° of Taurus, he is 21° high about three-quarters after six A.M.

Ver. 15215. At the side of this verse is written in the margin of MS. C., ‘ Petrus Comestor,’ to intimate, I suppose, that this maxim is to be found in the ‘ Historia Scholastica ’ of that author, who was a celebrated commentator on the Bible in the twelfth century. (See Fabricius, ‘ Bib. Med. Ætat.’ in v.)

Ver. 15221. ‘ A col fox :’ Skinner interprets this ‘ a blackish fox,’ as if it were ‘ a cole fox.’ (Gl. Urr.) It is much easier to refute this interpretation than to assign the true one. ‘ Coll ’ appears, from ver. 15389, to have been a common name for a dog. In composition it is to be taken ‘ in malam partem,’ but in what precise sense I cannot say. See Chaucer’s ‘ H. of F.,’ b. iii. 187, ‘ Coll-tragetour ;’ and in the ‘ Mirr. for Mag. Leg. of Glendour,’ fol. 127, b., ‘ Colprophet’ is plainly put for a false, lying prophet. Heywood has an epigram ‘ Of Coleprophet’ (Cent. vi. ep. 89) :—

> ‘ Thy prophesy poysonly to the pricke goth :
> Coleprophet and colepoyson thou art both.’

And in his ‘ Proverbial Dialogues,’ p. i. ch. x., he has the following lines :—

> ‘ Coll under canstyk she can plaie on both hands :
> Dissimulation well she understands.’

I will add an allusion of our author, in the ‘ Test. of Love,’ (b. ii. fol. cccxxxiii. b.,) to a story of one ‘ Collo,’ which I cannot explain : ‘ Busiris slewe his gestes, and he was slain of Hercules his geste. Hugest betrayshed many men, and of Collo was he betrayed.'

Ver. 15240. 'But what that God:' This passage has been translated into (rather elegant) Latin iambics by Sir H. Savile, in his preface to Bradwardin, ' De Causâ Dei,' Lond., 1618. (See the ' Testimonies,' &c., prefixed to Ed. Urr.) Our author has discussed this question of the Divine prescience, &c., more at large in his ' Troilus,' b. 4, from ver. 957 to ver. 1078. It is an addition of his own, cf which there is no trace in the ' Philostrato' of Boccaccio. (See ' Essay,' &c., p. lxxxi., note.)

Ver. 15277. 'Physiologus:' He alludes, I suppose, to a book in Latin metre, entitled, ' Physiologus de Naturis XII. Animalium,' by one Theobaldus, whose age is not known. (Fabr., ' Bib. Med. Æt.' in v. ' Theobaldus.') There is a copy of this work in MS. Harl., 3093, in which the ninth section, ' De Sirenis,' begins thus :—

> ' Sirenæ sunt monstra maris resonantia magnis
> Vocibus et modulis cantus formantia multis,
> Ad quas incaute veniunt sæpissime nautæ,
> Quæ faciunt somnum nimia dulcedine vocum,' &c.

See also ' R. R.,' ver. 680.

Ver. 15318. ' In Dan Burnel the ass:' The story alluded to is in a poem of Nigel Wireker, entitled, ' Burnellus, seu Speculum Stultorum,' written in the time of Richard I. The substance of the story is in Gl. Urr., v. ' Burnell.' The poem itself is in most collections of MSS. The printed copies are more rare, though there have been several editions of it. (See Leyser, ' Hist. Po. Med. Ævi,' p. 752, 753.)

' Burnell ' is used as a nickname for the ass in the Chester Whitsun Plays (MS. Harl., 2013.) See the note on ver. 3539. In the pageant of Balaam, he says—

> ' Go forth, Burnell, go forth, go.
> What? the devil, my asse will not go;'

and again, fol. 36, b.—

> ' Burnell, why begilest thou me?'

The original word was probably ' Brunell,' from his brown colour; as the fox (below, ver. 15340) is called ' Russell,' from his red colour, I suppose.

Ver. 15341. 'By the gargat:' The Editt. have changed this into 'gorget;' but 'gargat' is an old Fr. word. 'Rom. de Rou,' (MS. Reg., 4 C. xi.) :—

> 'O grant culteals e od granz cuignees
> Lur unt les gargates trenchies.'

Ver. 15353. 'O Gaufrid:' He alludes to a passage in the 'Nova Poetria' of Geoffrey de Vinsauf, published not long after the death of Richard I. In this work the author has not only given instructions for composing in the different styles of poetry, but also examples. His specimen of the plaintive kind of composition begins thus :—

> 'Neustria, sub clypeo regis defensa Ricardi,
> Indefensa modo, gestu testare dolorem.
> Exundent oculi lacrymas ; exterminet ora
> Pallor ; connodet digitos tortura ; cruentet
> Interiora dolor, et verberet æthera clamor :
> Tota peris ex morte sua. Mors non fuit ejus,
> Sed tua ; non una, sed publica mortis origo.
> *O Veneris lacrymosa dies !* O sidus amarum !
> Illa dies tua nox fuit, et Venus illa venenum.
> Illa dedit vulnus,' &c.

These lines are sufficient to shew the object and the propriety of Chaucer's ridicule. The whole poem is printed in Leyser's 'Hist. Po. Med. Ævi,' pp. 862-978.

Ver. 15451. 'As saith my Lord :' Opposite to this verse, in the margin of MS. C. 1, is written 'Kantuar,' which means, I suppose, that some Archbishop of Canterbury is quoted.

Ver. 15468. 'Said to another :' I have observed, in the 'Discourse,' &c., § XXXVII., that in MSS. Ask. 1, 2, this line is read thus :—

> 'Seide unto the nunne as ye shul heer.'

The following are the six forged lines which the same MSS. exhibit by way of introduction to the Nun's Tale :—

> 'Madame, and I dorste, I wolde you pray
> To telle a tale in fortheringe of our way.
> Than mighte ye do unto us grete ese.
> Gladly, sire, quoth she, so that I might please
> You and this worthy company,
> And began hire tale riht thus ful sobrely.'

Ver. 15514. 'Out of release:' All the best MSS. concur in this reading, and therefore I have followed them, though I confess that I do not clearly understand the phrase; unless perhaps it mean 'without release;' 'without being ever released from their duty.' The common reading, 'withouten lees,' is a genuine Saxon phrase. 'Butan leas;' 'absque falso:' 'without a lie.'

Ver. 15518. 'Assembled is:' This stanza is very like one in the Prioress's Tale, ver. 13403–13410.

Ver. 15530. 'Son of Eve:' See the 'Discourse,' &c., § XXXVII., note.

Ver. 15536. 'Be thou mine advocat:' I have no better authority for the insertion of 'thou' than Edd. Urr. The metre, perhaps, might be safe without it, considering 'highe' as a dissyllable, but the verse would be very rough.

Ver. 15553. 'First will I:' The note upon this in the margin of MS. C. 1 is 'Interpretatio, &c., quam ponit Frater Jacobus Januensis in Legendâ Aureâ.' It has been observed in the 'Discourse,' &c., that this whole tale is almost literally translated from the 'Legenda Aurea.'

Ver. 15654. 'Louting:' i. 'latitantem,' Marg. MS. C. 1, from the Sax. 'lutan,' or 'lutian;' 'latere.'

Ver. 15675. 'On Lord, on faith:' I have adopted this reading in preference to that of the best MSS.—'O Lord,' 'O Faith,' 'O God,' &c.—in order to guard against the mistake which the Editt. have generally fallen into, of considering 'O,' in this passage, as the sign of the vocative case. 'On,' and 'o,' are used indifferently by Chaucer to signify ' one.'

Ver. 15738. 'And of the miracle:' I should have been glad to have met with any authority for leaving out this parenthesis of fourteen lines, which interrupts the narration so awkwardly, and to so little purpose. The substance of it is in the printed editions of the Latin 'Legenda Aurea,' but appears evidently to have been at first a marginal observation, and to have crept into the text by the blunder of some copyist. Accordingly it is wanting in Caxton's 'Golden Legende,' and, I suppose, in the French 'Legende Dorée,' from which he translated. The author of the French version had either made use of an uncorrupted MS., or perhaps had been sagacious enough to discern and reject the interpolation.

Ver. 15783. 'And we also:' It should have been 'us.' I take notice of this, because Chaucer is very rarely guilty of such an offence against grammar.

Ver. 15855. 'Your course is done:' So all the MSS. In Ed. Urr. 'don' is changed to 'run;' and I believe no modern poet would have joined any other verb with 'cours,' especially after he had used 'ydon' in the preceding line; but I am not clear that Chaucer attended to such niceties.

In the latter part of this line, the best MSS. read, 'your faith han ye conserved;' and I know not by what negligence I omitted to follow them.

Ver. 15966. 'Thine utter eyen:' 'Exterioribus oculis,' Marg. MS. C. 1.

Ver. 16023. 'Five mile:' So all the MSS. except E., which reads 'half a mile.' This latter reading must certainly be preferred, if we suppose that Chaucer meant to mark the interval between the conclusion of the Nun's Tale and the arrival of the Canon. But it would be contrary to the general plan of our author's work, and to his practice upon other occasions, that the Host should suffer the company

> 'To riden by the way, dombe as the ston,'

even for half a mile. I am, therefore, rather inclined to believe that 'five mile' is the right reading, and that it was intended to mark the distance from *some place*, which we are now unable to determine with certainty, for want of the Prologue to the Nun's Tale.

I have sometimes suspected that it was the intention of Chaucer to begin the journey *from* Canterbury with the Nun's Tale. In that case 'five mile' would mark very truly the distance from Canterbury to Boughton-under-Blee. The circumstances, too, of the Canon's overtaking the pilgrims, and looking 'as he had pricked,' or galloped, 'miles three,' would agree better with this supposition. It is scarce credible that he should have ridden after them from Southwark to Boughton without overtaking them; and if he had, it must have been a very inadequate representation of his condition, to say that 'it seemed he had pricked miles three.' Besides, the words of the Yeoman (ver. 16056, 16057)—

'Now in the morrow tide
Out of your hostelry I saw you ride—

seem to imply that they were overtaken in the same morning in which they set out; but it must have been considerably after noon before they reached Boughton from Southwark.

There is another way of solving these difficulties, by supposing that the Pilgrims lay upon the road, and that the Nun's Tale was the first of the second day's journey. It is most probable that a great part of the company, not to mention their horses, would have had no objection to dividing the journey to Canterbury into two days; but if they lay only five miles on this side of Boughton, I do not see how they could spend the whole second day till evening (see ver. 17316) in travelling from thence to Canterbury.

I must take notice, too, in opposition to my first hypothesis, that the manner in which the Yeoman expresses himself in ver. 16091, 16092, seems to shew that he was riding *to* Canterbury.

Ver. 16156. 'For Cato saith:' This precept of Cato is in l. i. dist. 17 :—

'Ne cures si quis tacito sermone loquatur ;
Conscius ipse sibi de se putat omnia dici.'

Ver. 16211. 'Through jupartic:' So MS. C. 1. I have followed it, as it comes nearest to the true original of our word 'jeopardy,' which our etymologists have sadly mistaken. They deduce it from 'J'ai perdu,' or 'Jeu perdu;' but I rather believe it to be a corruption of 'Jeu parti.' A 'jeu parti' is properly a game, in which the chances are exactly even. See Froissart, v. i. c. 234 :—' Ils n'estoient pas à *jeu parti* contre les François;' v. ii. c. 9, 'si nous les voyons à *jeu parti.*' From hence it signifies anything uncertain or hazardous. In the old French poetry, the discussion of a problem, where much might be said on both sides, was called a 'jeu parti.' See ' Poesies du Roy de Navarre,' Chanson xlviii. See also Du Cange in v. ' Jocus partitus.'

Ver. 16288. ' The four spirits,' &c.: Compare Gower, ' De Conf. Am.,' b. iv. fol. 76, b.

Ver. 16306. ' Ascaunce:' See the note on ver. 7327.

Ver. 16430. ' But all thing:' This is taken from the ' Parabolæ' of Alanus de Insulis, who died in 1204. See Leyser, ' Hist. Po. Med. Ævi,' p. 1074 :—

> ' Non teneas aurum totum quod splendet ut aurum,
> Nec pulchrum pomum quodlibet esse bonum.'

Ver. 16480. ' A priest, an annuallere:' They were called ' annualleres,' not from their receiving a yearly stipend, as the Gloss. explains it, but from their being employed solely in singing ' annuals,' or ' anniversary masses,' for the dead, without any cure of souls. See the Stat. 36 Edw. III. c. viii., where the ' chapelleins parochiels' are distinguished from others ' chantanz anuales, et a cure des almes nient entendantz.' They were both to receive yearly stipends, but the former was allowed to take six marks, and the latter only five. Compare Stat. 2 H. V. St. 2, c. 2, where the stipend of the ' chapellein parochiel' is raised to eight marks, and that of the ' chapellein annueler' (he is so named in the statute) to seven.

Ver. 16915. ' The secret of secrets:' He alludes to a treatise entitled, ' Secreta Secretorum,' which was supposed to contain the sum of Aristotle's instructions to Alexander. (See Fabric., ' Bibl. Gr.,' v. ii. p. 167.) It was very popular in the middle ages. Ægidius de Columnâ, a famous divine and bishop about the latter end of the thirteenth century, built upon it his book, ' De Regimine Principum,' of which our Occleve made a free translation in English verse, and addressed it to Henry V., while Prince of Wales. A part of Lydgate's translation of the ' Secreta Secretorum' is printed in Ashmole's ' Theat. Chem. Brit.,' p. 397. He did not translate more than about half of it, being prevented by death. (See MS. Harl., 2251; and Tanner, ' Bib. Brit.,' in v. ' Lydgate.') The greatest part of the seventh book of Gower's ' Conf. Amant.' is taken from this supposed work of Aristotle.

Ver. 16918. ' As his book Senior:' Ed. Urr. reads, ' As *in* his book;' which I should have preferred to the common reading, if I had found it in any copy of better authority.

The book alluded to is printed in the 'Theatrum Chemicum,' vol. v. p. 219, under this title, 'Senioris Zadith fil. Hamuelis tabula Chymica.' The story which follows of Plato, and his disciple, is there told (p. 249), with some variations, of Solomon: 'Dixit Salomon rex, Recipe lapidem qui dicitur Thitarios—Dixit sapiens, Assigna mihi illum. Dixit, est corpus magnesiæ—Dixit, quid est magnesia? Respondit, magnesia est aqua, composita,' &c.

Ver. 16961. 'Do him come forth:' So MSS. Ask. 1, 2, and some others. The common reading is, 'Do him *comfort*.' The alteration is material, not only as it gives a clearer sense, but as it intimates to us, that the narrator of a tale was made to come out of the crowd, and to take his place within hearing of the Host during his narration. Agreeably to this notion, when the Host calls upon Chaucer (ver. 13628), he says—

> 'Approachë near, and look up merrily.
> Now 'ware you, Sirs, and let this man have place.'

It was necessary that the Host, who was to be 'judge and reporter' of the tales (ver. 816), should hear them all distinctly. The others might hear as much as they could or as they chose of them. It would have required the lungs of a Stentor to speak audibly to a company of thirty people trotting on together in a road of the fourteenth century.

Ver. 16965. 'To sleepen by *the morrow*:' This must be understood generally for 'the day-time;' as it was then afternoon. It has been observed, in the 'Discourse,' &c., § XIII., that, in this episode of the Cook, no notice is taken of his having told a tale before.

Ver. 16991. 'Will ye joust at the fan?' Some MSS. read, 'van.' The sense of both words is the same. The thing meant is the 'quintain,' which is called a 'fan,' or 'van,' from its turning round like a weathercock. See Du Cange in v. 'Vana;' Menestrier 'sur les tournois,' as quoted by Menage, 'Dict. Etymol.,' in v. 'Quintaine;' and Kennet's 'Paroch. Antiq.'

Ver. 16993. 'Wine of ape:' This is the reading of MSS. HA., D., E., and Ed. Ca. 1, and I believe the true one. The explanation in the Gloss. of this and the preceding passage, from

Mr Speght, is too ridiculous to be repeated. 'Wine of ape' I understand to mean the same as 'vin de singe' in the old 'Calendrier des Bergiers,' Sign. l. ii. b. The author is treating of physiognomy, and in his description of the four temperaments, he mentions, among other circumstances, the different effects of wine upon them. The choleric, he says, 'a vin de lyon ;· cest a dire, quant a bien beu veult tanser noyser et battre ;' the sanguine, 'a vin de singe; quant a plus beu tant est plus joyeux.' In the same manner the phlegmatic is said to have 'vin de mouton,' and the melancholic, 'vin de porceau.'

I find the same four animals applied to illustrate the effects of wine in a little Rabbinical tradition, which I shall transcribe here from Fabric. ('Cod. Pseudepig. V. T.' vol. i. p. 275) :— 'Vineas plantanti Noacho Satanam se junxisse memorant, qui, dum Noa vites plantaret, mactaverit apud illas *ovem, leonem, simiam* et *suem:* Quod principio potûs vini homo sit instar *ovis* vinum sumptum efficiat ex homine *leonem,* largius haustum mutet eum in saltantem *simiam,* ad ebrietatem infusum transformet illum in pollutam et prostratam *suem.*' See also 'Gesta Romanorum,' c. 159, where a story of the same purport is quoted from Josephus, 'In Libro de Casu Rerum Naturalium.'

Ver. 16999. 'A fair chivachee:' A fair 'expedition.' See the note on ver. 85. The common Editt. read 'chevisance.'

Ver. 17112. 'Take any bird:' This passage is too like one which has occurred before in the Squire's Tale, (ver. 10925.) The thought is plainly taken from Boethius, l. iii. met. 2. See also 'Rom. de la R.,' ver. 14717–14734.

Ver. 17124. 'Let take a cat:' This is imitated from the 'Rom. de la R.,' ver. 14825.

Ver. 17130. 'Lo, here hath kind:' So MSS. Ask. 1, 2. The common Editt. read, 'lust.' 'Kind' is 'nature.' See the next line but one, and ver. 10922, 10924.

Ver. 17132. 'A she-wolf:' This is also from the 'Rom. de la R.,' ver. 8142 :—

> 'Tout ainsi comme fait la louve,
> Que sa folie tant empire,
> Qu'elle prent de tous loups le pire.'

Ver. 17173. 'Or any thief:' 'Any' is from conjecture only,

instead of ' a,' the reading of all the MSS. that I have consulted. The reading of Ed. Urr. is, ' or elles a thefe; ' whether from authority or conjecture I cannot tell, but even as a conjecture I should have adopted it in preference to my own, if I had taken notice of it in time.

Ver. 17278. ' My son, thy tongue: ' In the ' Rom. de la R.,' ver. 7399, this precept is quoted from ' Ptolomée :'—

> ' Au commencer de l'Almageste.'

See the note on ver. 5764.

Ver. 17281. ' The first virtue :' This precept is also quoted in the ' Rom. de la R.,' ver. 7415, from Cato. It is extant l. i. dist. 3 :—

> ' Virtutem primam esse puta compescere linguam.'

Ver. 17308. ' Be no author new :' This seems to be from Cato, l. i. dist. 12 :—

> ' Rumores fuge, ne incipias *novus auctor* haberi.'

It looks as if Chaucer read—

> ' *Rumoris* fuge ne incipias novus auctor haberi.'

Ver. 17316. ' Four of the clock :' See the ' Discourse,' &c., § XLI.

Ver. 17321. ' Therewith the moonë's exaltation,
            In meanë Libra, alway 'gan ascend :
This is a very obscure passage. Some of the MSS. read, ' I mean Libra.' According to the reading which I have followed, ' exaltation' is not to be considered as a technical term, but as signifying simply ' rising; ' and the sense will be, ' that the moon's rising, in the middle of Libra, was continually ascending,' &c.

If ' exaltation' be taken in its technical meaning, as explained in the note on ver. 6284, it will be impossible to make any sense of either of the readings : for the exaltation of the moon was not in Libra, but in Taurus. (' Kalendrier des Bergiers,' sign. i. ult.) Mr Speght, I suppose, being aware of this, altered ' Libra' into ' Taurus ;' but he did not consider that the sun, which has just been said to be ' descending,' was at that time in Taurus, and that consequently Taurus must also have been descending.

' Libra,' therefore, should by no means be parted with. Being
in that part of the zodiac which is nearly opposite to Taurus,
the place of the sun, it is very properly represented as ' ascending' above the horizon toward the time of the sun's setting.   If
any alteration were to be admitted, I should be for reading—

' Therewith Saturnë's exaltation,
I meanë Libra, alway 'gan ascend.'

The exaltation of Saturn was in Libra.   ('Kalendrier des
Bergers,' sign. K. i.)

Ver. 17354. ' I cannot gest, rom, ram, ruf :' This is plainly a
contemptuous manner of describing alliterative poetry ; and the
Parson's prefatory declaration that he is ' a southern man,' would
lead one to imagine that compositions in that style were, at this
time, chiefly confined to the northern provinces.   It was observed
long ago by William of Malmesbury, (l. iii. ' Pontif. Angl.') that
the language of the north of England was so harsh and un-
polished, as to be scarce intelligible to a southern man.   ' Quod
propter viciniam barbararum gentium, et propter remotionem
regum quondam Anglorum modo Normannorum contigit, qui
magis ad Austrum quam ad Aquilonem diversati noscuntur.'
From the same causes, we may presume that it was often long
before the improvements in the poetical art, which from time to
time were made in the south, could find their way into the
north ; so that there the hobbling alliterative verse might still
be in the highest request, even after Chaucer had established the
use of the heroic metre in this part of the island.   Dr Percy has
quoted an alliterative poem by a Cheshire man on the battle of
Flodden in 1513, and he has remarked, ' that all such poets as
used this kind of metre, retained along with it many peculiar
Saxon idioms.' (' Essay on Metre of P. P.')   This may, perhaps,
have been owing to their being generally inhabitants of the
northern counties, where the old Saxon idiom underwent much
fewer and slower alterations than it did in the neighbourhood of
the capital.

' To gest' here is ' to relate gests.'   In ver. 13861, he has
called it ' to tell in gest.'   Both passages seem to imply that
' gests' were chiefly written in alliterative verse, but the latter

passage more strongly than this. After the Host has told Chaucer that he 'shall no longer rhyme,' he goes on—

'Let see whe'r thou canst tellen ought in gest,
Or tellen in prose somewhat at the lest.'

'Gest' there seems to be put for a species of composition which was neither rhyme nor prose; and what that could be, except alliterative metre, I cannot guess. At the same time, I must own that I know no other passage which authorises the interpretation of 'gest' in this confined sense. In the 'H. of F.' (ii. 114), Chaucer speaks of himself as making

'bokes, songes, ditees
In rime, or elles in cadence,'

where 'cadence,' I think, must mean a species of poetical composition distinct from rhyming verses. The name might be properly enough applied to the metre used in the 'Ormulum,' (see the 'Essay,' &c., p. lxxi. note,) but no work of Chaucer in any such metre, without rhyme, has come within my observation.

Ver. 17378. 'Had the wordes:' This is a French phrase. It is applied to the Speaker of the Commons in Rot. Parl. 51 E. III. n. 87: 'Mons. Thomas de Hungerford, Chivaler, qi *avoit les paroles* pur les Communes d'Angleterre en cest Parlement,' &c.

P. 189, l. 6. 'Forlete sin ere that sin forlete them:' The same thought occurs, by way of precept, at the end of the Doctor's Tale (ver. 12220):—

'Forsaketh sin ere sinnë you forsake.'

P. 214, l. 20. 'Saith Moses:' I cannot tell where. Perhaps there may be some such passage in the Rabbinical histories of Moses, which the learned Gaulmin published in the last century (Paris, 1629, 8vo), and which, among other traditions, contain that alluded to by St Jude (Ep. ver. 9).

P. 215, l. 26. 'In the thurrok:' The Editt. have changed this word, in this place, into 'timber,' though, in another place (p. 254, l. 3), they have left it; and Mr Speght explains it to mean 'an heap.' It is a Saxon word, which the Glossaries render 'cymba,' 'caupolus;' originally, perhaps, 'campulus,' as it was sometimes written. (Du Cange, in v. 'Caupulus.') It seems to have signified any sort of 'keeled' vessel, and from thence, what we call 'the hold' of a ship. The following explanation of it, from an old book entitled 'Oure Ladyes Mirroure,' (Lon., 1530, fol. 57, b,) will fully justify Chaucer's use of it in both places, in the first literally, and in the second metaphorically: 'Ye shall understande that there ys a place in the bottome of a shyppe, wherin ys gathered all the fylthe that cometh into the shyppe—and it is called in some contre of thys londe a *thorrocke*. Other calle yt an *hamron*, and some calle yt the *bulcke* of the shyppe.' I know not what to make of 'hamron.'

P. 221, l. 6. 'Outrageous array of clothing:' What follows should be read carefully by any antiquary who may mean to write *de re vestiariâ* of the English nation in the fourteenth century.

P. 282, l. 16. 'So high doctrine I let to divines:' See before, ver. 17366–17371, and below, p. 292, l. 14, 'The exposition of this—I betake to the masters of theology.' The secular clergy, in the time of Chaucer, being generally very ignorant, it would not have been in character, I suppose, to represent the Parson as a deep divine, though a very pious, worthy priest. The Friar, whose brethren had the largest share of the learning which was then in fashion, is made to speak with great contempt of the parochial pastors (ver. 7590):—

> 'This every lewed vicar and parson
>   Can say,' &c.

And yet in the Parson's character (ver. 402), we are told that

> 'He was also a learned man, a clerk.'

It may be doubted, therefore, whether in these passages Chaucer may not speak for himself, forgetting or neglecting the character of the real speaker.

P. 296, l. 29. 'Now pray I to them all,' &c.: What follows being found, with some small variations, in all complete MSS. (I believe) of 'The Canterbury Tales,' and in both Caxton's editions, which were undoubtedly printed from MSS., there was no pretence to leave it out in this edition, however difficult it may be to give any satisfactory account of it.

I must first take notice, that this passage in MS. Ask. 1, is introduced by these words :—

'Here taketh the maker his leve ;'

and is concluded by these—

'Here endeth the Personnys Tale.'

In MS. Ask. 2, there is a similar introduction and conclusion in Latin; at the beginning, 'Hic capit auctor licentiam,' and at the end, 'Explicit narratio Rectoris, et ultima inter narrationes hujus libri de quibus composuit Chaucer, cujus anime propicietur Deus. Amen.'

These two MSS., therefore, may be considered as agreeing in substance with those MSS. mentioned in the 'Discourse,' &c., § XLII., in which this passage makes part of the Parson's Tale. One of them is described by Hearne, in his letter to Bagford, App. to 'R. G.', pp. 661, 662.

In Edit. Ca. 2, as quoted by Ames, p. 56, it is clearly separated from the Parson's Tale, and entitled—

The Prayer.

In the MSS., in which it is also separated from the Parson's Tale, I do not remember to have seen it distinguished by any title, either of 'Prayer,' or 'Revocation,' or 'Retractation,' as it is called in the preface to Ed. Urry. If we believe what is said in p. 297, l. 13, Chaucer had written a distinct piece, entitled his 'Retractions,' in which he had revoked his blameable compositions.

The just inference from these variations in the MSS. is, perhaps, that none of them are to be at all relied on; that different copyists have given this passage the title that pleased them best, and have attributed it to the Parson or to Chaucer, as the matter seemed to them to be most suitable to the one or the other.

Mr Hearne, whose greatest weakness was not his incredulity, has declared his suspicion, 'that the Revocation, meaning this whole passage, is not genuine, but that it was made by the monks.' (App. to 'R. G.,' p. 603.) I cannot go quite so far. I

think if the monks had set about making a Revocation for
Chaucer to be annexed to 'The Canterbury Tales,' they would
have made one more in form. The same objection lies to the
supposal that it was made by himself.

The most probable hypothesis which has occurred to me for
the solution of these difficulties, is to suppose that the beginning
of this passage, except the words 'or read it' in l. 30, and the
end, make together the genuine conclusion of the Parson's Tale,
and that the middle part, which I have enclosed between hooks,
is an interpolation.

It must be allowed, I think, as I have observed before, in the
'Discourse,' &c., § XLII., that the appellation of 'little treatise'
suits better with the Parson's Tale taken singly, than with the
whole work. The doubt expressed in p. 297, l. 3, 'if there be
anything that displeaseth,' &c., is very agreeable to the manner in
which the Parson speaks in his Prologue, ver. 17366. (See the
note on p. 282, l. 16.) The mention of 'very penance, confession,
and satisfaction,' in p. 297, l. 29, seems to refer pointedly to the
subject of the speaker's preceding discourse; and the title given
to Christ, in p. 298, l. 1, 'Priest of all priests,' seems peculiarly proper in the mouth of a priest.

So much for those parts which may be supposed to have originally belonged to the Parson. With respect to the middle
part, I think it not improbable that Chaucer might be persuaded,
by the religious who attended him in his last illness, to revoke
or retract certain of his works; or at least that they might give
out that he had made such retractions as they thought proper.
In either case, it is possible that the same zeal might think it
expedient to join the substance of these retractions to 'The
Canterbury Tales,'—the antidote to the poison,—and might
accordingly procure the present interpolation to be made in the
epilogue to the Parson's Tale; taking care, at the same time, by
the insertion of the words 'or read it,' in p. 296, l. 30, to convert
that epilogue from an address of the Parson to his *hearers* into
an address of Chaucer to his *readers*.

But, leaving these very uncertain speculations, I will say a
few words upon those 'enditings of worldly vanities,' which are
here supposed to have sitten heavy on our author's conscience.

P. 297, l. 13. 'The book of Troilus:' It has been said, in the 'Essay,' &c., page lxxxi., note, that the 'Troilus' is borrowed from the 'Filostrato' of Boccaccio. This is evident, not only from the fable and characters, which are the same in both poems, but also from a number of passages in the English which are literally translated from the Italian. At the same time, there are several long passages, and even episodes, in the 'Troilus,' of which there are no traces in the 'Filostrato.' Of these, therefore, it may be doubted whether Chaucer has added them out of his own invention, or taken them either from some completer copy of Boccaccio's poem than what we have in print, or from some copy interpolated by another hand. He speaks of himself as a translator 'out of Latin,' (b. ii. 14); and in two passages he quotes his author by the name of 'Lollius,' (b. i. 394–421, and b. v. 1652). The latter passage is in the 'Filostrato;' but the former, in which the 102d sonnet of Petrarch is introduced, is not. What he says of having translated 'out of Latin' need not make any difficulty, as the Italian language was commonly called 'Latino volgare,' (see the quotation from the 'Theseida,' 'Discourse,' &c., p. cx., note); and Lydgate (Prol. to Boccaccio) expressly tells us that Chaucer translated 'a boke, which called is "Trophe,"

     " In Lombard tonge, as men may rede and see." '

How Boccaccio should have acquired the name of 'Lollius,' and the 'Filostrato' the title of 'Trophe,' are points which I confess myself unable to explain.

Ibid., l. 14. 'The book of Fame:' Chaucer mentions this among his works in the 'Leg. of G. W.' (ver. 417). He wrote it while he was Comptroller of the Customs of Wools, &c., (see b. ii., ver. 144–148,) and consequently after the year 1374. (See App. to Pref. C.)

Ibid. 'The book of five-and-twenty Ladies:' This is the reading of all the MSS. If it be genuine, it affords a strong proof that this enumeration of Chaucer's works was not drawn up by himself; as there is no ground for believing that 'The Legend of Good Women' ever contained, or was intended to

contain, the histories of 'five-and-twenty' ladies.   (See the note
on ver. 4481.)   It is possible, however, that xxv. may have
been put by mistake for xix.
    P. 297, l. 15. 'The book of the Duchess :' See the note on ver.
4467.   One might have imagined that this poem, written upon a
particular occasion, was in all probability an original composition;
but upon comparing the portrait of a beautiful woman, which
M. de la Ravaliere ('Poes. du R. de N.,' Gloss. v. 'Belee') has
cited from MS. du Roi, No. 7612, with Chaucer's description of
his heroine (ver. 817, *et seq.*), I find that several lines in the
latter are literally translated from the former.   I should not,
therefore, be surprised if, upon a further examination of that
MS., it should appear that our author, according to his usual
practice, had borrowed a considerable part of his work from
some French poet.
    Ibid. 'The book of Saint Valentine's day,' &c. : In the Editt.
'The Assemblee of Foules.'   Chaucer himself, in the 'Leg. of
G. W.' (ver. 419) calls it 'The Parlement of Foules.'   (See the
note on ver. 1920, and App. to Pref. C. p. xxviii., note.)
    Ibid., l. 17. 'The Tales of Canterbury,' &c. : If we suppose
that this passage was written by Chaucer himself, to make part
of the conclusion of his 'Canterbury Tales,' it must appear
rather extraordinary that he should mention those tales in this
general manner, and in the midst of his other works.   It would
have been more natural to have placed them either at the
beginning or at the end of his catalogue.
    Ibid., l. 18. 'The book of the Lion :'   This book is also
ascribed to Chaucer by Lydgate (Prol. to Boccaccio), but no
MS. of it has hitherto been discovered.   It may possibly have
been a translation of 'Le dit du Lion,' a poem of Guillaume de
Machaut, composed in the year 1342.   ('Acad. des Insc.,' t. xx.
pp. 379, 408.)   Some lines from this poem, as I apprehend, are
quoted in the Glossary to 'Poes. du Roi de N.,' v. 'Arrousers,'
'Bacheler.'
    Whether we suppose this list of Chaucer's exceptionable
works to have been drawn up by himself, or by any other person,
it is unaccountable that his translation of the 'Roman de la
Rose' should be omitted.   If he translated the whole of that

very extraordinary composition, as is most probable, he could scarce avoid being guilty of a much greater licentiousness, in sentiment as well as diction, than we find in any of his other writings. His translation, as we have it, breaks off at ver. 5370 of the original (ver. 5810, Ed. Urr.), and beginning again at ver. 11253, ends imperfect at ver. 13105. In the latter part we have a strong proof of the negligence of the first editor, who did not perceive that two leaves in his MS. were misplaced. The passage from ver. 7013 to ver. 7062 inclusive, and the passage from ver. 7257 to ver. 7304 inclusive, should be inserted after ver. 7160. The later Editors have all copied this, as well as many other blunders of less consequence, which they must have discovered, if they had consulted the French original.

A bachelor, who dances with Franchise, is said to resemble

'The Lordes sonne of Wyndesore.'
'R. R.,' ver. 1250.

This seems to be a compliment to the young princes in general, rather than to any particular son of Edward III., who is certainly meant by 'the Lord of Windsor.' In the French it is simply 'Il sembloit estre filz de Roy.'

ABBREVIATIONS BY WHICH THE WORKS OF CHAUCER AND
SOME OTHER BOOKS ARE CITED IN THE NOTES, &c.

A. B. C.	Chaucer's A. B. C.
A. F.	Assembly of Fowls.
An.	Annelida and Arcite.
Astr.	Treatise on the Astrolabe.
Bal. Vil.	Ballad of the Village.
Ber.	The History of Beryn.
B. K.	Complaint of the Black Knight.
Bo.	Translation of Boethius.
C. D.	Chaucer's Dream.
C. L.	Court of Love.
C. M.	Complaint of Mars.
C. M. V.	Complaint of Mars and Venus.
C. N.	Cuckoo and Nightingale.
Cotg.	Cotgrave's Fr. and Eng. Dictionary.
Conf. Am.	Gower's *Confessio Amantis.*
C. V.	Complaint of Venus.
Du.	The Book of the Duchess, commonly called, *The Dream of Chaucer.*
F.	The House of Fame.
F. L.	The Flower and Leaf.
Gam.	The Tale of Gamelyn.
Jun. Etymol.	Junii Etymologicon Ling. Angl., by Lye.
Kilian.	Kiliani Etymologicum Ling. Teuton.
L. W.	Legend of Good Women.
Lydg. *Trag.*	Lydgate's Translation of Boccaccio *De Casibus Virorum Illustrium.*
M.	The Tale of Melibœus.
Magd.	Lamentation of Mary Magdalene.
P.	The Parson's Tale.
P. L.	Translation of Peter of Langtoft, by Robert of Brunne.

P. P.	Visions of Pierce Ploughman.
Prompt. Parv.	*Promptorium Parvulorum sive Clericorum.* MS. Harl. 221.
Prov.	Proverbs by Chaucer.
R.	The Romaunt of the Rose.
R. G.	Robert of Gloucester's Chronicle.
Sk.	Skinner's *Etymologicon Ling. Angl.*
Sp.	Speght, the Editor of Chaucer.
T.	Troilus and Cresseide.
T. L.	Testament of Love.
Ur.	Urry, the Editor of Chaucer.

THE END.

BALLANTYNE AND COMPANY, PRINTERS, EDINBURGH.

www.ingramcontent.com/pod-product-compliance
Lightning Source LLC
Chambersburg PA
CBHW021715110726
47902CB00005B/1206